THE SHADOWS ARE DARKEST

M. R. PRITCHARD

MIDNIGHT LEDGER

The Shadows are Darkest Copyright © 2025 by M. R. Pritchard
Excerpt from *These Thorns are Sharpest* Copyright © 2025 by M. R. Pritchard
Veil of Shadows Copyright © 2014-2025 by M. R. Pritchard.
Cover Art and Interior Art: Stockphotos from DepositPhotos. Elements, Filters, Fonts and digital manipulations with Canva.
Photographs by M. R. Pritchard.
Edited by: Kristy Ellsworth
Midnight Ledger
Publishing
14391 Spring Hill Dr. Suite 203
Spring Hill, FL 34609
MidnightLedger.com
First Edition September 2025
ISBNs: 978-1-957709-80-2 (Hardcover)
978-1-957709-81-9 (Paperback)
Printed in the United States of America

About "The Shadows are Darkest"

The Shadows Are Darkest is a standalone dark fantasy romance with vampires, morally gray characters, and a slow-burn love story tangled in danger.

Though it can be enjoyed on its own, this is also the third book in the Next Generation Veil of Shadows series, where blood is currency, monsters walk beside kings, and love is as dangerous as any curse.

For those who crave every secret and tangled thread, begin with The Sky is Starless, The Night is Endless, and the original thirteen-volume Veil of Shadows saga. Step carefully because once you enter, the darkness won't let go.

A bite in the dark.
   A curse awakened.
   And now, the only way out is through him.

Layla was just searching for a book until something bit her in the basement of the Library. Since that night, her fingertips have darkened with strange veins of shadow. For her safety, she's sent to a remote ranch in Montana where the skies are wide, the secrets run deep, and her new housemate is a dangerously powerful princeling with a short fuse.

He's a cursed prince.
She's the girl unraveling his control.

Thrush is cursed with ancient magic that burns just beneath his skin. With every flare of temper, every spark of emotion, he risks unleashing something he can't contain. He's training to control it. To survive it. But then Layla arrives and she's too human, too curious, and far too tempting.

A bite runs deep.
A soul is split.
And now, she's caught between realms where nothing is safe, including her heart.

The Shadows are Darkest is a dark fantasy romance perfect for fans of cursed monsters, forbidden attraction, slow burning tension, and the kind of gothic longing that leaves you breathless.

He's a cursed prince.
She's the girl unraveling
his control.

THE SHADOWS ARE DARKEST

M. R. PRITCHARD

CHAPTER 1

LAYLA REACHED UP ON HER TIPTOES AND PRESSED a book into place. Reshelving was a bitch without her stepstool. But those were the new rules from the manager, James, who'd just taken over Loyola Library. Layla used to have freedom in her work. She could make her own schedule, take lunch when she wanted, grab a coffee mid-afternoon. Not any longer.

Now she found herself avoiding the sniffling man at the front desk. He always had something negative to say. She was too slow, spoke too long to guests, took too long reshelving. He blamed her slowness on the stepstool she dragged around and forbid her from using it any longer. Well, joke was on him; at five foot one, Layla couldn't reach much on the top shelves and climbing the bookshelves resulted in her slipping and scraping her shins.

Her arms ached from reaching up so high. She set the big book back on the cart and brushed curls out of her face. She was going to walk this cart back to James and let him know she wasn't going to risk her life climbing the shelves with a book that was bigger than her head.

Layla marched back to the front desk, short blonde curls bouncing right along with her irritation. She wanted to give the guy a piece of her mind, but she didn't want to lose her job. There weren't many libraries left in Baltimore, Maryland. She thought about the abandoned Peabody Library downtown and wished she'd been able to work there before it was shuttered.

Layla turned the corner and slowed to control her cart. James was at the front desk, typing on the computer and ignoring the girl standing there. Layla recognized the student who'd requested an interlibrary loan on a fifteenth-century art book. Layla's heartbeat picked up; she didn't like that James was ignoring the girl. She pushed the cart into place and went to the counter.

"Here to get your loaned book?" she asked the girl.

"Yeah. I thought it would never come in." She checked the time. "Is it right here? I've been waiting a while. I have class starting in a few minutes."

The girl glared at James.

"It's on this shelf. One sec." Layla went to the hold shelf and grabbed the book. She scanned everything and passed it to the girl. "Enjoy."

"Thanks." The girl was putting the book into her backpack when James turned.

"Make sure you return that by the due date." He turned to Layla. "Where have you been?"

"Reshelving." Layla was about to log out of the computer.

"Then why are there still books on the cart?" James

pressed a finger to the glasses sliding down the bridge of his nose.

"I can't reach the top shelves. That's what my stepstool was for and you took it away." Layla's heart was beating a hundred miles a minute, fueled by anger and annoyance.

James looked her up and down like she could do something about her height before rounding the counter and walking off with the book cart.

Layla sighed.

She despised that man.

A notification dinged from the computer. She turned and saw a message from Rue, one of the Archeology doctorate students. Layla and Rue had an understanding; many of the ancient books Rue had been requesting weren't supposed to leave the library, but Layla had been sneaking them out. They were books no one had touched in ages.

She squinted at the request Rue had emailed. The title was in another language that looked like Latin and strange symbols.

"What the heck..." Layla printed the request and found that the book was at Loyola, but it was in storage in the basement. She shivered. The basement was super creepy. The lighting was bad and the old books held a strange energy that she couldn't place. If it weren't for Rue, she'd make James go down there.

"You are gonna owe me one hundred coffees," Layla muttered as she folded Rue's request and put it in her pocket.

CHAPTER 2

THE TRAINING YARD BESIDE HELL'S CASTLE sweltered with heat and magic, the air thick with the scent of scorched rock and blood. Thrush's breath came ragged as he squared off against another Hellion, a bigger one this time. Still wasn't bigger than him. The weight of his blade was steady in his grip. His opponent lunged but Thrush was faster, twisting out of the way and bringing his blade down in a brutal arc. Sparks flew where steel met steel.

Thrush should have had control, should have been able to stop at the right moment, but the anger boiled beneath his skin like molten lava. Something inside him twisted harder, dark and volatile. A heat unfurled in his chest, spreading through his veins. The Hellion in front of him stumbled back, eyes widening in horror as sparks flew out of Thrush's fingers. The air crackled.

"Thrush, back down." Remington's voice cut through the yard.

Thrush gritted his teeth, but the magic didn't stop. It

surged outward in a violent wave toward the Hellion he had been battling. The creature lunged to the side just in time.

Energy like lightning flew across the yard, singeing the grass and spraying soil in the air.

A scream rang out. Evelyn.

The sparks lashed toward her like a gasoline fueled fire. She scrambled backward, but it was too fast. Before the rush of magic could touch her, a massive scaled body surged between them. Remington's basilisk slammed its tail into the ground, sending up a cloud of dust as it herded Evelyn away, its body coiled around her like a living shield.

Remington moved just as fast, shadows unfurling as he stepped into the storm of Thrush's magic. The dark tendrils pushed against the streak of light, crackling in defiance.

"Stand. Down." Remington warned again.

Thrush sucked in a sharp breath, but the magic wouldn't settle. His pulse hammered. His hands trembled.

"I can't," he ground out.

The magic rippled, the sparks flying from his fingertips desperate to consume and destroy.

And then Remington was in front of him, gripping the front of his shirt, shaking him hard enough to snap him back to reality. The darkness in Remington's eyes burned, his fury barely leashed.

"You almost killed her!" Remington shouted. "Control it. Now."

Thrush tore free, breathing hard. "I didn't mean to."

"Doesn't matter. Your magic doesn't give a damn about your intentions. If you can't control it, you're a danger to everyone here." Remington was searching Thrush's face. "It wasn't like this before. What is happening to you?"

Thrush ran a shaking hand through his sweat-drenched white hair. He could still feel it, coiling at the edges of his consciousness, waiting. "I don't know." His voice was raw. "I can feel it slipping. Every day, I feel like I'm losing control." He glanced at Evelyn. "I'm sorry. I didn't mean to hurt you."

Evelyn moved behind Remington. "I know. But you need to fix that problem, wild boy."

For a long moment, there was silence between them. The basilisk still coiled protectively near Evelyn, its tongue flicking, watching Thrush as though deciding whether or not to strike.

Thrush ran a hand through his hair. "You said the curse was going to clear when I took my turn as a Hellion. Your parents told me the same."

Remington was watching him for a moment before he let out a slow breath and took a step back. "We need to fix this."

Thrush swallowed hard. He wasn't sure if it could be fixed.

But if he didn't find a way to control it, someone was going to die. And next time, there might not be a basilisk to save the most innocent around them.

Thrush squeezed his eyes closed and held in a tic. His jaw clenched and unclenched while his shoulders quivered, fighting off shudders that would rattle his teeth.

CHAPTER 3

THE AIR IN THE LIBRARY BASEMENT WAS ALWAYS oddly cold. Layla hugged her cardigan tighter around herself as she descended the narrow stone steps, the bulb overhead flickering just enough to raise goosebumps along her arms. She didn't remember it being this cold before, but James probably turned the temperature down to save money.

The ancient archives were tucked in the oldest wing of the building, untouched by modern convenience. Here, the smell of dust and ancient leather bindings clung to the walls, the shelves bending under the weight of books that hadn't seen daylight in centuries.

Layla had Rue's request tucked into her pocket; an ancient text with a title in something that resembled Latin, though parts of it were composed of symbols that shimmered faintly under certain light. Layla had triple-checked the catalog index upstairs. There was only one copy. Her footsteps echoed as she scanned the labels on the bookshelves.

She found the correct row and skimmed the spines until her fingers paused over the leather-bound volume wrapped carefully in a dark, silk-like cloth. There was no title on the binding, just a single black seal burned into the cover. A peeling and yellowed label clung to the cloth, ready to fall off any minute.

"Here you are," she murmured. "You look out of place here."

She carefully lifted the book from the shelf, surprised by how *warm* it was, like it had been waiting for her. A whisper of unease curled at the base of her neck. She ignored it. This was for Rue. She'd had a knack for requesting sketchy books from all over. Usually Layla had to request them from libraries near Appalachia. She was surprised this one was on site. A shiver danced up her spine.

As Layla slid the book into her satchel, her fingers brushed the edge of the cloth.

Something cold rippled up her arm.

The world tilted. Bookshelves shifted in her vision. Nausea struck. The shadows in the room deepened unnaturally, swallowing the faint light from the hall and stairs. A low sound echoed from the walls, like distant chanting or the hum of something *alive*.

Layla stumbled back, clutching her head as a pressure loud as a thousand voices pressed into her skull. The book pulsed through the bag like a heartbeat. Something moved in the corner of the room.

She turned just in time to see a tall, shapeless figure surge from the shadows made of smoke and twisting limbs. It reached for her with a hand like a claw, no, not a hand. Not *human*.

Her hand shot out to protect herself but the thing was huge. Something sharp hit her wrist.

Layla screamed.

And everything went black.

———

SHE WOKE ON THE STONE FLOOR, COLD AND aching. The bag still hung from her shoulder, her satchel's strap tight across her chest. Layla rolled, feeling the heavy book in her bag flop against her side. The world was blurry. She searched for her glasses and found them next to her head. She grabbed them and put them on.

There was a distant shout. Footsteps pounded down the stairs.

James appeared at the bottom of the steps, lips curled in his usual sneer. His gaze swept the scene with immediate disdain.

"Unbelievable."

Layla groaned as she struggled to sit up. "James, I..."

"Sleeping on the job? In the *restricted archives*?" He threw his hands up, pacing. "Do you have *any* idea how important these volumes are? You could've damaged something priceless!"

"I wasn't sleeping!" she snapped, forcing herself upright. "I came down here to retrieve the book Rue requested, and something happened."

He crossed his arms. "Something happened. Of course. Do you have *any* idea how ridiculous you sound right now?" He motioned to the stairwell. "There is a line of

9

people at the desk. I've been swamped and you are nowhere to be found for hours."

"I think I'm sick. I blacked out, I swear." She faltered. She sounded unhinged–even to her own ears. Her voice was unsteady.

James snorted. "You're lucky I'm not filing an official grievance against you. I've had it with your excuses, Layla. You've been poking around where you shouldn't for weeks. That ends today. Pack your things. You're done here."

"But!" Panic swelled. Her mouth opened but she didn't know what to say. For weeks she'd dealt with James yelling at her behind closed doors and micromanaging her work. Most days she had headaches and stomachaches.

"Save it. This has been a long day coming. You're fired." He turned and stormed up the stairs without a backward glance.

Layla sat there stunned in the cold dark for a moment longer, her hand trembling as she reached for the flap of her bag and folded it over the opening, hiding the book.

A spark ran up her arm like a jolt of electricity. Her heart skipped. What was happening? This was like a bad dream. She could barely think, stumbling as she made her way to the stairs. The walk to the cubby where she kept her belongings seemed endless. She swallowed hard, holding in tears and collecting her jacket and lunch bag. She snuck out the back door, avoiding the walk of shame and the familiar faces of students who came in every afternoon. She definitely wasn't going to make it to the weekly book club meeting tonight. She'd suffered through a biography book for nothing.

Layla slammed the trunk of her car shut, her breath fogging in the cold evening air. The satchel sat on the passenger seat beside her, the book now buried beneath her scarf. She hadn't dared to touch it again. Not after the jolt. Not after the shadows and the blackout.

She didn't cry until she hit the main entrance to campus.

Tears burned down her cheeks, hot and furious. Fired. Just like that. After everything she'd done for that library, for *James*. And no one would believe what happened. No one could. She'd worked her ass off for years, running the place when there was no manager. She knew most of the students by name. She'd created clubs and engaged the students with read-ins and study halls. Sure she'd snuck books out of the library for Rue, but they hadn't been touched in ages. It wasn't going to hurt a soul. She always returned them.

Layla grabbed her phone at the next red light and called Rue.

"Layla?" Rue sounded surprised. "Hey, what's…"

"I got the book." Her voice cracked with the strain of keeping it together. "But something happened. Something's wrong with it. Or with me. I don't know."

"Whoa, slow down. Are you okay?"

"No. I'm not. I just got fired."

"What?" Rue's voice sharpened. "Where are you?"

"Coffee Connection. Or I will be in ten minutes." She wiped angrily at her eyes. "Just… meet me, please?"

"I'm on my way."

LAYLA WAS ALREADY AT A CORNER TABLE WHEN Rue arrived, the battered satchel clutched tightly in her lap like it might bite someone if she let it go. Her hair was windblown, her cheeks and eyes red from crying.

Rue slid into the booth opposite her without a word and set two drinks on the table. Black coffee for Layla. A pumpkin spiced latte for herself.

Layla offered a weak, tear-hardened laugh. "Still psychic, huh?"

Rue gave her a small smile. "Just predictable." Her eyes dropped to the satchel. "Show me."

Layla hesitated, then slowly unzipped the bag and carefully pulled the wrapped book into view. The cloth shimmered faintly under the café's warm lights.

Rue's face lit with excitement.

"That's it," she whispered. "That's the one I asked for."

"No offense," Layla snapped, "but your freaky old book nearly killed me. I touched it and blacked out. James accused me of sleeping on the job. I was on the damn floor." A sob escaped her throat. "What the hell is wrong with that creep?"

"When did you black out?" Rue asked.

"After I touched this book. Something weird happened."

"I believe you."

Layla froze halfway through another angry breath, and she looked up at her friend.

"I believe you," Rue said again, leaning closer, her voice low. "That book isn't written in Latin. It's written in Enochian. And those symbols? They're protective runes, worn and broken. It probably hasn't been disturbed in centuries."

"I disturbed it," Layla whispered. "What's Enochian?"

Rue nodded slowly. "Enochian is an angelic language; some view it as occult. There's not a lot published. Malcolm told me about it, he said he's been trying to get his hands on anything that might help us decipher the runes in the caves and dig sites. We've been finding a lot of marked stone."

Layla stared down at the cloth, fear worming into her gut.

"I think it did something to me," she whispered.

Rue's eyes went wide. "Are you feeling different?"

Layla nodded.

"The book might help us fix it," Rue suggested. "The runes in this book are supposed to hint at an ancient magic system. Astral magic. We haven't studied it much." Rue paused. "What are you doing?"

"Huh?" Layla looked up from staring into her coffee, blinking like she'd just surfaced from underwater.

Rue didn't answer right away. Her gaze had locked onto something–Layla's hand. She reached across the table and gently took her wrist.

"Layla, look." Rue lifted her hand into the light. There, beneath Layla's fingernails, streaks of red stood out starkly against her pale skin. "You were scratching your arm."

Layla frowned, confused. "I wasn't..."

But her voice trailed off as she looked down. Her sleeve was bunched slightly at the elbow. With a trembling hand, she tugged it up.

Her eyes widened. "What the hell?"

Faint red lines ran down the length of her forearm, fresh and raw. The scratches were jagged, like she'd clawed at herself in her sleep. When she rolled up the other sleeve, Rue sucked in a breath.

Just above Layla's wrist, in the soft flesh of her upper arm, were twin punctures. Round. Deep. The skin around them was discolored; a sickly gray-green bruising spreading outward like ink in water.

Rue leaned in, all levity gone. "That's a bite mark." She paled.

Layla stared. "But I didn't feel anything. I don't remember anything!" Her voice pitched up, panic starting to rise in her chest.

"Whatever happened in that basement wasn't just magical residue." Rue sat back, eyes scanning the café as if suddenly paranoid they were being watched. "Something touched you." Rue's expression twisted into deep concern.

"I thought I just passed out. There could have been a snake or a spider down there. It was so dark I could barely see," Layla whispered.

"No. I don't think that's what happened." Rue was shaking her head.

"I don't understand... What are you trying to tell me?"

Rue hesitated, then reached across the table again. "I need to tell you something about myself. About my family. I think I just dragged you into the mess that is my life."

Layla closed her eyes, trying to slow her breathing, but the scent of blood felt too strong now. Her skin itched. Her arms burned. Her *throat* burned.

And in the back of her mind where thoughts should be quiet, something was whispering.

"What's wrong with your family?" Layla asked.

Rue took a deep breath before reaching for her phone and sending a message.

Strangely, the coffee shop began to empty out. Layla blinked a few times. "What did you just do?"

Rue smiled before standing and scooting into the booth seat next to Layla. The door opened and Rue's boyfriend entered.

Layla hadn't seen the guy in a few days, but he always seemed attached to Rue's hip. Dacre was his name and he used to be her bodyguard.

"I need to tell you a secret." Rue reached out to touch Layla's arm. "And you can't tell a soul."

Layla nodded, wiping at her eyes and adjusting her glasses. "Okay."

"I'm a princess."

"Well, that's kinda cool," Layla's voice was flat. "I kinda expected something more with the way you're acting."

"There is more."

Dacre slid into the seat across from them and nodded a greeting to Layla.

"We're from a different realm." Rue paused. "My parents are the Queen of Hell and a King of Heaven."

Layla broke out in laughter. "That sounds ridiculous."

She went still when she noticed Rue was serious.

"Oh crap." Layla's hand flew to her mouth. "Oh god you're telling the truth." She glanced to Dacre. "And you? What about you?"

Dacre smiled. "I'm something that's a little harder to explain."

"But you both look so human."

Rue and Dacre smiled.

Layla was nodding and took a deep breath. "Okay... so you're a princess. But what about all of this research you've been doing?"

"A lot of history has been hidden and lost to my family. I'm trying to dig it up. There is so much we don't know." Rue released Layla's arm and reached for her coffee cup. "Are you gonna be okay?"

"Wait... is this why Evelyn disappeared? You all were inseparable and now I hardly see her." Layla was searching Rue's face.

Rue nodded. "Evelyn was very sick and she bled on a stone that caused some very dangerous creatures to come after her."

"Well, where did she go?"

"She's with my brother."

"That really tall guy with the blonde hair?"

"No, he has dark hair. The blonde one is my cousin." Something strange flashed in Rue's eyes. "You remember him? You only saw him once. I'm surprised."

"He was just... really tall and looked troubled."

Rue glanced at Dacre.

"The real reason I'm telling you this, is that you're in danger now." Rue leaned closer. "Layla, I'm sorry, I didn't know the book would do something to you."

"Well, what did it do to me?" Layla asked, taking a sip of her coffee. "And you never finished with what happened to Evelyn."

"Oh. Evelyn is very happy. She's with my brother."

"Where?"

"In Hell."

CHAPTER 4

CHEL GLANCED DOWN AT THRUSH. "SHE SAID, 'My office. Now.'"

Thrush stopped cleaning the blade in his hand and turned to set it on the rack behind him.

He clenched his fists, jaw tight. The stone walls around him felt like they were closing in, pulsing in time with the barely restrained magic in his veins.

Magic he couldn't stop.

Couldn't slow.

Couldn't control.

He shoved the door open to the corridor, storming past two other Hellions who quickly stepped aside. Whispers followed him. He didn't need to hear them to know what they said. He'd almost incinerated a training ring with Evelyn nearby. He lost control. Again.

He didn't even remember what set it off. Someone hit him wrong. The heat rose. His hands burned. The air cracked.

"Calm down," Chel shouted from behind him. "She

may be your aunt but she will send you to meet your parents if you don't control yourself."

Thrush was half-Angel, half-Astral, born of something so strange that the old records stuttered when trying to trace how he'd been created. There was power in his bones older than anything they knew. He'd survived the fast-zombie war. He'd claimed a basilisk. He'd survived the war with Lucifer. He should be in control.

So why did he feel like he was coming undone at the seams?

The door to Meg's office loomed ahead, tall and carved with images of lambs and demons. The Hellions at the entrance didn't speak, just stepped aside with careful neutrality. They'd heard. Everyone had. It was no secret that Thrush, the cursed princeling, had come home and was slowly losing his mind.

Thrush raised a hand and knocked once.

"Come in," came Meg's voice, calm. Too calm.

He pushed the door open and Chel followed. Giant leathery-wings flexed as he greeted the Hellions standing guard.

Meg sat behind her desk, surrounded by burning candles and scrolls. The scent of brimstone clung to the air like incense. She didn't look up immediately, finishing whatever note she was writing with a scrape of her pen. Great, she was already on edge. It was something Thrush and his aunt had in common: quick to temper.

Thrush stood there, pulse pounding. His shoulder ached, the muscle fluttering and eager to twitch.

Finally, she looked at him. Her hair was shorter, her

leather jacket new. She stripped it off revealing arms and shoulders scattered with tattoos, runes, and scars.

"You're losing control." Not a question. A truth. She stared at him, blue eyes blazing. "I didn't rescue you from certain death multiple times during your childhood only to lose you now."

Thrush's jaw flexed. "I'm *fine*."

"No, you're not." She gestured toward the empty chair in front of her. "Sit before you melt the floor."

He hesitated, then dropped into the seat like it offended him.

Meg studied him for a long moment. "You've hit your limit. And you're pretending it's not happening. That's dangerous. Living like a wild animal for all those years was bad enough. You should have come home a long time ago so we could help you."

"I'm not pretending," he growled. "I'm just trying to contain it."

"That's not control," she said sharply. "That's repression. And repression with this bloodline leads to combustion. You saw what happened to your uncle Sparrow. You lived through the same history as us. I won't ignore what's happening to you like others have ignored their children."

"I'm not your child."

Meg snapped her fingers and stood. "Close enough. I risked my life for you just like I did my own children. Your father was my *best* friend."

Thrush looked away. "What do you want me to say? That I'm scared? That I feel like there's something crawling under my skin every time I breathe? That I don't even trust my own hands anymore?"

Meg's expression softened. Just a little. "I want you to admit you need help. That's always the first step in some twelve-step bullshit recovery program. Saying it out loud makes you finally believe it and accept the help."

The silence stretched between them, heavy and unforgiving.

"Fine. I need help." He exhaled through his nose. "So what? You're kicking me out?"

"I'm sending you to Jed," she replied. "He's dealt with this kind of thing before. Jed's bloodline is closer to yours than anyone else's here."

Thrush scoffed. "You're sending me to a ranch in the middle of nowhere to talk about my feelings? With a half-breed scum and a human? On the Earthen plane?"

"I'm sending you somewhere you won't kill someone while trying to figure yourself out," Meg snapped. "You're not being punished. You're being protected. And so is everyone else." Her eyes narrowed on him. "And Jed is not 'half-breed scum.' He brought your mother back from nothingness. He helped save you and Rue and Remington. I suggest you watch your tongue or I'll cut it out myself."

He looked away again, this time toward the candle on her desk. The flame twisted violently as he stared at it.

"...When do I leave?" He stood.

"Now." There was a beat. "One second."

Thrush waited.

"The Hellions tell me you won't drink the blood."

Thrush looked to the floor. "I'm afraid it will make me more powerful. I'm barely holding on without it. Could you imagine me filled to the brim with blood? I'd be a monster."

Meg was staring at him, her mind working. She finally glanced to Chel and tipped her chin toward the door without another word.

Chel moved closer to Thrush and gripped his weapon, noticing the faint light glinting from Thrush's fingertips. "Let's go, princeling. Head out. Don't make me send you to the Astral and soil the new tile. Your aunt just had it replaced."

THRUSH FOUND SPARROW IN THE ARMORY.

He stood at the far wall, inspecting a blade as long as his arm and twice as scarred. His black wings were tucked in, but there was still something massive about him. He filled the space.

Thrush hesitated in the doorway.

"You going to say something, or just stand there brooding like a ghost?" Sparrow asked without turning. "Like my sister used to do?"

"You'd know a thing or two about ghosts," Thrush muttered as he stepped inside.

Sparrow chuckled, low and dry. "Yeah. I would."

He set the blade back in its place and turned. His eyes were always watching, always waiting for something worse to come around the bend.

"So," Sparrow said, crossing his arms. "You're going to train with Jed."

"Word travels fast," Thrush grumbled.

"Course it does. Hellion gossip is more reliable than Hellion mail." Sparrow studied him for a moment then walked over, the weight of his boots echoing in the quiet room. "I figured this would happen eventually. I just hoped... not this soon."

Thrush clenched his jaw. "You think I can't handle it."

"I know what you're handling." Sparrow's voice softened, but there was no pity in it. "The curse didn't start with you, Thrush. It didn't even start with me. It runs back generations, maybe further than any of us even know, but it always shows up the same way. Anger like a second heart. Power like a loaded weapon. Voices that aren't yours. A tic in the neck and shoulders we can't contain." Sparrow stretched his neck and the bones cracked. "I lived with it long enough."

Thrush said nothing, but his shoulders hunched under the weight of it.

"I didn't want this for you," Sparrow continued. "When you were born... your mother used to say you had this light inside you. Not just power; light. Like something was untouched by the curse." He paused. "Maybe it still is. She was all light. She had a spunk. I'm sorry you never got to see that side of her."

"Whatever it is," Thrush shook his head, "...feels like it's eating me alive."

"Don't let it win." Sparrow stepped closer, placing a heavy hand on Thrush's shoulder. "You fight it. Tooth and claw. You learn how to control it, to master it. Not just for you. For them." He nodded toward the direction of the Astral realm. "For the ones watching."

Thrush swallowed hard, his throat tight. "And if I can't?"

"You can." Sparrow's voice was iron. "Because you're

not alone. You've got people who want you to win this, even if you don't see it yet."

Thrush didn't answer, but the heat behind his eyes told him everything he needed to know.

Sparrow pulled him in suddenly. A one-armed hug carried all the weight of a thousand unsaid things. It was rough and quick.

"You're still my family," Sparrow muttered. "Even if you're a pain in the ass."

"Yeah," Thrush rasped. "You too. I'm sorry I ran away."

Sparrow smiled. "Our family does that sometimes. Time to set things straight."

———

THE CORRIDOR LEADING TO THE LIBRARY WAS quiet now. Most of the creatures in the castle avoided eye contact as Thrush passed, like he was a loaded weapon with a hair trigger. Maybe they weren't wrong.

Chel's footsteps still echoed behind him. The Hellion had become Thrush's shadow as he said his goodbyes.

He stopped at a familiar carved door. The library. He hesitated, then, then knocked twice.

Evelyn answered almost immediately.

She looked tired; her blonde hair pulled into a loose braid, a smudge of ink across her wrist from whatever research she'd been buried in. But her eyes widened slightly when she saw him.

"Thrush."

"Hey," he said, voice low. "Can I... talk to you?"

She nodded and stepped aside to let him in.

The room smelled like old paper and leather. He stood awkwardly near the shelves, shoulders tense, hands in the pockets of his jacket like he was trying to contain himself physically as well as magically.

"I wanted to see you before I left," he said.

Evelyn crossed her arms. "I heard you're going to the Earthen plane."

"Yeah. Jed's going to try and fix me, I guess. Meg said something about a twelve-step program."

He looked away, jaw tight. "I came to say I'm sorry. For... almost hurting you. For losing control. I can never apologize enough."

"You didn't mean to."

"That doesn't matter."

"It does," she said, stepping closer. "But so does what you're doing now. *Trying*. I know what it's like to feel something inside you breaking loose. You don't have to go through this alone. I know we haven't known each other long but Rue and Remington, they care for you–a lot. I wish you could have heard the way they talked about you before you finally agreed to return."

Thrush finally looked at her, and something cracked in his expression. A shadow of guilt. "I didn't mean to almost hurt you. I could've killed you."

Evelyn nodded. "The curse doesn't own you."

"I'm not sure I believe that."

"Maybe Rue can help. She's knee deep in the history of your family."

"Knee deep isn't that deep for her." Thrush's voice was thick with sarcasm.

"Might be deep enough if her foot was in your ass." She

laughed hard, hand on her chest. "Ah, I'm so funny some-times." She cleared her throat, serious again. "Then borrow my belief until you can." She smiled.

He blinked, a little stunned. No one had ever said that to him before. Not like that.

After a long moment, he said quietly, "I don't want to become what I saw in my parents. I don't want to vanish into the same void they did."

"You won't." Her voice was steady. "And when you feel like you might, you call someone. Me. Rue. Sparrow. Meg. Even Remington, though he might punch you first."

That earned her a faint smirk.

Evelyn stepped forward and, without asking, hugged him.

Thrush stood stiff for a second, then slowly wrapped his arms around her. "Be safe out there," she murmured. "And don't be a stranger. Maybe we will come visit and throw off the balance between realms a little. Don't make me come to Lame Deer to check on you."

He grinned, the first real one in days. "I wouldn't dare."

REMINGTON STOOD NEAR THE PORTAL CENTERED in the castle gardens. His arms were crossed, his basilisk curled around a nearby tree like a silent sentinel. His expression was unreadable, stone carved into flesh.

Thrush approached slowly, his bag slung over one shoulder.

"Didn't think you'd come say goodbye," he said.

"I didn't," Remington replied. "I came to make sure you left."

Thrush huffed a bitter chuckle. "Fair."

They stood in silence for a beat.

Remington's eyes drifted over him, sharp and assessing. "You could've killed her."

"I know." Thrush's voice was low. "I didn't mean to."

"Doesn't matter. Intent doesn't fix damage. Only action does."

Thrush met his gaze. "That why you're letting me go?"

Remington nodded once. "That, and because I've seen what happens when something like us ignores the storm inside. Meg says you're going to the ranch. Jed'll help. Shay too."

"And if he can't?"

"He will." Remington stepped forward, expression firm. "But only if you let him. You fight Jed, you fight yourself. You give up, I come find you."

Thrush gave a crooked smirk. "Wouldn't want that."

"No. You wouldn't."

They locked eyes in an uneasy truce that wasn't brotherhood, but more like a shared burden.

Then, after a moment, Remington extended a hand.

Thrush looked at it.

Then took it.

The basilisk hissed and slithered aside as Thrush stepped through the gate.

And Hell was behind him.

Chapter 5

The apartment was quiet.

Layla sat cross-legged on the couch, her laptop perched on a pillow with half a dozen tabs open to job listings: bookstores, archives, library research assistant positions– none of them promising. She scrolled mindlessly, her fingers hovering over the keys but never clicking.

A cup of tea sat untouched at her side, growing cold.

"What now?" she whispered to herself, dragging a hand down her face.

Since the library, everything had felt... off. She missed her job and the smell of the books, the familiar faces, the new ones. Now she had nothing. She kept catching glimpses of movement in the corners of her eyes.

And sometimes, just beneath the surface of silence, she could hear something.

Maybe she needed psych meds.

The headaches and stomachaches had stopped. Working with James had truly been hell on earth. Layla was sure the man had given her some type of traumatic stress disorder.

She shook her head and focused on the screen again, typing half-heartedly: "remote librarian positions + occult archive experience."

The results loaded, but her vision blurred before she could make sense of any of it.

"Layla."

She froze.

The voice was whispering through the walls like smoke through cracks.

Her hand twitched violently. Her tea cup tipped over, spilling cold liquid onto the rug.

The shadows in the corners of the room deepened. Tendrils snaked out like arms reaching.

"No," she whispered, standing up too quickly. Her knees knocked the laptop to the floor with a dull *thud*. She took off her glasses and rubbed her eyes.

"I didn't open anything. I just touched the damn book."

The shadows twisted.

Pain spiked in her wrist.

Then the world went black.

KNOCKING. HARD. REPEATED.

Layla woke with a gasp. She was sprawled on the floor beside her overturned laptop. Her breath came in short panicked bursts, and sweat slicked her hair to her neck. Her fingers dug into the carpet, her arms trembling.

KNOCK. KNOCK.

She dragged herself up, dizzy and disoriented, and stumbled toward the door.

"Layla?" a voice called. "It's Rue! I need to talk to you!"

Layla fumbled with the lock and opened the door.

Rue stood there, eyes wide and frazzled, her jacket half-zipped like she'd thrown it on mid-run. Behind her was Dacre; tall, unreadable, leaning one shoulder against the hallway wall like he wasn't casually radiating *you-might-die* energy.

Layla blinked. "What are you doing here?"

"I had a vision," Rue said quickly. "Sort of. It was blurry. I'm still learning how to... process them. But something was wrong. Something with you."

"You saw me?" Layla asked, voice hoarse. "What did you see?"

Rue hesitated. "You. Blood. The sound of voices. Something dark, opening."

Layla took a shaky step back. "I blacked out again."

"Again?" Dacre's voice rumbled low, dark eyes narrowing. "That's the second time in less than a week."

"I don't know what's happening to me." Layla snapped, more out of fear than defensiveness. "I just... I just touched the damn book you wanted."

"Then we need to find out what that book is," Rue said, already stepping inside. "And fast. Because whatever's attached to it, it's coming for you."

Layla sighed. "I need to find a new job. I can't find the books you need without a job. I can't pay my rent without a job." Layla picked her laptop up off the floor and the screen illuminated. "And from what you told me days ago, your

29

research isn't going to stop anytime soon. I like helping you." She walked to the table and set the laptop down. "But I think you're going to have to find a new book dealer."

Rue glanced at Dacre and Layla noticed.

"Why are you two making eyes at each other?" Layla scowled. "I've been around you both long enough to notice that wasn't just a love-glance."

Dacre sighed. "You're going to need protection."

Layla blinked.

"More than we can offer here." Dacre moved closer to Rue. "We know people you can stay with."

"What kind of people?" Layla asked. "Angel people? Hell people?"

"Well, one of them is human. Mostly. We're just out of options." Rue stepped closer.

"I need to call my parents. I still haven't told them I got fired."

"Wait," Rue urged. "You don't want to worry them."

Layla paused, adjusted her glasses. She was overthinking again. What if the book hurt her parents? No, she couldn't have that.

"Okay," Layla said. "I'll wait."

CHAPTER 6

THE PORTAL SPAT THRUSH OUT WITH ALL THE grace of a punch to the chest. It was as if the portal didn't even want his bad energy traversing realms. He tried not to take it personally. But one moment Thrush was surrounded by brimstone and pine, the dry heat of Hell scorching his skin, and the next he stumbled forward into shadow and dust. His boots hit old linoleum with a *thud*, and the sharp scent of mildew and forgotten paper filled his lungs.

The portal had opened inside the backroom of an abandoned bookstore in Lame Deer, Montana. Meg had mentioned it once in passing, one of a handful of thin places still tethered to Hell's ley lines that were close to Jed and Shay.

Thrush adjusted his pack on his shoulder. He hadn't packed much. He had a few weapons, the few clothes he owned, and a notebook from childhood with spells written in scraggly childhood handwriting. It was tucked inside his jacket pocket, warm against his ribs.

He made his way through the abandoned bookstore,

pausing next to the shelves and rubbing his thumb over the spine of a book. He didn't recognize the title and something in his chest ticked, wishing for more time with the old books tucked away in the library at the castle. A life of reading seemed relaxing, like a way to escape the drama of this world. He walked away, pushed open the back door, and stepped into the late-summer dusk.

The sky was bruised with clouds stretched thin over the prairie. Wheatgrass whispered in the breeze. Far off, he could hear the groan of an old windmill and the distant bark of a dog. The air smelled like sage and soil. Clean.

He winced as the sun touched his skin. His body, used to Hell's dull ochre haze, recoiled from the open sky.

Still, he started walking. There were people driving by in trucks, a few walking along the sidewalks. His size earned him a few glances but Thrush was quick to look away, wishing he knew a spell to hide himself. He didn't belong here. He was far from human and he hoped the residents of Lame Deer couldn't tell. Feeling the flush of magic fill his fingertips, he tucked his hands into his pockets and looked for a road sign.

Jed's ranch was in Colstrip, about thirty miles north-west. Normally someone would've met him. But Meg had said, "*You need the walk. The space. Let the earth shake off the hellfire.*"

He hadn't argued.

The gravel roadside stretched ahead in a silver ribbon, cutting through fields that burned gold in the light. Thrush fisted his hands deeper in his pockets. That flickering magic was under his skin, volatile and itching to lash out. It was as if his soul might blow away with the prairie wind.

No flames here. No voices. Just the creak of trees and the far-off call of a hawk.

It made the silence louder.

He walked for an hour before he passed the faded sign welcoming him to the outskirts of town. Another hour and the sun dipped behind the mountains in the distance, turning the sky to molten amber. Dusk swam over everything, painting the world in shadow and peace. He hadn't found peace in years–not since before the war. His last sense of peace was running through the graveyard in Hell where the small stone chapel was set, his childhood home. That was peace. He'd spent his days exploring with his cousins and training with the Hellions, many of whom teased him for being half ghost. He always corrected them. He was half-Astral; there was a difference. And the Hellions would all laugh.

Thrush breathed in the sharp scent of turned soil, and it settled deep into his bones. His body urged him to do something he didn't understand. Maybe it was the Earthen plane trying to get a grip on what he was. There was so much he wasn't understanding. And the longer he walked, the more it felt like something unseen was walking with him. He looked up, then checked the shadow like of the forest. His parents were watching, afraid to reach out.

"Leave me alone," he muttered as sparks lit his fingertips. "Go."

The sense dissipated.

He paused once, halfway up a low rise where the grass grew wild and stared out at the darkening horizon. The land stretched out before him, vast and indifferent. It didn't care what blood he carried. It didn't care that his magic was broken or that he was barely holding it together.

Maybe that's why Meg had sent him here.

To be healed.

To be humbled.

Thrush muttered something under his breath in Hells-peak-half curse, half prayer.

Eventually, the outline of a distant ranch took shape against the bluing night. Faint lights burned in the windows like stars.

He walked down another dirt road that led to the ranch. He turned at a mailbox and from there it was an uphill trek. Horses ran by in the distance. His gaze followed them and he noticed there was an unnatural looking mound near the tree line, dotted with white headstones. He shivered, remembering the private conversations he'd over-heard from Jed and Shay. Her parents were buried there. A demon had dealt them an unnatural death a long time ago, leaving Shay orphaned and alone. All she had left was Jed. And her horse, Nero. Orphaned. The term repeated over and over in Thrush's mind. His parents were dead. But not gone. He could see them if he wished. It was just... he didn't want to disappoint them. He'd gotten so good at disap-pointing those around him.

The ranch came into view slowly, like a memory creeping back into the folds of his mind.

Thrush stood at the edge of the gravel road, boots scuffed with dirt, hands clenched in his pockets. The sky above him had turned a deep cobalt, the kind of blue that only came just before full dark. Stars began to flicker into existence, shy and scattered. It reminded him of the Astral plane. He wondered if his parents were still watching him.

Hellsky was never like this—never so clear. He had a sudden memory of the brightness of the Seven Kingdoms of Heaven and flinched inwardly. That was too bright. It was so bright it hurt and burned something deep within him. It burned a piece of him right off until it dropped back to Hell.

The main house sat a few hundred yards ahead, nestled between the shadowed swell of hills and the lean stretch of pasture beyond. Porch lights cast a warm, amber glow over the wooden steps. The screen door creaked open briefly as someone stepped out; a tall figure with a familiar shape.

Jed.

Thrush didn't move.

He stayed still, crouched behind a thick Oak trunk, half-shrouded in tall grass.

Inside the house, another figure passed in front of the windows with a smaller silhouette and blowtorch-blue hair pulled into a bun.

Shay.

Laughter drifted toward him; muffled, but not hard to recognize. Easy. Natural.

Thrush stared at the scene like it was something fragile, distant, something that might break if he breathed too hard. It might break if he didn't control himself. The ranch buzzed with quiet life; the faint murmur of cows in the paddock, the clink of dishes, and a song playing low from a radio in the barn, too faint to catch.

He hadn't realized how long it had been since he'd seen

anything this... normal. It was like the old movies Meg used to watch when they were kids.

And maybe that's what unsettled him. His normal had become the wild mountains of Hell. He'd felt safe there. Hidden. Unfound, even. Shame was easy to hide amongst the pine trees of Hell. Shame fit just right in the cave he'd called home.

The curse had become noise, heat, chaos. Anger was easier to hold than hope. And now, standing on the outskirts of a place built on trust, hard work, and roots, he felt like a trespasser in his own redemption arc.

Thrush looked down at his hands. They were steady for now. But the magic was always there. Humming. Waiting like a caged thing pacing inside him.

What if it spilled uncontrolled again?

What if he hurt someone? He'd nearly killed Evelyn. He squeezed his eyes shut. No. He would control it. He had to. A hard shiver ran across his shoulders and sprung up his neck. He couldn't control the tics that the curse gave him.

A gust of wind rustled the grass beside him, carrying the scent of sagebrush and horses. He closed his eyes for a moment and let it pass through him.

The screen door creaked again. This time, it stayed open. Chickens and goats made noise, alert but not alarmed.

Jed stepped out onto the porch, scanning the dark horizon. He wasn't looking for trouble. But somehow, Thrush knew he was looking for him.

Still, he didn't move. Not yet. He was trying to regain control.

"Will you just stand there like a tree, waiting to be struck by lightning, or are you going to enter?"

Thrush turned at the sound of the strange voice and recognized Nero.

Nero was a giant black horse. A demon-horse. A Cross-roads Demon to be exact. Thrush knew the beast could talk but it had been so long since he'd heard the creature's voice that it startled him.

"Christ," Thrush muttered. "How did you manage to creep up on me like that?"

Nero nodded his head in the direction from which Thrush had walked. "I've been here the entire time. Maybe you should open your eyes."

Thrush turned. "I never saw you."

Nero whinnied softly. "Maybe you need glasses."

"Never realized you had such a sense of humor." Thrush shifted the pack that was slung over his shoulder.

Nero huffed and pawed the ground. He was watching Thrush warily, like he was watching a bomb getting ready to detonate. Finally, he said, "Come with me."

The giant horse walked towards the ranch and Thrush followed.

"Meg sent a message," Nero warned. "I must remind you that this is a sanctuary to us." Large black eyes looked at him for a half step before Nero looked away again. "You have an *energy*."

"Sure do." Thrush rubbed his fingers together as if smoldering out a flame.

"Have you eaten? Shay made the biscuits. She always brings us some after dinner but looking at the size of you I'm guessing she'll offer them to you."

On cue, Thrush's stomach growled.

"The White Horse will be disappointed. She loves the buttermilk biscuits." Nero whinnied in annoyance.

CHAPTER 7

"MONTANA!" LAYLA EXCLAIMED, DROPPING A stack of folded shirts onto the bed. "What's in Montana?"

Rue stood at the foot of the bed, arms raised in a gesture of peace. "There are people there who can protect you. People I know very well. They're like family."

Layla shook her head, grabbing a worn pair of jeans from the floor and flinging them into her half-packed suitcase. "But... I've never been to Montana. What's even there? I need to find a new job. I can't just disappear to some... horse town in the middle of nowhere!"

She paused, turned sharply, and pointed at Rue. "Also, hello? Who's going to help you find your weird, ancient books now? I've been helping you since you started your research project." She paused and went still. "Are you going to replace me? Are you firing me too?" Panic and disappointment were rising in Layla's voice.

"No. Not at all," Rue said, softer now. "Your safety matters more than my research project."

Layla scoffed, trying to ignore the gnawing chill still

clinging to her spine from earlier; the blackout, the voices, the dark pressure that seemed to press into her chest when no one else was around.

She rifled through a drawer, pulling out socks that didn't match. "This is ridiculous. I'll just go stay with my parents."

"No," Dacre's voice cut in from the living room. Calm. Firm.

Layla stilled. "Excuse me?"

He stepped into the doorway, arms crossed over his chest. "We don't want to put them in danger."

Layla narrowed her eyes. "What kind of danger are we even talking about here? I touched a book. *A book*. Now you're acting like I'm cursed or marked or something. Like she who cannot be named." She used air quotes.

Neither Rue nor Dacre responded right away.

That silence said more than Layla was ready to hear. They didn't know what she was referring to. She'd have to gift them some reading material.

Layla swallowed hard, her fingers curling around the zipper of the suitcase. "You think something's after me, don't you?"

Rue exhaled, stepping closer. "I had another vision after we left your place. It was fractured, but... I saw something moving through your walls. I saw you." her voice cracked slightly. "You were screaming. And then you were gone. Dragged somewhere actually."

The room dropped into a heavy silence.

Layla sat down on the edge of the bed, the suitcase now forgotten. "What's really going on? All of this sounds very Poltergeist." Layla looked up at Rue. "This is very strange."

She took a deep breath and muttered to herself about fucked up fairy tales.

"We don't know," Dacre answered quietly. "Let's remember the details. You touched the Enochian book, you blacked out, then woke up with a bite mark on your wrist."

Layla moved her sleeve and rubbed two fingers over the faded marks. It was nearly gone. She was still not convinced it wasn't just a spider bite.

"Something bit you," Rue reminded her. "In my visions, whatever it was is hunting you."

Layla was shaking her head. "You said that book was connected to angels. And the books I've been digging up for you for the past year have dealt with demons and religion." She paused. "I thought Angels were good."

Rue frowned. "That's not always the reality."

"So you're telling me Angels are bad?"

Dacre leaned against the doorframe. "Some are despicable. Some are decent. They have free will just like humans."

Layla touched her chest. "But I'm human."

"And that's why we need to protect you," Rue said as she sat next to Layla.

"And Montana is your answer to that?" Layla asked.

Rue nodded. "Jed and Shay are like family. They protected me and my brother when we were kids. Jed is... he's half Angel."

Layla's eyes went wide. "You just told me some Angels are bad."

"Not him." Rue shook her head.

Layla looked between them. Her world was unraveling one thread at a time, and she could feel herself hanging just above the drop.

"I don't want to run," she said finally, her voice small. "I just got my life on track. I loved my job at the library."

Rue sat beside her. "I know. But you won't be running forever. You'll be safe, just long enough to figure this out. Then you can come back. I promise."

Layla looked down at her hands, at the faint mark still on her arm; a bite that hadn't fully faded. Her stomach twisted. "But Evelyn never came back."

Rue touched Layla's arm. "Evelyn is happy and in love. She didn't come back because she didn't want to leave Remington. She still is involved in the research. You should see the library my brother built."

She nodded as a single tear welled in the corner of her eye. "Fine," she whispered, "Montana," as she lifted her glasses and wiped the tear away.

Are we there yet?" Layla groaned, her forehead pressed against the car window.

"You asked that five minutes ago," Rue replied without looking up from the tattered book resting in her lap.

"I know, but I thought maybe time had sped up since then," Layla muttered, shifting in her seat. Her knees were practically up to her chest, a hoodie rolled behind her head like a sad excuse for a pillow. "My butt's asleep. My brain's melting. And there's nothing but cows and grass out here. No coffee shops. No bookstores. Not even a good murder mystery podcast signal."

Dacre, at the wheel, didn't say a word. He stared ahead,

stoic as ever, like the stretch of empty Montana highway owed him something and he intended to collect.

Layla threw an arm over her eyes dramatically. "Remind me again why we didn't just fly?"

Rue glanced over the top of her book, one brow arched. "You hate flying. You said, and I quote, 'Planes are just fancy metal coffins with stale pretzels and expired ginger-ale.'"

"Okay, yeah, but I didn't know the road would be this long. Or this flat. Is this even a real state? This feels made up."

"It's not made up," Dacre said dryly. "It's just... under-populated."

"Underpopulated?" Layla repeated. "There are more tumbleweeds than people."

She sat up straighter, craning her neck to look behind them, then ahead again. "How much longer?"

"Another hour or two," Rue said. "Depending on how many times you keep asking."

Layla groaned again and flopped sideways, kicking her shoes off and tucking her feet under her. Her glasses slid down her nose, but she didn't bother fixing them.

"I'm gonna lose it. I swear I'm gonna summon a demon just for the entertainment." Layla wasn't sure why she was saying stupid things. She just couldn't stop.

"Please don't," Dacre said, eyes still on the road. "You're already drawing enough attention."

That shut her up for a moment. It gave her something to overthink about.

She hugged her arms around herself suddenly remembering the whispering voices, the sharp pain in her arm, the cold chill that hadn't left since she touched that damn book. "Do you think they'll know what's happening to me?" she asked quietly. "This Jed guy?"

Rue didn't answer right away. She closed the book in her lap and placed a hand gently over Layla's.

"I think we'll figure it out. But you need to be patient. Trust them."

Layla gave a soft huff. "Trust. Yeah. That's different."

But she didn't pull her hand away. She leaned to the side, resting her head on Rue's shoulder. "Sorry I'm being obnoxious. It's because I'm nervous. Let's read together."

Rue opened the paperback and held it so Layla could read along.

Outside the window the sky was beginning to turn gold at the edges, stretching wide across the empty plains. The wind carried the scent of grass and something wilder underneath. Homey, almost.

Layla glanced away from the book and squinted at the distance. Somewhere out there past the dust and the silence, a home was waiting with the promise of safety. She just wasn't sure if it was going to save her or swallow her whole. Plenty of women had disappeared in the mountains–Layla had listened to a million podcasts about them. She shivered and glanced across the seat at Rue. No, her friend would never do that to her. Rue might be from another realm or dimension or from space but Layla had always felt safe in her presence. Even with her giant, scary boyfriend lurking around. She didn't know anything about Jed and Shay but if Rue trusted them, then Layla probably would as well.

DACRE DROVE UP A LONG GRAVEL DRIVE FLANKED by old fence posts and overgrown prairie grass. A rusted sign hanging on a gate read *Crossroads Ranch*, its letters half-faded.

Layla peered out the window, adjusting her glasses as a tall wooden farmhouse came into view. It looked brand new and charming with a wraparound porch crowded with potted plants, wind chimes, and what looked like a... sword hanging next to the front door. Odd.

"I thought you said these people were ranchers," Layla said, eyeing the sword warily. "That looks like someone's ready for a medieval invasion."

"They are ranchers," Rue said. "Sort of. They dabble in darkness between the realms."

"Oh. Of course. That's totally normal," Layla muttered. "Why not throw in circus performers while we're at it?"

Dacre cut the engine and climbed out. Rue followed, already stretching her legs and giving a small wave toward the house.

Layla stepped out cautiously, gravel shifting under her boots. The Montana heat was different from home, not heavy or humid but dry and golden, the kind of heat that soaked into your bones without making you sweat. The smell of wild sage and horses filled the air. Wind blew the curls out of her face.

The front door creaked open.

A woman emerged first; tall, lean, with blowtorch blue hair in a braid down her back. Her jeans were worn, her boots dust-covered, and tattoos on her arms. Her eyes locked onto Layla instantly, sharp and assessing.

"Shay," Rue said with a warm smile.

Shay returned the smile, and it softened her face. "You brought the librarian."

Layla blinked. "Layla," she introduced herself.

Shay nodded. "Layla. Pretty name. Rue called ahead. Come inside and we'll get you settled."

"Friendly," Layla muttered under her breath as she hoisted her backpack.

From around the side of the house, a tall man emerged. Jed. His sleeves were rolled up, arms dusted with hay and something like soot or ash or... dirt. His presence was quiet but powerful, and when he glanced at Layla it felt like he was already seeing straight through her.

"You've touched something," he said without greeting. "Something angry." He reached for her hand.

Layla froze mid-step.

Rue stepped behind her. "It's okay."

Jed gave a slow nod and took Layla's hand. "It's stained your fingertips."

Layla glanced down. "My fingers are clean." She only saw smooth skin.

"No," he pulled her index finger straight, "here, on the tip." His light eyes stared into hers. "What did you touch?"

Layla swallowed hard. "A book."

"It was written in *Enochian*. And the symbols looked very much like protective runes, worn and broken. It probably hadn't been disturbed in centuries." Rue was at Layla's side, peering at her fingertips. "I didn't know it would do anything to her. I asked her to get it for my research."

Jed frowned. "Seems to be the way of things lately." He

glanced up at Shay then back to Rue. "Why wasn't that book at the Peabody Library?"

"There are no books there. Peabody has been closed for years." Layla looked at Rue like she should know.

Shay cleared her throat. "You brought Layla to the right place." She smiled wide and motioned for everyone to follow.

Inside, the house was a strange blend of rustic charm and arcane edge. Shelves lined the walls filled with old leather-bound books, bottles with handwritten labels, and what might have been a taxidermy gryphon head mounted above the fireplace.

Layla squinted and realized it was a boar. "Okay. This place is... interesting."

"Safe," Shay said behind her. "Which is what you need right now."

Dacre remained near the door, ever the sentinel. He glanced over his shoulder a few times as though he was expecting someone. Rue was already shedding her jacket and settling in like she'd been there a hundred times before.

Layla hovered near the couch, uncertain. "So, uh... where do I sleep? Or am I being sacrificed to a demon goat tonight?" She forced a laugh.

Jed actually smiled. "Room's upstairs. Second door on the left. And we don't sacrifice to goats here." He smirked. "Other things, maybe."

Shay stepped forward, her expression softening slightly. "Something happened to you, Layla. But that doesn't mean you're doomed. We've dealt with worse."

"Great," Layla muttered. "That's comforting." She glanced at Rue.

"Want me to come with?" Rue asked. "Or do you need a moment?"

Layla's stomach tightened. She knew Rue wasn't staying so she decided to take the moment to check out her room and set her mind straight.

"Nah," Layla said. "I'll check it out and come back down."

"You all staying for dinner?" Shay asked.

Rue nodded.

"I'll get it finished." Shay crossed the room and headed to the kitchen.

Layla felt something shift. Here, in this desolate place, maybe she could start to understand what had actually happened when she touched that book. Maybe she could learn to understand whatever trouble Rue had dragged her into, not that she hadn't gone willingly. Searching for the old books had pulled her out of the mundane ho-hum daily tasks she'd fallen into since landing the librarian position on campus. It was exciting, even if it had just changed her life.

Layla headed up the stairs with her backpack slung over her shoulder.

She noticed the shadows didn't move here like they did at her apartment and the basement of the library. She sighed in relief.

THE GUEST ROOM SMELLED FAINTLY OF CEDAR AND fresh linens.

Layla sat cross-legged on the bed, her backpack open at her feet, its contents spilled out across the patchwork quilt.

A half-unzipped hoodie. A half-used notebook. A romance novel with a cracked spine.

She needed a moment to breathe.

She stood and walked to the window and pulled it open. The wood window frame creaked. Outside, the Montana sky stretched endlessly, a wash of deepening blue streaked with gold. Horses grazed in the distance, their tails swishing lazily. A breeze rustled the tall grass, carrying the scent of hay, pine, and something... strange. She noticed strange markings carved into the wood of the window frame and traced them with her fingertip.

Layla let out a slow breath. "Okay," she murmured. "It's not so bad here. It's cozy at least."

The house creaked around her. It didn't look old enough to creak as much as it did since she stepped foot inside. She could hear the muffled voices of Rue and Shay talking in the kitchen, the clink of mugs, laughter, and the deep voices of Jed and Dacre. She smelled coffee. It made Layla miss her parents. She picked up her phone to call them but there was no signal. Strange.

She took off her glasses, cleaned them absently with her shirt, then moved to the small writing desk tucked against the wall. She opened her notebook and wrote:

Day One: Not dead.
Pros: No demon goats. Dinner smells good.
The bed is comfy.
Cons: I feel weird. Book might have infected me. Possible spider bite on arm??? TBD.

Still not sure why Rue trusts these people. But they seem... okay.

Shay could kill a man with a glance. Jed has cryptid vibes but not in a bad way.

I think I needed this. Silence. Space. Sky.

Maybe I can figure out what's wrong with me here.

Maybe I'm not crazy.

SHE TAPPED HER PEN AGAINST THE PAGE, THEN underlined the last sentence twice just to feel like she meant it. She hadn't journaled since high school and doubted that she'd keep up with it. But it did feel nice to write down a few thoughts.

The wind picked up outside, rattling the windowpane. Layla looked out again, frowning.

Far off, just at the edge of the fields, the horses had stopped grazing. They stood stock still; ears perked, heads lifted as if listening.

The breeze shifted again, brushing cool against her skin, and something invisible passed just beneath it. She had a sensation like just before lightning strikes. The hair on her arms rose. Her fingers twitched.

She stepped away from the window slowly.

Layla's breath caught. Her heart thudded hard once against her ribs.

Then a knock came at her door.

"Layla?" It was Rue's voice.

Layla stared at the door. She swallowed. "Y-Yeah?"

"Dinner's ready. Can I come in?"

She turned back to the desk and closed her notebook, pressing her palm to the cover like she could seal her thoughts in there, safe.

"Yeah. Come in."

The door handle turned and Rue stepped inside. "This is cute." She glanced around the room. She walked straight to the window and closed it. "Do you recognize these markings at all?" She turned to face Layla.

Layla shook her head. "I just got you the books. I didn't study them."

"These are protection runes. Jed is also going to line all the windows and doors with salt until they figure this out. Don't break the salt line."

Layla swallowed hard. "Is this like... a Supernatural show or something?"

"Close." Rue forced a smile. "There's definitely danger and ... creatures." Rue focused on Layla's arm. "Are you cold?"

"I don't know. It just felt like a storm was rolling in or something."

Rue looked out the window. "I don't see any rain clouds."

A chill went up Layla's back and she shuddered slightly.

Rue exhaled a breath. "Okay so I'm about to tell you some crazy shit."

Layla's eyes widened.

"You might want to sit down."

Layla shook her head. "I prefer to stand when someone is about to say something crazy."

Rue giggled. "Okay." She began pace. "There are ancient creatures that live on this ranch. Well, one that I know is actually ancient."

"Is that why it feels like lightning is about to strike?" Layla asked.

Rue stilled. "Probably. But... umm... you won't be alone here."

"Right because Shay and Jed are here."

Rue shook her head. "Someone else is arriving today."

Layla crossed her arms. "Who? Some weirdo?"

"My cousin. Thrush." She paused. "Me and Dacre are going to head home after he gets here. I want to see him."

"Oh." Layla's thoughts were spiraling. She could feel the storm circling again.

Thrush. She'd seen him once before. And never forgot. He was very handsome and stoic. He looked like some kind of military guy on leave who didn't know what to do with himself. Layla bit her lip. What were the odds the most attractive man she'd ever crossed paths with was about to live under this roof with her?

DINNER WAS SURPRISINGLY WARM AND FAMILIAR. The long wooden table was set simply with ceramic plates chipped in places, mismatched mugs, and a massive cast-iron skillet in the center filled with bubbling venison stew. A basket of golden buttermilk biscuits sat beside it, still steaming.

Layla had already eaten two.

Shay moved around the table with ease, refilling mugs

and shooing Dacre away from trying to do the dishes early. "Not in my kitchen," she warned, raising a brow. "Go sit down."

"I'll be sitting in the car the entire way home," Dacre argued. "I need to do something."

"The stalls need cleaning," Jed said between bites of stew.

Dacre sighed then stepped back without argument and seated himself beside Rue, who looked completely at home with her bowl in one hand and a spoon in the other.

"These biscuits are incredible," Layla said around a mouthful, blinking behind her glasses. "What's the secret?"

"Cold butter," Shay replied. "And love. In that order."

Jed chuckled quietly, spooning more stew into his bowl.

"I usually bring the extras out to the horses after we eat," Shay added, wiping her hands on a towel. "They love the smell of the biscuits. One of them, Nero, likes to pretend he's too dignified to beg, but he always ends up nosing the basket."

Layla lit up. "Wait. There are horses here? I saw them out the window but I thought they were from a nearby ranch."

"Nope," Jed said. "We've got three hundred acres here."

"I love horses," Layla said, suddenly sitting straighter. "Like, irrationally. I used to beg for riding lessons when I was a kid, but my parents said it was too expensive. So I just... collected plastic models and cried over Black Beauty."

Jed and Shay exchanged a quiet glance. It was subtle, but there was a flicker of something in Shay's eyes.

"Well," Shay said gently, "you'll meet a few of them tomorrow morning if you're up early enough."

Rue leaned over, nudging Layla's arm. "We're just glad you're here. And safe. This place... Jed and Shay will help. You'll see."

Shay had just turned toward the sink with the empty stew pot when her body went still.

Jed stood slowly, eyes narrowing as he moved toward the nearest window, brushing aside the curtain.

Outside, the last blush of sunset painted the horizon in burnt rose and violet. A soft wind moved through the fields, brushing the tall grasses in waves.

But it wasn't the wind that caught Jed's attention.

A massive black horse was walking toward the house from the far edge of the property. The horse's coat shimmered like midnight.

And beside him walked a figure.

Tall. Broad-shouldered. His pale hair caught the fading light like silver fire.

Jed's jaw tensed.

Shay's voice was low. "Nero's brought our next guest."

Layla, still seated, blinked. "Wait. Nero? You named the horse Nero?"

"I was a kid when I named him," Shay said.

But Rue was already standing. "It's him."

Dacre moved toward the front door, face hardening. "He's late."

"Heard Meg told him to walk in from town," Jed chuckled.

Layla looked from face to face, her fingers tightening

around her biscuit. "Okay. Um. Why do you all look like someone just lit a warning beacon? Who's him?"

Jed didn't answer.

Rue stepped toward the door, her voice softer now. "It's Thrush."

Layla's brows pinched. "Why are you all so worried?"

Dacre opened the door and the cool air rushed in.

Outside, Nero stopped just a few feet from the porch, the man beside him pausing as well.

His eyes lifted toward the house.

Toward her.

Layla felt something inside her chest shift.

Rue's warm fingers touched her arm. "Come on," she whispered. "Let's say hello."

CHAPTER 8

THE SCREEN DOOR SLAMMED AS RUE DASHED outside, boots thudding down the porch steps.

"Thrush!" she called out, running toward him, throwing her arms around him before he could brace himself.

He caught her in a stiff surprised hug, blinking as she squeezed tight. Rue had always been full of this unshakable warmth. Like sunshine on a stormy day. He didn't know what to do with it.

"We've been waiting for hours." she said, stepping back, her grin wide and teasing. "I thought you got lost or ran away to the forest again."

Thrush shrugged, his voice low. "Your mother told me to walk from Lame Deer."

Rue's smile faltered just a little. "Is it that bad?"

He didn't answer at first, just looked down at his hands. His palms itched, the magic under his skin stirring even now. "I can't control it, Rue. I thought I could. I've tried everything. Meditation, exercise, training drills... nothing works. It just builds and builds and builds. I almost hurt Evelyn."

Rue's expression softened, and she touched his arm. "Then you're in the right place. Jed and Shay will help. You're not alone, Thrush. You never were. Me and Dacre will help too."

Behind them, Shay stepped onto the porch with a towel slung over her shoulder, eyes twinkling. "Well," she said, "looks like we're going to have a full house. Good thing I made extra biscuits."

Jed appeared beside her, arms crossed, but there was the smallest twitch of a smile under his beard. "Finally got help for the morning chores."

Thrush raised an eyebrow. "You expect me to shovel horse shit to fix this?"

Jed didn't blink. "Think of it as penance."

Shay snorted and looked toward the door. "Well, don't just stand there, Layla. Come out and say hi."

Thrush turned as the screen door creaked open.

Layla stepped out cautiously. Up close, she was even smaller than he'd remembered. But every bit a human woman. She squinted up at him like she was trying to solve a puzzle she didn't remember signing up for.

Her voice was quiet. "You're Thrush?"

He tilted his head. "Last time I checked."

She blinked, eyes looking magnified behind her glasses. "You look like you sleep in caves." She was studying him.

Thrush barked out a surprised laugh. "Sometimes accurate."

Dacre leaned against the porch railing, smirking. "He

does. Literally. For years at a time. Kid was practically raised by wolves."

Layla took another bite of her biscuit and muttered, "Of course."

"Is nothing a secret?" Thrush grumbled.

"Your boy Remm told me." Dacre chuckled.

Rue grinned between them, clearly enjoying herself.

Thrush shoved his hands in his pockets unable to keep his eyes off Layla. "I remember you. From the coffee shop."

Layla looked up, startled. "You do?"

"You brought in a stack of books bigger than yourself."

A flush crept up Layla's cheeks. "Oh. Yeah. I remember."

He shrugged, looking away. "You stood out." He glanced at her hair then the dark-rimmed glasses perched on her nose.

The porch fell into a moment of awkward silence, the kind that wrapped around them like a pause in a song. And Thrush had a sudden memory of a conversation with Evelyn rush to the forefront of his mind.

EVELYN TAPPED A FINGER ON HER CHIN. "BUT YOU have a bit of a darker kinda prince kinda vibe going on."

Thrush laughed under his breath. "That's the nicest thing anyone's ever said to me." Then, tilting his head, he asked, "You got any single friends?"

Evelyn snorted. "Why? Thinking about settling down?"

"I like options," he said with a smirk. "And Remm seems happy for the first time in years. I've been watching him."

"Mm." She crossed her arms, narrowing her eyes. "You

should see Rue. Are you going to do your time, or are you just going to wander around making bad jokes? I'd hate to watch you slowly go crazy. We just met, after all."

NERO WHINNIED SOFTLY BEHIND THRUSH, AS IF impatient to move things along.

Shay clapped her hands once. "Alright! Let's get you settled, cave-boy. We've got a guest room ready, and tomorrow Jed's going to make you cry before breakfast."

Thrush muttered, "Can't wait," and followed Shay toward the house.

As he passed Layla, their eyes met again and something flickered between them. An echo. A thread neither of them knew the shape of. But it was there.

THRUSH CLOSED THE BEDROOM DOOR WITH A quiet *click* and leaned against it for a long moment, letting the stillness settle over him.

The walls were bare, the linens smelled clean. A single bed was tucked into the corner, and a wide desk stretched beneath a window that overlooked the pasture. The scent of sagebrush drifted in with the late summer breeze.

It was... peaceful. It reminded him of the forest. Minus the clean bed.

He didn't trust it. Didn't trust much these days. Didn't trust himself. Energy surged to his fingertips and he fisted his hands, took a deep breath, and forced it to stop. He focused on the mountains in the distance, the open window, anything but the magic.

His boots creaked on the floorboards as he moved, fingers trailing along the carved runes etched subtly into the windowsill and the doorframe. Jed's handiwork. He recognized a few protection runes.

He traced one with the edge of his thumb, letting a thread of magic skim the surface. It sparked faintly, reacting to his touch, then settled.

They were active. Of course they were.

"Good," he muttered.

He moved to the dresser, where his worn duffel bag sat half unzipped. He pulled out clothes and spare boots; the usual gear. But at the bottom, beneath a folded flannel and a black T-shirt, he found what he was really looking for.

A battered soft-cover notebook, its edges curled. The spine was broken in two places. The pages were stuffed with clippings, half-legible notes, and hand-drawn runes in black ink. The leather cord he'd wrapped around it years ago still held, barely.

Thrush sat down on the edge of the bed and slowly undid the tie.

Inside, his childhood stared back; desperate; desperate scribbles from where he'd rushed to make notes after watching Jed in action, bits, bits of spell work copied from Jed's own notebook,, and frantic attempts to gather spells while he had felt the chaos swirling inside him as a teenager. He'd always known he was going to run. Always known he held darkness. Always known it would end in disaster. It became more evident the moment they sought refuge in the Seven Kingdoms of Heaven before the war with Lucifer.

He had felt himself crumbling apart back then. His parents had fled to Heaven and Thrush had began training with the Legion of Angels. They were brutal. Thrush had hated it. Then Heaven's sun had turned his hair white and it felt like his soul was burning up inside his body. He couldn't leave that place soon enough.

He flipped to the middle of the notebook where a section had been added later, more organized with bits of spells and theory he'd gained from the mountain Demons... and others he'd dare not speak of. Yes he'd fled to the forest and the mountains because he'd been afraid and dangerous, but he was also seeking answers. Creatures who'd been in hiding since Lucifer's reign had few answers. Many were still afraid to discuss details about magic. And then there was the fact that he couldn't control what was happening to him. There were plenty he'd accidentally hurt over the years. Some who deserved it. Thrush's head twitched and it sent a sharp pain blasting into his skull. The family curse had lessened since he'd returned to do his time as a Hellion, but it was still there; lingering, waiting for him to abandon his duties again.

Thrush sat on the bed and flipped through the notebook.

He recognized Evelyn's handwriting, neater than his, marking theories about some of the rune spells. He'd shown her the notebook when he'd recognized books in the castle library with some of the same symbols. Evelyn was knee deep in research related to angelic heritage and giants on the Earthen Plane. There was plenty of history and magic that had been lost and hidden and buried. And killed. Jed was legend to that. The Nephilim was the only surviving one on any plane. All others had been killed by their sires or died during childbirth. After a lifetime on the run, Jed had grown into a powerful magic wielder.

Thrush traced a line Evelyn had drawn between two opposing runes. She'd written: *If one energy outweighs the other, destabilization occurs.* Underneath, she'd scrawled: *You are not broken. You just don't have all the pieces yet.*

His chest tightened. Maybe she was on to something. Thrush's father was a creature of the Astral. His mother was a princess of the Seven Kingdoms of Heaven. Thrush was something no one had ever come across before.

Remington was a lucky bastard.

He closed the notebook and leaned back on the bed, staring at the ceiling as the hum of the wards settled into the background. They dulled the edge of his magic, kept it wrapped in something secure like an anchor or a warm blanket.

Beneath it all, the storm still churned.

And in the quiet breaths between he swore he felt the shift in the air again. Cold. Familiar.

A whisper against the wall. A flicker in the corner of his vision.

He sat up sharply, eyes scanning the room.

Nothing.

But the space behind him suddenly felt too full.

His parents were watching. He could feel them hovering on the edge of the veil. Their presence was undeniable, like a pressure behind his ribs or like being watched by a memory.

"Please go," he whispered.

He stood and crossed to the window, flinging it open wider. Wind rushed in, brushing across his face. The tension ebbed, just a little.

Thrush looked out across the darkening land. A few horses were grazing near the fence. The sky was bruising with twilight, streaked with gold and soft indigo.

He placed the notebook on the desk carefully and whispered, "Not tonight."

No ghosts. No spells. No more digging into things he didn't understand.

He glanced in the mirror over the desk, noticing his eye color was changing again, blue to green to silver. A storm. He closed his eyes and took a deep breath.

Not tonight.

He didn't know what was waiting for him here: training, chaos, maybe redemption. But for the first time in what felt like forever, he wasn't running.

And that had to count for something.

CHAPTER 9

THRUSH HATED THE BED.

The mattress was too soft. The pillow smelled like lavender. The blankets were too clean. He'd tossed and turned all night, sheets twisted around his legs like shackles. Sleep never came. His mind hovered on some periphery between sleep and wake and aggravation.

At some point, just before dawn, he gave up.

Now he stood in the kitchen of the ranch house, barefoot and bleary-eyed, rubbing at the ache in his shoulder like it might disappear if he glared hard enough at the coffee maker wishing it tasted like the coffee from Hell.

The twitches and confusion had lessened when he showed up for Hellion training. Heck, the confusion was nearly all gone. Meg had told him that this training still satisfied the curse. But what did she know about it...

There was movement upstairs; small feet padding to the bathroom above. Layla. Thrush swallowed hard. He could hear her every movement from across the hall. She was small like a mouse, her sounds were just enough to remind him that she was here. Why was she there? She stood out like a sore thumb in a place like this. A city girl on the ranch. It didn't make sense. Although, he couldn't ignore the fact that something had lightened in his chest when he saw her yesterday. He never thought he'd get the opportunity to see her again. The little librarian. Quiet as a mouse and a million times too pretty for this ranch.

Thrush spun at the sound of footsteps in the kitchen.

It was Jed. He handed Thrush a basket with something wrapped in a dish towel.

"Biscuits," Jed said. "You'll need 'em."

Thrush raised an eyebrow. "You are bribing me with carbs at the ass-crack of dawn?"

Jed arched a brow right back. "Not for you. They're for Nero and the White Horse."

Thrush blinked. "The horses?"

Jed gave a single nod and then crossed the kitchen to pour himself a mug of coffee. "The Earthen plane is the White Horse's. You don't belong here so you need to ask permission to stay."

"Meg didn't do that?"

"Why would she when you can do it yourself?" Jed helped himself to the fresh coffee ahead of Thrush. He lifted the mug to his lips and took a sip. His eyes seemed to brighten. "You're a man now. Time to do manly things."

"Right." Thrush looked down at the basket on the counter, then back up at Jed, narrowing his eyes. "So what's the catch?"

"You're here to train," Jed said simply. "And this place is sacred to Her."

Thrush stared.

Jed took another sip of his coffee. "Before we begin, you'll take those biscuits and go out to the east barn. They'll be there, waiting. She *always* knows when someone new arrives."

"What do I do? Bow? Beg? Sacrifice a small creature?"

Jed smiled. "Offer them the biscuits. Ask for permission to remain." He paused. "You've known Nero for a long time. I'm sure they've already had a discussion about you."

Thrush huffed. "Fucking horses making a decision about my life."

"You know they are more than horses."

Thrush went still. Yes, he knew. Nero was a demon now. A Crossroads Demon. And so was Shay. They were bound, tethered by a strong bond. It was strange though, a creature like the White Horse shacking up with a demon horse. He sighed. But then there was Meg and Sparrow. Seemed light and dark had an affinity for each other.

Thrush muttered something under his breath and shoved his boots on. He hated being told what to do but he knew better than to challenge Jed these days. If he had a chance in Hell at getting his body under control, it was here.

Basket in hand, he stepped out onto the porch.

The sky was still streaked with lavender and orange, the sun barely rising above the horizon. Fog clung to the grass like a blanket. The air was cool, biting against his skin.

He followed the dirt path east, the fog thinning with every step, until he reached the fence line.

There was a soft whinny.

Nero stood outside the door and he noticed the White Horse inside, luminous and still as a statue. The white of her coat shimmered faintly, ethereal, like moonlight woven into flesh. Her mane was impossibly long, almost touching the ground. She was still. Her black eyes fixed on Thrush as if she'd known him forever.

Thrush exhaled slowly.

He walked inside.

Nero moved closer. The White Horse stayed at the far side of the barn, watching.

Thrush crouched, setting the basket on a nearby table and pulled back the cloth. The smell of buttermilk and honey drifted into the air.

"I came to ask permission to stay," Thrush said, straightening his shoulders.

The White Horse only watched.

"I'm not here to cause trouble," Thrush said after a beat. "I don't know what's happening to me. And I don't know how to fix it. But... I want to. I don't want to be lost to the darkness."

The words came out quieter than he meant them to, like a secret not meant for anyone to hear.

Finally, the White Horse moved. One slow step. Then another.

She crossed the open space, elegant and eerie, until she stood just a few feet from Thrush.

Thrush didn't breathe.

The horse stared into his eyes, blinked once, then turned toward Nero. "Tell him if he destroys this place, I will destroy him."

Thrush swallowed hard.

Nero repeated what the White Horse had said.

Thrush exhaled hard, relief washing over him like a cold

shower. He wasn't sure why the White Horse refused to speak directly to him. Why did she need to speak through Nero? Perhaps she didn't trust him. No one should trust him. He was barely holding on as it was.

"Understood," Thrush muttered, tipping his head down.

"One more thing," the White Horse said.

"You must promise to protect the girl at all costs."

"Who?" Thrush asked.

Nero blinked and nickered in disgust. "Layla. The girl who is here under our protection. Promise you will protect her."

"She's under your protection?" Thrush asked.

Both horses stared, not offering any answers.

Thrush nodded. "Of course. I'll protect her."

Both horses nodded in satisfaction as the words left his lips.

Jed was waiting outside. "Don't get too comfy, caveboy! I've got a shovel with your name on it." He tossed a large shovel in Thrush's direction, the tool drifting through the air as though it were nothing but a feather.

CHAPTER 10

It had been nearly a week of waking with the sunrise, eating eggs and coffee, tucking her short, curly hair under a baseball cap and heading out to do chores with her new blue-haired friend. Layla watched Shay's back as they walked to the henhouse. She noticed movement on the far end of the cattle field and recognized the outlines of Jed and Thrush. They looked like giants even from this distance. Standing near them was more off-putting. Both men towered over Layla and made her feel exceptionally short.

The hens clucked as Shay opened the door to the hen house. Layla wasn't sure how many chickens in total there were, she'd counted nearly fifty the other day. They all filtered out of the small shed. Layla gripped her basket and began looking for eggs.

"Oh crap," Shay muttered. "Lucy here hid some eggs. Guess we've got chicks now."

Layla moved closer and smiled as tiny chicks peeked their heads out from under the reddish colored hen.

"They're so cute." Layla reached out but the hen named Lucy pecked at her hand.

"Don't be rude, Lucy," Shay scolded as she searched the nesting boxes for more eggs.

Layla moved on, searching the opposite side of the hen house nesting boxes.

Something outside cracked like lightning, but when Layla looked out the window the skies were clear and blue.

"You doing okay?" Shay asked. "I know ranch life isn't much like what you're used to."

"I miss the library." Layla set three eggs into her basket. "Don't get me wrong, it's nice here. And I'm appreciative. I just... I had a life plan and that's all seemed to have gone to shit now."

"That happened to me once," Shay said.

Layla turned and noticed the woman was completely still and staring off into the distance.

"Do you want to talk about it?" Layla asked.

Shay smiled and shook her head. "It's a long story. Some other time."

LAYLA WAS FRESHLY SHOWERED AFTER A MORNING of chores and sitting on her bed, reading. There was a knock on the door.

"Can I come in?" Shay's voice said from the other side of the door.

"Sure." Layla closed her book and sat up.

Shay walked into the room with a smile. "I have something to show you." She waved. "Come on. We're headed to town for a few hours."

Layla slipped her shoes on and grabbed her bag. "Is there cell phone service? I'd like to call my parents."

Shay nodded. "Yeah. There should be."

Layla followed Shay out of the house and to an old truck.

The black horse named Nero was watching them from near the fence.

Shay put the windows down and drove slowly to town.

"Who names a town Lame Deer?" Layla asked.

"Well, this is native land," Shay said. "There are a lot of tribes around here. There was a casino in Lame Deer and a reservation nearby. Some of the people were like family. There was this old lady, Grandmother Crow we called her. She was kinda like a spiritual being. Made teas and talked really suspicious about reality."

"Sounds like someone I'd like to meet."

"Well, she's gone now. She died back when the dead walked." Shay glanced at Layla. "That was probably before you were born." Shay sniffed. "One of her sons used to work for my father on our ranch."

"Where's he?"

"Also dead."

Layla turned to look at Shay. "This is concerning. Is anyone alive?"

Shay chuckled. "Yes. I'm just not as close with the tribes that survived. Maybe one day, after we rebuild relations. When they lost Grandmother Crow, everything changed."

Shay turned left at a stoplight.

Layla recognized the town they'd driven through on the way to the ranch a week ago.

Shay drove down main street. Most of the buildings were empty. Old shops and restaurants.

"The casino is over there," Shay motioned. "That's where I first met Jed."

Layla noticed a burnt and crumbling building in the distance. "Romantic."

Shay shrugged. "Not really at all. But he was handsome. The moment I set eyes on him I froze up like a snake was about to bite me."

Shay slowed the truck and pulled into a parking spot.

The sign overhead was crooked and read "Books."

"This town could use a bookstore. And a portal to the other realms in the back room would be an added bonus." Shay opened her door. "Come on, let's take a look."

Layla scrambled out of the truck and followed.

Shay pulled a key from her pocket and used it to unlock the front door. They went inside.

The old bookstore was dusty, the air stale. But there was something about it that sang familiar to Layla.

"I'm used to the library but this could work..." Layla trailed off as she noticed the aged computer on the shelf. "It's going to need some work and upgrades."

"Money shouldn't be an issue. Rue's family owns this." Shay ran her finger over a shelf thick with dust. She brushed it off and turned. "What do you think?"

"I could still request the books Rue needs for her research if we upgraded the computer systems." Layla wandered the shop. It had good lighting. A deep cleaning and some fresh paint would brighten the space. New books would bring in customers. She glanced out the window. Only a few cars had driven by. There was no foot traffic. Layla didn't know much about business but it didn't seem like there would be many shoppers. She glanced at the computer again. Maybe online fulfillment would be the major income here. Maybe she should take some business classes?

"What are you thinking?" Shay asked, walking closer. "I can see your mind is moving a mile a minute."

Layla shrugged. "Just... money."

"Don't worry about money. Rue said that keeping you able to find her the books she needs for her research would be worth plenty." Shay sighed. "I think we're gonna have to have to order some cleaning supplies and mops."

Layla smiled and she adjusted her glasses. "Okay." She rubbed her hands together. "I'm in. Let's do this."

She pulled out her phone. "Oh, there's service here. Give me a sec. I want to call my parents."

Shay bit her bottom lip. "Please don't tell them about the ranch."

Layla paused before tapping the screen. "Does anyone know about the ranch?"

"Only those who need to know." Shay tucked a strand of blue hair behind her ear.

A chill passed through Layla. "Okay. I'll just tell them I have an apartment here." She looked at the ceiling. "Maybe above the shop. Is there a space up there?"

Shay nodded.

"Okay. I just don't want them to worry."

Shay was biting her nail as Layla tapped on the phone screen and held it up to her ear.

CHAPTER 11

NEARLY TWO WEEKS OF NOTHING BUT DIGGING holes for fence posts was grinding on Thrush's subconscious. He came here to learn how to control his magic not work as free labor. He'd learned how to throw hay bales, shovel shit in the barns, herd the cattle and horses, shoot coyotes lingering around the hen-house and prepare their pelts for sale. And he wasn't allowed to use a spec of magic for any of it. Jed had forbidden it. Still, the power lingered in his fingertips, threatening to burst free. The ache in his shoulder from the too comfortably uncomfortable bed grew each day. Many nights he'd moved to the floor to sleep as though he were in a cave in Hell or the Hellion barracks. He woke with every creak in the house, every movement from across the hallway. Agitation was bubbling up inside him.

"Hey," Jed shouted. He was nearly a hundred yards away, twining wire around fenceposts. "We gotta finish this by sunset."

"If you'd just use magic it would be done already." Thrush shouted back.

"Not here." Jed was frowning.

"Why not?" Thrush countered.

"Because I said so."

Rage surged and sparks of white suddenly flew from Thrush's fingertips.

"Put that away," Jed scolded.

Thrush couldn't take it anymore. A tic hit him hard, pulling the muscle in his shoulder that had been aching for weeks. It felt like it was tearing in half. The shudder and pain were too much.

"How much of this shit are you going to make me do?" Thrush yelled. "I've been here for weeks doing nothing."

Jed stared, his lips curved downward as he watched Thrush unravel.

"You half-breed scum!" Thrush shouted. He couldn't control the anger, the pain, the magic shooting through his body. White lightning shot out of his fingertips and hit Jed.

Jed stumbled backward. Thankfully, the Nephilim had covered his skin with runes of protection. His magic was as strong as it had ever been but it was nothing compared to the young man in front of him, who was losing his shit and throwing a tantrum like some ethereal toddler with a hell of a lot of ancient magic coursing through his body.

Jed frowned and never took his eyes off the man in front of him. "I have never been so disappointed in you. You of all people should know better. I protected you from death and darkness. I spent my life on the run from Archangels and demons. Who knew I'd have to add you to the list-" Jed stopped.

Thrush opened his mouth but words did not come, only hate for himself. He picked up the shovel and began digging again.

———

THRUSH DIDN'T RETURN TO THE RANCH AT DUSK. Shay was watching out the window as his large form continued digging holes for the fence posts.

"Is he going to stay out there all night?" Shay asked.

"He better," Jed grumbled, rubbing soreness out of his chest. "He'll be sleeping in the barn next."

Shay went still. "That's cruel."

"Not for a creature like him. He lived in the forests and mountains of Hell for nearly ten years, like a wild animal. Maybe the wild is where he belongs."

Shay touched Jed's arm. "He can't control much of it. Remember Sparrow?"

Jed looked down at Shay. "He must learn how to control it."

CHAPTER 12

"WHY IS HE STILL OUT THERE?" LAYLA WAS standing next to Jed in the dark hours of morning. "I could barely sleep with that pounding sound."

Jed pushed the button on the coffee maker. "He's working things out."

Layla glanced up as Jed reached for an insulated mug. The coffee maker beeped as the aroma of fresh coffee filled the kitchen.

"Maybe you could bring him this."

Jed poured hot coffee into the travel mug and scraped it across the counter in Layla's direction.

"Me?" Layla swallowed hard. "Why me?"

"Why not you?" Jed's gaze was unnerving.

"Maybe he should eat something?" Layla offered. "He's been out there all night."

Jed smiled. "You're right." He crossed the room and opened the freezer, then pulled out two breakfast sandwiches and went to the microwave. "Don't tell Shay about my stash."

Layla smiled. "You have a secret stash of frozen breakfast sandwiches?"

"Our secret." He heated them up for a minute in the microwave then wrapped them in a towel. Layla slid on a pair of boots and grabbed her jacket from a hook near the door.

"Do you think he'll be mad?" Layla asked.

"He's too ashamed to be mad." Jed didn't make eye contact as he took two mugs of coffee and walked toward the bedroom he shared with Shay.

Layla stepped out into the cool morning. Fog drifted around her boots as she headed for the field in the distance.

The sun was already a pale haze above the horizon when Layla found him. The fence line stretched behind him in a half-finished row of posts and wire, sharp against the morning mist. He was crouched beside a wooden post, his shirt soaked with sweat, his hands streaked with dirt and blood. His blonde hair clung to his forehead, and a faint shimmer looking like a water mirage pulsed around him like heat waves.

He didn't notice her.

She watched him work. Muscled arms flexed, sweat dripped down his back. Layla licked her lips. He was a wild thing, that was easy to see. Wild and...

He suddenly went still and turned to face her. "What do you want?" His voice sounded like a growl.

"I brought you breakfast and coffee." She held them out. "It's fresh."

He walked closer, dirt streaked across his skin and smelling very male. Like... woodsmoke and pine trees. It reminded her of the mountains.

78

Silver eyes focused behind her.

Layla turned and recognized the giant black horse named Nero had followed her. She hadn't heard him. The creature had stealth.

Thrush smiled, though it seemed forced.

"I suppose I should just say thank you."

He was too close, looking her up and down.

Layla shivered before holding out the food to him again.

She didn't miss the white glow to his fingertips. Or the beat of electricity that slid up her spine when his fingers brushed her hand as he took the thermos and warm towel wrapped around breakfast sandwiches.

"Why did you work all night?" Layla asked.

Thrush stepped back and she missed his closeness. Even though he seemed on edge, she wasn't afraid of him. She found him interesting, curious, something like a puzzle with jagged pieces.

"Because I needed to."

"You needed to build a fence at night?" She pushed her glasses up.

"Yeah. Something like that."

"What happened?"

Nero moved closer and rubbed Layla's arm with the side of his nose affectionately.

Thrush's eyes narrowed.

"They didn't tell you what happened?"

"You tell me. Why did you work all night?" Layla asked.

Thrush glanced up, his gaze sharp and wary. "Because I needed to."

He stepped back, a few feet of distance immediately between them. She caught the shift and frowned.

"You *needed* to build a fence at night?" she pressed, pushing her glasses up. "Under the moon and stars? I guess that sounds relaxing."

"Yeah. Something like that." He let himself sink cross-legged into the grass, yanking open the cloth covering the breakfast sandwiches. He grabbed one, chewing without any real enthusiasm. "Don't know if Jed will let me back in the house."

"What happened?"

Nero nudged Layla's arm with the side of his nose—a gentle, almost affectionate gesture. Layla smiled, brushing her fingers through his dark mane. The horse seemed to preen under her touch.

Thrush's eyes narrowed. "When did you become so close to that horse?"

Layla shrugged. "He seems to like me. He kinda reminds me of you. Big and lurking but..."

"Do you even know what he is?" Thrush chuckled as he took a bite of the sandwich, his brow rising when Layla didn't reply.

"He's a horse," Layla whispered as she covered Nero's ear and lowered her voice. "Don't embarrass him." She giggled.

"Sure he is." Thrush took a sip of the coffee.

She watched him carefully. "Did you... do something?"

"Yeah." His voice was rough. "Lost my cool." He stretched his neck.

"Lost your cool?" Layla tilted her head, and a wild curl

slipped from behind her ear. "You mean, like... threw a tantrum?"

His jaw clenched. "Sure. Let's call it that."

"And because of that, you think Jed won't let you back in the house?"

"It's better that I stay outside," Thrush muttered. His fingers dug into the grass, magic sparking faintly between the blades, leaving a dark, ashy mark in its wake. "I almost hurt him." He sighed. "Just like I almost hurt Evelyn." He glanced up, eye color shifting. "You should leave before I hurt you too."

"You didn't hurt them. Whatever happened was an accident."

"I could have," he snapped, then immediately looked away, staring at the distant hills, his shoulders tense. "It's not a game, Layla. I lose control, and people get hurt. Jed knows that. I know that. So yeah, I worked all night. Because it's better than sitting inside, waiting to blow up again. I should have never left the mountains. I was better off there with the wild animals than trying to fix this curse. I'm damned. I should have left it at that."

"You're acting like you're a monster," she said quietly. "But you're not. You're just..."

He laughed but it was bitter, a rough sound that scraped his throat. "You don't get it, do you? I've got an ages old curse inside me turning me crazy that I can't control. It doesn't listen to me. One wrong moment, one flash of anger..."

"Then control it." She stood.

He looked up, stunned. "It's not that simple."

Layla moved a step closer, then another, her boots

rustling against the tall grass. Nero's nose brushed her shoulder and she scratched him absently, eyes never leaving Thrush.

"Maybe it is." Layla crouched down to his level, her voice calm but steady. "Maybe you've convinced yourself it's impossible, so you never really try. You spent years running from reality and how long have you spent actually dealing with it?"

Thrush's eyes darkened, the color flaring silver to blue. "You don't know what you're talking about."

Her gaze was searching his, waiting, mesmerized by the change in his eye color.

"It's been a few months."

She smiled. "Maybe give yourself more time. A day heals nothing. A week heals little. And a month is only good for reminiscing. Maybe evaluate everything in a year."

Thrush stared at her, the words hanging between them like a fragile bridge. He hated it, hated how easily she spoke, how lightly she stepped into the storm of his rage without a second thought.

And yet... that same quiet defiance held him there. Grounded him. Kept the chaos at bay.

"Fine," he muttered, pushing himself to his feet. "But when you get hurt, don't say I didn't warn you."

"I won't." She looked away, brushing off the dirt on her jeans. "Maybe you should stop pretending you're a lost cause."

The tension snapped like a taut wire. He leaned in, eyes locked on hers; his breath a sharp, heated whisper against her cheek. "Careful, Layla. You don't know what you're playing with."

"Maybe I do," she whispered back, finally looking up.

For one long electric moment, the world shrank to just the two of them. Layla's heartbeat was loud in her ears and she didn't look away, even with the angry shimmer of magic in his eyes or with his towering frame and clenched fists.

Thrush was the first to break, turning sharply away, his breathing unsteady. "You're gonna get yourself killed."

"No," Layla whispered, watching his back. "But maybe I'll figure you out."

Nero snorted softly, brushing his mane against Layla's cheek as if to comfort her. She reached up to pat his nose, but her gaze stayed on Thrush; on his hunched shoulders and the way he gripped his own hands to keep them from shaking.

"Eat your breakfast," she called, letting the teasing tone return. "Maybe I'll come out tomorrow with breakfast and a lecture again."

"Lucky me," he muttered, but there was no heat in it.

As Layla turned to walk back toward the ranch house, she found herself smiling.

CHAPTER 13

Day Fourteen: Delivered forbidden freezer biscuits to a cursed man-beast. Survived. Would do it again. 4.5 Stars.

Pros:

Coffee successfully delivered. Unspilled.

Did not get eaten by Thrush or the giant horse.

Learned Thrush has a tragic streak to match his eyebrows.

Nero let me scratch his mane again. Very validating.

Cons:

Apparently, I look like I'm "playing with fire." (...Is that a threat or a compliment?)

Thrush is still convinced he's too dangerous to be around me.

He worked all night building a fence to avoid people. That's... deeply saddening.

I may be developing a soft spot the size of Montana for a cursed wild-boy with anger issues and very nice shoulders.

Let's be honest: he looked wrecked. Not in a bad way, more like a storm-tossed lighthouse that hasn't realized it's still standing. I couldn't stop thinking about him working through the night. What's wrong with me?

His fingers brushed mine when he took the coffee. Sparks. Also: his eyes changed color. That probably should've freaked me out more than it did. They were kind of pretty, in a handsome way.

But the thing is... I don't think he realizes how not afraid I am of him.

He's trying so hard to keep people away-out of fear, not cruelty. He's not lashing out; he's trying to protect us. Which would be noble if it wasn't so lonely. If I've learned anything from books (and libraries and those strange books Rue orders), it's that isolation makes monsters of all of us eventually.

Maybe what he needs isn't another warning. Maybe he needs someone to bring him breakfast and say, "Hey, I see you. And no, you're not too far gone."

Even if he thinks I'm reckless. Even if Nero's a literal giganta-horse that wouldn't leave my side. Even if he glared at me like I was some puzzle he didn't want to solve but couldn't walk away from.

Whatever happens next... IDK but it feels dangerous.

LAYLA SOFTLY CLOSED THE COVER OF HER journal. Damned man.

Chapter 14

She'd brought him coffee and breakfast again. And argued with him. Again. It was about something stupid like him talking about his feelings.

Thrush watched Layla walk back to the farmhouse alone, short curls blowing in the morning breeze. She was stupid. And... beautiful and brave and small and *human*. And far too innocent for his world. He didn't want to hurt her. She made all the feelings in his chest intensify. He missed having Evelyn around; her kind words, her quick laughter. He pulled the notebook from his back pocket and opened it.

You are not broken. You just don't have all the pieces yet.

Nero whinnied.

Thrush focused on the horse. "What?"

"She stood up to you."

"And she doesn't know what you are." Thrush smirked before bending and pickup up the second breakfast sandwich he hadn't eaten.

"I am a horse. That's all she needs to know."

"Why not tell her more?" Thrush ate, not offering any to Nero. "Why did you follow her out here?"

"To make sure you didn't damage her. She is a creature of the White Horse. Fragile and human. Hurt her and you'll end your chances of ever setting that twisted head straight on this dirt. You promised us."

Thrush stopped chewing. "I told her to stay away from me. I can't control much else that happens. She has free will."

"Oh, but you can, princeling."

"I am not a prince."

"But you are." Nero whinnied and it sounded like a laugh, a heckling. Mocking, even. Then Nero turned and galloped toward the mountains in the distance, picking up speed until he was running so fast he looked like nothing more than a shadow from a cloud passing under the morning sun.

Thrush looked down at his half-eaten, cold sandwich. Why did she have to bring him breakfast?

CHAPTER 15

LAYLA WIPED A THIN LAYER OF DUST OFF THE shelf, her fingers tracing the cracked leather spines of old paperbacks. The smell of the small, cluttered bookstore reminded her of the library. She finally felt a little bit at home. Sunlight filtered through the streaked front windows, cutting across the space in golden slants.

Her thoughts wandered back to the field yesterday and to Thrush, sweaty and angry. She smiled. He looked worse for the wear, way more disheveled than the first time she saw him at the coffee shop. He was troubled. She remembered the way his jaw had clenched when she'd pushed him to stop being so hard on himself.

Her thumb traced a long, cracked line on one of the books, her mind pulling between curiosity and concern. He was dangerous, he'd said as much himself. But there was something else beneath the temper, something that made her heart ache even though she barely knew him. He'd said he was cursed. Layla thought about all the strange things she'd come across since meeting Rue. Heaven and Hell were real. Monsters did exist. She glanced at her fingers. She couldn't see what Jed had seen—her fingertips looked fine, just as pink as ever.

Layla pulled another book from the shelf, wincing at the faint plume of dust.

At least she wasn't bored. She wondered if her old boss at the library was enjoying doing everything himself since he fired her. She was certain the library was in utter calamity right now. Restocks were probably piled up, inter-library loan requests unfulfilled. Good. He deserved the chaos.

She looked around. The bookstore had been a mess when she started; stacks of books scattered and forgotten, a few so old their bindings had crumbled. She had ten garbage bags full of books that couldn't be salvaged. She couldn't even give them away for free. Maybe she could craft with them?

She thought about a book arch or open page mural on the wall as she began dusting the shelf, a chill prickling along the back of her neck.

"*Layla.*" A soft voice called to her; faint, like whispers just beyond earshot.

A chill ran up her arm.

"No," she whispered, pressing her palms to the counter. Her head throbbed, and her vision blurred for a moment. She felt like she was going to pass out. She felt the same as when she first touched that book in the library basement. She focused on the book she'd just set down. It was nothing more than a mass market thriller by an author she'd hadn't read in ages.

Her fingers tingled, cold and stiff. Layla looked down

and her breath caught as the air in front of her face fogged like it was freezing.

"What the heck?" Panic surged through her and she stumbled back, knocking a stack of books off the counter. Her breathing quickened, her heart pounding against her ribs.

Her legs gave out and she slumped against the side of the counter clutching her wrist, trying to force the darkness away. Her vision doubled, the room around her twisting. The shadows compressed then swirled around her like a tornado.

"No!" She squeezed her eyes shut, pressing her forehead against her knees. "Leave me alone! Please."

The bell above the door chimed. Warm air swept in and with it the whispers scattered. The darkness on her fingers receded like ink seeping into her skin. The pressure in her head faded, leaving her trembling and soaked with sweat.

"Layla?" Shay's voice broke through. "I brought you lunch."

Layla gasped, blinking rapidly, forcing her breathing to steady. She didn't move immediately, her forehead still pressed against her knees. She took off her glasses and rubbed her eyes until she saw stars.

Suddenly Shay was standing next to her. "Are you okay?"

"Yeah... yeah, just... just tripped. Knocked over some books."

Shay's boots clicked against the wooden floor. Layla heard the shuffle of books being picked up. "Well, you've definitely got a mess here."

Layla forced a smile, wiping her damp forehead and

trying to stand. Her legs were shaky, but she steadied herself. "You didn't have to bring me lunch."

"Yes I did." Shay set the basket on the counter, her bright smile warm and motherly. "I'm afraid to leave you alone for too long. You know, with everything that happened."

Layla tried to laugh, but it came out a little too breathy.

Shay's gaze flicked over her, sharp and assessing. "Did something happen? You look pale. Like you've seen a ghost or a monster."

Layla swallowed.

Shay's look didn't soften. "Well, eat something. And if you need a break, come back to the ranch for a bit. I know the bookstore is... well, it's got its charms, but you can't work yourself to death over this. Lame Deer hasn't had a bookstore since I was a kid, a few more weeks worth of waiting won't hurt anyone."

"It's fine," Layla said, leaning on the counter. "I like the work. It fills the void of missing the library."

"I'm glad." Shay grinned, opening the basket and pulling out a wrapped sandwich. "You've been hanging around Rue too long. She's always working herself half to death and drinking so much caffeine."

Layla tried to laugh, but the sound was weak. "Yeah... she does that."

Shay handed her the sandwich and Layla took it, forcing herself to bite and chew, even though her stomach twisted. Shay's presence was a comfort with her gentle humming as she continued to straighten the scattered books.

Layla noticed Shay walked with a slight limp sometimes. Like now, after she bent to pick up a stack of books. She rubbed her thigh and groaned.

"Shay?" Layla asked, trying to sound casual. "Did you hurt your leg?"

Shay chuckled, unaware of Layla's concerned expression. "Oh, Christ, that's a long story."

Layla nodded, her fingers tightening around the edge of the counter. "I've got nothing but time."

Shay pulled a ponytail holder from her pocket and twisted her long blue hair up into a knot on top of her head. She exhaled, hands on her hips. "You really want to hear this?"

Layla nodded.

Shay cleared her throat. "I don't tell many people this."

"Does Jed know?"

Shay laughed. "He was there."

"Oh. Okay. Sorry to interrupt. I just like to know when I'm not supposed to repeat something." She tapped the side of her head. "I just let it fall out my other ear." Layla took another bite of her sandwich.

"I broke my leg years ago. I was... in Hell."

Layla choked a little. "Did you die?" Her eyes went wide.

"No. Nothing like that. Me and Jed were in hiding. Angels were hunting him. Actually, they'd been hunting him his entire life."

"Why would they hunt him?" Layla asked.

"Because he's Nephilim. Forbidden. He's been on the run his entire life. Anyway, he was traveling through these parts and my father invited him to stay on the ranch for a bit."

Layla smiled. "How romantic."

"Not really. But, he was very handsome. Then... things happened and I found myself traveling with him to California."

"Wait," Layla interrupted, "was this during that time before I was born? You met at the casino, right?" Layla hadn't been born yet but her parents had told her about the time when corpses walked and attacked. It sounded like a horror movie.

Shay was nodding. "Yes."

"Wait, so what happened to your father and the ranch?"

"My father died. So did my mother." Shay swallowed hard. "Sorry I haven't talked about this in a long time. But, so many died. Jed helped me and I helped him. We survived together. The ranch was nearly destroyed. We still own it. It's in the northern acres. Abandoned."

Layla was wide-eyed. "I'm sorry."

Shay tossed her hands in the air. "Can't do much about it now. But, we met some people. Rue's parents. And her mother gave us sanctuary in Hell. It wasn't easy being the only human there. Those were different times." Shay rubbed her thigh. "A demon kicked me and broke my leg, some of its poison is still lodged in my scar."

"Does it hurt?"

"Sometimes. When thunderstorms roll in or when the winter chill gets unbearable." Shay paused, waiting for Layla to ask more questions but she began eating again. "It changed me. I'm no longer fully human."

Layla was nodding along, taking it all in. She knew Rue wasn't human and that Evelyn changed. She'd never imagined her daily conversations would turn into this.

"I'm part Crossroads Demon now. When someone, anyone, human or demon or whoever calls the Crossroads Demon to make a deal, I go. Sometimes I just, disappear."

Layla swallowed hard and pressed fingers to her lips. "Oh my god. I don't even know what to say."

"Does it scare you?"

"I mean, it's freaking weird but my head is spinning with all the strangeness I've learned about these past few months. I guess it's just life now. Fiction is life. Does it hurt when you get pulled away?"

"No." Shay was shaking her head. "It's just... I can't control it so sometimes it happens in the middle of conversations, or chores or... dinner." Shay shrugged. "I just wanted you to know, in case it happens around you."

"Do you think something like that is going to happen to me?" Layla was looking at her fingertips.

"We are going to do our best to make sure nothing happens."

CHAPTER 16

RUE TOSSED AND TURNED IN HER BED, THE sheets twisted around her legs like creeping vines. Sweat beaded on her forehead, and her breathing came in sharp, uneven gasps. Behind her closed eyelids, the darkness gripped her; flashes of light, the shimmer of silver sparks, and a tether whipping in the air. She saw a crown of thorns, twisted and cruel, pressed down on a shadowed figure's head.

The scene shifted. Layla's face appeared, her eyes wide with fear and her hands reaching out, fingers blackened as if stained by ink.

Layla's scream pierced the darkness, and Rue jolted awake, her heart pounding. Her hand flew to her chest, her pulse a rapid drum beneath her fingertips.

Dacre stirred beside her, immediately alert. "Rue?" His voice was low, warm but cautious. "Another vision?"

Lucipurr, her little black cat, jumped onto the bed and meowed in concern.

Rue nodded, swallowing hard. "Yeah. Another...

another vision. It's Layla." Rue rubbed her eyes. "I wish I could have seen more."

Dacre sat up, his muscular frame casting a shadow against the moonlit room. "What happened?"

"She was screaming." Rue rubbed her forehead. "Her fingers were black."

Dacre's expression darkened. "That doesn't sound good." He pressed his lips together. "Jed said that her fingers were black when we brought her to the ranch."

Rue pushed herself out of bed, her bare feet touching the cool wooden floor. She crossed the room to her cluttered desk, grabbing a notebook filled with hasty, frantic sketches and scribbled notes. Each page was a chaotic mix of symbols, dream fragments, and questions she didn't yet have answers to. She could see the future but it was a gift she'd only just become aware of within the past year. She had so much to learn about it still. Half the time she wasn't sure what she was seeing until it was too late.

"I keep seeing her hands," Rue whispered, flipping through the pages. "Blackened. Like ink... there was a tether. Like a rope but it was made of shadow."

"Have you told Layla?"

"No... I don't want to scare her," Rue admitted. "Not until I know what it means."

Dacre's hand rested on her shoulder, his touch steady and grounding. "Let's figure it out."

Rue leaned into him for a moment, letting his warmth chase away the lingering chill of the dream. "I need to do some more research. I gave the book she touched to Evelyn. It's safer in Hell. Whatever it did to her, however it marked her, I didn't want it on the Earthen plane."

Dacre nodded. "That was a good idea."

Rue's fingers drummed against the open pages. "I remember seeing something about curses and tethers. Maybe something from the Astral Plane?"

Dacre frowned. "The Astral Plane?"

"She touched that book, and ever since then..." Rue shuddered. "I think she activated something."

"A tether?" Dacre's expression grew more serious. "If she's tied to the Astral Plane, she could be in serious danger. That is the spirit realm. No humans go there. Only certain souls of the dead."

Rue's gaze snapped to his. "Then we have to solve this before something terrible happens."

Dacre pulled a pair of jeans off the floor and stepped into them.

"What are you doing?" Rue asked.

Dacre smiled. "I know you're not going to sleep for a second until you figure this out. So we might as well get started."

Lucipurr meowed from the bed as if agreeing with Dacre.

RUE AND DACRE STEPPED INTO THE OPAQUE shimmer of the portal, a shiver running down Rue's spine as the world twisted around them. The chill of Baltimore was replaced by the scent of brimstone.

Dacre's hand gripped Rue's, steadying her. "You probably should have eaten before we left."

"I'll get a coffee here," Rue muttered, brushing her hair

back. Her pulse quickened as they walked through the garden and toward the door to the castle. A giant Hellion recognized Rue and nodded, opening the door for them.

"You know, coffee isn't a meal," Dacre teased. "I've been reminding you of that for a long time now."

"Do you think Evelyn's in the library?" Rue ignored the teasing. She was going to get a coffee. Maybe even two.

"Evelyn is always in the library if princeling doesn't have her tied up with other things," a familiar, booming voice echoed in the hall.

Rue turned and smiled as Chel walked toward them. The giant Hellion had known her since she was an infant, had been a protector of her mother, Meg, since she first took the throne of Hell.

"You're home?" Chel greeted Dacre with a slap on the shoulder before grabbing Rue and lifting her off her feet with a bear-hug. "You didn't call."

Rue squirmed to get free. "Set me down, you big lug. What's with the affection?"

Chel set Rue on her feet. He rubbed his neck. "Nothing. It's just nice to see you both."

"We were just here a few weeks ago." Rue tugged at her shirt.

There was a beat of silence.

"Oh," Dacre turned to Rue's bag, "he wants to see Lucipurr."

There was a soft meow from Rue's bag when Dacre reached in and pulled out the kitten. Lucipurr looked like a mouse in Chel's giant hand, but he brought the black kitten to his cheek and rubbed.

"Are you okay?" Rue narrowed her eyes.

Dacre pulled Rue away. "He's fine. Just give him a moment."

Rue stumbled as Dacre dragged her toward the hallway that led to the library. "What's with him?"

"I think he's sad. Remington said something about Chel having a crush on an Angel and she keeps avoiding him."

Rue made a face. "An Angel?"

Dacre nodded.

"That's surprising."

Dacre shrugged. "I'm sure stranger things have happened on this realm."

"Who is it?" Rue asked.

"Bros don't kiss and tell."

Rue stopped dead in her tracks and looked up at Dacre. "Someone *kissed* him?" She gagged a little.

"Jeeze he's not that bad looking."

"For a Hellion!"

The door to the library swung open. "I hear people," Evelyn's face appeared and she smiled wide as she recognized her friends.

"Evelyn!" Rue called, her voice carrying through the vast, echoing hallway.

Evelyn's head snapped up, her face brightening immediately. "Rue! Dacre!" Her smile was warm, but it quickly faded when she saw their expressions. "What's wrong? You didn't call."

Rue glanced at Dacre, then stepped forward. "We need your help. It's Layla. I think... I think she's somehow connected to the Astral Plane."

Evelyn's brow furrowed, and she carefully closed the

library door after Rue and Dacre entered. "Connected? How?"

Rue had already filled in Evelyn and Remington on how she'd sent Layla to find the ancient book and the events that happened afterwards.

"I had a vision," Rue explained. "She was screaming and there was a shadow that looked like a tether."

Evelyn's gaze darkened, her fingers absently tracing the spine of one of the books. "A tether isn't unheard of. Your mother and Thrush's father, Noah, had a soul tether, and Noah was of the Astral. Nero and Shay have a soul tether."

"Yes," Rue said. "This seems different. Dangerous."

Dacre stepped closer. "What about a summoning tether tied to the Astral Plane. The Enochian book could have done this to her. Maybe it wasn't for humans to touch."

"I've been doing some research since you brought me the book for safekeeping." Evelyn's lips pressed into a thin line. "If it's a tether, that's incredibly dangerous. The Astral Plane is a realm of spirits; echoes, lost souls, it's very impressionistic. If something is trying to anchor itself to her..."

"I did this to her," Rue said fiercely. "I have to figure out how to make it stop."

Evelyn's gaze softened. "I might have a place to start." She gestured for them to follow, leading them toward a section of the library where the shelves were older, the books thick with dust and magic. "There's a text... It's one of the most detailed collections on Astral Plane lore we have here. It's mostly theory and history, but it could give us a clue. I traded a mountain gypsy for it."

"What did you trade him?" Dacre asked.

Evelyn's gaze shot to Rue. "You don't want to know."

Rue giggled. "Embracing the darkside, are you Ev?"

Evelyn shrugged. "I blame your brother."

Rue smirked. "Me too. He's a bad influence."

Evelyn scanned the shelves, her fingers running along the ancient tomes. "There are a few sections on Astral tethers, how they're created, what they feed on, and how they can be severed. If Layla's been marked, we need to know if she's calling the tether somehow."

"Calling it?" Rue's stomach twisted.

"Potentially," Evelyn murmured, her expression tense. "If it's connected to her soul or her emotions, it could be draining her life force. Whatever makes her who she is."

Evelyn's hand stilled on one of the higher shelves, and she nodded. "Here." She pulled down a massive, silver-edged book. Its cover was dark blue, and a silver spiral twisted into a star shimmering on the front.

Evelyn carried it to the large, dark wood table. "It's not an easy read, but there are more answers here. I scanned a few pages but some of these runes I've never come across before."

Dacre leaned over the table as Evelyn flipped it open, the pages covered in densely written text and swirling illustrations of the Astral Plane; a chaotic sea of spirits, twisting pathways, and towering shadows.

"Here," Evelyn pointed to a section, her finger tracing a passage. "It speaks of tethers. Bonds that can be created intentionally or by accident. Sometimes through ritual, other times through cursed objects."

Rue's heart pounded. "So Layla activated it just by touching the book?"

"It's possible." Evelyn's voice was grave. "Some objects

are latent, waiting for someone with the right spark—an echo of magic, a trace of spirit. Something about Layla must have been enough to trigger it." Evelyn looked up at Rue. "What do you know about Layla's family history?"

Rue made a face. "She's too small to be Nephilim. Too innocent to be part demon. And the White Horse would not be so protective of her if she weren't full human."

"How do we break it?" Dacre asked.

Evelyn flipped through a few more pages. "It depends on the strength of the tether. If it's a more complex bond..." She paused, her eyes darkening. "We might have to sever the connection to the Astral Plane directly."

Rue felt a cold knot form in her chest. "Dangerous for Layla?"

"And for anyone who tries to help her," Evelyn warned. "If we try to sever the tether and fail, it could rip Layla straight into that realm." She tapped the book. "Or so that's what the literature says."

Rue's knees felt weak and she leaned against the table. "My Archeology studies did not prepare me for this. We were just supposed to be digging up in the mountains. Not this." She glanced up at Evelyn. "We aren't prepared for something like this."

"That's true," Evelyn said. "But you have a powerful Nephilim."

"I think we need more than that." Dacre muttered.

"You have Thrush." Evelyn straightened.

Rue was shaking her head. "No. He's... out of control. He's barely hanging on. He can't help her. He's the one who can hurt her the most."

"He doesn't want to hurt anyone," Evelyn said. "He's

struggled for a long time but I don't think anyone here knows what's going on with him. There has been too much lost history."

Rue was nodding along. "I agree. I just don't trust him like I used to."

Footsteps echoed and a deep voice said, "You would if you'd seen the way he prepared to go back into Hell to find you after you'd been kidnapped."

Remington.

Rue turned and greeted her brother. "Those were different times."

"For all of us." Remington's head tipped to the side. "You didn't call. I would have had dinner prepared. Told mom and dad. Maybe they would have come back from wherever they flew off to."

Rue rolled her eyes. "Right. They have been forever on a honeymoon since we started taking care of ourselves."

"From what I've heard, they kinda deserve it." Evelyn looked between Remington and Rue.

There was a beat of silence before Rue sighed and turned back to the book. "We have to find another way."

"There may be one," Evelyn said, a spark of hope in her voice. "Jed is really skilled at tattoos of runes." She motioned to the runes tattooed on the skin peeking out from Remington's button-down shirt.

Dacre frowned. "Layla doesn't seem like the tattooed type."

Evelyn hesitated. "We could talk her into it."

Rue and Dacre exchanged a look.

"She's headstrong," Dacre murmured. "Weak. More of a press-on tattoo type." He chuckled.

Evelyn touched Rue's arm. "Be careful. From what I've read here, the Astral Plane's influence can be subtle... or it can be devastating. Being half astral hasn't worked out well for Thrush."

The room went silent.

It was true, though none of them had thought much about Thrush's makings. His mother was Nightingale, the daughter of the Archangel Remiel and the sister of Sparrow, the Raven King.

Thrush's father was Noah, Meg's best friend from childhood who had died in a bus accident on the way to state prison. Noah had been tethered to Meg in Hell, her manservant of sorts. He got her food and kept her spirits up, helped her sort out her new life. They were the best of friends and happy to have each other during those years of confusion and discovery.

Everything fell apart when Nightingale died during the Fast-Zombie War. Meg pulled Thrush from his dying mother's arms before the dead sent him to an early grave as well. Thrush was parentless and in grave danger.

Except he wasn't completely parentless. He had his father, Noah. But Noah was of the Astral. Meg questioned how a ghost could get an Angel pregnant, but during those times of chaos and war, no one seemed to care much. No one ever listened to her. They were all too quick to blame and judge and ignore. In the end, Thrush was faced with a family curse and lineage none had seen in ages, if ever.

CHAPTER 17

THE BELL ABOVE THE BOOKSTORE DOOR GAVE A faint, muffled chime as the wind outside picked up, rattling the windowpanes. The glow of the sunset cast an amber hue through the dusty glass.

Layla adjusted her glasses, her fingers brushing over the spines of the books she was rearranging. She'd been working for hours, grateful for the distraction–anything to keep her mind off the fact that she was in a strange place with strange people and her life had been forever altered. She wasn't sure strange was even the correct word for it. Bizarre maybe. Peculiar. She sighed, wishing she had a dictionary to find the right word to describe it all.

Her mind wouldn't shut up. She was overthinking everything; every moment, every word, every look. Her brain was a jumble of words.

"Christ I think I need a doctor," Layla muttered to herself, wishing there was someone else there to distract her mind while she worked.

Shay had left a while ago, called to the Crossroads. Shay

had warned Layla that it could happen. It finally did and Layla had never seen anything like it in her life. One moment Shay was talking and laughing, the next she was gripping her stomach, face twisted in concern as she shouted for Layla to call Jed to the Bookstore.

She'd tried. The old landline rang and rang and rang. Cell phones didn't seem to work on the ranch. The keys to the truck had gone with Shay. She wasn't walking back to the ranch. She wasn't that kinda girl to walk fifteen miles in the dark. Nope, sir.

Layla turned, her breath hitching when she saw her pale reflection in the window. For a moment, it looked wrong. Her face was shadowed, the eyes a touch too dark. She blinked and the illusion was gone.

"You're just tired," she whispered to herself. "It's fine. Everything is fine." She rubbed her face. "My life is just a dumpster fire right now. But it's gonna be fine."

But just as she tried to reassure herself, the overhead lights flickered once, twice, then went dark.

"Oh crap," she muttered, fumbling with her phone for a flashlight. The tiny beam was pale, barely enough to light the immediate area. Her heart raced but she forced herself to breathe, focusing on the shelves, the dust, and the comforting smell of old paper.

A sudden, muffled thud came from the back of the store. Her head snapped around, the light trembling in her hand. The portal was back there. Layla had never seen it used before but anything could come through, Shay had warned. That's why they didn't want her there alone.

"It's probably just... something fell. Maybe a book." But even she didn't believe that. "It's not a monster. It's not a monster. *It's not a monster*," she muttered to herself. "Monsters are not real." It was a lie. She knew that as soon as the words left her lips. She'd just learned monsters were absolutely real.

The air grew colder, the shadows deepening around her. Her phone flickered and then died, leaving her in near-total darkness.

"Layla."

The voice seemed to come from everywhere and nowhere. Her breath caught.

A spark of light flared at the front of the store and Layla's gaze shot toward it. A warm, golden glow pulsed in the darkness then stabilized into a steady, gentle light. At the center of it stood Thrush, his tall, lean figure outlined in the cool radiance of his glowing fingertips.

"Thrush?" she whispered, relief flooding her voice.

He didn't look at her immediately. His gaze was fixed on the darkness, his other hand raised as a faint shimmer of silver energy pulsed from his fingers. The shadows seemed to writhe. They shrunk back, recoiled into the corners of the store.

"What was that?" Layla whispered.

He glanced at her. "Stay back."

Her breath caught.

"Just stay there," he ordered, stepping forward, his fingertips moving in strange dance as he whispered barely audible words that sounded like a rainstorm on a windy night.

When he was done he said, "Jed sent me to check on you. You were both supposed to be back for dinner. Where is Shay?"

"She was called to the Crossroads."

"So why are you waiting here alone?" He looked annoyed.

"The truck keys were in her pocket." Layla snapped. Then she raised both hands and proceeded to snap her fingers aggressively. "I don't have cool tricks like you."

Thrush's lips pressed together and he glanced out the window, face softening in recognition. "Well. That's some shit."

Layla should have been afraid. Normal people didn't trickle light from their fingertips. But instead of fear, a deep sense of curiosity overwhelmed her.

"You... you're not like Rue or Dacre," she whispered.

"No. I'm not." He turned toward her, the light casting dark shadows over his sharp cheekbones. "Are you afraid?" His voice was a low rumble, his frown deepening as he stepped closer.

He was so tall. The mess of his white hair, and the intensity in his eyes were hard to look away from. She wondered if he noticed how long she stared at him when she'd brought him breakfast to the fence line each morning.

Layla instinctively backed up, her shoulder blades pressing against the shelf behind her. Her heart fluttered wildly, but she didn't look away. "No."

His lips curved into a faint, wry smile. "Confident for someone who doesn't know what I am."

"Do you even know what you are?" Layla's voice was a touch breathless now, her pulse pounding. "You seem confused most of the time about yourself. But I do know you're not a monster."

Thrush stepped even closer, the light from his magic

casting warm, flickering shadows over his face. He leaned down, his face mere inches from hers. "What makes you so sure?"

"I just... am," she said, her voice barely above a whisper. His presence was overwhelming, but not in a terrifying way. It was like standing on the edge of a cliff, dangerous and exhilarating.

His gaze searched hers, the air between them charged. Neither could deny it.

"I'm not of your world, Layla," he whispered, the warmth of his breath brushing against her cheek.

"I know."

"Then tell me to leave," he challenged, his voice low and dangerous. "Tell me you don't want me here. Tell me to go away."

She opened her mouth, but no words came out. She didn't want him to leave, didn't want to be alone again with her racing thoughts and overthinking. She was glad he arrived to scare away the darkness and shadows.

A faint, dark pulse rippled across the floor. A shadow was creeping and stretching toward them.

Thrush's gaze snapped down.

"Don't move!" he ordered.

Layla didn't need to be told twice. She held her breath.

With a sharp gesture, Thrush carved a line of light along the floor. The shadows hissed, recoiling, and then vanished into the back of the bookstore.

"It came back so quickly." Layla's voice was full of concern. "What is that thing?"

Thrush ran a hand through his hair, the faint glow in

his palm extinguishing. "Whatever that was... it wanted you." He was staring at her like he wanted her too.

Layla shivered, unsure of what to say when he was looking at her like that. Saying something awkward was always in her repertoire. "How can you be so sure? Maybe it wanted you."

Thrush's gaze lowered. For a brief fragile moment there was something raw in his eyes, an emotion she couldn't quite name, then a light. His lips moved like he was holding in a smile.

"You're not safe here," he murmured.

"Now you sound like Rue." Layla pushed away from the bookshelves and stepped to the side, putting distance between them. "Are you okay?"

"Fine. I could have lost control again." He rubbed a hand over his face but his eyes locked onto hers, then roaming to her hair and her neck, he scanned down to her feet. "I told you. You should be afraid of me."

"I'm not." She took a step forward.

He stared at her for a long moment, the tension between them thick, almost suffocating. A flash of white left his fingertips and blasted the floor, cracking the laminate. He pressed his eyes closed and stepped back, letting the space between them fill with the cool, empty air. Silence.

"You're not very smart for a human," he whispered.

"Really?" She pushed her glasses up. "That's rude, even for a..." she looked him up and down judgingly, "whatever you are. Drama. That's what you are. High drama." She wanted to say more, like handsome high drama. Darkly handsome. She forced her mind to go blank.

He smirked. "Watch it."

"You," she challenged, bending to move a stack of books from the floor.

"I am."

There was a beat of silence.

Layla pushed curls off her face and grumbled. "These need to be moved off the floor before we leave. Maybe you could make yourself useful."

There was a soft noise then the books surrounding Layla lifted off the floor.

"Where do you want them?" Thrush asked.

"On the counter along the back of the store." She started walking with the stack in her arms.

Books followed, floating. When she set the stack down, the rest followed.

Layla pushed the books against the wall then turned.

"Look at you. All this time who knew you were good for something other than breaking things and being rude."

When she looked back at Thrush his eyes were on her, his mouth slack, caught between a smile and a frown. His hands were shoved in his pockets.

"Are you going to use those hot hands to get the truck started or did you bring a spare set of keys?" Layla asked, motioning to Shay's truck that was parked outside.

"Maybe we should walk," he offered, his tongue brushing over his teeth.

"No." Layla wiped her hands on her jeans. "I've been busting my ass all day, I don't have the energy to walk." She looked up at him. "And you'd move faster than me. Probably leave me in the dark alone. I'd be eaten by a wolf."

"Maybe not a wolf," he muttered.

"What?" Layla shot back. She might have been barely half his height but she wasn't going to stand down. She was having too much fun teasing him.

"I drove Jed's truck," Thrush said loudly.

"Do you even know how to drive?" Layla pestered.

Thrush headed for the door. "Let's go." He held the door open and looked down as she passed under his arm, watching as she stepped out onto the dimly lit sidewalk.

Thrush stepped out behind her, letting the door swing shut with a soft chime. The evening air was cool, a light breeze stirring Layla's curls. The street was quiet, the soft hum of crickets filling the silence and the sky stretching wide above them, dark and glittering with stars.

She turned to lock the door, feeling the heat of Thrush at her back.

Layla had never seen a night like this in Maryland. There was too much light from the nearby cities to see the stars this clearly.

Layla's fingers tugged at the strap of her bag, a nervous habit she barely noticed. Thrush walked beside her, his stride slow and measured. There was a restless energy around him. She stole a glance, catching the sharp angle of his jaw. What was up with this guy and why did she feel drawn to him in the worst way? She felt it the moment she first laid eyes on him back at the Coffee Connection on campus. She wondered if he felt the same way or if he was simply toying with her. *Stop thinking*, she scolded herself.

"You didn't answer my question," she said, trying to dispel the tension thickening between them. "Do you even know how to drive?"

"I know how to do a lot of things." His lips quirked in a slight smile.

"So mysterious." She laughed lightly, her voice a bit louder than she intended. Nerves. That was all it was. She worried about being stuck in the vehicle with him on the drive back to the ranch. There had always been plenty of space between them. In the truck, there wouldn't be.

He led the way to Jed's truck that was parked under the weak glow of a streetlamp. He moved to the passenger side and opened the door, motioning for her to get in.

Layla figured she should probably say thank you, but she didn't anticipate the chivalry. And frankly, it shocked her.

Layla climbed into the passenger seat, the leather cool beneath her legs. Thrush slid in behind the wheel, the old truck creaking slightly under his weight. He used the key to start the engine–like a normal person. Then he shifted into gear and pulled onto the road leading away from the bookstore.

The road stretched out before them through the center of Lame Deer. Then he turned right and the road turned into a winding ribbon cutting through shadowed fields.

Layla leaned back, letting the gentle rumble of the engine soothe her nerves. "So... are you gonna tell Jed and Shay about the shadow thingy in the bookstore?"

Thrush's fingers tightened on the steering wheel. "I should."

"I don't want you to. The bookstore is all I have right now," she said quietly. "I've lost everything, I don't want to lose that too..."

There was a beat of silence. He murmured. "It's clearly not safe there."

Layla glanced at him, the faint glow of the dashboard lighting his face, casting shadows over the strong lines of his profile. The brooding silence was killing her. Why couldn't the guy just carry on a conversation?

The tension between them eased, just slightly. The truck bumped over the gravel, the headlights tracing the road ahead. Layla let her gaze drift out the window, watching the dark fields pass by, the distant shapes of trees swaying in the wind.

But even in the quiet, her thoughts kept drifting back to Thrush and the way he watched her with a hunger he seemed determined to keep buried. Maybe he hated her. She was having a hard time figuring him out. Not that she'd had much practice. Librarians weren't a hot commodity in the dating world these days.

When they finally pulled up to the ranch, the porch light spilled soft gold across the gravel. Layla hesitated, her fingers lingering on the door handle.

"Thrush?" she asked, her voice softer now.

He turned, the shadows playing over his face. "Yeah?"

"Do you think I'm going to die? Are those shadows going to kill me?" She held her hand up, looking for the blackened fingertips. She couldn't see it. But she noticed he focused there. She knew he could see it.

"Not if I can help it," he murmured.

She looked away. "Okay. I'm glad you were there tonight."

"Just doing what Jed told me to." The tone of his voice made it sound like he didn't care.

"Right." She swallowed, forcing a smile. "Well, thanks anyway."

He nodded, his gaze lingering on her just a moment longer before he looked away. "We should go inside."

Layla slipped out of the truck, the cool night air brushing her cheeks. As she walked up the steps to the porch she glanced back, adjusting her glasses. Thrush hadn't moved. His gaze was fixed on the road, his hands still gripping the steering wheel like he was about to take off and drive somewhere else.

CHAPTER 18

THE DARKNESS IN THRUSH'S ROOM WAS THICK, oppressive, settling around him in a suffocating shroud. The ranch was quiet. But for Thrush, it was anything but peaceful. He missed the chirping of the crickets outside his cave, the sharp snapping of twigs from nighttime creatures exploring Hell. That was a lullaby, this was... *torture*.

He lay on the narrow bed, staring up at the ceiling, his fingers gripping the soft blanket beneath him. Sweat beaded along his brow despite the cool air from the cracked open window. His shoulder throbbed a dull, twisting ache that sent sharp jolts down his arm. But worse than the pain was the familiar, crawling sensation beneath his skin. The slow, relentless pulse of something dark and hungry twisted through his veins like living shadow.

Tick. Tick. Tick.

His jaw clenched, the sound almost audible in his ears; the curse's rhythm, the pulsing heat that refused to fade. He rolled onto his side, gripping his shoulder, his breath ragged. This was supposed to be his reprieve, his training, his escape from Hell's chaos. This was supposed to cure him. But he was still a prisoner of his own body, a prisoner of this curse brought on by his grandfather who'd refused to do what was required. The bastard.

But, it wasn't just the pain keeping him awake.

It was the noises across the hall.

It was Layla.

Even through the thick walls of the house he could hear her soft restless movements; the quiet padding of her footsteps as she got ready for bed, the gentle rustle of pages turning, and the faint creak of her bed as she shifted. He tried not to listen, tried to shut it out, but every tiny sound was driving him insane.

He hated that he couldn't banish her from his mind, hated the way his thoughts twisted back to her again and again. The stubborn set of her jaw when she argued with him, the light in her eyes when she teased him, the way she'd looked at him in the darkness of the bookstore, defiant and fearless and... he thought he'd seen something else. She couldn't be that stupid to see anything attractive in him. He was a monster, a beast, scrambled brains and all. In the shadows of Hell his shadows were *darkest*.

Thrush pushed himself upright, his fingers digging into his scalp. He needed to sleep. He needed quiet. He needed to stop thinking about...

A soft sound.

A gentle sigh.

Her sigh.

His teeth snapped together and a chill surged to his

fingertips. He shoved the blanket aside and stood, his body tense, energy crackling beneath his skin like static. He paced the narrow room, the floorboards creaking beneath his feet.

The turning of a page.

The wet sound as she licked her finger.

Thump, Thump, Thump. Her heart beat louder than anything.

He tried to force himself back to bed—twice—but the ache in his shoulder and the ceaseless thrum of his magic made it impossible. Every time he closed his eyes, he saw her face with those wide curious eyes, the faint blush that touched her cheeks when he stepped too close and the way she pushed her glasses up and how she pushed all of those curls away from her face.

He ground his teeth, and they felt sharper. Impossible.

This was stupid. He was being stupid.

He stood again, moving to the center of the room. It didn't stop. None of her noises stopped. They kept going and going and going and it was all he could hear echoing in his mind.

Then the clock on the nightstand read 3:07, and something in him snapped. His hand was on the door handle before he even realized it, his feet carrying him across the narrow hallway. He barely noticed the cool wood under his feet, barely noticed the faint sliver of moonlight pooling through the window at the end of the hall.

He knocked. Once, twice.

There was a muffled rustling, a soft thud, the door easing open, and there she stood. Layla; bleary-eyed and adorable, her curls a wild sleepy mess, her glasses perched crookedly on her nose. She wore an oversized T-shirt, the sleeves swallowing her arms, and a pair of worn leggings. Her bare feet were tiny.

"Thrush?" Her voice was soft, husky with near sleep, and something twisted in his chest.

"I can't," He broke off, his own voice raw, strained. He didn't even know what he meant to say.

"You can't what?" She rubbed at her eye, adjusting her glasses, blinking up at him. "Did something happen?"

"Yeah," he muttered. "Something happened. I can't sleep. I can't think. I can't. It's you."

"Me?" Her voice was a touch sharper now, but not unkind. "I didn't do anything."

"Not when you're across the hall," he snapped, the words spilling out before he could stop them.

Layla's mouth fell open. "Excuse me?"

"I mean," He swore under his breath, pressing his palm to his forehead. "You're... you're loud."

"Loud?" She folded her arms, the loose sleeves bunching up. "I was reading! Sorry for existing, Your Majesty." Her eyes narrowed. "Or should I call you Princeling?"

"I can hear you breathing," he shot back, frustration and embarrassment tangling together in his chest. "Every time you turn a page. Every time you move in the bed. Every beat of your heart."

"That sounds like a you problem." She crossed her arms tighter, the oversized sleeves hiding her hands. "If you can't handle your supersonic hearing, go sleep outside!"

"Maybe I will." He leaned against the doorframe, trying to keep himself from stepping closer, trying to keep his voice steady. He didn't want to yell. He and Jed yelled at each other enough all day long and he was tired of it. "Or maybe you could just... just..."

"Just what? Be quiet? Disappear?" Her voice was a mix of anger and hurt. "I didn't ask to be here. I had a nice cozy apartment with no giant man-beasts living across the hallway."

"No." His voice softened, his fingers curling against the doorframe. "I don't want you to disappear. That's the problem."

The words hung in the air between them, heavy, raw. Layla's breath caught, her glare softening. "What?"

He shook his head, stepping back, one hand massaging the ache in his neck. "I shouldn't have come here."

But as he turned to leave, her hand shot out, gripping his wrist. "Wait."

Her touch was a shock of warmth that seemed to ripple up his arm. He froze, his pulse pounding in his ears.

"What's really wrong?" Her voice was softer now, her gaze searching his face. "Tell me what's going on."

"It's nothing." His voice was rough. "It's just the curse. It's always the curse. Driving me mad. Boiling me from the inside out."

"Then let someone help."

"No one can help." Shadows flickering at the edges of his vision. "You can't fix this, Layla. No one can. I'm a mess. I'm... I'm dangerous." His fingers began sparking.

Her eyes searched his face, a mix of fear and something else, something he couldn't name. "You're not dangerous."

"You don't know." He took a step closer, his face inches from hers, his breath mingling with hers. "You don't know what I am, what I could do. One wrong moment, one slip, and you..."

"Don't slip." Her fingers were warm against his wrist.

"Don't you get it?" he whispered, his voice a raw tremor. "I'm..."

She didn't flinch away from him. Her other hand reached up, brushing the wild strands of his white hair from his face. "Then let me help."

His breath caught. For a heartbeat, the world seemed to stop with just her touch and her steady gaze. He was drowning in it, burning beneath her calm. She was too fragile. Too human. He'd crush her in more ways than one.

He leaned in, his forehead resting against hers, his eyes slipping shut. "I don't know what's happening. You should stay away from me."

"I can't. We are living here, under the same roof." Her voice was a whisper; a soft, dangerous promise. "I can't go anywhere."

Silence stretched between them as his ragged breaths echoed. He was fighting something.

Then, with a low shuddering sigh, he stepped back, her fingers slipping from his wrist. "Go back to reading, Layla. I won't bother you again."

"Where are you going?"

"Don't worry about it." His voice was a rough whisper.

He turned and walked back to his room, the ache in his chest worse now. The pain in his neck and shoulder was unbearable as he held in a shudder. Thrush grabbed his boots and left the room, closing the door softly as he stomped to the stairs. He ran down them and outside.

Jed was in the kitchen, sneaking a breakfast sandwich

out of the freezer. He paused just long enough to see Thrush run out the door, but he didn't say a thing.

Thrush ran across the yard, leapt over the fence, and headed to the field in the distance.

Not long after, the night echoed with the sounds of him pounding fence posts.

CHAPTER 19

Day... I can't remember how long it's been: Emotional whiplash achieved.

Pros: Still not dead. Still no goat attacks. Shay made tea. Jed didn't grumble at me today.
Cons: Thrush. Just... Thrush. Also, I may be the problem? TBD.

Tonight, he showed up at my door looking like a storm bottled in a person. White hair wild, that twitch in his jaw like he was holding back the moon from crashing into Earth. He said he could hear me breathing. That I was loud.

Note to self: breathing is now considered a threat to princeling stability.

He practically accused me of existing too close to him. And for a second, I was furious. But then he said he didn't want me to disappear and that he couldn't stop thinking about me.

So... naturally my heart did the stupid flutter thing like this was a paperback romance and not a weird prince from Hell reality.

He looked so tired, like he hasn't really slept in years. I wanted to be angry, I did. But he's unraveling and for some reason, I feel like I'm part of the thread.

He said I can't fix him. But maybe I don't need to.

I could try. It can't be that hard to listen. Maybe if he would just... be still.

He said I should stay away.

But I can't.

Not because we're stuck under the same roof, though... yes, that too. But because he looked at me like I was the only thing keeping him tethered to earth.

Maybe he scares me because I want to be that anchor.

Maybe I'm the one slipping.

Anyway.

I'm not dead.

I'm not afraid.

And I think I've officially lost control of this situation.

And if he comes back again, I'm not sure I'll send him away.

Update: Possible emotional infection.

Definitely not spider bite-related.
Will report again tomorrow.

LAYLA SLAMMED THE COVER OF HER JOURNAL closed and rubbed her eyes.

Damn man.

CHAPTER 20

GOLDEN AFTERNOON LIGHT SPILLED THROUGH the dusty bookstore windows, casting amber streaks across the scattered rows of books. Layla stood behind the counter, a stack of leather-bound volumes open in front of her as she worked on her inventory sheet.

Shay was on her knees, sorting a box of donated books, occasionally muttering under her breath about the poor condition of some of them.

The bookstore was coming together. They'd cleaned most of the dust. The windows were next for a deep scrub. Layla was looking at the tote of cleaning supplies and wondering if some hot water would get the job done so she didn't have to go to the store for window cleaner.

The little bell above the door chimed and Layla glanced up, smiling when she saw Rue and Dacre stepping inside. Rue's dark hair was tied back, her face bright when she laid eyes on Layla.

"Hey!" Layla waved. "I didn't know you were coming to visit."

Rue glanced back at Dacre before saying, "I wanted to surprise you. And see the bookstore."

Dacre followed, his towering form shadowing the doorway. There was a tightness in his expression.

"Oookayyy." Layla was watching them. "You two look like you're about to tell me something I won't like."

Shay stood and cleaned her hands on her jeans. "It's always better to rip the band-aid off."

Rue exchanged a look with Dacre, then approached the counter. "It's... complicated. But yes, it's serious."

Shay moved to the counter, setting down a stack of books. "That's not ominous or anything."

Dacre's lips tightened. "We've been doing some research. The book you touched, Layla, it's tied to the Astral."

Layla's smile faded. "The Astral?"

Shay moved closer.

"Yes," Rue said. "And it's not just any ordinary artifact. It's a tether. We think."

"Tether?" Layla's voice rose, her heart racing. "What even is the Astral?" Layla asked.

"It's a spirit realm," Shay said.

Layla rubbed her face. "Oh gosh. I don't know if I can deal with this new information."

"We've never come across anything like this before. Rue and Evelyn have been doing a lot of research to figure it out," Dacre explained.

"Is that what happened in the basement of the library? When I blacked out?"

"It could have been. There is no portal that we know of on campus. The book might have knocked you out until the tether could find you." Rue reached out, taking Layla's hand. "We can protect you. But we need to take this seriously."

Shay stepped closer. "I don't like the sound of this."

"That's why we want Jed to mark you with runes of protection," Rue continued, squeezing Layla's hand. "It would keep you grounded here, keep the Astral from grabbing you again." She pulled down the collar of her shirt and showed Layla her own runes. "These help me. Jed did them when I was a teenager."

Layla's stomach dropped. "Tattoos? No way." She pulled her hand back, folding her arms over her chest. "I'm not... I don't even have any tattoos. I don't want any."

"It's not about style, Layla," Dacre said, his voice low. "This is about your safety."

"And who's going to even see them?" Rue asked, a hint of desperation in her voice. "They could be small, hidden. But they'd keep you safe."

"I shouldn't have to carve things into my skin just because of some creepy ancient book," Layla argued, feeling her pulse quicken. "There has to be another way."

Rue shook her head. "We've researched other ways. This is the strongest option."

"Just think about it," Dacre added, his expression concerned. "Please."

Layla shook her head, her heart pounding. "I, no, I need time." She sighed and pushed curls away from her face. "My parents would be pissed."

Rue chuckled. "Your parents? You're an adult."

Layla paused. "That's true. I am an adult. I guess." She

let out a breathy laugh. "Still. I don't want to mark my skin."

The air grew thick, a faint chill crawling up Layla's spine. The shadows in the room seemed to lengthen, and a quiet rustling sound echoed from the far corner of the store, near the back hallway.

Shay turned, her brow furrowing. "What was that?" She stepped toward the hallway.

"What's *that*?" Layla's voice was a whisper, her gaze locked on the darkness gathering in the hallway and spreading across the floor.

A shadow slithered out, thin as smoke but reaching with clawed tendrils. Layla's breath hitched.

"No, no, no," she whispered, stumbling back. "Not again."

"Again?" Shay and Rue shouted in unison.

"Rue, get out," Dacre grabbed Rue and dragged her to the door. "Layla!" Dacre shouted, pulling Rue behind him. "Get over here."

Layla's eyes were wide as she glanced toward the hallway and the shadows moving.

"I can't–" She was behind the checkout counter. There was countertop, window, a wall behind her, the only way out was to move toward the shadow.

"Over the counter, Layla!" Shay shouted.

Layla struggled. The counter was high and she was short. She searched for something to stand on. She pulled down a stack of books and they thudded onto the ground. She bent to stack them. She stood, trying to jump and lift her body with her arms but she didn't have the strength.

"Help her!" Rue shoved Dacre.

Dacre ran across the bookstore in a few long strides. He motioned for her arms. Grabbing them, he started to lift her like a child and dragged her across the counter.

Layla inhaled a sharp breath as the counter edge cut into her stomach.

Just as Dacre was pulling her to the other side, the tendril snapped out, seizing Layla's ankle. Ice shot through her leg, the cold so intense it felt like fire. The shadows twisted around her leg, dragging her back.

"Layla!" Rue screamed.

"Let her go!" Shay's voice was fierce, her hand outstretched. She had a pistol and shot at the shadows. It did nothing. "Shit. Fuck." Shay holstered her weapon and grabbed a book then threw it at the shadow.

Layla's shoe dropped to the floor, her fingernails digging into Dacre's skin as she was dragged.

Pain seared through her ankle, and it felt like her leg was going to be pulled off. She made a noise deep in her throat that sounded like a cry. She wasn't sure what to do, she felt like she was being pulled apart.

The door burst open. Jed and Thrush stormed in. Jed's hand raised, glowing with light. He shouted something that sounded like the crashing of waves against rocks. A burst of light surged from his palm, striking the shadows. The tendrils recoiled, shuddering and then evaporating with a hollow wail.

Layla fell forward, gasping.

Dacre pulled her the rest of the way over the counter and carried her to the door.

Thrush was at her side in an instant, his own dark

magic thrumming beneath his skin. "Layla... are you hurt?" His voice was rough.

"I'm," Layla swallowed, her vision blurring. "I don't... I can't..." Her glasses were crooked.

Thrush reached forward and set them straight.

Jed crossed the room to collect Shay, his expression a mix of anger and concern. "You have to leave this place."

"I'm fine," Shay argued. "I can handle whatever it is."

"I don't care if you can handle it." Jed's voice was rough. "I don't want either of you here until we figure this out."

Shay pointed to the dark hallway. "The tether came from the portal. Layla said it's happened before."

Everyone paused and turned.

Rue's voice trembled. "She needs those runes."

Layla's gaze met Thrush's. "I didn't want... I didn't want this..."

"Doesn't matter what you wanted," Thrush muttered, his voice a rough whisper. "This is the second time that I know of."

Shay moved closer and knelt beside Layla, brushing a lock of her curly hair out of her face. "Listen to me, Layla. Jed can help protect you, but you have to let him." She pushed up a sleeve and showed Layla her own runes. "I promise, they'll help."

Layla nodded, tears burning at the corners of her eyes. "Okay... okay. Do it."

Jed leaned down, his expression softening. "It won't hurt, I promise. But we can't wait."

"I don't care." Layla's voice shook. "Just... please..." She broke down and started crying. "Get me out of here." She buried her face in Thrush's shirt.

His hand spanned her back, rubbing the tension away until she stopped crying.

"We'll fix this," he whispered against her ear. "I won't let them take you."

Layla went still in his arms when she heard the concern in his voice.

CHAPTER 21

Day 34: The shadows came back.

Pros:
Still alive.
Got to cry into Thrush's shirt. That wasn't embarrassing or anything. He smelled good.
Did not lose leg.
Everyone is okay. Mostly.

Cons:
I was dragged across a counter by a living shadow.
My ankle feels like it was frozen and lit on fire at the same time.
Almost got swallowed by whatever's haunting the damn portal.
Also: one shoe down. RIP, favorite boot.
Tonight was... a blur. No, not just because I

still have blurry vision half the time. Something else happened. I felt it when the shadow touched me, like it knew me. Like it had been waiting. I couldn't move, couldn't breathe. And I panicked. I froze. This lifestyle is not for me.

It wasn't like before. This was stronger. Hungrier.

Dacre saved me. I'll never tell him this, but I owe him. Shay fought like hell. Rue screamed like her heart was breaking. Jed and Thrush showed up like a damned cavalry, and I cried. I cried. In front of everyone.

I'm so weak...

But I also said yes.

Yes to the runes.

Yes to the protection.

Yes to staying alive.

It wasn't the way I imagined it, but... I don't think I care anymore. I'm tired of pretending this isn't real. The shadows are coming for me.

Thrush looked at me like I was going to vanish right there in his arms. I saw it on his face. The fear. The helpless rage. I don't think I've ever seen anyone that angry and that scared at the same time.

He was warm. Solid. Safe.

(How ironic, considering he might actually be part monster.)

And I realized something while I was clinging

to him like a loser: *I don't want to go back to my old life. I've always felt different. Odd. My doctor always blamed it on reading too much since I refused any type of diagnostic evaluation or psychological assessment. Maybe this is why. Maybe I was meant to be part of Rue's world. I like the idea of something new and exciting.*

Maybe it's because I finally believe him when he says he won't let anything take me.

Final update: One rune about to be down. One broken boot. One scary as heck demonic tug-of-war. I'm still here.

LAYLA SLAMMED HER JOURNAL CLOSED. WHO WAS she kidding? Tomorrow she'd still be a freaking mess.

CHAPTER 22

THE SKY WAS STREAKED WITH DUSKY LIGHT, THE
first hints of night covering the endless horizon. A thin mist
curled along the grassy fields, but the world was quiet,
empty; a corridor between worlds. Reality softly shifted.

Thrush stood at the Crossroads. A patch of open land
lay just beyond the main pastures where the air felt thinner,
the ground colder. This place was where deals were made
and souls were sold.

Thrush's breath misted in the cool air, his heart racing
beneath his ribs. He used a stick to draw the summoning
runes into the dirt. He'd never called a Crossroads Demon
before, but he knew how.

He didn't know what else to do. Because the darkness
gnawing at him felt stronger than ever, the pressure beneath
his skin threatening to burst, the relentless pulse of magic
turning to madness. He was out of options, especially after
what had happened at the bookstore. Twice now.

A gust of wind swept past, rustling the dry grass, and
then they arrived. Shay stepped into the moonlight, her

familiar calm presence like a soothing balm in the chill. Behind her, the massive black horse followed, Nero's dark eyes glinting, his hooves barely making a sound. They looked so different in their demon forms.

Shay was tall, hair so blue, eyes darker than night. She wasn't a terrifying Demon like her horse, no, she was a warrior; intimidating and absolutely stunning.

NERO WAS ALREADY HUGE BUT IN THAT SECOND he doubled in size, his long black tail and mane stiff as needles and sharp as razorblades. His veins became giant ropes of obsidian, twining and swirling under his skin like protective armor. And he looked *hungry*. Thrush had heard stories of the Demon horse eating Hellions whole and he'd witnessed the creature breathing fire like a dragon during the war years ago. He hoped the horse wasn't going to barbeque him right here, right now.

"You should be in bed," Shay greeted, her voice warm, though touched with concern.

Thrush forced a smile. "Couldn't sleep."

"You haven't been sleeping well for a while." Shay crossed her arms, her gaze steady. "We hear you at night." She looked him up and down. "We hear her as well. Something is happening between you two."

"That's none of your concern."

"Don't tell me what is of our concern, Princeling. You called us here for a reason, Thrush. What's on your mind?"

He hesitated, his fingers curling into fists. "I need to make a deal."

"A deal?" Shay's voice was gentle. "I didn't expect this. I haven't made a deal with a prince before."

"The curse. Make it stop."

"What?" Shay's expression didn't waver. "Take it away? Give you an easy out?" She shook her head. "That's an Archangel curse. I can't touch that sucker."

"Why not?" Thrush's voice rose, anger flaring. "What's the point of all this if I'm just going to end up hurting someone? Hurting her? Killing someone? I can't do this."

"Her?" Nero's deep voice rumbled, his gaze fixed on Thrush. "You mean Layla."

Thrush's jaw tightened. "I can't be around her. I can't." He was shaking his head. "I want..."

"You want to be free of your own soul?" Shay stepped closer, her expression softening. "Thrush, that's not a deal we make here. That's not a price anyone should pay. You are too young for a deal like that. If we make a deal, you'll owe us. Out of the eater will come something to eat. And out of the strong will come something sweet. We'll call on you when we desire. Last time we called upon a deal it was for war."

There was a long silence.

"I have to do something." Thrush's voice broke and he looked away, his shoulders tense. "Every time I'm near her, it feels like the darkness claws deeper. Like I'm losing control. I can't stop it."

"And what do you feel when you're away from her?" Shay asked.

His breath caught, a bitter laugh escaping. "Worse. Like fire is inside me. Torture. Like everything inside me is being demolished."

Nero's gaze seemed to pierce through him. "That means something."

Thrush glared at the horse, heat flashing beneath his skin. "Spare me the lecture. I know what I am. I know what I become; wicked and cursed and crazed. She doesn't deserve that. No one does. I tried to hide but you all wanted me to come back. Now look at me. Look at this mess."

"You are afraid," Nero continued, his voice a deep rumble, calm and unwavering. "Afraid of the darkness within you. Afraid of the light she brings."

"She doesn't have a light. She's a human. There's nothing powerful or magical about her. She's weak and soft and fragile. Something is hunting her and I can't stop it."

"Thrush." Shay's voice cut through. "Running from your own magic won't save you. Making a deal to hide from yourself won't free you. And Layla... she sees something in you. Something worth saving. Being human isn't so terrible. I was once completely human and Jed found me. We've made it work."

"She doesn't know *what* I am."

"That's not fair. *No one* knows what you truly are. You can't hold that against her."

Thrush's heart thundered in his chest. "She'll hate me. She'll be afraid." Thrush pinched his eyes closed.

"Then let her be afraid." Shay said. "But give her the choice. Don't make it for her."

Silence stretched between them, the wind rustling through the tall grass the only sound.

Thrush looked away, his hands shaking. "Just make the deal with me. That's what you do. You've made deals with others."

A soft huff of breath escaped Nero, almost a chuckle. "If you wish to make a deal to hide from yourself, I refuse. I will not barter with fear."

Thrush's chest tightened, a mix of shame and anger burning through him. "So that's it? I'm just supposed to suffer? To watch her get hurt because of me?"

"No." Shay's voice softened and she stepped forward, resting a gentle hand on his arm. "You're supposed to learn."

Thrush stared at the ground, his vision blurring. "I don't know if I can."

"Then stay. Train. Try." Shay's voice was a whisper. "But don't give up before you've even tried."

Nero stepped forward, lowering his massive head until his dark eyes met Thrush's. "Running will not save you. You must stop running. She might help you."

"A human?" Thrush scoffed, but his voice lacked the usual bite. "I don't think that's possible."

Shay's smile was warm when she asked, "Will you try the blood?"

Thrush stood there, the cold wind brushing against his skin, the mist swirling around his feet. His pulse still raced, the darkness still trembled beneath his skin. Teeth pinched the inside of his cheeks. "No. It will make me more powerful. It will put all of you in danger."

"Are you sure?" Nero asked. "Meg says you refused to drink it all this time."

Shay took a step closer. "Rue became more powerful. Remington too. Maybe stop running from your fate. Stop running from your destiny. Both of their lives changed when they gave in."

"Not until the curse clears." Thrush looked up. "I can't trust myself with the curse."

"What if it never clears?" Shay asked.

Nero whinnied. "The Raven King still suffers from tremors and more after all these years of curing his curse. Maybe you should speak with him. Maybe this is the way things will always be and you worry for no reason. You're trying to cure something that can't be cured any further."

Thrush pressed his lips together and thought. "You think I will always be this way?"

"There are some things you can control," Shay said. "Others you can't. I can't control who calls me to the crossroads. It interrupts a lot of my life with Jed and the ranch. But this is *my* life."

"You are significantly less wild than you were when you arrived weeks ago," Nero said, wagging his head up and down.

Shay nodded. "Must be the fence making. Who knew pounding fence posts could tame a wild man?"

Nero whinnied in laughter.

"I still want a deal," Thrush said. "Take my magic. Clear the curse."

"And deny you the experience of life?" Shay was shaking her head. "No. I will not make a deal."

Nero nodded. "I won't make a deal." His voice was quiet, almost a whisper.

Thrush swallowed hard, his gaze drifting toward the ranch house in the distance. The faintest hint of light glowed in one of the upstairs windows. Layla's window.

"Maybe you should check in with Meg," Shay

suggested. "Your aunt and uncle went through Hell. You're not alone in trying to figure things out."

CHAPTER 23

LAYLA'S BREATH CAME FAST AND SHALLOW, HER gaze fixed on the flickering light overhead. The smell of baked bread and herbs hung in the air and she could hear the muffled sounds of the ranch; horses and chickens outside, a faint rustle of wind against the kitchen door.

Jed stood across from her, his sleeves rolled up, a delicate silver needle between his fingers. Intricate patterns of protective runes were already inked into his own forearms, twisting and curling with a quiet glowing shimmer. She'd never noticed before–he'd kept them covered around her.

Layla was fidgeting.

"Deep breath, Layla," he murmured as he sat, his low voice a warm and steady rumble. "This won't hurt. The magic will do most of the work." He whispered something that sounded like spring rain on a Sunday afternoon.

Layla nodded, trying to relax her shoulders. Her gaze dropped to her wrist where he had already begun marking the faint outline of the runes, ancient words she couldn't understand but looked just like the markings on the books she used to locate for Rue.

"Where's Shay?" she asked, a faint tremor in her voice.

"You want her here?" he asked, looking up.

"It doesn't matter." She swallowed hard.

"I've done this a lot," Jed replied, dipping the needle into a shimmering black ink. "I spent most of my life running, hiding from angels and demons both. I learned to protect myself, to stay just out of reach. I've been doing the tattoos for a long time."

"Running from angels?" Layla's lips twitched in a nervous smile. "I always thought angels were... I don't know, the good ones. Rue told me otherwise."

Jed chuckled. "Good and bad don't quite work the same way when you're dealing with these creatures. Just because something sparkles doesn't mean its kind. Some of these creatures live within unbendable ancient rules."

Her smile faded and she stared at her wrist. "I didn't even know any of this was real until Rue showed up in my life. I only read about this kind of stuff in fiction books or watched it on TV shows."

"You're adapting fast," Jed noted, pressing the silver needle to her skin. "It wasn't easy for Shay, either." A gentle warmth spread from the needle, the ink glowing before sinking beneath her skin. There was no pain, just a faint soothing hum. "You've been dragged into something strange, but you're still standing. That's important."

A breathy laugh escaped her lips. "I feel like I'm falling."

Jed's gaze softened. "Sometimes falling is just the first step to learning to fly."

"I can't fly." Layla's lips quirked in a faint smile, but the worry still haunted her eyes. "What if it comes back?"

He moved to her other wrist, beginning the next set of runes. "These marks will protect you. But they'll only do so much."

"They'll hide me from a shadow." Layla's voice was a whisper.

Jed's hands stilled and he leaned back slightly, his sharp eyes studying her. "We're still trying to understand it. The runes aren't fool proof. It's just a starting point until Rue discovers more about what's after you."

Layla glanced down at her fingertips and blinked, her stomach twisting. The dark staining she couldn't see before was visible now, a faint inky shadow stretching from her fingertips toward her palms. She rubbed at them, trying to wipe it away but it remained, cold and unnatural.

Jed noticed her frantic movement, his gaze hardening. "Layla... that's spreading." He looked up at her. "You can see it now."

It disappeared. Layla nodded. "I could see it just for a second. Maybe it's the runes?"

Jed leaned closer, his brows knitting together. "It was just the tips of your fingers before."

Her throat tightened. "So these runes won't even help?"

"They'll help," Jed assured her again, finishing the last delicate curve of the rune. "But until we know what's causing this... we have to be careful." Jed muttered. "It's possible the tether is trying to root itself through you. It might be trying to gain access to this realm."

"Root?" She shivered. "That sounds... bad." A hollow ache settled in her chest. "So what do I do?"

"For now, stay away from that bookstore."

"But..."

"No," Jed's tone was firm, almost fatherly. "Until we know why it's trying to connect to you, you can't go near that place. We'll figure this out. Rue, Dacre, even Thrush. They're all working to protect you." He cleared his throat. "Eventually you'll be able to go back. Just not right now."

"Thrush won't help." Her heart skipped, and she tried to ignore the warmth that rushed to her cheeks.

"He's here for training and he will help. He wants to."

"Oh." Layla tucked a strand of curls behind her ear. She stared at the runes along her wrists, tracing the delicate patterns with a finger. "It's just... so much. So fast." So much had changed in her life these past few weeks.

Jed's hand rested on her hand, his touch reassuring. "I know. But you're stronger than you think. We've all survived some shit. You will too."

Layla's shoulders slumped. "I don't feel strong."

"Strength isn't about feeling powerful." Jed's voice was soft, but his words carried weight. "Sometimes, it's about refusing to give in. No matter how scared you are."

Tears stung her eyes, but she forced a smile. "I... I'll try."

"Good," he whispered, leaning back and giving her space. "We'll figure this out, Layla. One step at a time."

"My first tattoos," she whispered.

Jed pulled down his sleeves. "Wear long sleeves," he said. "Cover them. Or I can do another set to make them invisible to the human eye."

"It's okay for now. But I'll need to hide them when I finally see my parents." Layla stood up. "They've been asking about what's going on."

Jed nodded slowly. "Welcome to living a double life."

"I'm going to go read." She headed for the stairs.

"Wait," Jed grabbed her arm. He pulled her closer and twisted her wrist. His finger rubbed the skin over two tiny scars. "I didn't notice these before today." He pressed two fingertips over the marks. "What bit you, Layla?"

Layla went still. She hadn't thought about it since the day she blacked out in the library and got fired. Memories flooded back. That day she was scratching the marks until they bled. And then, they just went away.

"What bit you, Layla?" Jed asked again.

"I... I don't know. I think it was a spider."

He scowled. "That is not a spider bite."

CHAPTER 24

WOODEN BOARDS WERE WARM BENEATH LAYLA'S bare feet as she lounged on a rocking chair. A gentle breeze stirred the pages of her book. Beside her, Shay leaned against the railing, her own book balanced on her knee. They had settled into a comfortable silence, the sunlight catching in Shay's blue hair, the scent of fresh hay drifting from the nearby barn. There was a cherry pie in the oven and fresh bread rising on the stove. It smelled divine.

In the distance, Layla could hear Jed's gruff voice barking orders and the unmistakable clipped replies of Thrush. The clang of metal, the rustle of straw, and the occasional curse from Thrush made a steady background rhythm.

Shay snorted, lowering her book and grinning. "Think they'll end up fighting?"

Layla chuckled. "I'm betting on it. They both look like they're ready to throw punches half the time."

"They do," Shay agreed, turning a page. "Poor boys. Thrush didn't used to be like this."

Layla leaned back, letting the gentle wind ruffle her curls. But her smile faded slightly. "I miss the bookstore. It's been weeks... I feel like I'm losing a part of myself just sitting here doing nothing."

"Hey, you've done plenty. We've done chores, cleaned the barn. Picked the garden." She paused. "We should start canning for the winter months." She bit her lip and tension crossed her face.

Layla's gaze softened. "Has anyone figured out what's wrong with the portal?"

"Jed and Thrush have been going out every other night to mark new runes." Shay looked off in the distance.

Layla had a hint of guilt in her voice. "It feels like I brought trouble to you all."

"Not your fault." Shay reached over, giving Layla's knee a comforting squeeze. "Sometimes trouble finds you, whether you ask for it or not. I learned the hard way." She rubbed her thigh absently. "Trouble has found me before and I only survived because of the people around me now."

Layla traced the edge of her book, her eyes drifting to the barn. The sight of Thrush hauling hay bales, his shirt damp with sweat, muscles taut, was more distracting than she cared to admit. His arms had grown with all the manual labor, his shirt stretching tight over them. The faint hum of power seemed to ripple off him like heat shimmering off the desert salt pan. He was very nice to look at, even if he was frustrating as hell. Layla had never met a man like him, one who looked like that, one she couldn't keep her eyes off of, and one she found it hard to speak around.

"Ever ridden a horse before?" Shay's sudden question pulled her from her thoughts.

Layla blinked. "No, never. There aren't many horses where I grew up in Maryland. Well, in the city at least."

Shay's lips curved in a mischievous grin. "Well, I think it's time you learned. Want to take a break from worrying and try something new?"

"Are you serious?" Layla's pulse skipped.

"As a Hellion," Shay declared, pushing herself away from the railing. Then remembered Layla had no context to that joke. "Come on. It'll be fun. I'll teach you everything you need to know. Been riding my whole life."

Layla hesitated for only a moment before sliding off the chair and following Shay toward the barn. The scent of hay and leather hit her immediately, along with the soft snorts and occasional whinnies of the horses in their stalls.

Thrush and Jed were around the back of the barn still arguing about some repair work, and neither seemed to notice the two women slipping past.

Shay led Layla to a tall, sleek mare with a chestnut coat and a white star on her forehead. "This is Stella. She's gentle, won't give you any trouble. I'll saddle her up for you, and I'll ride Arrow."

As Shay worked with ease, and Layla watched in awe. "You make it look so easy."

"It is easy," Shay replied with a grin. "Just gotta be patient. And do it a million times. I'll saddle up Stella for you this time, next time you'll do it."

Layla nodded.

She tightened the straps and led Stella out of the stall, passing Layla the reins. "Here, give her a pat. Let her know you're here, that you're her friend."

Layla reached out, her hand trembling slightly, but Stella's warm velvety muzzle pushed against her palm and a surprised laugh bubbled out of her. "She's so... soft."

"See? She likes you. Now, put your foot here and swing up. I'll help if you need it."

Shay held onto the saddle and waited for Layla.

Layla's first attempt was awkward–her boot slipped, her grip was weak, but with Shay's patient guidance she managed to climb into the saddle without Shay lifting her.

"Okay... this is... this is higher than I expected," she muttered, gripping the reins tightly.

"Relax," Shay coaxed. "Just keep a light hold. Trust her. She knows what she's doing."

Shay swung up onto Arrow's back with an easy grace, then turned. She reached down to pat the old mare. "This one's good for slow walks."

Layla was watching. "You make it look so easy. I'm pathetic."

"No, girl, I've been riding horses my whole life. You should see me get on Nero, now that's a struggle." Shay giggled.

"Nero? That horse is giant. I would need a ladder."

"I make do." Shay clicked her tongue and loosened the reins. Arrow started walking and Stella followed along.

For a few minutes, they walked in slow, easy circles, Layla's tension gradually melting away as she adjusted to the sway of the horse.

"Want to go ride in the fields?" Shay pointed to the span of land between the ranch and the mountains in the distance.

"Okay." Layla nodded hesitantly.

Shay taught Layla how to pick up speed and within a few minutes the horses were trotting past the driveway and toward the prairie.

"See, it's easy!" Shay was smiling as she turned to look at Layla.

But then, a sharp, metallic clang echoed from the far side of the barn. Either something was dropped or someone lost their temper. There was a loud boom and dirt shot into the air. A lot of dirt. It rained down on them like a hailstorm.

Stella's ears flicked back, her head snapping up, and in a heartbeat she surged forward.

"Whoa! Whoa!" Layla yelped, her grip tightening.

"Layla, hold the reins. Keep your balance!" Shay shouted, nudging Arrow forward to catch up. She wished she'd picked a faster horse, the old mare wasn't made for running.

Stella was already picking up speed, her hooves pounding against the dirt, Layla's panic rising with every stride. Her hands slipped and she fought to remember Shay's instructions, but everything felt like a blur.

"Stella! Stop! Please!" Layla begged.

Of course the horse didn't listen, her wild eyes fixed on the open field beyond then the nearby forest. Layla's breath came in desperate gasps, her body bouncing in the saddle, her vision shaking. Her glasses bounced until they were crooked.

The fence rushed toward them. Layla leaned forward, clutching the horse's mane, her heart in her throat.

"Layla!" Shay's voice was distant, drowned by the

thunder of hooves. "Hang on tight. My horse can't keep up."

And then, just as they neared the fence, Stella's muscles bunched, and she leapt.

Layla's scream tore free as the world seemed to fall away.

They cleared the fence. The impact on the other side jarred Layla's teeth. Her balance wavered. Thankfully, she didn't fall. She used her shoulder to push her glasses up and looked back. Shay wasn't there.

No one was there.

"Oh no." Layla worried. "Slow down. Slow down." This was a bad idea. Layla was never going to ride horses again.

She gripped the reins and ducked as Stella ran straight for the forest. "Please don't go there. Please." She muttered.

The trees blurred as they whipped past, a smear of green and shadow.

Layla clung to the saddle horn with white-knuckled desperation, her thighs screaming as she bounced against Stella's galloping back. She watched the reins bounce, too afraid to reach for them. The mare was panicked, her ears pinned flat, eyes wild. Layla didn't know what to do.

"Stella, whoa! Please, stop!"

But the horse didn't slow. Didn't even hear her. Branches lashed across Layla's arms and scraped her cheek as the trees grew thicker and the forest grew darker. She ducked as one snapped across her glasses, knocking them off. She gasped, blinking through the sting, trying to stay upright. She wasn't built for this. Not for wild animals. Not for danger.

Her fingers ached as she clutched the leather. Her breath came sharp and panicked, her heart hammering against her ribs. She couldn't see where they were going, just shapes and shadows, and then she felt the sudden jolt of the mare leaping over something.

It was an old fence, splintered and half-buried in weeds.

Stella landed hard on the other side and it jerked Layla. She slipped sideways, her foot catching in the stirrup before wrenching free. Stella bucked and threw Layla off her back. Layla hit the ground, hands down to catch herself. A sickening crack shot pain through her left arm.

She screamed.

The forest behind her and empty prairie ahead of her swallowed the sound.

She lay there for a moment, dazed, eyes squinted against the sunlight filtering through the overhang of trees. Her breath trembled in and out of her lungs. Every nerve in her body sang with panic and pain.

Her arm throbbed from her wrist to her elbow. It had to be broken. She tried to flex her fingers but couldn't. Pain zipped up her arm to her shoulder.

Stella had vanished, gone in a blur of hooves and shadow. Somewhere far ahead, a branch cracked. But nothing came back for her.

Slowly, Layla rolled onto her good side, sucking in a breath as she sat up. The clearing stretched out around her, overgrown and oddly quiet. In the distance, through the trees and weeds, she saw a blurry and blackened skeleton of a house.

Burned and forgotten, it leaned sideways, bones of

wood and ash half-buried beneath creeping vines. A memory, long erased.

She sat still in the dirt, blood on her cheeks, sweat stinging her eyes, arm cradled tight against her chest. She told herself she was just going to catch her breath, give herself a minute, and then she'd try to find her glasses. The world was a blur of light and dark. She cursed herself for not getting laser eye surgery last year when her parents offered it up as a Christmas present.

She ran the fingers of her good arm over her aching arm and hissed as she felt a bump under the skin. She pressed on it, moaning when sharp pain lit up her arm. It was definitely broken. She crossed her legs and sat up straight, taking in a few deep breaths and cradling her arm.

"I'm going to be fine. The ranch can't be that far away." She peered into the forest and only saw darkness. She looked up, the afternoon sun was dipping. Shay would be putting that bread in the oven for dinner and then night would come faster than she expected. She didn't have anything to create a sling, so she held her injured arm close and moved to stand, hissing again as pain shot up her back. She was just glad the fall didn't kill her.

Layla looked down. The grass was up to her knees. She stepped forward and blinked. Her vision was always terrible at twilight, especially with her glasses off. She started walking into the forest but felt something warm dripping down her forehead. She wiped at it with her good arm. Blood.

"Did I hit my head?" she asked herself, remembering the branches and bramble that had licked her face. Suddenly she felt lightheaded and nausea flooded her stomach. Maybe it was the pain, maybe it was the adrenaline. Layla sat immediately and pressed her back against a tree trunk. She squeezed her eyes closed.

"This fucking sucks," she muttered to herself. She glanced at the runes tattooed on her wrists. They didn't do shit for falling off a horse.

CHAPTER 25

STELLA RETURNED TO THE RANCH. RIDERLESS. Thrush was tossing hay into the stalls with stiff movements. His body was taut with lingering tension, the muscles in his back bunching beneath his shirt. He'd been holding in tics from the curse all day and it was taking a toll on him. His temper had never been shorter. And now he was going to have to fix the giant hole he'd blasted into the dirt behind the barn.

Shay was running toward the men, shouting.

Jed was leaning against the doorframe, arms crossed. He stood up straight and took in the scene. Shay had the old mare Arrow, who was only good for grazing and slow walks. The chestnut mare followed closely behind them, head hung low.

Jed started toward her. "What happened?" He noticed there was no Layla.

"I have to get Nero," Shay shouted. "Something spooked Stella while we were riding and she took off with

Layla." Shay scowled. "I'm guessing it was you two fucking off with your magic and making loud noise."

"And the mare returned without her." Jed took the mares reins.

Thrush straightened, brushing the hay from his hands. "What happened to her?"

"I'm going to go find her," Shay said as she took the saddle off Arrow. "Can you get these two settled for me?"

"Which direction did they go?" Jed asked.

Shay's back went stiff before she nodded north. "The forest. Toward the old ranch."

There was a moment of silence.

The old ranch held terrible memories. That was the plot of land where Shay had grown up. Her parents were preppers and had taught her how to survive anything and everything. When tragedy struck Shay survived, but they didn't. While Shay loved the land, she couldn't bear to go back to that scene. Her parents were buried there near a mass grave of the dead. The house had burned. Trees and prairie grass had grown in and overtaken the property. While Shay owned the land, she didn't travel there. She swallowed hard thinking of seeing the old house now.

"No." Jed's hand wrapped around her wrist. "You're not going up there alone."

"I won't be alone, I'll take Nero," Shay said, refusing to look up at Jed.

"No." He looked across the barn. "Thrush will go."

"Thrush?" Shay's face flexed in confusion.

"It will be good for him. And her."

"What happened to Layla?" Thrush asked again.

"I want you to take him," Jed pointed to Nero, "and go find Layla."

The hay fork slipped from Thrush's grasp, clattering against the stall door. "She's been left alone?"

Jed didn't flinch. He gestured at Thrush. "You need to go. Now."

Thrush's jaw tightened. He didn't want to admit the anxiety pooling in his gut, the nagging fear that his magic was too volatile, that he was a danger to everyone around him. Especially her. Especially now.

"What if I hurt her?" Thrush growled.

"What if she's already hurt?" Jed countered.

Thrush's face paled. He grabbed his flannel off the nearby hook and shrugged it on.

"Nero will send you back to Hell if you hurt her. That's why he's going with you." Jed took a saddle from Shay and set it aside.

"Stella ran toward the north forest." Shay pointed the direction.

"One sec," Jed shouted as he grabbed a flashlight off the nearby bench and tossed it to Thrush. "Nightfall is coming."

A rumbling nicker caught Thrush's attention. Nero was at the door of the barn, his dark mane a rippling shadow, his restless hooves churning the grass.

Thrush exhaled sharply and tucked the flashlight into his pocket. "Fine." In a few long strides, Thrush was beside Nero.

"Get on," Nero grumbled. "Walking is too slow."

He grabbed the back of Nero's neck, his fingers trembling slightly. The horse leaned down, his dark eyes meeting Thrush's.

"Yeah, I know." Thrush muttered, swinging up onto the horse's back. "Let's go."

Nero needed no more encouragement. The moment Thrush's knees touched his sides, the stallion broke into a swift gallop, the wind tearing at Thrush's hair, the land blurring past. He tried to focus, to quiet the frantic rhythm of his thoughts. It was of little use.

Layla had to be fine, just lost. She'd probably get mad at him for overreacting. He told himself this over and over, but the tension in his chest only grew.

Nero was running so fast that Thrush had to wrap the horse's mane around his fists and lean down.

Nero sniffed the air. "Stella took her this way. Don't fall off," he warned.

The giant horse ran through the forest, trees passing by in a blur. Thrush smiled; he'd ridden Nero as a child but the beast had never revealed his true speed. Not even close. Adrenaline pumped through both of their veins until a subtle snap echoed from under Nero's hoof. He came to an abrupt stop.

"That wasn't a stick," Nero warned.

Thrush slid off his back and began searching the forest floor. It was getting darker. The shadows from the forest canopy danced across the ground. Light sparked from his fingertips.

"Use the flashlight or risk a fire," Nero warned.

Thrush pulled the light from his pocket and shined it onto the forest floor. There was debris, leaves and sticks. And... a pair of dark-rimmed glasses, the lenses cracked.

Thrush picked them up and tucked them into his shirt pocket.

Nero sniffed the air again. "There's blood." He turned to stare at Thrush. There was concern etched in the horse's features.

"The blood won't bother me," Thrush assured him.

"Because it's never bothered your kind?"

"Because I've never given in to the desire." Thrush pressed his lips together and felt the sharp points of his teeth. No, he'd never given in, never tasted it, but there was something about the scent in the air, *her blood*...

"Snap out of it," Nero grumbled.

Thrush rolled his shoulders and started walking, following the smell and trail of broken branches and tipped saplings.

The tree line wasn't far and beyond Thrush could see the outline of the mountains in the distance. He searched.

"She's close," Nero warned.

And then he saw her. A crumpled figure at the base of a tree.

"Layla!"

Thrush ran forward, his boots skidding against the dirt. Layla's arm was bent at an awkward angle, her face pale, and her breathing shallow. Her lashes fluttered, her lips trembling with a faint gasp. There was so much blood dripping down her face.

Something burned in his throat. He ignored it.

"No... no, no, no." Thrush's hands hovered above her still body, afraid to touch her, afraid of making things worse. Power churned beneath his skin, desperate to escape, to fix this. He held it in. That power was darkness, chaos. He'd never used it to fix a thing. Ever.

His teeth felt sharp against his lips again. He swallowed hard and ignored it. He had to ignore it. He *must* ignore it.

"Thrush..." Layla's voice was a faint whisper, her eyes barely open. "I though Shay or Jed would come."

"They sent me."

"Oh." She tipped her head away, revealing a small pool of blood in the hollow of her collarbone.

He sucked in a sharp breath, the air crackling around them. "There's a lot of blood."

"Are you... mad at me?" she mumbled, her brow furrowing. "You're always mad and grumpy. I don't think I can get up." Her head lolled to the side and her body slumped further. "I'm really tired."

"No. No, I'm not mad." His voice broke. "Just... hold still. Please."

"Um hm," was all that came softly from her throat.

The darkness clawed at his chest, a soft glow curling around his fingers.

Heal, not harm.

Heal, not harm.

Heal, not harm.

Nero whinnied softly. Another reminder.

The beast would turn him into a cinder without another thought if this went wrong.

He pulled the notebook out of his back pocket and flipped through it, searching for a spell for broken bones or healing. It was something Jed had passed on to him years ago when he was a child.

There it was. He set the notebook next to his knee.

He pressed his hands against her broken arm, his heart hammering. He whispered words that sounded like mist in the morning, like tiny bells, like softness. His magic surged, the faint light pulsing into her skin.

For a moment, Layla's face contorted with pain but then her breathing steadied and the twisted angle of her arm straightened beneath his touch.

He pulled his hands back and her arm appeared healed but she was still pale. The cut on her head was still leaking blood. He took her by the shoulders and moved her small body, maneuvering her until she was laying in front of him.

Layla's eyes opened fully, her gaze meeting his. "Thank you," she whispered. "Are you going to kill me now?"

"Why would you ask that?" He couldn't stop staring at the blood.

"You keep telling me to stay away from you. That you'll hurt me. But, you never have." She sighed and touched her rib, coughing slightly.

"I won't hurt you." Thrush's voice was hoarse. "I promise."

"Okay." Layla nodded slightly.

She reached up, her fingers brushing his cheek. "Is it the blood bothering you? I've never seen you so still."

He couldn't lie. "Yes." The blood was bothering him. A temptation. A desire. A calling.

His breath caught and he leaned into her touch, his eyes closing. "You don't know what I am... what I'm capable of."

"It's okay. I don't need to know." She touched her face then looked at the sticky blood on her fingertips. "Will you close the wound?"

A bitter laugh escaped him. "You trust me to do that?"

"You fixed my arm." Her fingers tightened against his cheek, forcing him to look at her. "I'm not afraid."

"Stop." His voice wavered, his heart pounding like a war drum. "Stop touching me. Please." He licked his lips.

"Sorry." She looked away. "I think I hit my head when the horse threw me. I can't think straight. My brain is all fuzzy."

He held his hands over the cut on her forehead and whispered the healing spell again. The bleeding stopped. His hands moved to his thighs and gripped them, relieved. She was still covered in blood. It coated her face, down her neck. Her neck. It was so pale and smooth. And she was sure warm. Yes, she was warm and smelled so good and that mouth of hers... he was sure her lips were as warm as the rest of her body.

"Why are you staring at my neck?" Layla swallowed hard.

He squeezed his eyes closed and turned his head. It was a bad idea as the sound of blood coursing through her body got louder.

"Do you... do you drink blood like Rue?"

"No. Yes. I can. I just have never."

"And now you've drained your magic and you're weak?"

"I'm not weak. I just need a moment." He took a deep breath.

"Blood would make you stronger."

"I'll be fine. I don't need it."

She held out her wrist. "Are you sure?"

He licked his lips and clamped his teeth together. What

was wrong with her? Offering herself up like this? She must've hit her head really hard.

"Let me thank you." Layla moved faster than he expected. Her lips were warm, her touch gentle as her fingers threaded into the hair at the back of his scalp. For an instant, the world fell away. The whispering shadows, the fear, the confusion; all gone. All that existed was her–the little librarian who haunted his dreams.

Thrush's shock melted into hunger. His hands slid to her waist, pulling her closer, his lips answering her with a desperation he could barely contain. He kissed her like she was his lifeline, his only tether to sanity in the swirling chaos of his world.

But the sharp ache in his chest brought him back. He felt the sharpness in his mouth; wanting, waiting. He broke the kiss, pulling back, his breath ragged. "Layla... I..."

"Thank you." Her voice was soft, her fingers gripping his shirt. "If I never get to tell you. Thank you."

"I'm not leaving you."

He stared at her, his chest tight. She was so fragile, so human. But she was the only thing that made him feel real. He leaned in, his forehead pressing against hers, his breathing slowly calming.

"Sorry," she whispered, and he felt the faintest crack of a smile on his lips.

"You shouldn't do things like that."

Nero snorted behind them, nudging Thrush with his large velvety nose, and the moment shattered with a soft awkward laugh from Layla.

"I think he's telling us to get a move on," she murmured.

Thrush stood, carefully helping her to her feet. His touch lingered, his thumb brushing against her wrist where the faint runes of protection glowed beneath her sleeve.

"You seem calmer out here near the forest. In the wilderness." She was staring at him.

Thrush took a deep breath. "It's from all the time I spent alone in the mountains of Hell. It feels like home to me. Much more than the ranch or the castle or the Hellion barracks."

"Do you want to stay longer? We don't have to go back." She touched her head like she was dizzy. Thrush could tell she couldn't stay out here. She needed to get back to the house.

But the *blood*.

There was blood on the grass. Blood on her skin. On his hands. He looked in the distance and noticed an old water pump.

"Let's get you cleaned off and then we'll head back."

CHAPTER 26

THRUSH WALKED SLOWLY WITH LAYLA LEANING against his side, her weight pressing into him more heavily now that the adrenaline had worn off.

She was quiet. Too quiet.

He glanced down. Blood had dried across her temple and neck. Her shirt was torn at the sleeve, her jeans ripped. But it was the blood. Its scent sharp, metallic, and warm in his nose. It gnawed at him now. It wouldn't stop. This was bad.

His body thrummed with hunger.

Thrush exhaled and turned his head away.

They weren't far from the old ranch's pump beside a rusted basin half-sunk into the earth. The low moonlight caught the glint of its handle.

Nero was following slowly behind them.

"It's not far," he muttered. "Can you still walk? Nero can carry you."

Layla blinked up at him. "I'm fine."

"You're covered in blood."

She tried to smile. "You've said that a few times now. I think it's bothering you."

Thrush looked away. "It's fine," he muttered.

He led her to the pump, bracing her as she stumbled then leaned against the basin. The pump groaned in protest as he worked the handle. Water sputtered out, brown at first, then clearing.

"Hold still," he said. He stripped off his flannel and hung it on the pump, then motioned to her shirt. "Take it off."

"My shirt?" Layla moved slowly as she gripped the hemline. She looked up at him, blinking.

"It's covered in blood."

"Oh." Layla started pulling the shirt up, shivering as the cool summer night air touched her skin.

"I'll be quick." Thrush promised. He helped her get the shirt over her sore arm.

Layla stood in just a bra as Thrush rinsed her shirt, the water in the basin turning red. He glanced at her.

"I can just rinse myself off. I'm short enough." Layla moved closer as Thrush pumped the handle on the spicket. She put her arms under the flow of water, sucking in a breath as the cold well water touched her skin. "Christ is this water straight from the artic?"

"I'll get the blood off your back." He dipped her shirt into the water and gently wiped at the back of her neck and spine. He noticed lots of bruising from her fall.

She hissed but didn't pull away. "That bad?"

"No." His voice was rough. "Just... distracting. You really got hurt. You probably shouldn't ride any more horses."

She gave him a curious look.

He didn't answer. Instead, a large hand gripped her shoulder and turned her. He focused on cleaning the streaks down her throat, keeping his eyes on the task and not on the pulse beneath her skin or on the way her breath hitched when his fingers grazed her collarbone.

When she spoke again, it was softer. "You don't have to be afraid of yourself, you know."

He stopped. "I'm not afraid of myself. I'm afraid of what I'll do to someone else." He closed his eyes and took a breath. "Before I came here, I lost control during training and almost killed Evelyn. I'd never forgive myself for hurting an innocent."

The water slowed to a trickle. He handed her the shirt and turned to pump the handle until water flowed again.

"You can't see well in the dark, and I don't want you tripping and snapping your other arm or taking another branch to the face. You should ride Nero back."

"Actually, I can't see well without my glasses." She pointed to the forest. "They fell off back there. I was going to try and find them, but I couldn't move since my arm hurt too much."

Thrush held up his finger. "I almost forgot." He grabbed his flannel and pulled her broken glasses from the pocket. Then he passed the jacket to her. "Put this on."

"My shirt—"

"It's wet. Here." He held the flannel open until she sighed and pressed her arms into the sleeves.

"You found my glasses?" she asked as she buttoned the flannel.

"Well, Nero did. He stepped on them."

Layla frowned. "Can you fix them?"

"I can try." Thrush pulled the notebook from his pocket. He'd used the magic to break plenty of things, not necessarily fix them. He found a piece of a spell that might work. He set the glasses down on the side of the basin and rubbed his hands together.

"Step back," he warned Layla.

Nero started acting antsy. The giant horse was whinnying low and pawing the ground.

"I think he wants to leave," Layla said.

"This will just take me a minute." He whispered words that sounded like glass melting. A blue light spun from his fingertips and her glasses began to repair. The crack in the lens disappeared and the earpiece moved back into place.

Nero got louder, nudging Thrush's elbow and back. Whinnying louder.

———

NERO DIDN'T WANT TO SPEAK IN FRONT OF LAYLA, he didn't want her to know what he really was. Horses didn't speak in Layla's world. But Nero had a bad feeling. This place was cursed. There was darkness here... Nero remembered...

Then...

Jed woke in the darkness with an uneasy feeling. He cursed himself for sleeping for so long. He'd only planned to rest his eyes like the old folks would say. Now the moon was high and shining through his open window.

Open?

Jed didn't leave the window open. He'd checked the locks and had planned to set some wards but never did.

The floorboards creaked.

Jed knew that uneasy feeling he'd woken with. He wasn't alone in the dark room. He glanced to his bag at the foot of the bed. He needed the big knife with the runes etched into it. Just as he had the thought, his bag started slowly moving, being pulled off the foot of the bed.

It was now or never.

Jed clapped his hands and twisted his fingers into shapes like stacked pyramids. He spat words that sounded like the hiss of fire igniting. Light erupted from the foot of the bed and as it did, Jed launched himself forward to grab his bag and pull the knife out. The creature on the floor scurried to the wall and hissed back.

"You don't belong here," Jed said.

The creature jabbered in Hellspeak. It sounded pissed and hungry.

Jed secured his bag over his shoulder, gripped the knife, and moved toward the lesser Demon as it crouched, trying to escape the ball of light.

"What are you doing here?" Jed asked the Demon, settling the tip of the knife at the base of the Demon's throat.

"Something sweet to eat," it garbled.

"You don't belong on this plane." Jed slid the knife down the creature's neck, but stopped when he heard a struggle in the living room. "How many of you are there?"

"More than me."

"How many?" Jed pressed the tip of the knife in. It required more pressure to pierce the Demon's thick hide.

"We are four of the crossroads."

The ball of light was starting to fade. The Demon watched it, muscles twitching, ready to fight when it went dark again.

Jed slammed his knife through the Demon's heart. "Not today, shithead."

The Demon's body slouched against the wall and inky blood pooled between its legs on the floor.

Jed looked at the open window, then the door. Old habits were hard to break. He climbed out the window. Whatever happened in the living room, he was sure the other Demon had won from the sounds. The chewing of human bone was a distinct sound, and Jed was sure whoever was out there wasn't chewing on the Demon's bones.

Jed glanced at the gate to the ranch. He could be gone quickly and save his own hide. He'd done it enough times throughout his lifetime. He glanced at the main house and the window on the second floor.

Shay.

Damn it.

Jed knew better than to get attached. But he knew Shay would die if he left now. At least he could try. He remembered the feel of her energy under his palms as he healed her forehead, the glimmer in her eyes as she joked about saving him. No, he couldn't leave Shay to die. Being eaten by a Demon was never a good way to go.

Jed inched along the guest house exterior. He watched the shadows for movement.

One Demon slunk out of the front door of the guest house. Another left the horse barn. A third moved from the kitchen window inside the house.

Jed moved. He ran to the house. The other two Demons

made it to the front door before him. They blasted through and began wrecking the interior of the house, searching for blood.

Jed began climbing the railing. He jumped to grab the roof overhang of the front porch and pulled himself up. Arms aching, he was running on pure adrenaline. He climbed onto the roof and went to Shay's window. He tried to open it, but the frame didn't move. He tapped on the glass.

"Shay, wake up," he said just above a whisper.

Jed didn't want to make too much noise and draw attention, but he needed Shay to wake up or next he'd be breaking the window.

He tapped the glass harder. There was movement inside. On the bed, then the floor.

His stomach sank. He was too late.

But then footsteps moved closer. The window unlocked and opened.

"Jed?"

"Thank God you're okay." He moved back. "Get out here."

"Why?"

A large crash and the sound of Momma screaming broke through the night.

Shay ran back into the room. She rounded her bed and pulled a shotgun out from under the bed.

Without a chance of getting her out of the window, Jed climbed in.

"Shay," he warned. "There are creatures here."

"Oh no, the dead?" her face paled. "Are Momma and Daddy dead?"

"I don't know. But you're about to see something you've never seen before."

Jed was interrupted by the door blasting open. One demon charged into the room like a lion leaping to attack prey.

Shay shot it. Shotgun pellets left a blast hole in the creature's chest. She turned to Jed. "What the fuck was that?"

"A Demon." He moved closer to the corpse on the floor, used his knife to stab it through what was left of the heart, just to be sure. "Nice shot, by the way."

"Daddy didn't raise no sissy." Shay loaded the shotgun chamber, opened her nightstand drawer, pulled out a box of shells, and tucked them into her pocket.

They heard the sounds of Nicholas fighting and shouting from the bedroom downstairs.

Shay ran out of the room without another word. Jed followed.

Momma was lying in a pool of blood. One of the Demons crouched near her shoulder, feeding from her neck like a vampire.

"Get out!" Nicholas shouted as he grappled with the other Demon. Blood was dripping down the side of his head. "Run."

Both Demons turned to Jed and Shay. The one near Momma rose. "Out of the strong will come something sweet." The Demon focused on Shay, body twitching, ready to pounce.

Jed tried his previous spell; it subdued the first one. He clapped his hands and twisted his fingers. He spat the words that sounded like the hiss of fire igniting. Light erupted in the center of the room. The Demons shrieked and scurried to the far wall. Jed leapt over to the bed to confront the Demons.

"*Who summoned you here?*" Jed had a knife in each hand, tips touching the leathery necks of the beasts.

"*One who desires what he does not have.*" The Demon's eyes flicked to Shay.

"*A name.*" Jed pressed harder with each knife.

"*Clyburn,*" the Demon hissed.

Jed recognized nothing special about Clyburn, just that the guy had a serious hard-on for Shay and no boundaries.

"*What is Clyburn?*" Jed pressed the tips of each knife until dark blood dripped from the necks of the Demons.

"*A foolish man with a plan.*"

"*Just a man?*" Jed asked.

"*Nothing more than Earthen plane scum,*" the Demon on Jed's left said as it began moving, trying to escape. The creature had grabbed a lamp cord and swung it, the lamp colliding with Jed's back.

"*Move right,*" Shay shouted.

Jed stooped and twisted, felt the force of buckshot scrape the air.

The Demon to his left slid down the wall, head tipped to the side and half of its face and neck dripping.

Jed's ears were ringing. He shook his head, hoping it would pass. His hand was steady on the knife holding the last Demon.

"*A deal is a deal.*" The Demon focused on Shay. "*The ranch and the girl.*"

"*Focus, creature.*" Jed slapped the Demon on the side of the head. "*You can't have her.*"

"*Out of the eater will come something to eat. And out of the strong will come something sweet. A deal is a deal.*" The Demon knew he was outnumbered. There was nothing but death for him in this room, but he was driven by desire for something he could never have on the plane of Hell. A fresh human to eat. Nothing was sweeter or more filling. The crossroads Demon was going to get what he was promised. Taloned feet dug into the carpet as he readied himself.

The ball of light in the middle of the room faded.

The creature launched himself, twisting away from the tip of Jed's knife.

Jed twisted, grabbed the Demon by its ankle, slamming it to the ground.

Nicholas grabbed the Demon's shoulders and helped hold it down.

Jed stabbed it in the heart. As the Demon was dying, it howled like a wolf in the night and a wisp of a soul left its body, flying out the broken window and disappearing into the moonlight.

Jed looked the Demon over, making sure it was dead. He touched its hand with the golden ring and chain connected to a golden bracelet. He rarely came across Demons wearing anything like this. Jed cut the Demon's arm at the wrist, just above the golden bracelet.

"What are you doing?" Nicholas asked.

"Saving this for later." Jed stood and went to the kitchen. He searched the cabinets and drawers for a large Ziploc bag and put the Demon hand inside.

When Jed returned to the bedroom, Nicholas and Shay were stooped over Momma's body. Jed hadn't seen a man like Nicholas cry in a long time and he felt uncomfortable watching.

Jed waited in the hall as they said their goodbyes.

Nicholas and Shay closed the bedroom door as they walked toward him.

"We should check the rest of the ranch and make sure we got them all," Jed suggested.

"There's more?" Shay asked.

"I killed four." Jed headed to the back door on the far end of the kitchen.

A black shadow galloped by.

"That's Nero." Shay ran forward and out the door.

Now

Thrush held up Layla's repaired glasses. Mostly. "They're still a little crooked." He frowned, disappointed with his work.

She slipped them on, blinking as the world came into focus. They sat bent on her nose.

"Thanks. Now I can see the creepy shadows better," she muttered. "I'll have to get to the optometrist in the morning. I hope they have one nearby."

He gave her a look.

She smirked. "Joking about the creepy shadows. Mostly."

But even as she spoke, a cold ripple passed through the air. It was so faint she thought it might have been her imagination. She turned toward the fence behind them. Beyond it, mist clung low to the ground, curling unnaturally at the edges of the clearing. There was a large pine with shadows that looked like puddles under its canopy.

Thrush noticed it too. He straightened, one hand instinctively going to the runes inked into his forearm.

"I think we need to go. Now." Thrush warned.

Layla started to move, but something slithered from the tall grass. A black tendril, thin, wet, and writhing like smoke made flesh.

Before she could scream, it coiled around her ankle and yanked.

Nero whinnied loudly.

Layla cried out as she was dragged toward the pine tree. The flannel was torn down her shoulders. The top button popped off. Her sore arm flailed helplessly as dirt scraped her back.

"Thrush!" she shouted.

He was already moving. Nero too.

Layla cried out as she was dragged across the dirt toward the watery shadows in the distance. The tendril jerked her farther into the darkness. Her body scraped over jagged roots. A split opened on her cheek where a sharp stone caught her skin.

"Thrush!" she screamed, her voice hoarse with pain and terror.

It all happened so fast.

The ground groaned beneath Thrush's boots as he raced after her. His heart pounded with fear and fury. Not again. He would not let the shadows take her. He wouldn't lose her to the Astral.

Another tendril wrapped around her ankle. Then a third around her middle.

"Let her go!" he roared, skidding to his knees and slamming his palms against the ground.

Power exploded from his body in a sharp pulse. The first tendril shrieked and hissed away, but it wasn't enough. It just moved faster. He was weak. He cursed himself.

The earth beneath Layla was no longer solid.

"Careful!" Nero barked.

Layla's eyes went wide and her face was beyond pale.

A gaping crack had formed at the base of the pine, barely visible in the dim light; a dark sinkhole. Layla's body jolted as her foot disappeared into the void.

"No!" she cried, clawing at the ground.

Thrush dove forward, fingertips brushing hers, but it was too late.

The tendrils yanked and the ground gave way completely.

With a scream, Layla was pulled under.

The earth sealed behind her like a mouth closing over prey, leaving only silence and a jagged blood smear where she'd been.

Thrush dropped to the dirt, digging wildly, throwing debris aside with shaking hands. "No, no, no," he muttered. "Layla!"

Then he smelled it.

Brimstone and pine and... blood.

Hell.

He could feel it in his bones. Something dark had slithered up from deep underground, sick and ancient. A tunnel, a forgotten artery of the underworld once used by demons to cross between realms had been reopened.

Thrush gripped his knees, breathing hard, his hands

still glowing with uncontrolled magic. He didn't know what to say or do next.

"Come now, Princeling," Nero ordered. "We must tell Jed and Shay and go find her." He whinnied in annoyance. "The White Horse will not be happy with this."

"What was that?" Thrush asked.

"When the balance between realms is tilted, the Veil becomes thin. Creatures can get through."

"But there is balance." Thrush moved to his knees.

"Must not be." Nero motioned for Thrush to get on his back. "Don't let go," he warned taking off like a bolt of lightning before Thrush had a grip on him.

Thrush didn't have a chance to think about how he was going to find Layla. In the blink of an eye the breath rushed from his lungs and then they were at the ranch with Shay waiting on the porch. That's how fast Nero could move.

CHAPTER 27

LAYLA HIT THE GROUND. THE AIR LEFT HER LUNGS in a ragged gasp and the impact sent pain flaring through her ribs. Dirt and ash coated her skin. Her ears rang. For a moment, she couldn't move; couldn't think.

She adjusted her glasses, took them off, and noticed they were cracked again.

The scent of sulfur filled her nose, metallic and sharp like lightning about to strike. The ground beneath her was rock.

She pushed herself up onto her good elbow, gritting her teeth against the pain in her ribs.

She was in a cave, wide and uneven, the ceiling low and jagged, slick with some kind of black moss. The only illumination came from the opening in the distance.

Layla's breath caught.

The shadows in the far corner moved.

At first, she thought it was her vision. She was having trouble focusing with the crack in her glasses lens. There was something there. Tall. Still. Watching.

"Hello?" Her voice was raw from screaming.

Nothing answered.

But the shadow shifted again, just barely, like a figure breathing in the dark. A tendril of shadows slithered out into the open.

Layla crawled backward until her back hit the wall. Her heart slammed in her chest. She blinked through the blurriness. It couldn't be a person. She didn't want it to be a person. Not here, wherever she was...

"Where...where am I?" she whispered.

The stone under her palm was warm.

A shiver ran up her spine.

This place wasn't just underground.

This was somewhere else. Somewhere wrong. It was the kind of wrong that made her blood feel too thick and her thoughts swim like she was underwater. Nausea churned in her stomach.

Her thoughts raced. Rue and her brother were from Hell. Thrush had come from Hell. Hell was a real place. She'd been dragged under the dirt and fell through a space that seemed like air. She'd felt terribly nauseous.

Layla looked up again. The shadow was gone.

No, not gone. Moved.

Now it was closer. It was still blurred by distance and her wonky vision, but there. Watching.

She scrambled to her feet. Her legs shook. "Stay away," she said.

Still nothing.

Silence pressed down like a weight. No wind. No echo. Just her voice swallowed by the cave like it had never existed.

Then, low and rumbling from the darkness, a whisper that sounded like, "You belong here."

She froze.

"Where am I?"

No response.

"Let me go," she said, trying to keep her voice from cracking. "Please."

The shadow moved again.

It was closer now.

She could see the vague outline of a man; tall, broad-shouldered, unmoving. Strange, like the edges of him didn't fit right in the space. A ripple of cold passed through the cave. She clutched Thrush's jacket tighter around herself.

Her chin lifted. "If you're going to kill me," she said, heart hammering, "just do it."

The figure didn't move.

Then, almost softly, "No."

The shadows receded again, as though melting back into the cave wall.

Layla sagged to the ground, shaking. Her ribs throbbed. Her head spun. She didn't know how long she had or if anyone would find her in a place like this.

CHAPTER 28

"SHE WASN'T ALONE," THRUSH SAID, JAW TIGHT. "She was with me. And I failed."

Jed looked like he might punch a hole through the wall. "I wish you would have stayed away from the old ranch."

"Why didn't you tell me what happened there?" Thrush asked, voice low and sharp.

Jed's eyes darkened. "Because we buried that history for a reason. We didn't think anything would ever stir there again."

"Well, something did," Thrush said. "And it took her. It crawled through the ground and dragged her under."

Shay stepped forward. "Find her. Bring her back."

"I will," Thrush said without hesitation.

"She might already be..." Jed started.

Thrush growled, low and deep. "Don't."

Jed held his gaze for a long moment. Then finally, he nodded. "You'll need someone to get you in and out. Nero goes with you."

Nero snorted. "Obviously." He walked away. "I'm going to tell *her*."

"Come with me." Jed motioned for Thrush to follow.

He crossed the yard and entered a root cellar. There were rows of jars filled with preserved food. Baskets awaited the fall harvest of potatoes and carrots to make it through the winter.

Jed walked to the weapons rack and pulled out a carved blade, handing it to Thrush. The hilt was engraved with protective runes. "Take this."

Thrush gripped the blade. "This looks familiar."

"It's basilisk bone. Carved by the Raven King. Your uncle. You carried it into war. Remember?"

Thrush turned the blade over in his hand. Back then was when he'd started turning, when his thoughts went dark, when the sunlight of the Seven Kingdoms of Heaven had bleached his hair white as a ghost. The Legion of Angels had bullied him. He had hated Heaven. He'd always felt out of place and couldn't wait to leave.

Memories flooded his mind: hate and pain. He'd killed during the war, plenty of demons died on the edge of his blade. His parents were overwhelming and too focused. It drove him mad. The sunlight drove him mad. The curse... Thrush slammed his eyes closed and walked out of the cellar.

"Bring her home," Shay whispered.

"I will," he said, mounting up behind Nero.

"The White Horse is not happy with the current situation of one of her humans," Nero muttered. "Seems the Veil may have thinned because of you."

"I'll fix this." Thrush jumped and threw a leg over Nero's back. "We'll bring her back."

Nero whinnied. "Hold on tight, Princeling."

Nero took off; he was faster than a speeding bullet, faster than lightning, faster than the speed of sound. Nothing in the three realms moved faster than Nero.

He took off for the mountains.

"The portal at the bookstore," Thrush coughed out, the wind filling his mouth.

"There's a tiny tear in the Veil. It will be faster." Nero was faster than lightning, faster than the speed of light, faster than a black hole. Trees bent away from him before he passed them, hoofprints appeared in the soil before his gallop hit the ground. The ground in the distance shook before the black blur passed.

They had passed the forest; the mountains were close and in the darkness. Nero could see the tiny tear. A spec, a mirage.

"That looks small," Thrush warned.

"Don't. Let. Go." Nero leapt through.

CHAPTER 29

LAYLA WOKE TO THE SENSATION OF WARM STONE beneath her cheek and every muscle in her body aching from the ride, the fall, and the sheer terror of being dragged underground. Her ribs throbbed with every heartbeat. Dust clung to her clothes and skin. Dried blood cracked against her neck and temple where new wounds had been scraped open as she was pulled through realms. She sat up slowly, blinking into the dim cave.

A shadow moved in the corner.

No, paced. Not drifting or slithering like smoke. It had form. Height. Shoulders. Arms. It was the outline of a man, but more jagged. It stopped when she looked at it directly but resumed once she turned her gaze elsewhere. He was always pacing, always watching. It seemed familiar.

Layla crawled backward until she felt the jagged cave wall scrape her back.

"Tell me where I am." Her voice cracked. "What is this place?"

No answer.

She stood, wobbling. "I have to leave. I can't stay here."

The shadow surged forward, not attacking but blocking her from getting closer to the mouth of the cave. Its edges wavered, as if caught between this world and another. Still, it made its intentions clear.

She jumped away. "You're keeping me prisoner?" she whispered.

It nodded.

She glanced toward the mouth of the cave, where a thin shaft of light pierced the gloom. Outside she could hear strange noises, low guttural growls, screeches in the wind. They were the kind of sounds no living creature should ever make. She backed away from the opening instinctively, dread crawling over her skin like ants.

The shadow was shaking its finger and head as if to say no.

"I need food," she said, her voice louder now. "Water. I can't stay in here and starve to death."

The shadow tilted its head.

"I don't know what you want, but I won't die in this cave."

The shadow looked away.

"Do you want me to die?"

The shadow shook its head.

"Then let me go."

The shadow shook its head again and pointed across the cave, instructing her to go back.

She turned like she was going to follow orders. She waited for the right moment, the light outside shifting slightly as what little sun Hell had moved across the sky. The shadow moved to the far side of the cave. She remembered how it had avoided the sunlight in the bookstore and how it had waited until nightfall to drag her underground.

It avoided the light. Layla pushed her glasses up and snapped the flannel as high as it would go. She waited for the light to move, widen, illuminate the entire mouth of the cave.

Then, she ran.

She was out of the cave and into the wilderness. The ground was uneven, scorched, and cracked in places. Strange flora clawed at her boots. She limped down a narrow slope, thorns scraping her legs, and followed the distant gurgle of water. The air was heavy with smoke and something sweeter, rotting fruit and ash. And rotting meat. There were strange sounds of moans and the echo of something dragging.

Layla paused by a tree trunk and held her breath. It was coming from the left. She ran to the right, toward the sound of rushing water. She was so thirsty. Her hand felt strange. She lifted it in front of her eyes and noticed her fingertips were nearly black.

"What the..."

Layla wasn't made for this, she was out of breath too quickly. Her head felt heavy and stars were threatening to obstruct her vision. The crack in her lenses made focusing even worse. Still she ran, afraid of that shadow finding her again and stealing her away. She was afraid of the moaning and dragging sound and the strange yelps and howls she'd heard.

After what felt like hours, she stumbled out of the forest and bramble and found herself at the banks of a dark, sluggish river. It shimmered like black silk; obsidian black. She'd never seen water that looked like ink before.

She fell to her knees and reached toward the water. Her hands shook. Her lips were dry. She was so thirsty. As she took deep breaths, her stomach growled. She'd missed dinner yesterday.

She reached into the water.

A ripple tore through the surface.

She froze, focused on the movement.

Another ripple. Something moved beneath.

No, many things moved beneath.

A head broke the surface–serpentine, elegant, crowned with black ridges and glowing yellow eyes.

She'd never seen a creature like this in her entire life, only read about it in fantasy books. It was like a dragon or a giant snake.

Layla's heart nearly stopped. The creature rose slowly, its long neck undulating. It could gobble her up whole.

She screamed.

Scrambling back, she tripped over a rock and tumbled into the dust, tearing the skin of her palms again. She launched to her feet and ran, branches clawing her face. She found a crumbling road with dark pavement. Recognition sparked, wherever she was they had roads.

She never saw a car, didn't hear the rumble of an engine. She took to the road, glanced back, and relief flooded her when the giant snake monster didn't follow.

Layla slowed, bending and gripping her knees, taking deep breaths. She wiped her forearm across her forehead and cheek, noticing there were faint streaks of blood–probably from the branches and rocks she'd been dragged across.

Something snapped near the edge of the road. Layla stood up and braced herself.

A figure stepped out from behind a blackened tree; tall, humanoid, but wrong in every detail. Eyes too black. Smile too wide. Teeth too sharp.

"Well, well," he said smoothly, tilting his head. "What have we here?"

Layla's breath caught.

"You're not supposed to be here. But I suppose you'll do just fine." He looked her up and down, black eyes focused on the blood streaks across her face. He tipped his head. "A human?" Brows rose in interest. "Humans don't come here unattended. Not with their blood showing." He paused, looked down the road then at her again. "Fresh blood." Black eyes sparkled.

Layla's glasses slid down her nose and terror flooded her body.

CHAPTER 30

THRUSH GRIPPED NERO'S MANE TIGHTER, HIS JAW set as Nero galloped through the ochre haze of Hell, hooves throwing up dust against the blackened prairie. Neither of them spoke.

Thrush was sure he couldn't get the words out even if he tried. He couldn't compete with the wind.

Nero finally slowed. "Do you sense where she is?"

Thrush went still. "I can't... I don't sense her. How could I?"

"Her blood. Can you smell her blood?" Nero clarified.

"Not here."

Thrush recognized the landscape–they were far from the castle.

Hell was nothing more than a dark reflection of the Earthen plane. They were still in the Midwest of Hell just like they'd been in the Midwest on the Earthen plane.

"We need help. Meg will know what to do," Thrush suggested.

"And if she's off gallivanting across the realms with Sparrow?"

"Remington will know what to do."

Nero muttered something about stupid children being left in charge before taking off.

They thundered through the expanse of Hell. Over mountains, across rolling hills, through towns that had come alive with demons and creatures that had remained in hiding during Lucifer's reign. Thrush's aunt, Meg, had brought hope to Hell. She'd defeated Lucifer, taken the throne, and brought peace to the realms.

The castle came into view, cut from the burning caves, with its high towers piercing the ochre sky.

Before they reached the main gate, the doors slammed open with a violent crash.

Remington burst out first, a blade in one hand and his other arm shielding Evelyn, who followed close behind.

The Hellion named Chel barreled out behind them, already shouting. "What happened?" Chel's voice echoed like thunder, eyes wild as he stormed down the steps. "Is it Shay? Did you hurt Shay?"

Thrush barely had time to dismount before Chel grabbed him by the collar.

"You were supposed to control yourself!" Chel roared.

"I know," Thrush growled, shoving him back. "It's Layla. She was taken. Shadow demons, I think. It wasn't supposed to happen. I was standing right next to her."

"Then why did it?" Chel shouted, wings half-flared, his fists trembling.

Evelyn stepped forward quickly, placing a hand on Chel's arm. "Let him speak."

Nero snorted and pawed the ground. "We stopped at Shay's old family ranch. Something crawled out of the ground and dragged her under."

Remington interrupted, narrowing his gaze. "You took her there? Explain."

Thrush and Nero began telling the story of how Layla was horseback riding with Shay and the mare had gotten spooked and ran off. Thrush rubbed his face, knowing exactly why she'd gotten spooked. He'd lost his temper on a tractor engine. It was his fault. It was always his fault.

"We found her at the edge of the forest, she had a broken arm and probably a concussion," Nero said. "She was covered in blood." Nero turned to look accusingly at Thrush.

Thrush looked away. "She was bleeding. I had to get it off her. The sight of it, the smell, it was..."

Remington was watching his cousin. "The blood has never bothered you before."

Evelyn touched Remington's arm. The two of them knew exactly how someone's blood could affect one of the princelings. Evelyn's had driven Remington crazy until he'd claimed her. And although Rue wasn't there at the moment, she'd had a similar experience with Dacre.

Nero finished for Thrush. "It drew something out of the ground." He nodded in Thrush's direction. "He used his magic but didn't want to hurt her. I couldn't even use fire to stop it. It was dark and fast. Then she was gone."

Chel muttered something under his breath, a curse in Hellspeak.

"There must be an access portal beneath that ranch,"

Nero said grimly. "An old one, probably used by the demon who kidnapped Shay."

Chel stalked away, fuming. "I'm glad Shay is okay. But that tiny human." He shook his head. "You should have never let her out of your sight." Chel glanced at Remington. "You should have brought her here for protection."

Remington shook his head. "My mother would not have allowed that again."

"The White Horse said no," Nero said. "There is something about Layla, she didn't want the human here."

Thrush stared up at the castle, guilt crushing his chest like armor too tight. "She has to be in Hell. Somewhere. I felt it in the ground when she was taken. It smelled like the mountains here."

Remington sheathed his blade. "Then we start asking the local demons. We comb every tunnel, every ruin, every cave."

"Someone from the market might know," Evelyn suggested.

"It's a good place to start."

"Let's go," Thrush said, stepping forward. "She's injured."

"You better find her quickly," Chel growled, spinning back toward him. "She'll be sold to the skin trades in an instant."

"Oh not Layla." Evelyn gripped Remington's arm harder. "She's too kind for those creatures. They'll tear her apart in an instant."

Thrush rubbed his face. Evelyn was right. Layla was too sweet for Hell, too fragile. He had to find her. "I'm going now." He paced toward Nero.

Then Remington nodded once.
"Gear up. We leave in one hour."

CHAPTER 31

"LEAVE ME ALONE," LAYLA SAID AS SHE PUSHED her glasses up.

The creature clicked his tongue. "You shouldn't be here alone. I'll help you."

"No." Layla backed away. "Skedaddle. Weirdo creep."

The creature smiled. "You don't want to be alone out here. The basilisk hatched weeks ago, they'll be looking for food."

In the distance, she heard what sounded like a goat.

Layla glanced to the left. The road was winding and riddled with potholes. She could run but it would be rough without being able to see well. Fuck it. She had nothing else to lose.

A moaning sound came from the forest.

The creature walked closer and she was sure as shit it was a demon, just like from the movies. Which would mean she *was in Hell*.

"You better watch out for those dead things," the creature warned. "One bite and you're done for."

Layla took off running. She wasn't made for sprinting or marathons. The most she'd exerted herself was with moving books. Her legs began burning immediately. Her chest and ribs pinched. Water splashed from the direction of the river.

Layla's heart was beating so fast. She didn't want to die like this; in Hell, running from creatures that only haunted nightmares. And... alone. Her breath caught, muscles ached. She felt like she was running in quicksand. It was like a bad dream. She glanced to the left, the Demon was following her. She looked to the front, felt her footing slip and her knee give out. She put her arms out to catch herself and, remembering that was how she'd broken her arm yesterday, she tried to twist to the side but something grabbed her leg. Layla's chin hit the pavement. She saw stars then darkness.

LAYLA WOKE IN A SMALL, DAMP ROOM. THE FLOOR was dirt. Outside she heard farm animals; goats and chickens and the guttural sounds of demons speaking. She rolled to the side, her hand moving to her chin. There was a fresh wound crusted with blood. She moved her jaw and winced, remembering hitting the pavement when she tripped. Well, at least the demon hadn't killed her. She blinked a few times, noticing the wooden furniture. There was a glass of water and a half-loaf of bread on the table.

The voices moved closer.

Layla crawled to the door to listen.

"A human?" a voice said with a grunt. "You think it's the Princeling's?"

"Don't know." She recognized the voice of the Demon who'd found her along the road.

"What will you do with it? Eat it?"

"Too small for eating. Doubt she's got enough blood to sustain much. She's small."

"A child?"

"Definitely not a child. Could tell when I carried her back here."

Layla shivered. The demon had touched her.

"What will you do with it?"

"She'd bring a pretty penny from the skin trades. She has that light colored hair that they like. But she can't see worth shit. She's mostly blind, I think."

There was a pause and grumbling.

Layla was immediately offended. She could see quite well when her glasses weren't broken.

"If she's the Princeling's, you'll be in a world of hurt. Especially after he replaced your herd twice. The Queen might even come after you. Then you'll be dead in an instant."

"This can't be his. He has a female and she never leaves his side. This human is from somewhere else. Maybe she escaped the skin trades. They'll give me a reward for returning her."

"Possibly. But there is another Princeling."

"That one is gone. I will sell her back to them."

Something knocked against the door.

Layla scurried back, hiding in the corner of the room.

"I need help moving her. She runs, but she's stupid and clumsy."

Layla didn't realize she could be even more offended until then. She sucked in a breath as anger flooded her veins. She was not stupid.

The door opened but just before light flooded the room, she noticed movement in the shadows to her right; a flutter, a ripple of something darker than the gloom. Her heart stuttered. She turned her head but the figure, if there had been one, was already gone. It vanished back into the wall, or her imagination...

"Get up." The demon stepped into the room. His eyes narrowed when they landed on her. Another demon, taller and bulkier with curling horns, followed behind him.

Layla didn't move.

The tall one huffed. "She's awake. That's good. Don't want the Princeling mad that she died."

That word again.

Princeling.

Her blood chilled. What if they meant Thrush?

Her mind reeled back to the woods, to the way his hands trembled when he healed her and the way he always seemed so close to the edge. He'd said he didn't trust himself. He'd said he would hurt her.

"Move." The demon shoved her up, none too gently.

She stumbled to her feet, vision still fuzzy and unfocused. "Where are you taking me?"

Neither of them answered.

They led her down a corridor carved from dark stone, lit by flickering torches that made the walls dance with shadows.

Then, as they turned a corner, she felt it again.

Movement.

Not physical—it was more like a shift in the air, the pressure of someone watching her. It was the shadow-man from the cave, the one who dragged her through the ground and into Hell. She was sure of it now. He was here. He was following her. Again.

But if he meant to help her... why hadn't he stopped this?

They reached another room. This one larger, empty. They shoved her inside and slammed the door.

The demons were speaking in that strange language again. She didn't have a clue what they were saying but it didn't sound good.

She was alone again.

Her knees gave out and she sank to the floor, wrapping her arms around herself.

The room was cold and quiet. She kept her back to the wall, watching the shadows twitch and shift across the stone. Her skin itched with dried blood and sweat, but it wasn't the filth that unsettled her.

It was the silence. The unknown.

The shadows rippled. She took off her glasses and tried to clean the dirt off them but one of the lenses cracked further and fell apart in her hand.

"Dammit," Layla swore to herself. She put the glasses on again and blinked. She could only see good out of one eye now. The other was blurry. Damn the need for glasses.

Footsteps echoed down the corridor. Measured, confident, expensive. That's the only thing she could think. That wasn't the sound of boots. It was the sound of dress shoes coming for her.

The door creaked open.

A tall man entered dressed in a sharp-cut coat of velvet black, hair slicked back like ink, his eyes nearly all black. He didn't look like the others. No horns, no scaled skin. He looked human but only if a human had been sculpted from seduction and sin.

He glanced at her once, dismissively, like a jeweler eyeing a flawed gem.

"Asmodeus," the demon said, worrying his hands. "She's mostly unharmed."

Layla stood, her fists clenched at her sides. "I'm right here. Maybe speak to me instead of around me like I'm some... object."

Asmodeus smiled thinly. "You're exactly that. Right now, you're a free human in the realm of Hell. Nearly unheard of." His voice was smooth, velvet or venom. "How did you get here?"

"I'm not for sale," she snapped.

The demon guard chuckled. "Everything in Hell is for sale."

"Since you didn't answer me. I'll assume you are the goat herder's property." Asmodeus turned toward the demon. "How much?"

"She's healthy," the demon replied.

Layla stepped forward. "Don't talk about me like that."

The demon named a price. A favor, something about goats owed and protection broken. Layla didn't understand the language of Hell, but the words ownership and binding stood out like knives.

She could not believe she was about to be traded for a herd of goats.

"You don't get to decide this!" she shouted. "I didn't ask to be here. I don't belong to anyone. Let me go!"

She lunged forward, but Asmodeus raised a finger. The air shimmered around her and she hit an invisible wall, falling backward with a grunt.

"Done," Asmodeus said.

"No!" she screamed.

But they didn't hear her or pretended not to.

Two giant Demons entered the room and she back-stepped. They looked like monsters with tusks and horns. They were so ugly. The guards grabbed her arms. Her injured one throbbed as they dragged her through the corridor. She fought every step, but Asmodeus walked ahead without a care, like a man collecting a parcel.

They led her through a wooden gate and out into an open courtyard. If it could be called that; there were chickens and cattle and goats grazing. It was more like a farm pasture.

A sleek, black vehicle waited near a pine tree.

The back door opened on its own.

Layla dug in her heels. "You can't just take me."

"I'm not just taking you," Asmodeus said with a soft smile. "I bought you. I'm rescuing you. You didn't want to stay with the goat herder. The things he would have made you do! Eventually, you'll see the difference."

One guard shoved her forward. She stumbled into the seat.

Asmodeus followed.

The door slammed shut.

And the vehicle sped off, rumbling over the crumbling road.

The interior of the car was too quiet.

Layla pressed her shoulder against the opposite door. Asmodeus lounged beside her, one ankle resting on his opposite knee, utterly relaxed as if they were driving to a dinner party and not kidnapping her.

"You're tense," he said without looking at her. "Understandable. But unnecessary."

"I've been kidnapped thrice in the last twenty-four hours," she snapped. "Forgive me if I'm not thrilled to be chauffeured by the Prince of Smarm."

That earned a quiet laugh. "You don't even know who I am, do you?"

"I don't care. Let me go."

His black gaze slid toward her, amused and unsettling. "Then you should know I could have left you there. Or worse, taken you to someone far less charming. You should be grateful it was me and not some wild beast."

"Why?" she asked, hating the thin edge of fear in her voice. "Why take me at all? You should have just let me go."

"Because you're interesting," he said honestly. "Because something has touched you." He sniffed the air around her. "Something not of this place. Do you even know?" He glanced at her wrist. "Have you been bitten?"

"No." Layla stared at him. "What do you want from me?"

"I haven't decided yet."

The car dipped, descending into a valley as a sprawling

black silhouette loomed ahead. The mansion looked carved from obsidian, its spires like claws scraping at the ashen sky. Smoke coiled around its towers like living things. The path to the front door was lined with pale statues; winged, face-less things hunched in frozen screams.

"Home sweet home," Asmodeus murmured.

"Charming," Layla said dryly.

The car slowed and stopped in front of tall iron doors.

When the door opened he slid out first, then extended a hand to her like this was some kind of formal date.

She didn't take it.

Layla climbed out on her own, knees still shaky. The mountain air smelled of smoke and pine needles and scorched bone.

"Is this where you keep all your kidnapped guests?" she asked as he led her up the black stone steps.

"No," he said. "Only the valuable ones."

She hesitated at the door. "And what if I run?"

Asmodeus turned back to her, his voice velvet-dark. "You won't. And I suspect," he stepped closer "If you try you won't make it far. Not by a long shot." He pointed to the forest. "You have no idea what lies out there. You'll be dead before dawn."

Layla's skin prickled. He reached out, brushing his fingers near her temple, but not touching–like sensing a pulse beneath her skin.

"The question," he whispered, "is who will purchase you? Something who is hungry or something lonely?"

The doors opened.

And Layla stepped into the Black Mansion.

INSIDE, THE MANSION SWALLOWED HER WHOLE. The walls pulsed with a heat like something alive and... music. It was strange, rhythmic, intoxicating as it echoed faintly through the stone. They passed creatures she couldn't comprehend; draped in silk and bone, laughing with too many teeth, eyes glowing like fireflies caught in a jar.

And they all stared at her.

The human.

The lamb in a den of wolves.

But what shocked her most was not their attention. It was how something inside her responded. Her heart sped up.

There was... a pull.

Darkness had a rhythm. It was in the footsteps echoing off obsidian floors. It was in the way the women leaned close, whispering secrets into the hollows of men's throats. It was seductive. And Layla's body shivered. Suddenly, she felt incredibly thirsty. She swallowed. This was crazy. She didn't belong here. But something inside her wanted to see more.

Asmodeus led her to a room just off the main hall; low lighting, velvet couches, and a glass wall overlooking the black forest. There were three other demons already there, lounging with the kind of confidence that only came from ancient power and too much blood on their hands.

"This is the human?" one asked lazily.

Asmodeus said. "Fresh from the Earthen plane, like

fruit plucked from the vine and dropped in our basket. How lucky are we today?"

Layla's mouth went dry.

One of the demons stood and stepped closer, his pupils slitted like a snake's. "I can smell something on her. You brought us a delicacy."

"Let me see what we're working with," Asmodeus said, stepping behind her.

Layla froze.

His fingers brushed the side of her throat until they rested just over her pulse. She jerked away but he caught her chin with one hand, tilting her face up to his.

"This is how it works here," he said softly. "You are blood. And blood draws hunger. Blood draws power."

He leaned in. His lips brushed the hollow of her throat. Then, a shockwave tore through the room. Every candle flickered. The window shuddered. Asmodeus reeled back like he'd been slapped.

Layla stumbled, heart thundering.

"What was that?" one of the other demons hissed.

Asmodeus wiped blood from his lip. "Something's claimed her already."

He stared at her, eyes black as the void—not angry, but curious. His fingertips rubbed the skin of her throat.

Layla clutched her elbows, backing toward the far wall. "What does that mean?"

He didn't answer. Instead, he released her neck.

Asmodeus turned to the others and said, "Not for sampling, after all. But perhaps still for sale."

She pressed herself against the glass, trembling, but somewhere beneath the fear... was something else.

Something had claimed her. What the heck did that even mean?

And she wasn't sure whether to be terrified or grateful.

The Black Mansion settled into an eerie hush as night deepened. Somewhere far below, music played; slow, discordant notes on a piano echoing off stone.

Layla stood at the window of her locked room, hands clenched around the iron railing. Beyond the glass, Hell's sky glowed violet and bruised, churning with clouds. The forest below moved unnaturally like something beneath the trees breathed. She couldn't take her eyes off it.

The door behind her opened without a knock.

She didn't turn. "I'm not in the mood for another parade of monsters."

"You wound me," said the familiar voice, smooth as silk.

She turned slowly. Asmodeus stood in the doorway, now dressed more casually in a dark open-collared shirt and slacks. The absence of his suit didn't make him less dangerous, only more intimate–like a snake coiled closer.

"I'd like to speak with you," he said, stepping into the room and closing the door behind him. "Privately."

Layla crossed her arms, instinctively stepping back until her shoulder hit the windowpane. "You could have done that without dragging me through a room full of demons."

"True." He moved toward the table near the fireplace and poured two glasses of deep crimson liquid.

He offered her one of the glasses. She didn't take it.

Asmodeus sipped from his and let out a small, pleased

sigh. "Power rarely asks permission, Layla. It finds people like you. People who are unaware, unprotected, and full of potential. You are lucky it was me who found you."

"Is that why you bought me like cattle?" she snapped. "Because I am so lucky?"

"You were for sale," he said smoothly, "and I'm not in the habit of leaving valuable things in unworthy hands." He looked her up and down. "You should clean up nicely."

Layla's jaw clenched. "You don't know me."

He stepped closer, slowly and deliberately. "No. But I want to."

She froze as he reached up, gently brushing a lock of hair behind her ear. She hated how soft the gesture felt and the way her skin tingled in the wake of it. Visions of the creatures downstairs flooded her mind; the teeth, the drops of blood.

"I know you're not entirely human anymore," he said quietly.

Layla blinked. "What?"

"Something has happened to you. Your soul is not entirely human any longer."

She turned her head away, fighting the twist in her gut. "You don't get to talk about my soul. I'm pretty sure you don't even have one."

Asmodeus chuckled. "That's debatable."

There was a beat of silence, then his voice lowered more serious. "You can hate me if it makes you feel better. But you should also understand you're safer here than you are out there."

Layla met his gaze. "Am I safe from you?"

He didn't answer right away.

"That's not a yes."

He smiled faintly. "No. It's not."

She turned away again, her fingers tightening on the cold windowsill.

"I'm not yours," she said quietly. "No matter what you paid. I am not for sale."

Behind her, his voice softened. "That remains to be seen." He'd leaned in close, lips parted in something between interest and amusement. "You've been bitten," he said, voice curling around the word like it tasted sweet. "Something from Hell... and recently."

Layla jerked away, but she could feel the heat of his gaze lingering at the back of her neck.

Then the door opened and closed with a whisper of movement, and she was alone.

Her heart kept pounding long after he was gone.

She looked down at her blackened fingertips. She rubbed the skin on her wrist until she found the scars that she'd been certain were from a spider.

What had bitten her?

Silken drapes spilled like blood from the tall arched windows. There was velvet furniture and intricate papered walls. It should've been a suite in a gothic novel.

She sat on the edge of the massive bed, cradling her ribs. Her entire body ached and her head was starting to hurt.

Asmodeus had confirmed that something had bitten her. She never felt it. She'd been dwelling on it for hours.

He could be lying. Do demons tell the truth? She thought about how he looked. Maybe he wasn't a demon, maybe he was something else.

Her jacket and boots were gone. Her glasses were still busted, which meant the room was blurry and strange at the edges. She paced, trying not to panic, trying not to think about how long she'd been gone. Was anyone going to help her?

Thrush and Jed had to be looking for her. Right?

Twilight bled through the windows. The light grew softer, the kind of dusk from movies and TV shows where monsters felt brave.

Something moved in the far corner.

Layla froze.

It wasn't her imagination. A shadow rippled near the vanity. A shape paced slowly, almost as if agitated.

Her heartbeat thundered. "Who's there?"

Silence.

The shape edged closer, still made of shadows and not fully formed. She could make out a vague figure: tall and masculine, with long limbs and something like a cloak or wings dragging behind it.

The shadow man.

"Are you the one from the cave?" she asked, her voice barely above a whisper.

The shadow stopped and nodded.

"I'm not afraid of you," she lied. "But you can't just keep showing up and watching me like this. Who are you?"

It stared at her.

Still no reply. The energy in the room shifted to an anxious hum. Layla suddenly had the sense that it wasn't trying to frighten her. If anything, it was trying not to. It kept its distance.

It raised a hand slowly–a gesture of peace–and stepped closer to the bed. Moonlight hit its form for just a second, revealing the shape of a face, a smooth shadow where features should be. It was looking at her expectantly.

Layla backed up against the bedpost. "What do you want?"

The shadow tilted its head as if frustrated with its own silence.

It raised its hand again, gently pressed a palm to the center of its own chest, and then pointed to hers.

Her breath caught. Ok, it was communicating.

"What does that mean?" she asked, mirroring the gesture.

The shadow man repeated it a few more times, looking more and more frustrated when she didn't understand.

"I don't know what you're saying. My heart?"

It shook its head.

"My... body?" Layla's voice came out confused.

He did it again.

Layla sighed. "I've never been good at charades. I hate games. This is no fun for me."

He did it again.

"I don't know." Layla shook her head.

The shadow paced, pointed at the door and then pressed his palm to his chest again. His arms started moving frantically when Layla couldn't piece together what he was trying to say.

She took a step back. "Oh, wait, You're trying to protect me?"

It nodded.

"Ok." She blinked quickly. "Why me?"

No answer. Only stillness.

The door creaked.

The shadow vanished in a blink, dissolving back into the dark corners of the room.

Layla didn't move.

She was bait. She was marked. She was about to be put up for sale.

When the door didn't open, the shadow moved closer. It paused and held out his hands, palms up.

"Sure," Layla muttered.

It motioned again, holding out a bent wrist and pointing with its free hand.

Layla moved her arm. The faint scars from the bite were there. "How do you know about this?"

The shadow was still.

"This got me fired from my job. A job I loved. I was a librarian on campus..." She looked up. "Do you even know what that means? I worked at a college. I met some wonderful people." She paused. "Actually, I met someone from here. Rue. She's been a great friend."

The shadow stepped closer.

"I need to get out of this mess."

The shadow walked its fingers across a palm.

"I can't leave here. They locked the door. What is that guy going to do with me? I saw things in this mansion. Creatures, blood, sharp teeth. What is going on here?"

The shadow-man's shoulders slumped. He began pacing.

Layla was watching his every movement. The edges of

his form were blurred but he seemed familiar. He ran a hand through his hair and Layla suddenly knew.

"What are you?" she asked.

The shadow went still again.

"Are you someone I know?"

Nothing.

"Are you related to Thrush? You move like him but you seem less angry."

It was so still.

"Are you related to him?" she asked again.

The shadow didn't move.

"What's wrong with me? Maybe I am stupid." Layla exhaled. "You can't even speak." She touched her head. "I must've hit my head really hard when that horse threw me."

She closed her eyes and leaned back. Her head was throbbing and her eyes ached. She took off her glasses and tucked them into the flannel jacket she was wearing. She pulled the collar against her nose and sniffed. It still smelled like Thrush–like woodsmoke and pine and something darker. Something like ozone.

"Magic," she whispered to herself. "He smells like magic."

When she looked up again, she couldn't see the shadow man, probably because her glasses were off and everything was blurry. She closed her eyes again.

"I just need to sleep for a few minutes, then figure out how I'm gonna get the heck out of here."

She felt her hair move, like a cool breeze brushing the curls away from her cheek.

"Is that you?" she asked, eyes closed on the edge of

sleep. "Why are you cold? Why didn't you tell me how dangerous it would be to leave that cave?"

She felt her hair move again. Something cool touched her wrist; like fingertips massaging the bite scars on her skin.

"Careful," she warned. "My fingers are turning more and more blackened with each day. Whatever's wrong with me, it might be contagious." She giggled to herself, drunk on fatigue.

Her eyes flashed open and she sat up, holding her hand in front of her face.

"Oh my god." She looked for the shadow and found him hovering across the room. "It's not a stain." She pointed to him. "Is this a shadow taking over my hand? A shadow like you? Did whatever bite me... is it slowly turning me into a shadow? Is that what happened to you?" Breath caught in her throat. "This freakin' sucks. I don't want to be a shadow."

The shadow man slowly backed away until he disappeared.

CHAPTER 32

"YOU'RE IN TROUBLE NOW," REMINGTON WARNED, glancing at Thrush.

Before Thrush could reply, the door slammed open and Rue stood in the threshold. Her dark hair was in a messy bun and her face red with exertion.

Dacre appeared behind her a second later.

"I had a vision," Rue said as she took in the gear the men were strapping to themselves. "Appears it was correct."

She looked directly at Thrush. "It was you."

"I didn't do anything." Thrush slid a blade into the holster at his hip. "Yet."

"What took her?" Rue asked as she walked closer.

Dacre grabbed Rue by her shoulders. "Don't go after him. Give him a chance to explain."

"I saw it already." Lines of tension crossed Rue's forehead.

Remington stepped forward. "Explain it to us then," he motioned to Thrush, "because this one doesn't know where she is. The last he saw her, she was being pulled through the ground at Shay's old ranch."

"There's more." Rue said. "It's not making sense right now." She pulled away from Dacre and walked around Thrush. She glanced at the light overhead then the floor around Thrush. "Something bit her at the library months ago. Did you figure out what that was?"

"I didn't know." Thrush turned to face his much smaller cousin. She looked like an angry elf staring up at him. "Tell me what you saw in your vision."

"I can't. It's not the right time." She glanced to Remington. "You'll find her. But you need to go now."

Rue searched the room until she found Evelyn sitting near a window, watching the spectacle quietly; very unlike her. She walked to her friend and left the men to get ready.

"Is Dacre going with them?" Evelyn asked.

Rue nodded. "We need to go take another look at that book."

Evelyn uncrossed her legs and stood. "I'll never say no to a good research project."

There was a knock on the door before it swung open. A Hellion stepped through looking like he'd just flown in.

"What?" Remington asked.

"There's a human on the loose." The Hellion paused to catch his breath. "She's small. The goat herders caught her near the Black River."

"Fucking A," Remington muttered.

Thrush grabbed another blade. "You're about to lose some goat herders," he warned Remington.

The Hellion held up his hand. "There's more. He's selling her."

"Alastor is dead," Remington interrupted. "No one with half a brain would be willing–"

"The skin trades did not die with him, Princeling." Chel was moving toward the door. "Asmodeus has been waiting in the wings to pick up that industry for ages."

THE CARAVAN MOVED THROUGH THE DARKENED basin of Hell with a singular purpose: find Layla, and burn down whatever or whoever stood in their way.

Nero led the way with Thrush. His jaw was set, his eyes a storm as he took in every tiny detail of the terrain surrounding them.

Remington was driving behind him. The SUV was loaded with Chel and Dacre.

"We're close," Thrush muttered. "The trail leads toward the Black River. I can smell the basilisk, and something else... her."

Nero whinnied and picked up his pace.

A low whistle sounded from ahead. One of the scouts raised his arm, pointing toward a lean stone structure tucked beneath a craggy hill; a goat paddock, half-collapsed, half-burning. The smell of sulfur, sweat, and livestock rolled toward them.

Remington pulled over and parked, then got out of the vehicle in one swift motion, Chel and Dacre close behind.

The goat herder, a withered creature with long curling horns and eyes too large for his leathery face, froze in place as the Princes and Hellions approached.

He dropped the pail in his hands. "I ain't done nothin'.

Just a simple keeper of beasts that your water dragons have a habit of eating."

Remington stepped closer, shadows curling at his back like smoke. "The Queen will skin you alive. And I'm going to help."

The herder swallowed. "Princeling." He looked up at Thrush and sucked in a breath like he'd seen a ghost.

Remington's voice lowered. "Where's the girl?"

The herder's trembling gaze flicked to Thrush, then to Chel, and back to the blackened mountains. "I don't know."

Chel unsheathed a dagger slowly, its edge flickering with moonglow. "He asked you a question."

"The offer was too good. There was no claim on her."

Thrush's stomach turned. It was true.

Remington stepped in, took the herder by the front of his filthy tunic, and lifted him easily off the ground. "Where. Is. She?"

The herder squealed. "Asmodeus! He has her, he took her to the Black Mansion. He paid well! I didn't know she meant anything to you! She was alone."

"She wasn't for you to touch," Thrush growled.

The herder sobbed as Remington dropped him to the ground. "Which direction?"

The Black Mansion had a habit of moving locations depending on its owner.

"Th-the path with the black trees... north ridge above the river. Guarded now, twisted things. Hellhounds. The dead wander."

"Good," Remington said. "I like a challenge."

He turned toward the others, his expression unreadable. "We go now. No more delays."

Thrush tightened his grip on Nero's mane. The ache in his chest deepened, his heart beating in time with the rhythm of hooves hitting scorched earth.

Layla was close.

CHAPTER 33

LAYLA WOKE TO THE FEELING OF BEING WATCHED.

Her heart skipped as her eyes opened to the dim, opulent room. It wasn't the shifting shadows this time. It was the man who'd brought her here.

He stood at the end of the bed, dressed in a sharp black suit that clung to his lean frame like it had been stitched from the night sky. His eyes, darker than the suit, shimmered with a predatory stillness.

"You are pleasant to watch," he said, voice a soft purr. "Innocent."

Layla sat up slowly, wincing as her bruised ribs ached in protest. She leaned instinctively away from the hand he offered, her gaze narrowing.

"I'd like to leave now," she said, searching the nightstand beside her for her glasses. "I don't belong here."

"Ah, but you do," he murmured.

He stepped back and held up something that caught the soft lamplight: a dress. Black, simple, elegant, and definitely not hers.

"You'll clean up and wear this," he instructed. "I have guests who are very curious about you. Best not to look like you clawed your way out of a grave."

Layla took the dress reluctantly and walked to the adjoining bathroom, locking the door behind her. She was grateful to have space between them.

She turned on the faucet and splashed her face, gasping softly at the sting of cold water against raw skin. Then she caught sight of herself in the mirror and froze.

Bruises in purple and blue bloomed along her ribs, shoulder, and cheek. A cut split her lower lip. Dirt smudged her jaw, dried blood crusted in her hairline. Her eyes looked hollow.

She leaned in closer. "What are you doing, Layla?" she whispered to herself. "What is this place? You need to get out of here."

There was no answer, only the sound of distant thunder rumbling through the mansion's foundation.

She'd showered quickly, freshened her curls with water, and washed the dirt off herself. The entire time she watched the door, not trusting the handsome creature on the other side.

She dressed.

The gown clung in all the right places, the boat-neck design flattering her figure. And it had pockets.

Asmodeus was waiting, leisurely gazing out the window for a moment before turning to her. A pleased expression crossed his face.

"Turn." He motioned with his finger.

Layla spun slowly.

She found her glasses and slipped them on. They were terribly crooked and she couldn't focus.

Asmodeus reached forward without permission and slid the glasses from her nose with the ease of someone accustomed to taking what he wanted.

"I can't see very well without them," she snapped.

He studied the broken frames with distaste, then tossed them onto a nearby table. He glanced down at her bare feet then her face. "Leave them," he said again, gesturing toward the door with one hand.

"But..."

"Follow me," he said, with a tilt of his head that tolerated no argument.

Layla blinked against the haze of her vision, shapes doubling at the edges.

She quickly grabbed the glasses and tucked them into her dress.

He strode ahead without glancing back, and she had to skip every few steps to keep up.

They left the bedroom and entered a corridor that opened into a massive hall lit by flickering chandeliers. The walls were lined with etched obsidian panels that seemed to twist with movement as if alive with memory or monsters. She wasn't sure, her vision was too poor to make out.

She recognized the front door as they passed and moved down a hallway.

Then they passed through a pair of heavy double doors into a room that made the air shift.

Layla didn't know what to call it. A gathering place? A dining hall? A throne room?

No.

It felt like a *feeding ground*.

Conversations halted. Heads turned. Creatures she couldn't fully make out filled the room. Hunger rolled off them in waves. Some hissed, some grumbled, others swore as she walked by. A sinking feeling hit her stomach. This wasn't good.

Layla faltered.

"Keep up," Asmodeus warned, not turning. "One might grab you."

Her breath caught in her throat.

He moved faster. She broke into a half-run to stay near him, her bare feet echoing against the marble. She kept her gaze low, trying not to look at the teeth, the claws, and the eyes that gleamed too bright in faces that weren't human.

She felt like a child chasing after a giant.

Whatever he had planned, she wasn't ready for it.

And deep in her gut, she knew the worst was still coming.

Layla followed a step behind Asmodeus as they wove through the grand atrium. The ceiling arched high above, etched with old infernal glyphs, pulsing faintly like veins beneath stretched skin. The floor was obsidian, polished so smoothly she could see flickers of her reflection beneath the torchlight.

All around them, demons lounged and prowled, some draped in finery, others in nothing but hunger and teeth. They whispered when they saw her. Some laughed. One even licked their lips.

Asmodeus walked with the self-importance of someone bringing a prized beast to auction.

She hated him. She barely knew him but she hated him.

He clearly didn't have much respect for life, or at least for human life. Layla swallowed hard.

Her vision still swam without her glasses and she fought to keep close, to stay upright. Her ribs ached from bruises, her arm still sore. She didn't know how long it had been since she'd eaten; maybe a day, maybe two. She felt watched from every angle. Measured. Appraised.

Asmodeus raised a hand. "Fresh soul. Human-born." He paused for effect. "Bitten by something unknown."

A murmur rippled through the chamber like the hiss of wind before a storm.

Layla clutched her sides. She didn't dare look anyone in the eye.

And then, a hum.

Soft at first, like static building in the walls.

A breeze swept through the chamber. A strange, crackling wind lifted the edges of dresses and ruffled demon wings.

And then, light.

Blinding. Harsh. Not the flickering red-orange of fire-light, but white; cold and pure, like lightning sealed in glass.

Layla's hands covered her eyes.

Gasps echoed. Some demons fell to their knees, others stumbled back with hisses of pain. Layla squinted through her fingers, trying to make sense of what she was seeing.

Low and distant voices rumbled through the room. "Angel," they said in unison.

Layla's heart seized, remembering Jed's words. Angels didn't mean good.

The chamber stilled in perfect silence, broken only by the hiss of torches extinguishing one by one.

When she opened her eyes again, the room had changed.

She was alone, surrounded by piles of ash.

No Asmodeus. No demons. Just Layla and the impossible figure at the far end of the chamber.

"Angels aren't always the nice ones." She remembered Rue telling her.

It stood, glowing so bright it blurred at the edges, wings unfurled like fire made solid, like judgment made flesh. The silhouette pulsed, humanoid in shape but somehow more. Larger. Older. Wrong.

She couldn't breathe.

She couldn't think.

So she did the only thing that made sense.

She turned and ran.

Her feet slammed against the stone. Her ribs screamed in pain. She slipped once, caught herself, ran faster. The walls stretched and bent like she was trapped inside a dream or a cathedral underwater. She didn't know where the exit was. She didn't care. Anything was better than staying there with that thing.

The sound of wings beat behind her.

The light surged again.

Layla screamed and the world fractured.

She was suddenly thankful for bare feet that gripped the tile. She ran through a doorway, remembering that she'd seen the carved door as she'd followed Asmodeus to the room filled with... demons. They had to be demons. That was the only reasonable thing. She reached the door and pulled. It was heavy, but she pulled it so hard her shoulder hurt and the crack was just big enough for her to fit through. She ran down the steps, pausing as she took in her surroundings. She had no idea where she was. The SUV that Asmodeus had driven here was parked nearby. She ran to it, pulled open the driver's side door, and climbed in.

The keys were in the ignition. That didn't seem smart but Layla wasn't going to argue with fate. Although, she didn't realize that if someone was able to leave their keys in the ignition without fear, then they must *be* something to fear.

She scooted forward in the seat, started the SUV. She shoved the gear into drive and slammed her foot down on the gas. The SUV jolted forward, bouncing on the uneven gravel.

She blasted through the open iron gate with a shuddering clang, bits of rust and stone scattering behind her. Without hesitation, she turned right onto a narrow cracked road lined with skeletal trees and curling vines.

Her eyes strained in the dark. Everything was blurry, like looking through fogged glass. Her vision swam, shapes shifted and warped around her.

She gripped the wheel tighter, leaning forward, nose nearly to the windshield.

"Just get away. Just keep going."

But the road didn't want to let her go.

It twisted like a serpent beneath her tires. Dips turned into craters. The gravel snapped up, morphing into uneven dirt carved with deep ruts and claw marks.

She couldn't tell what was real and what wasn't.

Branches lashed the side mirrors. A glowing eye blinked in the brush to her left.

"No, no no."

Something leapt across the road. She swerved. The SUV tilted sharply on two wheels before slamming down again with a bone-jarring thud.

A jagged stone rose out of the ground too late to dodge.

The front bumper hit it dead-on.

CRACK!

The wheel twisted violently from her hands. Her shoulder smashed into the window as the SUV spun once, then skidded sideways into a shallow ditch.

Everything stopped.

Dust rose around the car like smoke.

For one perfect second, there was silence.

Then, they came.

Shapes moved in the shadows beyond the windshield. Not human. Not animal. Their limbs were bent wrong. Their eyes glowed yellow-white in the dark, unblinking and hungry.

One dragged a claw across the hood. Another pressed its face to the window.

Layla gasped and scrambled for the door, but it was jammed. Her breath fogged the glass.

What the Hell were those?

Her hand shook as she reached for the lock. She didn't know where she'd run only that she had to.

Then the first crack hit the windshield.

A second followed. Then a third, until the glass webbed with fractures like ice underfoot.

Layla's scream caught in her throat. She did the only thing she could. She went completely still.

Footsteps. They were soft, distant. A strange knocking and clicking sound reverberated off the cracked windshield.

It shook like it was going to cave in. If it did, the glass would fall on her leg. Layla bit her lips together. She couldn't move, couldn't make a noise.

Then she heard a voice.

Layla closed her eyes.

A blast of light as bright as the sun surrounding the wrecked SUV.

The creatures stopped with their tapping. Layla opened her eyes and was surrounded by piles of ash.

The angel was coming for her. It was going to kill her, she knew it.

She didn't move a muscle.

A groan and a strange beating noise came from outside. The ash blew as wind circled the wreck.

And then, silence. Layla exhaled. She was alone.

Chapter 34

A CRASHING SOUND ECHOED THROUGHOUT THE mountains.

All heads turned as the distant thud rippled through the stone and bone of Hell's northern mountains. Chel and the other Hellions took to the sky with a roar of movement. Their wings cut against the ochre air, blotting out the fractured moon like ash swirling in a tornado.

Thrush clenched his jaw and looked over at Remington.

"You thinking what I'm thinking?" Remington said, already scanning the ridgeline beyond the Black River.

"I'm thinking we should've eaten the goat herder," Thrush muttered.

"You should have let me turn him to charcoal," Nero muttered.

"No wings," Remington noted. "Again."

"On foot is safer," Thrush grumbled. His shoulder still ached from earlier. "A monster dropping out of the sky is only going to scare the shit out of her."

231

"She's already scared," Chel said, landing hard beside them, his boots crunching through burnt black grass. His long coat billowed with the gust of air from his descent. "But yeah. If one of our scouts dive-bomb her while she's running, it won't be good."

"She's out there," Thrush said quietly. "We must find her."

He didn't need to explain how he knew. Not to Remington. Not to Chel. Not to the Hellions gathering just beyond the ridge. He could feel her as a thrum in his blood like a second heartbeat that didn't belong to him. He'd had difficulty sensing her before but now he could and he wasn't sure how it was possible.

Chel crossed his arms and flicked his gaze toward the west. "I'll tell the others to only scout the area. No contact. No surprises. If she sees something with wings, she runs. If she runs again..." His eyes flicked toward Thrush. "You might not get to her in time."

Thrush's jaw tensed. "I will."

"You sure?" Remington's voice was low, a warning.

Thrush didn't answer. He just reached for the blade at his belt, then turned toward the direction of the crash.

He wouldn't fail her again. He wouldn't let the shadows drag her away, he wouldn't scare her, he wouldn't... Thrush realized he had to stop making promises that he might not be able to keep. It would only make things worse in the end.

THEY MOVED IN SILENCE THROUGH THE WOODS, boots crunching over blackened pine needles and brittle leaves. The trees thinned slightly ahead, revealing the jagged slope of the northern mountain ridge where Layla had last been seen.

Nero lifted his head abruptly. His nostrils flared.

"Wait," he said, voice taut. "Something's wrong."

Thrush stilled. "What?"

Nero turned slowly toward the east.

"There's an Angel at the Crossroads," Nero said quietly. "Beckoning."

Dacre's jaw tightened. "That's impossible."

"The timing is suspicious," Remington said grimly.

Chel snorted. "Or it's a distraction."

"Still," Nero murmured, eyes fixed on something no one else could see, "it shouldn't be here."

Silence fell over the group.

"I must go," Nero warned.

They all knew the Crossroads of Hell was no place for an angel. Not without permission. Not without starting war.

"We go," Remington decided. "If it's a threat."

"I'm not leaving her," Thrush cut in. His voice was low but final. "I'll keep looking."

Remington turned to him, uncertain. "Are you sure?"

Thrush nodded once. "If this is a trap, it's to draw us away from her. If it's not... it still doesn't change that I must find her. Now."

Chel grimaced. "If anything happens..."

"This is a distraction like Remm said," Dacre said simply. "That's all. We must end it."

The others moved toward the Crossroads, tension simmering in their wake. Soon, only the rustle of the trees and the hum of magic in Thrush's fingertips remained.

Thrush adjusted the strap on his shoulder, gritted his teeth, and turned toward the forest.

"Hold on, Layla," he murmured.

The trees in the northern hell-woods were all black bark and ash-draped branches. It was the kind of place even the demons didn't venture without reason.

Remington's boots crunched over something brittle as he ducked under a low branch. Burned bone. He didn't stop to look closer.

Dacre moved ahead without speaking, his gait unnervingly quiet for a man that size. He moved like a giant cat.

"We'll split," Dacre said. "If the Angel is creating an ambush, we'll have a chance. I can shift and confuse them."

"Good idea," Remington said.

Dacre was already turning away. Very few knew about Dacre. He was the last of his kind and could shapeshift into a panther-like creature. In that form, he could alter reality with subtle vibrations.

Remington sighed and moved east into the thick of the dead woods, eyes scanning the twisted roots and crumbling stones for any sign: footprints, broken branches, blood.

Time passed strangely here. The shadows deepened. The scent of sulfur thickened.

A gust of air broke the stillness.

Chel dropped from the sky with a heavy landing beside Remington, wings folding sharply against his back.

"You find her?" Remington asked, straightening.

Chel shook his head. "Worse."

Remington raised an eyebrow. "Define 'worse.'"

"There's a horde nearby," Chel said. "Walking dead. Old, rotted, not the quiet kind either. Something's riled them up."

Remington swore under his breath.

Chel continued, "She won't know what they are until they're on her."

"They'll hear her," Remington said. "She's practically ringing the dinner bell with every step she takes."

Chel nodded. "We need to find her before they do."

Remington pulled his dagger free, the blade glinting silver-blue with warding runes. "Get word to Thrush. Tell Dacre to circle north If they hear her, that's where they'll go. We might be able to make enough noise to lure them away from her."

Chel launched back into the sky without another word.

Remington's grip tightened on his blade. He could feel the tension building, the filled with magic, chaos, hunger. Whatever fresh hell Layla had stumbled into, it wasn't finished with them yet.

He just hoped this wasn't going to be a shit show of epic proportions. A missing human and an Angel in Hell; neither of those things had happened in years.

Chel flew low, weaving between the jagged treetops like a blade through smoke. His wings beat hard against the night. Nothing could match a Hellion in flight. Especially not him.

Below, the black trees gave way to a narrow clearing where he caught a glimpse of Thrush moving between shadows, blade drawn, shoulders tight with tension.

Chel landed hard, dust and ash kicking up around his boots.

Thrush spun, blade flashing but stopped short when he saw him. "You look like bad news."

"I am." Chel folded his wings. "There's a horde."

Thrush didn't blink. "How many?"

"Thirty, maybe forty. Did you warn her about the dead in this realm?"

"I didn't have a chance. And I'm not sure how she'd take that information."

Chel shook his head. "She's a sitting duck."

Thrush clenched his jaw. "I'll go faster. Have you seen her?"

Chel nodded. "They're moving toward the river bend. If anything, Layla's near there."

"She's blind without her glasses," Thrush said, voice low, feral. "She won't see them until they're ripping her apart."

Silence hung between them for a beat too long.

Finally, Chel gave a grim half-smile. "I'll take the skies and lead them off if I have to–if they'll follow me. Don't like the idea of sacrificing myself for a–" He stopped short and rubbed his mouth like he was going to say something uncouth.

Thrush nodded once. "Go."

Chel took off again, wings cracking the air like thunder.

Below, Thrush disappeared into the trees, moving faster now; his expression stony, his blade ready.

THE FOREST SWALLOWED THE SOUNDS OF THE others. Their voices faded, replaced by the creak of branches and the occasional rustle of something unseen darting through the underbrush. Every so often he heard a whistle or a knock as the others tried to lead the horde away from where Layla might be.

Thrush moved like a shadow, boots silent over the uneven ground. His pulse was a slow drumbeat in his ears. Every nerve felt pulled taut.

An owl hooted overhead. The scent of moss and damp ash curled in the air.

And something else.

Smoke. Not fresh; old, stained into the rocks. Magic.

His eyes narrowed.

He knew this place.

The path dipped, sloping into a shallow ravine just beyond the ridge. And there, half-hidden behind thorn-bush and a collapsed tree, was the crooked opening of a cave.

His breath caught.

No.

He hadn't realized how close they were to it. This stretch of wilderness had been his shelter for years.

His home was here while the curse slowly rooted in his head.

He stepped carefully, hand brushing the rock wall as he approached the mouth of the cave. Cold air whispered from its depths. It smelled of stone, old blood, and magic long suppressed. Runes he'd scratched into the rock years ago still faintly shimmered along the entrance, a pale echo of the boy he'd been then.

Thrush's throat tightened.

He'd lived here when he couldn't trust himself. When every nightmare made him wake clawing at his own skin. When the curse had eaten him raw and wild.

And now, she might've been dragged here.

He dropped to one knee and pressed his fingers into the earth.

Footprints. A smear of blood.

Layla's blood.

They were old, maybe by a day. He left the cave and continued searching for her.

CHAPTER 35

THE WINDSHIELD CRACKED THEN SHATTERED. SHE moved her legs just in time, avoiding the glass as it fell. Now the front of the vehicle gaped open like the mouth of a corpse. Layla blinked up at the starless sky, her ribs aching from the seatbelt's bite. Every part of her body throbbed.

Layla pushed the door open with a creak and stumbled into the gravel. Her bare feet stung as she rose and rocks poked into the sensitive skin. Broken branches clawed at her arms as she moved around the wreck, her eyes watering from the effort to focus. Ash spun around her feet, the piles of the creatures burned by the Angel disrupted by her steps.

My glasses... she remembered with a jolt.

She searched her dress pocket for them, they'd been further broken in the wreck. The remaining lens fell out and she caught it before it hit the ground.

"Great," she muttered. Everything was a blur of shadows and moonlight. Trees loomed like giants with twisted faces. The air smelled of ash and moss and something rotting just beyond her ability to place it.

She didn't wait to identify the scent.

She shivered, wishing she still had Thrush's big flannel on instead of the skimpy dress. A branch snapped. Fear zipped up Layla's spine and she took off running.

Branches cracked underfoot. She ducked under a low bough, heart pounding in her throat. Somewhere to her left, something groaned with a long, rattling breath that sent a chill down her spine.

What was that? She remembered the goat herder demon mentioning the dead. She swallowed hard and old movies flooded her mind with corpses wandering and biting and consuming. Her parent's stories always seemed like fiction, but she was beginning to understand how they'd felt with hell on earth.

She broke into a sprint.

Twice she tripped, once she fell, knees digging into cold dirt. She scrambled back up, one hand pressed to her aching ribs. Her vision swam.

"Don't cry," she whispered to herself. "Just keep going."

A hoot broke the silence.

She froze. An owl?

The sound came again, sharp and steady, not far off.

With no better choice, she veered toward it, limbs trembling. The forest deepened, moonlight streaking in patches through a skeletal canopy.

Then, something cold slid against her wrist.

Layla gasped, skidding to a halt.

There was no pressure. No threat.

Just cool skin... a presence. Familiar.

She turned slowly.

The shadows rippled near a low, gnarled tree. And from them, a shape peeled itself away; tall, cloaked in the dark, eyes flickering hollowed in the low light.

The shadow-man.

She took a shaky step back, but he didn't move.

He simply stood there, watching her. Concern lined the way he tilted his head, the way his form hovered just at arm's reach.

"Are you..." Her voice cracked, there was no one left to trust in this god forsaken place. "Are you trying to help me?"

He nodded once, deliberate and slow.

His hand lifted, beckoning her gently with two fingers. He glanced behind her, where the strange noises were getting louder by the second.

A sharp chill ran through Layla and she hesitated. Her pulse thundered. She couldn't see, couldn't think past the ache in her body or the fear swarming inside her.

There weren't many choices to make in this instant. She couldn't see shit, she had no idea where she was, and whatever was roaming this forest would surely put an end to her short life.

The shadow man beckoned again.

"Okay," Layla whispered with a nod. "Okay. I'll follow you."

CHAPTER 36

THE FOREST PRESSED IN. LAYLA STUMBLED forward, the shadow-man guiding her again with silent urgency. A dark hand motioned for her to move and when to stop. She couldn't see more than a few feet ahead, but she recognized the shifting outline of him–always just in front, never quite touching.

"Where are we going?" she whispered.

The shadow shook its head and held a finger to his lips.

"I don't exactly trust you," she said as a stick jabbed into her little toe. She hissed in pain then paused. "Was that a snake? Did I just get bit by a snake?"

The shadow motioned to a stick near her foot.

Layla exhaled. "This is ridiculous. I want to go home. I'm done with this bullshit."

The shadow made a hurried up gesture like he was quick to avoid something in the forest with them.

Her throat was raw, her body aching. Her vision blurred everything into foggy shapes. "I could really use some water."

No answer.

The only sound was the soft padding of her feet moving over the pine needles and dirt. The shadow man made no noise.

Layla rubbed at her temples, trying to blink away the haze. "You're not real," she muttered. "You're not even real. Maybe none of this is. Maybe I hit my head harder than I thought. Maybe I'm still in the road. Bleeding out. Am I dead? Maybe I died. Maybe I died in the library basement that day... This is all too strange."

The shadow-man paused.

She almost crashed into him–or through him. He turned and though she couldn't make out his features, she felt him looking at her.

He felt strangely solid.

"I'm talking to shadows," she said with a short, helpless laugh. "I've been kidnapped, nearly eaten by a giant snake in the river, sold by a demonic goat herder, and now, now I'm just following you to who knows where, like that makes any sense."

Still, no reply. Just the tilt of his head; a strange, almost sympathetic gesture.

Layla swayed on her feet. "Say something. Please. Anything. Just let me know I haven't completely lost my mind."

But the shadow only turned away and kept walking, motioning for her to follow.

She wanted to scream, but the cold had stolen her voice. She hugged herself as they wove between twisted trees and sharp rock outcroppings. Then through the dark, the familiar shape of the cave emerged, jagged stone like the jaw of some forgotten beast.

The place he'd taken her before.

The place she'd escaped from.

"No," she said, stepping back. "I'm not going back in there. I can't. You wouldn't let me leave."

The shadow didn't move. He waited, unmoving as stone.

"I can't live in a cave." Layla glanced behind her. Something cracked in the distance.

She swallowed hard. What choice did she have? Run away again? She was too tired for that. She'd seen enough of this realm.

Her legs carried her forward without permission. Up the small incline she went and into the wide mouth of the cave.

Inside the cave, the shadow moved to one corner, crouching low like a sentinel.

Layla sat down slowly on a stone ledge. Her limbs trembled. Every part of her felt stretched too thin, like she'd snap with one more breath. She pulled her knees to her chest.

"I want to go home," she whispered. "Not the ranch. Not even the bookstore. Home. Before I touched that damn book. Before everything broke."

The shadow looked up.

For just a heartbeat, something flickered across his form. It was a faint shimmer in the chest like a heartbeat beneath skin.

Layla stared. "What are you?"

The shadow didn't answer.

But he stayed with her as she cried, curling her fingers

into her arms and burying her face in her bare knees. She might as well have been naked in this stupid dress. He stayed as the sounds of the forest grew louder and as the hunger of Hell prowled just beyond the cave.

Something touched her shoulder and she turned, finding that the shadow was holding a thin, ragged blanket out to her. She took it and wrapped it around her shoulders.

And Layla, exhausted and shaking, finally gave in to sleep.

CHAPTER 37

THE AIR AT THE CROSSROADS LINGERED WITH unnatural stillness. Remington stepped just beyond the tree line, boots silent against scorched grass. Beside him, Dacre crouched low, blade drawn and ready. Chel hovered behind them, Hellion blade humming.

Across the wide, cracked clearing stood Shay and Nero and... an Angel.

The Angel wore no armor. He was dressed like a human: jeans and a button down shirt. His wings were tucked tightly against his back.

"I seek asylum," the Angel said. "I do not wish to unbalance the realms. I offer apology and explanation."

Nero tilted his head. "Explanation first."

"I was sent by the White Horse."

That made Remington's spine go straight. Behind him, Chel stiffened.

The Angel continued, "The girl was in grave danger. I moved to intervene before the darkness fed on her. I meant no offense to Hell. I waited as long as I could for your people to find her. It was too late. The Demons at the Black Mansion would have devoured her. Some were ready to pounce."

He glanced away, a shadow of guilt crossing his perfect features. "Many of the demons at the Black Mansion are no longer alive."

Shay and Nero glanced to each other before the Angel continued.

"I was tasked with protecting her, not only because she is vulnerable, but because she is essential. There is a prince among you. Torn between his birthright and his curse. The Veil between realms grows thin around him. He must contain himself. He must become whole. He will destroy the realms if he remains the way he is."

Shay's head tipped in understanding. "I know who you speak of."

The Angel's gaze lifted toward the trees, toward them.

Damn it.

"He will tear this realm in two," the Angel said softly. "The girl will help."

Dacre's expression twisted. "Layla?"

"Thrush," Remington murmured, realization falling like stone in his gut.

The Angel stepped back. "I do not wish to upset the balance of Hell. But this is not about borders. It is about survival of our worlds. A creature born of the Astral and Angel lineage has not been seen ever."

With that, he turned away from Shay and Nero, lifting his face to the sulfur-colored sky. "You may tell your Queen I will leave when the girl is safe."

His wings unfurled. Light shimmered briefly across the Crossroads.

And then he was gone.

Remington exhaled. Chel stepped up beside him, tense. "What the hell does that mean? 'Fractured prince'?"

Dacre just stared at the empty clearing. "Rue has been so worried. The visions she had of Thrush and Layla... I thought she was overreacting." He was shaking his head.

"Ah," Chel sheathed his blade, "the dark princeling, the chaotic princeling, I see. We should circle back and find them."

The group backed away from the crossroads and left Nero and Shay to their duties.

CHAPTER 38

THE LANTERNS IN THE LIBRARY FLICKERED. Evelyn shivered, curling her fingers around the book Layla had touched, the same book that had sent her friend collapsing to the floor weeks ago. Or so they had thought.

Rue stood beside her, stiff-backed and quiet.

"You okay?" Evelyn asked, brushing dust from the cracked cover.

Rue's fingers twitched. Her eyes were dark as stormwater. "Don't move."

Evelyn froze, hand hovering above the page.

Then Rue gasped, staggering back into a shelf. Books tumbled. Her body seized up, breath rasping.

"Rue?" Evelyn moved quickly and caught her. "Rue, breathe," she whispered, lowering Rue to the floor.

But the world behind Rue's eyes had already changed.

THEN...

. . .

THRUSH GRABBED THE SMALL BLADE CHEL HAD given him during training and tucked it into the pocket near his belt. He picked up his bag and secured it on his back. There was only time to grab a few things from his room; a few books he'd taken from the castle, clothes, small weapons, and snacks. His parents were pacing the living room when he finally left his bedroom.

Noah glanced at the clock, "We gotta go. It's getting closer."

His mother, Nightingale, was standing near the door. "Now, son. Quickly and quietly." She opened the door, careful that the hinges didn't squeak. They crossed the lawn and paused near the gate to the high fence that protected their sanctuary in the graveyard. Past the chain link, they saw snakes and bugs and small creatures of havoc headed toward the castle in the burning caves.

His father, Noah, mouthed, "Follow me."

Thrush nodded.

The gate opened silently, not drawing attention from the creatures on the ground.

Thrush ran as fast as his legs would carry him, his heart pounding in his chest like a war drum. He glanced at his mother beside him, her face set with grim determination. Since his parents were technically dead, they could flash where ever they wanted, but they stayed by his side. Thrush was grateful for it. They had their limitations being spectral beings and all, but they did their best. They still functioned as though they were very much alive.

"Stay close, Thrush!" Noah called out, his voice strained but firm.

Noah glanced back and Thrush could see the worry etched on his father's face. Nightingale's eyes darted around, scanning the Hellforest for any signs of movement. Escaping during the day hours meant the dead would be wandering.

The castle in the burning caves loomed to their right, a sinister silhouette against the ochre Hellsky. The cries of Demons echoed through the air, growing closer. And... there was another sound...

"No," Noah muttered, slowing to run by Thrush's side. He pointed to one of the dead. It wasn't ambling around looking lost like they usually were, this one was running toward the castle.

"Fast-dead," Nightingale warned. "Stay clear of them."

They ran faster, further.

"We are almost there," Nightingale said, her voice a mix of hope and desperation. "The portal is just ahead."

Thrush's legs burned with fatigue, but he pushed himself harder. He'd trained hard for this day. The portal was their only chance. It shimmered faintly in the distance, a beacon of hope in the darkness. But as they drew closer, he saw the dark shapes moving around it.

"Demons," Thrush said just loud enough for his parents to hear, pointing toward the portal.

Noah's jaw tightened. "We have to get through them. There's no other way."

The three skidded to a halt, hiding behind a jagged outcropping of rocks. Thrush peered around the edge, counting the Demons. There were five of them, grotesque creatures with leathery wings and claws that gleamed in the hellish light.

"We need a distraction," Nightingale whispered, her eyes narrowing as she formulated a plan.

Thrush's mind raced. He looked down and spotted a loose, heavy rock. It wasn't much, but it might just buy them the time they needed.

"I'll throw this," Thrush said, hefting the rock. "When they go to check, we make a run for it."

Noah nodded. "On my signal."

Thrush took a deep breath, trying to steady his trembling hands. He waited for his father's signal, the tension stretching out every second into an eternity.

"Now!" Noah hissed.

Thrush hurled the rock with all his might, watching as it arced through the air and crashed into a distant pile of debris. The Demons' heads snapped toward the noise. They moved to investigate.

"Go!" Noah urged, and they sprinted from their hiding place, making a beeline for the portal.

The Demons saw them and let out enraged roars as they ran toward the portal.

Thrush's heart pounded, adrenaline coursing through his veins. The portal was close, but the Demons were closing in fast.

Nightingale reached the portal first, her hand outstretched toward the shimmering surface. "Thrush, hurry!"

Thrush pushed harder, his feet barely touching the ground as he raced toward safety. Noah was right behind him, glancing back to see the Demons almost on them.

"No!" Nightingale shouted. She waved for Thrush to run around the portal. "The fast-dead are coming."

"*Change of plans,*" *Noah said, grabbing Thrush by his shirt.*

The fast dead didn't pick favorites, they went after whatever moved, whatever was closest, and the Demons had their attention.

"*Keep running,*" *Nightingale said, waving, "this way."*

Thrush lunged with a final burst of speed following Nightingale as she changed course.

"*Where?*" *Thrush asked between heavy breaths.*

"*The pond is the closest.*" *Noah was running by Thrush's side.*

The sounds of hundreds of feet running echoed through Hellforest. Thrush glanced from side to side, didn't notice the branches on the ground and tripped.

Noah was lifting him to his feet harshly. "Keep going," he urged.

Thrush limped for a few steps before swallowing down the pain in his ankle and resuming his previous speed.

"*It's not far,*" *Nightingale said.*

Thrush knew better; it was a good distance away and he wasn't sure he could keep running at this pace, but he'd try his hardest. They ran across empty roads and through forests littered with wandering dead.

Nightingale finally slowed near a shallow stream. "It's up here." She motioned toward the dark pond in the distance. "It's not much further."

Noah placed a hand on Thrush's shoulder, his expression a mix of pride and exhaustion. "You did it, son. We're out of here."

Thrush allowed himself a small, weary smile. They had almost escaped Hell but he knew their journey was far from over. There were still dangers ahead, still battles to be fought—

A fast-dead was running toward Thrush. He acted quick, not ready for the speed at which the fast-dead ran. His parents didn't notice in time. Thrush gripped his knife and slammed it into the skull of the fast-dead as it knocked him over.

Thrush groaned, trying to shove it off him but it was the corpse of a rather large man.

"No!" Nightingale shouted, grabbing at the dead man, and trying to get it off Thrush.

"It's dead," Noah said, dragging Thrush out from under the corpse.

Gore and blood stained Thrush's clothing. He shuddered, thankful for his training with the Hellions the past few years. He wiped his knife on his pant leg and secured it again. "Let's go," he said, making a beeline for the pond.

"The Basilisk," Nightingale warned. "There's two."

Noah pointed to the still surface of the pond. "They're not here."

"Go," Nightingale urged.

The trio ran for the pond.

Thrush dove under, a cold sensation washing over him as the soft current pulled them away.

Only... the faint outline of something clawing at the edge of the current lingered, something was being dragged away from Thrush's body. Up to the surface of the Nightjar's pond.

The vision twisted. Rue glimpsed Thrush's shadow self being hurled back to Hell, tossed like a scrap into the fire.

Split.

Forsaken.

. . .

SHE FELT IT, THE UNRAVELING. A SOUL TORN in two.

How did he not feel it?

Rue couldn't follow the shadow in her vision, she could only follow Thrush. So she stayed with him.

NIGHTINGALE, NOAH, AND THRUSH EXITED THE *fountain in the center of Babylon. Noah turned, taking in his surroundings.*

"Do ethereal creatures belong here?" Noah asked.

"I don't care," Nightingale replied. "Follow me." She skated over the water, turning to a stop before stepping down from the fountain.

RUE SENSED WARMTH FLOOD HER BODY, JOY AT seeing her aunt Nightingale like this—always with the roller-skates. She was cursed as well and her father decided it was best to hide her in the basement. She was odd in those early years of freedom.

"WHY YOU ALWAYS GOTTA SKATE ALL FANCY-like?" Noah asked Nightingale, appreciating the short shorts. "Why can't you just walk like the rest of us schmucks?"

"Because it's boring," Nightingale replied with an unimpressed tone.

Thrush stepped over the ledge of the fountain, his soaked

clothing leaving puddles as he walked. His parents were dry, like they'd never been submerged. Thrush followed the two toward a stone walkway. The lingering Angels of Babylon began noticing them and moving closer.

What Thrush couldn't see was the steam rising off his body like smoke, he didn't notice the smell of woodsmoke and pine. He didn't smell like Heaven, he smelled like Hell and everyone within a certain radius noticed. He didn't belong there and it was blatantly obvious. And as the bright sun of the Seven Kingdoms of Heaven shined down on them, all three walked without shadows. It was expected of Noah and Nightingale, they were of the Astral realm. Thrush was another story.

Thrush took in every motion of the surrounding crowd that had gathered to watch them. Thrush hadn't been to the Seven Kingdoms of Heaven since he was an infant. He wasn't sure what to expect, but he'd been trained by the strongest Hellions in Meg's court so he didn't miss one hand move-ment, one step fall, or one motion in his periphery. He gripped the small blade at his hip and adjusted the bag on his shoul-der. He wondered if they'd try and attack. Sure that he could take out a handful of them by himself, he worried if anyone would come to their rescue if an Angel attack overwhelmed him. He glanced at his parents. They'd have to draw on their Astral magic to protect him. Thrush hid his limp, not favoring his sore ankle that had twisted during their escape. He didn't want the Angels to notice any weakness.

He didn't realize the only thing they noticed was that he walked in this light without a shadow following him. Few knew what that meant, and they kept their distance.

"How far?" Noah asked.

"Maybe twenty minutes," Nightingale slowed to walk next to Thrush, his clothes drying quickly under the heat of Heaven's skies. The sun was intense.

They stopped at the gates leading to the Raven King's lands.

"Brother," Nightingale called. "Let us in, please."

Sparrow appeared in the distance, walking down a long winding driveway toward the gate. Nightingale was shocked at the sight of her brother. It had been years since she'd last seen him. He'd given them peace in Meg's realm, promised ceasefire. The smirk on his face led Nightingale to believe that everything was about to change.

Sparrow stood at the gate, his hand resting on the lock. "Shouldn't you both be in the Ethereal realm?" he looked from Nightingale to Noah before his eyes landed on Thrush.

"Let us in," Nightingale said.

"Just send the boy," Sparrow's eyes narrowed on Thrush. "He's due for training. He needs to be prepared for his future now that you've changed sides. He's been away from his rightful home for too long."

Nightingale called upon the same ethereal power she used to defeat the Nightjar. She began to illuminate, drawing light from the sun until her body glowed brightly.

"Neat trick," Sparrow said as he unlocked the gate and pushed it open.

"Raven King," Nightingale said. "This land is as much his as it is yours. This is family land. We are refugees of war."

Sparrow stepped back and motioned for them to enter. "What happened to Hell?" Sparrow glanced at her scarred cheek.

"We've been banished," Nightingale said, her voice cold.

She had an urge to remind her brother that the scars came from her death, bitten in the neck and face by the Fast-Dead.

Noah glared at Sparrow. "I remember a time when you weren't such a dick."

The corner of Sparrow's mouth tipped up in a half smile. Noah took that as a good sign. Maybe under Sparrow's dark façade he wasn't so different. Noah had seen the masks Meg had to wear as the Queen of Hell. There was a time that Sparrow and Noah were friends when Sparrow was doing his time as a Hellion and remained devoted to Meg. Times had changed. Still, it was hard for Noah to understand what Sparrow had turned into after all these years. He'd went from quirky and fun to dark and serious.

The lock to the gate clicked closed. Nightingale turned. "Thrush, this is your uncle Sparrow," Nightingale motioned to the Raven King.

Sparrow held out a hand toward Thrush. "Haven't seen you since you were a baby. You're practically grown now."

Thrush placed his hand in Sparrow's, wary with his free hand on the hilt of his hidden knife.

Sparrow glanced to the boy's hip and noted the weapon. One brow rose in interest. "Seems you've had some training."

Thrush smiled and it was just as dark as Sparrow's. Thrush wouldn't hesitate to draw a weapon, didn't want his uncle to think he had the upper hand, King or not.

"Don't mind Sparrow," Nightingale warned. "He went crazy a few times. But you can thank him for breaking the family curse." Nightingale touched the back of Thrush's head. "He's the reason why you aren't cracked in the head like the rest of us."

"Jury's still out on if it was a curse." Sparrow released Thrush's hand and began walking, black wings scraping the road in a constant shhhhhh.

RUE WONDERED IF HER FATHER COULD TELL THAT Thrush's soul had been torn and that his shadow was gone.

NIGHTINGALE GAVE SPARROW A DIRTY LOOK, AND Noah stayed protectively close to Thrush.

A house appeared in the distance. These were not the family lands Nightingale remembered. Their home was gone, destroyed in the Fast-Zombie War. That was also where Nightingale died, bit in the neck by the dead. Then Jack, Noah's brother, was bit. Meg rescued Thrush–kidnapped him really–and brought him to Hell.

Nightingale held back emotion. Returning to this place brought back too many memories and the realization of missed time after she'd died and strangers were left to raise her child. Nightingale moved closer to Thrush as they neared the house.

"I wasn't expecting guests," Sparrow said as he opened the door to the house. "Wait here while I have one of the surrounding cabins prepared."

Noah got Nightingale's attention. "Do you think this is safe?" he mouthed.

"It's all we've got." She focused on Thrush. "We can't take our son to the Ether and the Earthen plane is too dangerous."

Sparrow led them to a small cabin not far from the main

house. "Make yourselves at home," he said as he opened the door and entered. "Some things are similar to the way father ran the kingdom. The fridge will remain stocked. Clothes cleaned." He turned to look at Thrush. "You can start training with the Legion in the morning."

Thrush nodded.

"Are the training grounds in the same location?" Nightingale asked.

Sparrow nodded. "Welcome home, sister and family." He closed the door and left them alone.

Noah exhaled a large sigh. "Jesus Christ," his eyes were wide as he focused on Nightingale, "is it always this suffocating here? Everything is so quiet and proper and stoic and hot." He ran hands through shaggy blonde hair. "How did you survive this most of your life?"

Nightingale smirked. "Now you see why I was so eager to follow Meg to Hell. And don't worry, it will only get worse. You've only met one person so far."

"Yeah but there's a vibe." Noah rolled his eyes before nudging Thrush. "You doin' okay with all this?"

Thrush shrugged. "The Raven King sees me as a threat."

"No, no," Nightingale soothed. "He's just had his brains scrambled too many times." She rubbed Thrush's arms trying to calm him.

"Maybe we should have taken our chances with Alastor," Thrush suggested before saying, "I'm gonna find my room."

Thrush walked away from his parents to explore the cabin.

"He's just a teenage boy," Noah said to Nightingale. "We just took him away from the only home he's ever known. And the only friends he's ever had."

Thrush found a room in the back of the cabin. There was a large window that faced the forest and a private bathroom. He threw his bag on the floor before bending to unpack his things. He pulled out the books, wishing he'd wrapped them in something waterproof. The pages were soggy and limp. He set them out to dry and hoped they'd regain their original shape. He shook out his clothing and hung them to dry. Opening a small, zippered pocket, he took out a charcoal pencil and a pouch of salt and a small notebook with spells. The notebook hadn't fared so well after getting wet. He gripped the charcoal pencil and flipped through the pages, landing on a rune he knew quite well. He closed his eyes. Then he began to etch the door and the window casings with charcoal. When he was done, he took out one of the small blades given to him by the Hellions and began carving runes into the wood of the cabin.

NIGHTINGALE OBSERVED FROM A DISTANCE AS Thrush practiced with Sparrow's Legion. As though the darkness of Hell clung to him, plenty stared. He was starting to change; his hair had lightened to a white blonde in the weeks that they'd been in Sparrow's Kingdom.

The sun was starting to dip lower on the horizon, casting long shadows across the training grounds.

"You don't need to watch me so closely," Thrush mumbled as Nightingale approached him.

"I don't trust them," she said.

"They're harder on me when you are here. I need you to stop hovering. I'm not a child anymore." He stormed around

Nightingale, avoiding her and began jogging toward the path that led to the cabin.

Thrush raised his arm and pulled a leaf off a branch overhead and tore up the leaf in his hand, shredded it to a hundred pieces.

"Did the leaf deserve that?" a dark voice asked from the shadows.

Sparrow stepped out and Thrush came to a stop.

"It looked at me wrong," Thrush said.

A smile quirked Sparrow's lip. "Stupid leaf." He motioned for Thrush to follow him. "Training is going well I hear."

"Yeah," Thrush replied, glancing at the tall figure walking next to him.

"I told them to take it easy on you."

Thrush scoffed. "Tell that to my liver."

Sparrow's brow rose in question. "I also told them you might've been trained by the Hellions and to keep you on your toes."

"How do you know that?" Thrush asked.

"I was a Hellion." He paused. "All males of the Archangel families are required to do their time as a Hellion. Did your mother not discuss this with you?"

Thrush shook his head.

"When the time comes, you must go. You must learn true darkness to rule in the light. You must see bad to do good. I have no children of my own. As the next in line for this kingdom, you must prepare."

"And if I choose not to go?"

"You will curse this bloodline again. You will go."

"Why?" Thrush pushed. "There are no more children. My mother told me that I was the first in decades. It was a miracle. Doing time as a Hellion didn't make you good."

Sparrow turned to his nephew and found the boy glaring at him.

Sparrow glared down at the boy. "You should go home. Now," he warned.

Thrush turned and ran.

THRUSH TORE THROUGH THE DRAWERS OF THE small cottage, his movements frantic and agitated. His hair had grown unruly, a wild mess, just like his chaotic life.

Nightingale and Noah entered the cottage, sensing the tension even before they saw their son.

"Thrush, what are you doing?" Nightingale asked with a soft whistle, her voice filled with concern.

"Looking for scissors," Thrush snapped, slamming another drawer shut. "I need to cut this damn hair."

Noah stepped forward. "Thrush, calm down. Talk to us."

"There's nothing to talk about," Thrush shot back, his eyes blazing with frustration. "I can't go back to Hell. I won't. I hate that we're all scattered, that my friends are suffering, maybe even dead, who knows... and I'm stuck here."

Nightingale sighed, reaching out to touch his shoulder. "We know it's hard, but running away from your duties won't help. You are part of a bigger plan." She lowered her gaze. "If you don't do your time as a Hellion, the family curse will return. You don't want that on your shoulders."

Thrush pulled away from her touch, his anger palpable. "I never asked to be part of this plan. I don't care about some obscure rules between the realms. I just want my life back. If there is no one else to curse, what does it matter?"

"If you have children–" Nightingale started to say.

"I'd never bring a kid into this mess," Thrush spat.

Noah handed Thrush a pair of scissors he'd found. "If cutting your hair makes you feel better, do it. But know that it won't change what you must face."

Thrush grabbed the scissors and moved to a mirror. With determined snips, he started cutting away chunks of hair, the pieces falling to the floor like snow.

Nightingale stepped closer, gently taking the scissors from him and evening out his haphazard work. "I used to do this when you were a baby," she said softly. "Until you made me stop. You're not alone in this," she whispered, her hands steady as she trimmed his hair shorter. "We all have our battles, Thrush. But we face them together."

"We shouldn't be here." Thrush scowled. "We should be helping Meg. We should be with Remington and Rue. We shouldn't be separated."

"I miss them too," Noah said.

After a tense silence, Thrush pulled away from Nightingale and stormed out of the cottage.

"I'll go after him," Noah said.

"Please," Nightingale whispered, bending to scoop up the hair on the floor. It sifted through her fingers like snow.

Noah followed Thrush, the two walking toward the practice grounds. "I'll never get over this freaking sun. Thrush, I *understand you're upset. But avoiding responsibilities won't help."*

Thrush scoffed. "You don't get it, Dad. I don't want to be a Hellion. I don't want to learn darkness." He used air-quotes as he mimicked Sparrow's words. "I miss my friends and I hate that we are all split up."

Noah placed a hand on Thrush's shoulder, squeezing gently. "It'll be okay. We'll find a way through this. But you have to trust us, trust the rules of the realms."

Thrush scoffed. "Yeah, like you and Mom? Following rules got you both killed."

"Hey," Noah tugged on Thrush's arm. "I died on the way to prison. And your mom died protecting you."

"I don't want to talk about this anymore," Thrush said as he stumbled to a standstill. "Holy shit."

Both were stopped in their tracks by a chilling sight. Sparrow, exhausted and distraught, was carrying Meg's limp body. Her wings were gone, her form lifeless and bloodied. Sparrow's pants were saturated in blood. Smoke rose from their bodies and the scent of brimstone wafted in the slight breeze.

"Oh my God." Noah ran toward them. "What happened?"

Sparrow's eyes were hollow, filled with a mixture of rage and disappointment. "Alastor happened. We need to get her inside."

Thrush moved closer. "Is she..."

"She's alive," Sparrow said through gritted teeth. "But barely. We need to move, now. Don't you have somewhere to be?" Sparrow snapped at Thrush. "Go!"

"We'll catch up later," Noah said, motioning for Thrush

to head to training.

"I saw Meg sneaking out this morning," Noah said as he poured a cup of coffee and stared out the window like a forty year old dad checking out the neighbor's grass.

"She's going to the Earthen plane," Nightingale said. "Sparrow told me. He's going with her."

"She was alone when I saw her crossing the yard." He sets a pan on the stove and starts cooking for Thrush; eggs and sausage and leftover biscuits. "She probably tried to leave him behind."

"I can't say I blame her," Nightingale said as she crossed the room to sit at the breakfast nook.

"What do you think he's hiding?" Noah asked.

"I have to do some digging. He hasn't exactly trusted me with any secrets after I chose Hell over my family's kingdom."

There was shuffling in the hallway as Thrush readied for the day. He made an appearance a few moments later, grumbling about them being too loud.

"Good morning," Noah said as he grabbed a plate from the shelf and tipped the contents of the pan onto it. "You want coffee?" Noah asked Thrush as he sat.

Thrush nodded as he picked up a fork and began eating. He'd woken up with a sense of unease gnawing at him and spent the early hours of the morning staring at the ceiling, listening to the distant sounds of Sparrow's kingdom coming to life.

As he ate, he finally broke his silence. "I don't want to be here any longer," Thrush declared, his voice firm. "I can't stay here anymore."

Noah and Nightingale made eye contact, exchanging worried glances.

Thrush swallowed his bite of food. "I want to go to wherever Remington and Rue are."

Noah spoke first. "Thrush, this is the safest place for you. Alastor's forces are everywhere in Hell."

Nightingale nodded in agreement. "We only want to protect you, Thrush. This kingdom has the strongest defenses. Leaving would be too dangerous."

"You died here, mother. How safe could it be? I can't stand it here," he argued. "I need to do something, be somewhere I can make a difference. Our lives have been ruined by Alastor and we are just sitting here. Meg is going to go back to Hell to face Alastor and she's going to die."

"How do you know that?" Noah asked.

"I just know." Thrush stood up. "I need to do something, be somewhere I can make a difference."

Without waiting for their response, Thrush went out the door. As the day progressed, his distraction became evident. He narrowly avoided several accidents during battle drills, his mind consumed elsewhere.

The Legion Angels around him began to notice. They made crude jokes. "What's got you so distracted, Thrush. Is it a girl?" one of them taunted, making horns with his fingers, and throwing kisses in Thrush's direction.

Thrush pushed through the training with gritted teeth. By the end of the day, he was exhausted and bruised, his mind no clearer than it had been that morning.

At dinner, his parents tried to engage him in conversation. Noah mentioned exploring more of the Seven Kingdoms and possibly visiting Gabriel's kingdom for a few weeks. Thrush didn't participate more than a few nods of his head.

After eating, Thrush excused himself and went to bed. He lay there, waiting for the cabin to fall silent. Sometimes his parents went to the Astral plane at night, but never for long.

Thrush quietly slipped out of bed. He moved through the darkened halls. He didn't see his parents anywhere. Returning to his room, he grabbed his bag and began packing.

He tucked pillows under his blanket to make it look like he was sleeping in bed. Then he opened the window and climbed out.

There was a stone wall that bordered the Raven King's lands; he stuck to the shadows of the tree line and made his way to the trail that led to Babylon. He paused a few times listening for voices in the distance. Angels from the Legion barracks were wandering.

"Sneaking out to see your demon girlfriend?" one of the Angels had seen him.

Thrush went still, gripping the knife in his pocket. "Yeah," he said with a light chuckle.

The Angel laughed, then muttered something about filthy blood and walked away. The guy didn't care that Thrush was sneaking out.

He jogged down the trail that led to the gate of Babylon. He made his way to the nearby city center, navigating through the park-like sidewalks with ease. The sounds of water splashing echoed through the night. The fountain was straight ahead.

Thrush took a notebook from his pocket. He'd started collecting spells just like Jed. He flipped through his notebook.

Thrush stepped up on to the fountain, his boots hanging off the edge. He took a breath of the clean Heaven air and held a hand over the water while he chanted to spell.

The water bubbled and steamed for a moment before turning smooth as glass. Meg's image appeared as she exited onto the Earthen plane.

Thrush closed the notebook and tucked it in his bag.

Thrush took one last gulp of air before taking a half-step into the portal.

He paused as the water stirred. And then, a hand appeared. Thrush waited as someone came through. There was nowhere to hide so he stepped down and waited. He pulled the knife from his pocket. He took a defensive stance.

"Holy crap," he muttered. Securing his weapon and reaching forward, Thrush grabbed the hand and pulled them to the edge.

"Remm!" Thrush shouted, his voice cracking with emotion.

Remington's head snapped up. He looked up from the hand gripping his wrist and a grin spread across his face. He pulled Thrush in, closing the distance between them in a heartbeat.

"Thrush!" Remington cried, gripping his friend in a tight embrace. "I can't believe you're here!"

Sparrow watched the reunion with a guarded expression, his eyes flickering to Meg as she exited the fountain.

. . .

Rue wondered if her father had known back then. Why didn't he say something? Why didn't he help Thrush navigate these muddy waters?

The vision snapped again. Shadows screamed. Light fractured. Then silence.

   The curse of his bloodline had room to fester after all of that.

CHAPTER 39

Now.

RUE JOLTED AWAKE, CHEST HEAVING, FINGERS gripping the sleeve of Evelyn's cardigan. Her eyes were wide. "I saw it. I know what's wrong with him and Layla."

Evelyn blinked. "Tell me."

Rue nodded, pulling away. "His shadow was severed when we were teenagers, before the war, when we went into hiding. He fled to my father's Kingdom in Heaven. His shadow was thrown back to Hell."

Evelyn frowned. "So that shadow. The one following Layla. It's his? It's *him*?"

Rue stood, pacing. "Yes. It's a piece of him. Without it, he's been unstable. It's his shadow-self. It had no resistance, no balance. He never stood a chance at facing the family curse without it."

Evelyn's brow furrowed. "You never noticed before?"

"I never really looked," Rue admitted. "But in the

Hellion lair, right before they left to search for Layla, Thrush was the only one without a shadow. It hit me, but I didn't realize what it meant until now. His moodiness, his personality shift just before the war; he lost a piece of himself and we didn't know and instead of facing it he just... ran off."

"So how do we fix it?" Evelyn asked, still clutching the book.

Rue half-smiled. "We need to tell my mother. That this was never just a curse, it was a multitude of events."

Evelyn nodded, snapping the book shut. "Good luck. She's not here. You better call her, hopefully she'll answer from wherever she is."

Rue pulled a phone from her pocket and began messaging.

"The boys have been gone for hours, it will be daylight soon and they'll be hungry." Evelyn reminded her. "Also, where is the kitten?"

Rue pointed to the top of a bookshelf where Lucipurr was curled up sleeping.

Footsteps echoed in the hallway.

Rue turned to look at Evelyn.

"That's your mother," Evelyn smirked. "What did you text her?"

"Just that I had a vision about Thrush and knew what was wrong with him." Rue looked down at her phone. "She never even texted me back."

"Must be important information to her then." Evelyn stood and adjusted her sweater.

The door to the library flung open and Rue's mother entered. She recognized her father in the hallway, the edge of his large black wings peeking through the threshold. He was speaking in hushed tones to someone.

"Child," Meg moved to Rue, arms open, "I'm so glad you're home."

"Just until we figure this out." Rue's voice was muffled by Meg's shoulder as her mother hugged her.

Rue quickly told her mother everything about Layla and Thrush, and the visions and the book and Thrush being separated from his shadow-self.

Meg's expressions didn't reveal that she knew or didn't know any of the information. But then, Meg seemed to know plenty, somehow.

When Rue was done, Sparrow entered the room. "A Hellion just updated me. There was an Angel in Hell. They were at the Crossroads," Sparrow said. "The angel called Nero and Shay. He asked for protection, from you."

Meg turned, slow and controlled, but her fury shimmered like heat in the air. "He should have come to me directly."

"It was to protect the girl," Sparrow said. "He saved her from being sold into the skin trades. We've been searching for where the Black Mansion relocated to for a long time now. This might be a lead."

"Those fucks." She began pacing. "If the fracture in Thrush is weakening the Veil, then we are all in danger. And if that girl is the key to stitching him back together..."

"Then we can't let her be taken again," Rue finished.

Meg's voice dropped low. "No. We cannot. She's going to have to *change*."

CHAPTER 40

THE FOREST HAD GROWN DENSER THE FARTHER Thrush moved north. The trees here were older, the bark gnarled like bones, branches twisted like grasping hands. The deeper Thrush went, the more the terrain whispered to him. He knew this place.

The air was cooler here. Quieter too, like even Hell's creatures didn't dare disturb this stretch of wild. They didn't dare disturb his land.

He crouched, fingers brushing over a patch of disturbed moss and crushed leaves. Something had passed through here recently. Something human with small feet and a slight limp. His chest tightened. They'd passed each other? How? He turned back.

The cave wasn't far. He'd dipped into a little valley but could still see the mouth of the cave at the incline in the distance.

He stood and moved fast now, boots silent on the forest floor, eyes narrowed.

Layla.

She had come this way.

Thrush broke through the thicket and saw the mouth of the cave, gaping open like a wound in the mountainside. It was the very place he once called sanctuary, a place he swore he'd never return to.

And yet, here he was. Again and again it called him back like he'd left something here that he needed to survive.

He stepped inside.

The scent hit him first. Blood.

"Layla?" His voice was low, almost a whisper.

Then he saw her huddled in the corner, curled tight like she was trying to disappear. Dirt streaked her legs. Her hair was a tangled mess. Her face was pale and he could see cuts on her skin and bare feet. She wasn't wearing much in the way of clothing.

She didn't stir.

But beside her, in the shadowed corner of the cave, something moved.

Thrush reached instinctively for the dagger at his hip, eyes narrowing.

The shadow. That damn shadow was after her again.

It looked at him. For just a moment, it had shape; shoulders, a head, something vaguely human. And it radiated a surge of power, a threat.

Thrush growled. "What the hell are you?"

The shadow didn't respond, but it didn't attack either. It simply looked down at Layla once more then faded, vanishing deeper into the stone. This shadow wasn't new to Thrush. He knew this shadow well. He was sure it had been a figment of his fractured imagination for years. It had haunted his time in this cave, always watching him. Thrush blamed the shadow on the cure that was slowly driving him insane.

Thrush dropped to his knees beside her. "Layla," he said again, softer this time. "It's me. You're safe now."

She stirred, eyes fluttering open.

Her gaze was glassy, unfocused. She blinked rapidly, trying to bring him into view. "Thrush?" She rubbed her eyes. "My glasses are busted, I can't see very well in this darkness."

"I'm here." His voice caught. "I found you." He reached out to touch her, pushing the thin blanket away. "Why are you dressed like this?"

"Asmodeus was going to sell me." She rubbed dirty palms down the skirt of the dress.

"No shoes?"

Layla shook her head. "I'd appreciate some. But no." She flexed her foot.

"And your glasses?"

She reached into her bra and pulled out the busted spectacles. "I tried."

She reached out blindly. He caught her hand and held it gently. She was freezing. He pulled her closer, hoping his body heat might warm her.

"Are you real?" she murmured. "The shadow brought me back... I didn't know what was real anymore. I saw some really strange shit."

He pressed his forehead to hers. "I'm real."

But in the back of his mind, Thrush knew something was still wrong. That shadow wasn't just protecting her, it was acting like it was bound to her. And it was growing agitated. He watched it pace and flicker on the edge of his periphery while he held Layla close.

It wasn't his imagination. It never had been. That shadow had been following him for years.

THRUSH HAD BARELY BEGUN TO LIFT HER WHEN Layla shifted in his arms. "Wait," she whispered.

He froze.

She slowly raised her right hand into the thin light drifting through the cave entrance. Her skin shimmered dark. Not like bruising. Not like dirt. It was deeper; a stain.

Her voice trembled. "It's spreading."

Thrush stared. His heart dropped like a stone. "What the hell?"

Layla swallowed and reached up to show him the tiny spots on her wrist. A faint crescent-shaped scar peeked from beneath her wrist bone.

"I was bitten," she said. "In the library. I thought it was a spider. I didn't think it was important. But now..." She turned and pointed at the shadow near the back wall. "I think it was him."

Thrush stood. Cold anger shot through his chest like a lightning strike. "You let him bite you?"

Layla's chin lifted, but tears filled her eyes. "I didn't let him do anything! Oh my god you are such an asshole."

Thrush's vision tunneled. His fangs ached. His magic pulsed hot under his skin, too volatile to hold back.

"You're not becoming a shadow," he growled. "I won't let that happen."

"But what if I already am?" Her voice broke. "What if that's what's wrong with me?"

The shadow stirred.

Thrush's rage snapped.

"You touched her," he snarled, stepping toward the flickering figure. "You think you can mark her? Infect her? Hide in my realm and take her?"

The shadow coalesced, barely humanoid, wisps of black fog forming shoulders, arms, glowing eyes like twin moons. But it didn't strike. It stood its ground.

Thrush didn't wait.

He lunged.

His fist slammed into the side of the shadow-figure's head. It recoiled, light bursting from the impact like sparks from a flint strike. The cave shuddered. Rock dust rained from above.

The shadow retaliated. Not with claws or fists but with sheer force, a wall of unnatural cold slamming into Thrush's chest and hurling him backwards into the stone wall.

"Stop it!" Layla screamed. She huddled behind a jagged boulder. "Please, stop!"

But Thrush wasn't done. He surged to his feet, face wild, silver eyes blazing. "You're not taking her!" he shouted at the thing. "You're not making her like you!"

The shadow shifted again, flickering toward Layla, but not to attack.

To shield.

Thrush froze. His fists clenched. "What?"

"Don't you see it?" Layla said softly, tears streaking her dirt-smudged face. "He's not trying to hurt me."

The shadow reached toward her like it had before, a whisper of motion. Her skin reacted to it, pulling darkness around the bite mark.

Thrush's throat tightened. "He's changing you."

"He's bound to me," she whispered. "I think, because of the book maybe. I'm not really sure." She looked up at Thrush, eyes wide with terror. "But I don't know what he wants. He dragged me here."

Bodies moved.

The cave trembled beneath her feet.

Layla pressed herself to the stone wall, one hand braced against her throbbing ribs. In front of her, Thrush and the shadow circled each other like twin storms.

Thrush's fists pulsed with light. His veins glowed like they were filled with magma.

"You think you can mark her?" Thrush growled, voice reverberating unnaturally. "You think I'll let you claim her?"

The shadow didn't answer. It never had a voice, not really. But its posture shifted; shoulders drawing back, head tilting, as if listening and trying to explain.

Then Thrush attacked.

Magic ripped from him like a wildfire set loose. Flames surged outward, bright white edged with silver, and the heat slapped Layla in the face, searing the edges of her dress. She ducked behind a jutting stone just in time to avoid the worst of it.

The shadow countered; not with fire, but a pulse of Astral energy, black and silver and freezing cold. The ground fractured where it hit, roots of shadow veining across the cave floor.

The collision made the world go white.

A shockwave exploded through the chamber. The stalactites cracked above, raining down moss and rock. Light and shadow collided in a blinding fury. Layla screamed and covered her ears. The air rippled with energy, so much it made her head hurt.

And then, silence.

She coughed. When she opened her eyes, the cave glowed faintly orange. Smoke curled in the air. The walls were scorched black.

The air inside the cave pulsed with heat, a rift of magic crackling across scorched stone. Thrush staggered back, panting, fists clenched.

Across from him, the shadow stilled.

Then, it stepped forward. No, it ran and leapt before Thrush could react.

Thrush's eyes widened as the silhouette walked straight into him. No resistance. No battle. Just... return.

A breath caught in his throat.

His body locked in place as if bracing for impact, but there was only a strange bone-deep stillness.

The fury that had lived beneath his skin for years drained out of him in a slow exhale. The flares of anger and the wild lashes of magic that had danced uncontrolled along his fingertips zipped up his arms in lightning-like streaks and vanished into his chest.

Contained.

Centered.

Whole.

He gasped as the ground steadied beneath his feet. A

quiet hum spread through his limbs. His shoulders suddenly felt heavy.

He blinked.

And for the first time in years... there was no uncontrollable tremor in his neck and arms. The wrath that plagued him dissipated to a distant trickle and he saw the world clearly. Suddenly it wasn't too much to process all at once and the constant swirling in his mind stopped.

He collapsed.

Layla scrambled forward on her hands and knees. "Thrush!"

He lay motionless on the stone floor, surrounded by a circle of melted rock and singed feathers. His clothes were half-burned away. His skin glowed faintly, smoldering like coal after the heat of a fire has burned out.

Wings stretched out beneath him; blackened wings, charred at the edges, the feathers curled.

Layla gasped and reeled back on her knees. She couldn't see well without her glasses but this... this was something. She rubbed her eyes and looked again. She searched the cave.

The shadow was gone.

It was only her and this... what was he now? Before he was a man; handsome and angry and barely in control. Now he was... she wasn't sure.

She reached for Thrush, her fingers trembling. His pulse fluttered beneath her fingertips. He was alive, but barely. Whatever he'd turned into had kept his face the same, and his body... mostly. She was still drawn to him. Her only fear now was that he was nearly dead.

"Please," she whispered, pressing her forehead to his temple. "Don't leave me here. Don't you dare."

His breath stirred, faint and warm. Her hands moved to his chest. His skin was warm. She felt the slow beat of his heart under her palm. She tried to comprehend what had just happened. She'd never forget the scene of Thrush fighting the shadow man, or the moment when the shadow stepped into him as though it were coming home.

CHAPTER 41

LAYLA KNELT BESIDE THRUSH, BREATH CATCHING in her throat.

He looked like shit. Smoke still clung to his singed shirt, and the cave floor around him had blackened with the scorch of magic. One of his massive wings twitched, charred, but still whole. The other was curled protectively across his body, like it had shielded him from the worst of the blast.

She hovered. He'd been unconscious for what seemed like hours. She reached out and brushed dirt from his cheek. His skin was hot.

"Thrush?" she whispered.

No response. Just the faint rise and fall of his chest, as if he were suspended somewhere far away from her. His lips were parted slightly, his face too pale. He didn't look well at all.

With trembling fingers, she tilted his chin and studied him more closely. Her gaze fell to his lips... and then to his teeth. She touched his lip, remembering how she'd bravely kissed him after he'd healed her broken arm. He'd seemed so frightened of her afterwards.

Layla's fingers grazed his hair then smoothed down his cheek, and she pushed his upper lip back.

Fangs.

Not sharp like a vampire's in the movies, more subtle than that. They were set further back in his jaw, like a second set of cuspids but sharper.

She shivered.

"I should not be doing this," she muttered to herself.

But her eyes didn't stop roaming. Down his neck, the thick veins were still pulsing slow. His shoulders were bare where his shirt had been shredded, tattoos and scars laced across his chest. She touched his skin, found runes that were like the ones Jed had marked on her wrist. Protection runes. They looked old and Layla suddenly wanted to know everything he'd lived through in his life. She wanted to know why he was so angry all the time, why he seemed so uncertain around her one moment and the next completely charming. Why did he avoid drinking blood like Rue? It didn't seem right to deny what was natural to their kind. He was some kind of tormented puzzle, she'd always known it–she'd never feared the fact–but now she wanted to know *everything*.

Her gaze flicked to his wings. One had unfurled in the blast, smoke curling from the feathers. The other, half-opened, was glossy black and obsidian-edged. It was unnatural and magnificent.

Her breath caught again, this time for a different reason. She remembered the feeding room at the Black

Mansion; the press of demons, the low heat of hunger in the air and how part of her hadn't been horrified at all.

Now here, in the dark, beside this broken man that had fought for her, that hunger flickered again. Except it wasn't blood she craved.

But him.

She licked her lips and wondered what it would be like. Rue seemed happy, Evelyn too. It must not be that bad. Layla's throat suddenly felt dry.

He exhaled, weakly. His pulse slowed.

"No," she whispered, biting her lip. "No, no. You don't get to die now."

Frantic, she searched the cave and found his discarded knife near the firepit. Layla hesitated only a second before slicing the tip of her finger. Blood welled up, dark and slow.

She pressed it into his mouth.

He didn't move.

And then, barely, his tongue trembled.

A flush rose to his cheeks. His chest lifted more deeply.

Color bloomed beneath his skin.

Layla stared. "This is gonna cause trouble," she said aloud, trying to summon guilt. But her voice trembled with something else entirely. "What've I got to lose? I have no job, no glasses, no apartment. I'm in Hell with this... creature."

A breathtaking creature at that.

He groaned softly. The sound rippled through her.

"Damn it."

She pricked another finger and pressed it against his tongue.

He sucked.

Heat settled deep in her belly.

His tongue brushed the pad of her finger as if suckling. Her breath caught and she squeezed her knees together, stunned by how her body reacted to him. Even unconscious he ignited something primal in her.

She leaned closer, her forehead almost resting against his.

"I don't know what you are," she whispered. "But please don't leave me."

Outside the cave, thunder rolled low in the mountains, like Hell itself had felt the pulse of something returning.

CHAPTER 42

THRUSH FLOATED, WEIGHTLESS AS THOUGH disconnected from pain, from fire, from breath. The noise of the world dimmed to a quiet hum.

He hovered in a vast stretch of twilight, neither here nor there, suspended in the velvety dark between stars. The air smelled like ice and lavender and old paper.

And then... he wasn't alone.

Two figures stepped through the haze like light breaking through fog.

His chest tightened.

"Mother," he whispered, voice unsteady.

Her smile was soft, sad, radiant. She moved like song, elegant and slow, shimmering at the edges like something only half-tethered to the living world. Her hair was braided down her back in a dark chord. Her long fingers reached out.

"Thrush," she said, her voice music. "My beautiful, angry boy."

His father, taller and broader, approached. Smile wide. "Took you long enough."

Thrush blinked fast, shame creeping up his throat. "I'm sorry."

His mother cupped his face. "No more apologies. We understand now." She whistled a short trill like a songbird.

Thrush glanced away. "I was so angry with you both. For pestering me, for hovering, for suffocating me. For not explaining."

"We didn't know," his father said quietly. "None of us saw it until it was too late."

"It's back now," Nightingale said, brushing her thumb under his eye. "We saw it. The moment your soul stitched together again. We felt the shift. That lonely thread that's haunted our bloodline... it softened. A little."

Thrush swallowed. "The curse..."

Nightingale touched his chest. "You inherited my madness. My chaos. I'm so sorry for that. But it might not devour you now, not completely. The Raven King, your uncle, he lives with the effects of the curse every day."

His voice came out a cracked whisper. "You think it'll be easier now?"

"It won't be easy," his father said. "But it might not destroy you."

Thrush didn't respond right away.

The silence stretched.

Then, a shimmer appeared beside them like a tear in silk. The Veil ripped.

Through it, they could see his body sprawled in the cave. His skin was scorched, wings limp.

And above him a small, familiar shape hovered. Layla.

She was pressing her fingers to his lips. Blood. Her blood. She was healing him.

"She's okay," Thrush murmured, awe in his voice. "I didn't hurt her."

They watched as she whispered something to his body. Her expression was soft, determined, scared. And something else. She touched his skin, fingertips roaming over every part of him. She inspected his teeth, touched his hair and newly sprouted wings. It was intimate.

He wanted to touch her back but she was so far away.

The silence in the Astral stretched, a kind of peace that buzzed under his skin. His mother stood beside him, her eyes shimmering like star fields. His father watched from the edge of the stone archway, where Layla hovered beside his unconscious body.

Thrush's heart ached.

"She was never supposed to be part of this," he said quietly.

Nightingale shook her head. "That's not true."

He turned to her, confusion flickering across his face.

"She was the end of all this," Nightingale finished.

Thrush's brow furrowed. "I don't understand."

His mother placed a hand over his heart. "Your shadow. It's been searching for her."

Thrush went still.

"We've been watching the entire time but didn't understand." Nightingale's expression softened with something ancient and sorrowful. "It wasn't the book. It was her presence. Her closeness. It felt you waking up. And it followed the one thing it couldn't ignore."

"You mean…"

"She was near the portal. Both Peabody Library and in Lame Deer. The closest she's ever been to the Veil between your worlds," his father said. "Your shadow felt her. Recognized her. Hunted her. Reached out for her."

Thrush's throat tightened. He remembered the nightmares. The sleeplessness. The way his magic had flared wild and hot for weeks before Layla ever laid hands on the book.

"She was the missing thread," he whispered. "And I wanted her the moment I saw her. I didn't even know why."

His mother's eyes shimmered. "It's because a part of you already knew her. Already claimed her."

Thrush turned his gaze to the view below. Layla was brushing a hand through his hair, concern etched into her soft features. Even in the shadows of Hell, she glowed.

"She thinks she's ordinary," he murmured. "Just a girl who loves books."

Nightingale smiled faintly. "But your shadow knew better. It wanted her from the start."

"She steadied the pull inside you," his father added. "You're not unraveling anymore."

Thrush stared, stunned by the weight of it. Not cursed. Not just broken. Not alone.

He hadn't fallen for her.

He'd been drawn to her.

His shadow hadn't waited in the dark for vengeance or violence.

It had waited for *her*.

"She cares for you," Nightingale said, almost amused.

Thrush's throat tightened.

"I'm afraid," he admitted.

His mother raised an eyebrow. "Of what?"

"I'll hurt her," he said. "She's only human. She's break-able. Fragile. She doesn't understand what I am. What I've done." He pointed to the split in the Veil. "Look at me now. I have... *wings*."

His father chuckled under his breath. "Look again, boy."

Thrush peered closer through the shimmer of the veil and suddenly he saw her, really saw her. The lingering threads of a bond in her blood. The glowing scar on her wrist. The imprint left by the shadow. The bite.

His mouth went dry.

"She's not completely human anymore," his father said.

"She might be the only one who can survive you," Nightingale added softly.

Thrush turned back to them, his heart aching with confusion and hope and old fear.

"I don't know how to be whole," he said.

His mother leaned in and kissed his forehead. "Then learn, Thrush. She's already trying to love you. Stop pushing her away."

And then the light began to pull.

The veil rippled.

"I'm sorry," Thrush hush-shouted to his parents. "I'm sorry I pushed you away."

They were smiling, like they already knew.

And Thrush felt the weight of his body call him back.

CHAPTER 43

LAYLA SAT BESIDE HIM, KNEES PULLED UP AND resting her chin on them, watching the rise and fall of his chest with an obsessive kind of focus.

He was still alive.

She'd checked a dozen times.

Her blood still lingered on his lips. Some intuition in her had insisted it was the right thing. The only thing.

Now, he groaned faintly.

His body shifted.

He inhaled sharply.

Layla scrambled forward, heart crashing against her ribs. "Thrush?"

His lashes fluttered and he blinked once, twice. He grimaced, then licked his lips.

"What happened?" he rasped, voice low. "What... did you do?"

Layla bit her lip, nervous, but not sorry.

"I did the only thing that made sense," she said. "You were barely breathing. You were unconscious. You were dying. So I gave you..." she hesitated, then lifted her hand, showing the faint pink dot on her fingertip, "a little bit of my blood."

Thrush's eyes darkened—not with hunger, but something deeper. Anger? Regret?

"No," he growled, sitting up too quickly, face twisted in pain. "You shouldn't have done that. You don't know what that means."

"It's okay," she said quietly, not looking away. "I don't exactly have much going for me right now. It's the least I could do. I think. I wasn't going to watch you die." Her chin trembled and she felt hot tears collecting in the corners of her eyes.

Silence stretched between them, thick with tension.

Then he grabbed her.

His hands tangled in her dress, pulling her into his lap. Her gasp caught in her throat as she landed against his chest, his heartbeat thunderous beneath her palm.

"You're reckless," he said, voice low and furious.

"Librarians can be. I used to steal books for Rue all the time."

His mouth crashed against hers, fierce and desperate. He'd been waiting lifetimes for this moment. It was as if he didn't know how else to say thank you or I'm sorry or I want you so badly it scares me.

Layla melted against him, hands sliding across his shoulders and gripping the back of his neck, her body singing from the contact. She felt his wings shift around her like a shield. His breath hitched when she kissed him back just as hard.

When he finally pulled away, their foreheads pressed

together and breath ragged, she whispered, "I've been wanting you to do that to me for a long time now."

His voice was a broken prayer. "What are we doing, Layla?"

Her smile was soft, aching. "Surviving. Together. That's what we're doing."

His hands slid to her waist, still trembling. "You have no idea what you've done to me or what this means for you."

She met his gaze, unafraid. "Good. I guess it's the least I could do after you healed my broken arm and fixed my glasses that one time."

He kissed her again, hard. His mouth drifted to her jaw, teeth scraping her neck.

Layla's lips were still tingling when Thrush kissed her over and over again.

His hands were careful on her waist, as if afraid she might shatter beneath him.

Her voice trembled, part nerves, part desire, and complete curiosity. "Thrush... what are you?"

His brow furrowed, lips brushing hers as he whispered, "I'm not sure. Something different than what I've always thought. But... I saw my parents. In the astral."

She blinked, surprised. "Your parents?" She scanned his face. "The Astral. You were dead?"

He nodded, gaze slipping toward the mouth of the cave like he was expecting someone to walk in. "They told me... something's changed. I was missing a part of myself. But not any longer."

His tone turned hoarse, pained.

Layla reached for his face. "What do you want now? Now that you have that answer?

His reply was wordless. He kissed her again, hungrier. His hands tangled in her curls, wrapped around the back of her neck, and pulled her closer until their chests were flush.

Layla made a small noise in the back of her throat and then all clothes were shed in a frenzy of heat and shadow. Every touch between them burned; his calloused fingers against her soft skin, her lips along his jaw, both of them moving as if lit by fast burning fire.

He touched her throat, fingertips drifting to her collarbone, across skin, between her breasts. Down. Down. Down. He yanked the skirt of her dress up.

"Layla," Thrush whispered. "You should wear something like this for me."

She'd closed her eyes, unable to focus on anything besides the heat of his hands on her skin. She bit her bottom lip and nodded. "Anything you want."

"Anything?"

"Sure."

His hand slid up her thigh. "This?" Teeth scraped her shoulder.

"Please," Layla begged.

She hadn't wanted anything to touch her at the Black Mansion, but Thrush... she'd let him touch her all day long. She shivered in his arms, shifted her body so she was straddling him.

Then suddenly, he stopped.

"We can't do this right now," he murmured.

Layla sighed in disappointment.

"You deserve better than the stone floor of this cave." He looked down at himself. "And I'm filthy. And you're..."

"I'm fine," Layla said.

"You're bruised and injured and barely dressed. I don't know what you saw at the Black Mansion but you're probably traumatized." He looked around. "I wish I had clothing here for you."

"It's okay," her voice was soft. She'd never been so disappointed in her entire life but he was making sense. She could barely see without her glasses and they were both filthy and the cave wasn't exactly plush. She imagined she'd be covered in a million bruises if they'd gone much further. "What I saw at the Mansion wasn't nearly as bad as being dragged into the ground and being sold by a goat herder."

He frowned before leaning around her and checking outside. "Sunrise will be soon." He touched her hair. "Let's rest and we'll leave in the morning."

Layla nodded and moved off his lap.

She started to get further away but Thrush grabbed her around the waist and pulled her closer. He slipped his folded arm under her head like a pillow and tucked her tightly against his body. "You'll be warmer next to me," he promised as one dark wing shifted over them.

CHAPTER 44

LAYLA WOKE FIRST.

The cave was warmer, the heat from Thrush's body pressed along her back. She shifted and his arm tightened around her waist, tugging her back. His wings were half-draped across them both, catching little flecks of morning light.

"Stay," he murmured, voice rasped and heavy with sleep.

Layla tilted her head to glance back at him. His eyes, though still tired, watched her like she might vanish.

"We should get back," she said.

He snuggled against her. "I changed my mind. We can stay here. This was my home for longer than most places."

Layla moved up on her elbows and looked around. "You lived here?"

He didn't answer at first, just exhaled deeply and leaned forward, brushing his lips along the back of her shoulder. "I did."

They lay in silence for a moment, the faint drip of water echoing through the cave's stone belly.

"This place," he said eventually, gesturing vaguely at their surroundings, "was mine. For a long time. When I first ran away from everything. Hellion duties, my family trying to escape the curse. I came here."

Stone shelves lined the wall, holding mismatched pieces of pottery and canned goods. A long bench, clearly carved by hand, sat near the fire pit. A tarp was folded neatly beside a flat stone slab he'd probably used as a table.

"I stole that chair from a Hellion barracks two valleys over," he said with a crooked grin. "And the blankets from a spoiled prince's outpost. I stole most of the food too. But the basilisks, I claimed those fair and square."

Layla's brow furrowed. "Wait... basilisks?" She accentuated the s.

He nodded, amused. "I've got many."

She sat up, her voice caught in her throat. "There was a giant snake at the river. It nearly ate me. Maybe it was some kind of a dragon."

Thrush barked a laugh. "They wouldn't eat you once they figured out you were mine."

Layla shivered. "I wasn't exactly wearing a nametag."

Thrush sobered, watching her with something softer than humor. "I'm sorry you went through all of that alone. I wish I could have been with you."

"It's okay," she whispered. "Can't change it now."

Thrush's gaze sharpened. "Tell me what happened at the Black Mansion."

Layla hesitated. She twisted a strand of hair between her fingers, then let out a breath. "I wasn't harmed. Not really.

But they looked at me like I was fresh meat. Asmodeus showed me off like a prize."

Thrush's jaw clenched.

"I wasn't too scared," she continued. "I've heard Rue talk about the bloodlust. I saw it in action. It was everywhere. And I," she looked down, ashamed, "I felt different. I wasn't afraid. I was intrigued. I thought maybe..." She shook her head, chasing away the thought. "And then the angel came."

She looked up. "He killed everyone. And I ran."

Thrush sat up beside her, silent. The glow of the sunlight caught the edge of his jaw, his skin still dusted with char from the magic blast. Layla reached for his hand.

"The shadow was there too," she added quietly. "The one who kept saving me. The one I thought was haunting me."

Thrush's hand twitched under hers.

"That wasn't just any shadow," he said. "It was mine. My other half. We were split years ago. I think... I think I did it to survive. Sent it back to Hell to protect me from something I couldn't handle. But it left me unbalanced. Broken. I couldn't control anything. My magic, my anger, myself."

Layla swallowed. "But you're better now? I can tell. You seem...relaxed."

Thrush nodded slowly. "I think so. I felt it when you touched me. When the shadow came back."

She shifted closer, letting her forehead press against his. "Then maybe now... you can stop running."

His hand rose to her cheek, thumb brushing lightly under her eye. "Okay."

She smiled. "It was you at the Black Mansion. Your shadow, you: they are one in the same. So you were there, we just didn't realize it."

He was watching her.

"Do you think Asmodeus died?" Layla asked. "There was something about him I don't trust. I hope I never see him ever again in my life."

Thrush stretched, his wings brushing the cave ceiling, the joints flexing as if still getting used to their presence. The golden light of morning had begun to filter through the cracks in the stone, painting the cave in soft amber.

"We should get moving," he said, turning to Layla.

Layla, still pulling on her dress and brushing dust from the skirt, gave him a look. "I don't have any real clothing. No shoes."

He grinned, teeth flashing. "I've got wings now. I could fly you back, princess-style."

Layla straightened, eyeing the large, dark wings suspiciously. "Have you ever flown before?"

He paused. "Well... no. But how hard can it be?"

She narrowed her eyes. "We're walking."

Thrush laughed. "Suit yourself. You sure you don't want me to fix your vision?" he asked gently, tilting his head toward her. "It wouldn't take much."

She hesitated, touching her face as though her glasses were still there. "No. I like my glasses. They're part of who I am."

"Part of your charm, little librarian," he murmured, before clearing his throat and turning back toward the mouth of the cave. "Alright, then. Come on, four-eyes."

She laughed and swatted at him. "Rude." She pulled the busted frames from her dress and held them out. "Can you fix these again?"

Thrush held his big hand over hers, light pouring out, and when he moved it away Layla's glasses were repaired.

"You'll come in handy, I guess," she giggled as she put the glasses on. "Finally, I can see again."

She was staring at Thrush.

"What?" he asked.

"The wings. You... you're magnificent." She swallowed hard.

THEY LEFT THE CAVE, THE FOREST CLOSING around them. Thrush stayed close, one hand at the small of her back whenever the terrain shifted or tree roots threatened to trip her. Every sound made her tense; branches creaking or distant moans and howls, but he stayed calm with eyes scanning, ready to burn the world down if anything touched her again.

The trees began to thin and gravel crunched beneath their feet as a winding, narrow road came into view.

Layla exhaled. "Civilization."

"More or less," Thrush muttered.

She glanced sideways at him, lips twitching. "No flying."

"I get it," he said with a smirk. "But for the record... I would never drop you."

She gave him a look. "You already did." She rubbed her ribs. "Or at least your shadow did when it dragged me here. Dropped me right on the flooring of the cave. I think it bruised my ribs."

That shut him up for a beat.

"I can heal them," Thrush finally offered. "Your ribs. If they still hurt."

Layla tiptoed around sharp stones. "You can't just go on healing me and fixing my glasses and using all of your magic making yourself weak. I'll heal."

"I promised not to hurt you and I did." His voice was drawn.

"Hey." Layla reached for his arm, forcing him to stop. "I'm fine. Sorry, I was teasing. I'm fine." She held up her hand. "I'm no longer turning into a shadow so all is good. And I'm no longer being sold to demons so even better."

Layla stepped carefully, one hand grazing Thrush's arm now and then for balance.

"This looks slightly familiar," Layla muttered. "I hear the river." She backed away from the tree line, heart pounding. "I, I can't. That monster was in the river."

Thrush glanced toward the woods. "The Black River is on the other side of the road, past some trees."

"I don't want to go near it," she said breathlessly. "There was a thing. A giant snake thing. It almost ate me."

He stepped in front of her, his wings catching the light. "They won't come after you while I'm here."

Layla gave him a look. "That's weird."

Thrush smiled faintly and took her hand. "You're safe with me."

She exhaled and nodded once. "Okay. Okay. Let's just keep going."

They followed the road a little further until a figure came into view, hunched, familiar, leading a line of curious goats.

Layla stopped. Her blood turned hot.

"That's the goat herder who sold me."

The man saw them. Saw her. And went pale beneath the Helldust smudging his skin.

His attention turned to Thrush, confusion crossing his face.

"You!" she hissed, stepping forward. "Bastard!"

"I, I had no choice," the man stammered. "He paid well, Asmodeus paid."

Layla raised a hand like she might slap him from ten feet away.

Thrush stepped beside her, a shadow stretching tall and dangerous. "Want me to kill him?"

The goat herder's eyes bulged.

Layla blinked, caught off guard. "What?"

"Quick. Painless. Or not painless. Your call."

She looked at him in disbelief. "No! Of course not! You can't just kill people."

"That's a demon." Thrush shrugged, unbothered. "And this is Hell, Layla. Consequences look different down here."

"Yeah, well... I'm not sure how I feel about deciding someone's death." Her voice trembled.

Thrush watched at her for a long moment, head tilted.

His voice softened, just a touch. "You might need to stop playing by your human rules. Because down here..." He looked back at the goat herder, whose trembling hands were barely holding his herd in check. "Mercy is weakness."

"Don't ask me something like that. Especially now. I can't deal with it," Layla said, her chin lifting.

Thrush grinned. "Let's keep moving."

As they walked away, the goat herder dropped to his knees in relief.

And Thrush didn't stop watching him until they disappeared around the bend.

When they were out of earshot, he whispered to Layla, "You should have let me kill him because now the rest of his days he will live in torment, anticipating my return."

"I'm fine with that," Layla replied.

Layla never thought she'd be so happy to see a row of Jeep Grand Cherokees on the side of the road.

Three figures leaned against the vehicles, weapons at their sides, watching them approach.

Remington was the first to straighten.

"Well," he said, voice low and unreadable. "Looks like the prodigal asshole returns. With wings."

Thrush stepped into view, his wings flaring in the breeze behind him like storm clouds. "Yeah, yeah. Don't get jealous."

Remington's gaze narrowed. "I'm not jealous."

Chel, lounging against the passenger door, lifted one thick brow. "You sound jealous."

Remington shot him a look.

Chel just grinned. "He's older, Remm. Time comes for everyone. You'll get yours."

"You better hope so," Remington muttered.

Dacre said nothing. He nodded once at Thrush then gave Layla a long, searching look.

Layla wrapped her arms around herself, suddenly unsure what to say. These were the people Rue had trusted: Remington, Dacre, Chel. They felt like a pack. Tight-knit. Deadly.

Remington's tone gentled slightly. "You alright?"

"I'm fine," she said. "Wishing I had a coat, but fine."

Chel tilted his head before opening the door to the vehicle nearest him.

He pulled out a heavy blanket and passed it to Thrush.

Thrush shook the blanket out and draped it over Layla. She shivered as his fingers brushed her neck.

Thrush helped her into one of the back seats, then slid in beside her. His wings had to fold awkwardly, cramped between the seat and door, but he didn't complain.

Remington started the engine. "Everyone buckled in?"

Layla nodded.

"Good. Let's get you home."

Home. Layla's mind was swirling. She'd essentially lost her apartment. And her room at the ranch was far from here. This place... could it be a home?

Thrush reached across the seat and touched her hand.

The convoy growled to life. As they pulled away, the wheels kicked up gravel and ash. Layla rested her head against the cool window, watching the forest blur by. For the first time in what felt like days, she exhaled a breath of relief. She glanced at Thrush from the corner of her eye, studying him. He still seemed a bit broody, but calm. Way calmer than she'd ever seen him before.

CHAPTER 45

THE OFFICE WAS QUIETER THAN USUAL. THRUSH stepped inside, his posture rigid despite the new weight on his back. The wings felt foreign, like a heavy blanket draped over his shoulders.

Meg looked up from the head of the long wooden table, a flicker of satisfaction flashing in her eyes. "Well, well. Look who glowed up."

Sparrow leaned back in his chair with a smirk. "Took you long enough."

Thrush didn't respond right away. He folded his arms across his chest, wings shifting behind him. "It wasn't exactly a choice."

"Transformation rarely is," Meg said. She stood and circled him once, inspecting him like he was some rare magical artifact. "You seem different now. Balanced. I can feel it. Your magic isn't screaming to escape your body any longer."

He nodded once, tightly. "It was my shadow. It returned to me."

Meg was nodding. "Rue had a vision. She saw your shadow-self separate in the Nightjar's pond just before the war."

Thrush's head tipped to the side as memories came to the forefront. He remembered feeling out of sorts in Heaven when he was there as a teenager. He was so unlike himself that he couldn't handle being there and even planned to run away.

"And the girl?" Sparrow asked, voice deceptively casual.

Thrush hesitated. "Layla's... fine. A little rattled with the things she's seen." He ran a hand through disheveled hair. "I don't know what to do. She's torn between two worlds. She doesn't seem confused about any of this. It's strange."

"Some humans don't scare easily," Meg said with a shrug. "Some see things that would make our eyes fall out."

"I don't want her to go back." Thrush was looking out the window at Meg's back. "I want her to stay."

"Heard your shadow bit her." Sparrow looked up.

Thrush shifted his balance and looked down.

Meg sat, leveling him with her blue stare. "Bite her again, Thrush."

His eyes went wide. "What?"

"You heard me," Meg said, calm and lethal. "Go find an empty room and give her the night of her life. Give her the time of her life, please dear God. She's put up with your bad attitude for months. Poor girl deserves some fun, at least."

Sparrow snorted. "It's the least you can do after dragging her halfway through Hell."

Thrush's jaw tensed. "It wasn't intentional."

Meg ignored him. "You did this to her. She's marked.

The Astral left fingerprints in her soul. Do you know what that means?"

"She'll never be the same," Thrush said quietly.

"She might not care," Meg replied. "Losing a piece of herself to this, to you, might be worth it to her. She clearly has a thing for you."

Sparrow dropped his feet to the floor and stood. "She doesn't need to go home. She needs you. Whole. Claim her properly. Don't break the poor girl's heart."

The room was silent.

Thrush swallowed. His hands clenched at his sides, wings folding in close.

"I don't want to hurt her," he said.

"Then don't," Meg said simply. "But don't pretend ignoring her and the bond between you both is safer. Go. Or you'll break her heart and then wind up with one of those demon girls from the shops with no sense of purpose and horns. Pick Layla. She's cute. She'll look good in family pictures."

Thrush tapped his fingers, eager to let something surprising loose but, knowing better, he left the room with a purposeful stride.

Chapter 46

The water was still warm, despite how long Layla had been soaking. The massive clawfoot tub could've fit three people and the fragrant oils someone had left behind filled the air with the scent of smoke, clove, and something sweet she couldn't name.

Layla tilted her head back against the rim of the tub, water lapping at her collarbones. Her hair was now clean with no more blood or smoke clinging to the ends. Her body was sore, still tender from the bruises and scrapes and sleeping on the stone floor of the cave, but she felt more like herself again.

Mostly. Her fingers rubbed over the small scars on her wrist.

She turned toward the sink where her glasses sat neatly folded on a silk cloth. She'd spent too many days half-blinded without them. Having them far away generated an unease in her chest. She didn't like not being able to see.

She pushed herself from the water, wrapping one of the impossibly soft towels around her, then tugged on a warm robe. It was loose cotton that fell below her knees. Everything in this castle was huge, built and made for bigger people. No wonder Rue created a home on the earthen plane.

She looked in the mirror and wondered if maybe she should ditch the glasses. If Thrush could use his magic to heal her eyes, maybe that would be just fine. She put the glasses on and turned her head, and tucked the blond, wet curls behind her ears. She could always wear clear lenses if she got her eyes fixed. She took them off again, not really recognizing herself without them. Layla sighed. She wasn't going to make the decision today.

A knock came at the door. Two soft raps.

Her stomach flipped. "Please be dinner," she muttered, padding across the stone floor.

She opened the door.

It wasn't dinner.

Thrush stood there, white-blonde hair falling in his eyes, his clothes clean. His wings were tucked in tight, his arms tense at his sides.

Layla blinked up at him, clutching the edge of her robe. "Hey."

His eyes swept over her, gaze catching on the edge of her collarbone, the glasses back on her face. "You look..."

"Clean?" she offered with a small smile.

His lips twitched, but he didn't smile. "I didn't think you'd answer the door." He looked around the doorframe, noting the runes etched in the wood. "You should be more careful. I could have been a demon or... something."

"I thought you were a sandwich or steak or whatever it is you all eat for dinner here."

That earned her a real smile, small and crooked. So few times she'd seen Thrush smile. He looked like a boy.

They stood there in the doorway, the space between them heavy with unspoken words.

Layla's voice softened. "Did something happen?" She moved hair away from her face.

Thrush hesitated. "Can I come in?"

She stepped back without answering, pulling the door wider.

He entered like someone walking into a church-not slow, but humble. He looked around the room at the towels and the steam still curling in the bathroom. Her glasses were drifting down her nose as she pushed them up.

"Your glasses are still in once piece," he said. "Must be a record, it's been nearly a day."

"Yeah." She touched the edge of the frame. "Little miracle, I guess." She smiled.

His throat worked like he wanted to say something but couldn't.

So she filled the silence. "Are you okay? After everything? You seem different."

He nodded, but it wasn't convincing.

"I'm fine. You?"

She swallowed. "Umm, well, I think I'll survive but that was an adventure."

They looked at each other. Something between them drew tight and he moved closer.

"I didn't come here to talk," Thrush said finally, voice low.

Her heart jumped. "Oh?"

"But we can. If you want to."

Layla stepped closer, her voice barely above a whisper. "No... I think I know why you're here."

His eyes darkened, wings shifting slightly behind him.

She reached for his hand. "Close the door, Thrush."

The door latch clicked. The lock thudded into place.

"You still bit me without permission..." Layla was watching him. Her voice was soft but did sound a little desperate, a bit breathy. She couldn't help it. "A part of you did at least."

Thrush stood close enough that the heat from his body warmed the air between them. His wings arched slightly behind him like shadows braced to catch her if she decided to run.

He tilted his head, eyes half-lidded as he looked down at her. "Would it have mattered?" His voice was a husky rasp. "Permission, I mean?"

Layla blinked. Her heart hammered in her chest.

"I saw the way you looked at me in the coffee shop the very first time I saw you," he continued. "There was something there. Instant. Electric. You felt it, didn't you?"

She licked her lips, throat dry, and nodded in agreement. "Perhaps. I was completely exhausted that day though. After carrying those giant books for Rue, I might not have been in my right mind." She sighed dramatically.

Thrush took another step closer. He was crowding her, surrounding her.

"I'll ask now," he murmured, voice barely controlled. "Please, Layla... I'm begging. I'm aching. I'm burning up inside. Ever since the first moment I saw you, you've never left my mind."

A shiver crawled up her spine.

She bit her lip. "What... what will you do to me?"

He reached for her, his fingers brushing the side of her throat. She tipped her chin up without thinking, exposing the vulnerable line of her neck.

"I'm going to put my mouth right here," he said, his voice molten. "My teeth. I'm going to taste you like no one ever has."

Her whole body flushed, breath catching. Heat pooled low in her belly and she felt like her knees were going to give out. He sure had a way with words.

"Okay," she said, barely above a whisper.

He stilled. "Just okay? I will bite you. I will drink your blood."

Layla closed her eyes, heart pounding. "Please do it." The words came out as a whisper. A prayer.

He groaned softly, as if the word had gutted him. "It was trying to bring us together."

Her eyes fluttered open. "What was?"

He touched his chest lightly, as though feeling the spot where his shadow had once been torn away. "The other part of me. It was trying to connect us... the whole time."

"Why would it do that?" she asked, voice shaking, not from fear, but from something deeper.

"It must've known." He stepped in closer, his fingers brushing hair away from her face. "That even though you're snappy and small, and your hair is wild, and you can't see a damn thing without these..."

He gently plucked the glasses from her face, holding them like something fragile. Then, he set them gently on the bedside table.

"...I find you utterly irresistible."

Layla smiled, wide and unguarded, and it was the most beautiful thing Thrush had ever seen.

He leaned in. "May I?" He licked his lips. "I think I remember your taste. You fed your blood to me in that cave."

"I was afraid you were going to die." Layla shivered.

"You feared for my safety? All this talk of permission, Layla, and I think you gave it a long time ago." His voice was dark. "I think you *want* this."

Memories of writhing bodies in the Black Mansion fluttered through her mind. Heat flooded her veins. Things had gotten hot and heavy for a few minutes after he'd regained consciousness but she could tell he was holding back.

The room was quiet, bathed in the golden light from the windows. The shadows danced along the stone walls, but Layla only watched him. She watched the way his wings flexed and then lowered as he moved closer.

"We've played this game for months." Thrush's voice was rough.

"I agree." She reached out to grip his arm. "Will it hurt?"

A faint, crooked smile touched his lips. "I'll distract you. I think I can find plenty of ways to distract you, little librarian."

His mouth covered hers in a kiss that was not tentative, not gentle, but hungry. Desperate. His tongue slid past her lips, coaxing, claiming. She leaned into it, into him, gasping as his hands gripped her hips and pulled her flush against his body.

Her robe slipped to the side as his fingers found bare skin, dragging along her waist, his touch warm.

Her knees buckled, breath shuddering. He pulled her up and eased her onto the bed, never breaking the kiss. His body hovered over hers, heat rolling off him in waves, his wings spreading to either side of them like a dark shroud.

His lips left hers to trail down her jaw, over the pulse at her neck.

"I've wanted this," he whispered, voice like embers. "Since the coffee shop. Since the forest. Since you looked at me like I wasn't a monster even though I think I will always be one."

"I never thought you were," she breathed.

His hand curled behind her neck. "You should have. The White Horse will damn me for taking you. You are her creature."

He kissed the hollow of her throat and she gasped, her fingers fisting in his shirt. His teeth grazed her skin and she arched beneath him, the anticipation melting into need.

"I'll go slow," he murmured.

"Please don't," she said, surprising them both.

He growled softly, eyes flashing with something dark.

"I want to feel it," she added, voice shaking but firm. "I want to feel you."

"Layla..."

She reached for him, threading her fingers through his white hair, guiding his mouth back to hers. Her legs wrapped around his waist as she clung to him. Her hips rotated against his and he groaned, gripping her and forcing her to stop moving.

"I just..." His body went still. "I don't want to hurt you. Your body is much smaller than mine."

"Are you afraid you won't fit?" she asked. "You'll never

know until you try." She nipped his lips in jest. "Please try, don't leave me like this."

That was all he needed. He grabbed the tie of her robe and tugged it loose, revealing her body. He leaned back, taking her in, then rubbed his face.

Layla moved up on her elbows. "You better start moving, princeling."

He crawled over her until she lay back. His hand drifted up her leg, gripping her waist and squeezing, then up to her ribcage. His thumb brushed the underside of her breast and Layla shivered.

She reached for him, hands exploring his shoulders and the hard angles and planes of his sides and abdomen.

"When you touch me like that I want to explode," Thrush warned.

Layla's hand drifted down his front and reached into his waistband. She kept going until she found him hard and wrapped her hand around him.

Thrush groaned and pressed his forehead against hers. His hand moved to the vee of her thighs and pressed in, testing her. He pressed a finger inside as his mouth fell to hers, tongue exploring her mouth as his fingers explored below. Layla made small noises of pleasure, unable to stop her hips from moving as he tested and pressed a second finger inside, stretching her.

Layla broke away from his mouth, "Oh god, Thrush," she cried, "don't stop."

His mouth moved to her neck and he licked and sucked. She was frantically trying to unbuckle his belt and pull his shirt up.

"Why are you still dressed?" she asked.

He laughed lightly and pulled away, moving off the bed.

Layla made a noise of disappointment when his fingers left her.

He was watching her as he pulled the shirt over his head and dropped it. He kicked off his boots.

Layla licked her lips. He looked good, too good. No man should look like him. Pale skin, light hair, his eyes turned to blue. He smirked. So cocky.

Layla watched him from half-lidded eyes. "I'm getting bored," she warned with a smirk of her own.

He shucked his pants off and tossed them aside.

Layla's breath hitched as she took him in. The physique, the wings, the look on his face like she was the only thing on his mind.

He crawled across the end of the bed, grabbed her ankle, and jerked her down to meet him.

Layla squealed then moaned and arched her back as he started kissing and licking her belly. His mouth moved up, sucking the skin over her ribcage then the soft spot between her breasts.

"One day I will feed from you here," he promised.

"Okay," she gasped, "I can't wait."

Large hands slid under her back and down to her ass. He sat back and lifted her hips to his mouth. "And one day, from here."

Layla nodded before he licked her lips. She hissed and closed her eyes as his tongue probed and laved. She was hot and tingling, ready to explode. He was feasting on her and she couldn't move under his grip.

One throb in her lower belly struck as she was about to explode, then he pulled away.

"No," Layla begged.

He moved off the bed and dragged her down to the edge of the mattress. "Don't worry, we aren't finished," he promised.

Thrush grabbed her hips and flipped her, positioning her so she was on her belly, bent over the bed and her lower half dangling.

She looked back, felt the smooth nudge as he positioned himself and pressed inside.

"Oh god," Layla bit her lip, enjoying the stretch and the burn.

He went still.

"Oh god no," Layla begged, "don't stop. Don't stop now."

He leaned over her, chest to her back, his hand sliding down her shoulder and arm, threading his fingers between hers and pressing her hand into the mattress. "Tell me if it's too much," he said.

Layla nodded.

Thrush's other hand slid under her body. He brushed her nipple, pressed against her ribcage, then slid down her belly and between her thighs.

Layla was surrounded by him and it felt too good.

His hips shifted and he thrust into her as his fingers stretched to the nub between her thighs and rubbed slowly.

The heel of his hand pressed against her lower belly and she suddenly felt incredibly full. He moved again, thrusting softly, and Layla felt the scrape of his teeth against her shoulder. She tilted her head to the side, giving him access to her neck. He kissed her there, lips lingering.

"You feel so good," he whispered. "So tight. So wet. So hot."

She shivered. "Don't stop."

He didn't. His body moved with hers, his fingers working her over as he became incredibly hard inside her. Suddenly Layla felt her body flush and burn. She opened her mouth in silent scream as something sharp bit into her shoulder. It didn't hurt. It made the stars behind her eyelids brighter. It made her feel every inch of him. Every touch. Every place where his body touched hers. And when his hips rested against her backside and he throbbed inside of her, Layla smiled and sighed.

"Why did we wait so long to try this?" she asked, body tingling.

CHAPTER 47

THE FIRE IN THE HEARTH HAD NEARLY BURNED out, reduced to glowing embers. Warmth still clung to her skin. It was him.

Layla stirred beneath the blanket, her gaze already fixed on him.

Thrush.

He was facing her, one arm slung across the bed, hair mussed and wild against the pillow. His breathing was even, finally still, and she knew in the marrow of her bones that he hadn't slept like this in years.

She remembered the way he'd tossed and turned back at the ranch; the restless pacing outside the guest rooms and the night he'd worked on the fence in darkness rather than face sleep or his demons.

Now... he was whole.

His chest rose and fell with a steady rhythm, one that soothed her in ways she couldn't explain. She traced the slope of his bare shoulder with her eyes, watching the subtle twitch in the muscle there. The curse, she thought. It hadn't disappeared. Not fully. But maybe now that his shadow had returned, it could be healed. Softened. Not so brutal on him.

Her hand moved before she could think and she brushed her fingers along the edge of one folded wing.

It was softer than she expected, a strange mix of down, warmth, and weight. Her breath caught.

She glanced at her hand.

It wasn't black anymore.

No shadow stain. No eerie blotch tinting her skin. She turned it over, then over again, hardly believing it.

Her heart beat faster. She touched her neck where his mouth had been. No punctures, no lingering ache. Just skin.

She exhaled a breath.

She wasn't turning into a shadow.

She was still herself.

Still Layla.

After a long moment of stillness, she sat up carefully, pulling the blankets around herself. He didn't stir. His sleep held, deep and undisturbed.

She moved silently out of the bed, every muscle in her body aching after last night. She smiled to herself.

She found clothes neatly folded on the nearby dresser and put them on. She didn't want to leave and break the spell of their time together, but she needed answers. Rue and Evelyn might have them.

She cast one last look at Thrush before she opened the door, slipping quietly into the corridor.

She left it slightly ajar.

Just in case he came looking.

LAYLA STEPPED SOFTLY INTO THE LIBRARY, blinking as the golden light spilled across endless shelves. It smelled like old paper, lavender oil, and, merciful gods, coffee.

Evelyn looked up from a scroll at the main table and smiled. "Morning."

Rue popped up from behind a stack of tomes, holding a mug in each hand. "You're alive," she said, eyes twinkling. "And, more importantly, you're vertical. And your glasses are on!"

"I brought coffee," Evelyn added, as if that were the most important thing in the world.

It was.

Layla groaned gratefully and nearly collapsed into the nearest chair. "I could kiss both of you."

Rue handed her a steaming mug. "Maybe after we talk about why you look like you've just been through a dark fairytale and came out the other side beautifully ravaged."

Evelyn grinned.

"I have," Layla said, wrapping her hands around the mug. The first sip made her moan. "This might be better though."

Evelyn chuckled, settling beside her. "Are you okay?"

Layla went quiet for a moment, staring into her coffee.

"I think so," she said slowly. "I don't really feel that different. Not physically, anyway."

"But?" Rue asked, gently.

Layla looked up. "Thrush seems... different. Calmer.

Like he's not battling a hurricane inside his chest every second. I'm relieved. I'm happy for him."

"But you're worried," Evelyn guessed.

Layla nodded. "About the curse. About what it means for him. I still don't understand it completely, but I'm afraid it's lurking inside him, like it's waiting. Watching him. Like it might come back worse than before."

Rue folded her arms on the table, leaning closer. "You're not wrong. The curse is generational and Astral in origin. It doesn't just go away. But he's not alone anymore. That might be the difference."

Layla sipped again, this time slower. "He told me about his parents. About the cave. About stealing furniture and claiming basilisks like they were pets."

Evelyn frowned. "Yup, that's exactly what he was doing out there living like a wild boy. Saw it myself." She shivered and made a face.

"And I..." Layla hesitated. "I think I'm more afraid of what it'll do to him than anything else. He'd rather burn himself out keeping it inside than risk hurting anyone. He still doesn't believe he deserves peace."

"You gave him peace," Rue said softly.

"For now," Layla whispered. "But what happens when it flares again? What if the shadow separating was just a symptom of something bigger? What if he breaks all over again?"

Evelyn reached across the table and rested a hand over hers. "Then we help him. All of us. Together. Again."

Layla blinked hard, throat tight.

"Besides," Rue added with a smirk, "he looked like a wreck until you came along. If anyone's going to keep him grounded, it's the small snappy librarian who sees the world better than most people, glasses or not."

"And steals books from the rare books section," Evelyn teased.

Layla snorted. "Thanks."

Rue's expression turned serious. "Are you okay after the Black Mansion?" She glanced to Evelyn.

Layla's lips snapped shut.

"All three of us have been there. That place has touched us." Rue looked concerned. "They locked me in a basement and tried to drown me in a cage."

Evelyn raised her hand. "A demon named Alastor kidnapped me, drank my blood, then tried to sell me to the highest bidder."

Layla sucked in a gasp. "Oh my gosh, I didn't know. You both never told me."

"We didn't really have the context to tell you. If we just blurted it out over coffee before you'd been pulled into this mess, you would have thought we were absolutely crazed."

Layla shrugged. "You have a point."

"What happened to the ones who kidnapped you?" Layla asked Rue.

"Dacre killed them," she replied flatly.

Layla looked to Evelyn. "And what about the one who took you?"

"Remington slit his throat." Her voice had the same tone. "What happened to the one who took you?"

Layla cleared her throat. "Well, an angel showed up and burned everyone in the room. And then I ran as fast as I could out of there." She shrugged. "So, I'm not sure if he's truly dead."

"What was his name?" Rue asked.

"Asmodeus."

Rue moved closer and wrapped her arm around Layla's shoulders. "I'm sorry that happened. My parents have been trying to shut down the Black Mansion for a long time now. The building is enchanted, it moves from place to place every time someone takes over the skin trades."

"Explain the skin trades," Layla said.

"Well, human blood is forbidden in Hell. So of course, it's a delicacy. Some demons will pay greatly for human blood, and a real live human is worth so much more. They used to steal human women from the earthen plane and sell them, but that stopped when my mother took the throne."

"That is awful." Layla pushed a lock of curls behind her ear.

Evelyn touched Layla's hand. "Just know you're not alone if you need to talk about it. We've been there. We've seen it."

CHAPTER 48

THRUSH ROUNDED A CORNER TOO FAST, ALMOST knocking over a decorative vase as he stalked down the hallway barefoot and half-dressed. His shirt clung to his back, his wings still twitching with the aftermath of sleep– and the absence of the woman who should've still been tangled in his sheets.

Where the hell was she?

He turned another corner and almost slammed into Remington, who raised a brow and took in Thrush's very clear look of morning-after madness.

"She bolt?" Remington asked, sipping from a mug that definitely wasn't coffee.

Thrush scowled. "She's not in bed."

"I gathered that. Your wings are flaring. Tuck them in. You look obnoxious. Like a peacock."

Dacre leaned out of the Hellion lair doorway just in time to see the exchange. "He looks feral. Did you bite her too hard?"

"I didn't bite her too hard," Thrush growled. "And I didn't expect her to vanish."

"Oh, he's spiraling," Dacre said to Remington. "Maybe he fucked her too hard. Or not hard enough."

Anger flared through Thrush's veins and he stepped forward to grab Dacre.

Dacre laughed. "Whoa, princeling. I was just joking. I'm sure you did it just right." He winked.

Remington intervened. "Come on, we're calling a war council."

Thrush frowned. "For what?"

"Human women," Dacre said, grabbing Thrush by the shoulder and dragging him into the Hellion lair.

Remington tapped the table. "So. Humans are squishy."

"Emotionally volatile," Dacre added. "Not that I know because mine is far from human."

"They are also biteable," Remington said with a shrug. "And smell very nice."

Thrush narrowed his eyes. "What is this?"

"An intervention," Dacre said. "On behalf of her neck."

"You can't just feed whenever you're horny," Remington added. "That's not how it works. You'll fry her brain. Or worse, she'll get addicted and start sniffing your laundry when you're gone."

Thrush stared. "You are both so full of shit."

Remington tilted his mug. "Ask Evelyn. I caught her wearing one of my cloaks like a comfort blanket last week."

"Evelyn would never do that." Thrush scowled. "You don't even deserve her."

Remington slapped a palm over his heart. "Ouch. After all that pining and trying to avoid her."

Dacre raised a finger. "Back to the point. You need to pace yourself. Think sips, not gulps."

"Use a safe word," Remington said.

"She's a human," Thrush muttered. "She smells like temptation and everything I've never had."

"Don't romanticize it," Dacre warned. "That's how you end up writing poetry. And then we all suffer."

"I hate you both," Thrush said, rubbing his face. "She's probably in the library."

Remington nodded. "Good. Bring her coffee and don't stare at her neck the whole time."

Dacre crossed his arms. "And no more mysterious disappearances. If you're gonna vanish for soul-merging shadow magic, tell someone."

Thrush was already halfway to the door, but paused. "You two are the absolute worst creatures in all of the realms."

"Yet," Remington said with a grin, "still the best you've got."

Thrush groaned, flipped them both the bird and exited.

"Think he'll listen?" Dacre asked, sipping from Remington's mug. He coughed and paused making a face. "You start the day with straight fire whisky?"

"Some mornings require it," Remington shrugged. "I give it two days before the love birds are inseparable."

"Or she threatens to set him on fire."

Remington smirked. "True love." He took his mug away from Dacre and downed the rest of the fire whiskey in one gulp.

"Where's the Hellion?" Dacre asked. "He disappeared last night after we got back."

Remington shrugged. "I haven't seen him, but the table was covered in maps, an open bottle of something alcoholic, and, concerningly, a drawing of a woman's silhouette with various notes scribbled in the margins."

"Maybe you should ask the Queen where he is?" Dacre suggested.

"Nope. Don't want to get involved in that drama."

"I didn't think Hellions had time for drama." Dacre was headed for the door.

"This is Hell, it's total drama island all the time."

Chapter 49

Thrush strode into the library, breath still tight in his chest. He didn't bother to hide his steps or silence the rustle of his wings. He needed to see her. Now.

And then, there she was.

Curled in a window alcove with a steaming mug in hand, glasses perched on her nose, and talking softly to Rue and Evelyn, her face lit up when she saw him.

"You're awake," Layla said, standing quickly, coffee nearly sloshing over the rim. "I figured you'd sleep all day."

"You vanished," he said, a little more breathlessly than intended.

"You were asleep," she replied, taking a step toward him. "I didn't want to wake you. You finally looked at peace."

"I'm not at peace when you're not near me." His voice was low and rough as his arm curled around her waist.

Rue let out a hushed sound and slipped away with Evelyn, who gave Layla an encouraging squeeze of the shoulder on the way out.

They were alone now in the filtered glow of the library, ancient books surrounding them.

Layla smiled up at him. "Did you panic?"

"I almost broke a vase."

Layla touched his arm. "I'm here."

He caught her hand, laced their fingers together, and pressed her hand to his lips. "You're not going to vanish again, right?"

"I don't plan to."

"You seem more relaxed right now than I've ever seen you," Thrush said, looking her over.

"Well, I do love a good library." She motioned to the room around them. "And your cousins seem to have the most magnificent one I've ever stepped foot in."

But before he could kiss her, the air changed.

A quiet hush fell over the room, cold and heavy.

The doors creaked open.

Meg entered, Sparrow beside her, both dressed in black like twin blades of authority.

Thrush stiffened.

Layla instinctively stepped closer and Thrush inadvertently moved so she was just behind him.

"Did something happen?" she muttered.

Meg offered a small smile.

Sparrow cut a glance to Thrush. "We've come to speak with you both."

Layla's brows furrowed.

"About what?" Thrush asked.

Meg looked to Thrush. "It's time Layla returned to the Earthen realm."

"No." The word was out of Thrush's mouth before he could stop it.

His wings flared, his grip tightened on Layla's hand. "She stays here. With me."

Sparrow's brow arched. "Don't be dramatic."

"I'm not."

"She's not being banished," Meg said calmly. "But the balance between realms has been rattled. Your shadow-self ripped open a channel between Hell and the Earthen plane without our sanction. The White Horse has questions. You've taken her human without permission."

Thrush's jaw clenched. "But Remington took Evelyn."

Meg wagged a finger. "There are things you do not know that you should have learned when you spent all your time in the forest. Remington went straight to the White Horse and asked permission while you bringing Layla here was nothing more than a thought." She looked between Thrush and Layla. "You must learn to follow the few rules we have, princeling." Meg stepped closer to Sparrow. "You'll go with her. Both of you. Layla must return to her life, and you..."

"Have a conversation with the White Horse," Sparrow added, half-smirking. "A deeply annoying one, but wise nonetheless."

"Wait..." Layla looked confused. "There was a white horse at Jed and Shay's ranch."

"And a black horse," Meg said with a sly smirk.

"The white one can talk?" Layla's face was flexed in disbelief.

"Nero talks as well," Thrush said.

"Oh my god, talking horses." Layla looked at Meg then Sparrow. They both nodded.

Thrush looked down at Layla, heart pounding. "I don't want to leave Hell."

"You're not," Meg said gently. "You're just stepping between."

"Why now?" Layla asked.

"Because if you don't," Sparrow said, voice tightening, "we risk a tear in the Veil. Demons escape. Humans get stolen, eaten or hurt. Then the angels get angry. And then you won't just be a prince with a bloodlust problem, you'll be the reason Heaven, Hell, and Earth go to war again." Meg shook her head. "You don't want to be in that position. Believe me, I know."

Silence filled the room.

Finally, Thrush exhaled. His shoulders relaxed, but his jaw remained tight.

"Fine," he said. "But I'm not letting her out of my sight."

Meg smiled softly. "I wouldn't expect anything less."

Thrush's wings folded tightly behind him, his gaze still locked on Meg and Sparrow as if willing them to say no, you can stay. But the command had been clear.

Still, one last question pressed against his chest like a blade.

He looked to Sparrow. "What about the curse?"

Sparrow tilted his head. "What about it?"

Thrush rolled his shoulders, and the movement was stiff, sharp. "The shadow's back and I feel... more like myself. But the ticks," he rubbed at the tightness in his neck, where the muscle twitched like it had a mind of its own, "they're still there. The twitching, the burning in my spine, like something's still wrong."

He glanced at Layla, then quickly looked away. "I can't risk hurting her. Not if it comes back. Not if I lose control again. I almost hurt Evelyn once."

Sparrow stepped forward, gaze steady. "You think I don't know what that feels like?"

Thrush met his eyes, searching.

"I've had the same twitch in my shoulders for years," Sparrow said dryly. "Sometimes it eases. Sometimes it flares. But it never really disappears."

Meg leaned against the end of a long table, arms crossed, watching but saying nothing.

"It's not just a curse, Thrush. It's a wound that lives in the bloodline," Sparrow continued. "The shadow was only one part of it. Now that you're whole, you have a better chance at mastering it. But it won't happen overnight."

Thrush exhaled slowly. "So what do I do?"

Sparrow's voice dropped. "You wait. You endure. You don't run this time. You are not alone in this."

Thrush's throat worked around a bitter laugh. "That's your grand advice?"

Sparrow smirked. "No. My grand advice is this: do the right thing. Every time you can. Even when it hurts. Even when it's hard. Especially then. That's how you earn your way through a curse like this."

"Is that what you did?" Thrush asked.

"No." Sparrow's face was still as stone. "Definitely not. But Remington has tried his best. His symptoms are so mild you'd never know the curse touched his blood."

"And Rue?" Thrush asked, knowing that Sparrow and his mother Nightingale had both been affected.

"She's the best of us," Meg said. "No symptoms so far. You can tell that she is different than us. Sweet. Innocent. That's why she lives on the Earthen plane most of the time. So the darkness of Hell doesn't taint her soul."

"Maybe that's the secret to curing it?" Thrush said.

Sparrow was shaking his head. "No. Not at all. A few of us are allowed there with permission. We cannot disrupt the balance between the realms. The Earthen plane is not our home."

Thrush nodded slowly, still uncertain but holding onto the one solid thing he was sure of, Layla's hand in his.

"Okay," he said, glancing down at Layla for her answer.

She nodded.

"We'll go."

Chapter 50

The portal shimmered in the center of the garden like a pool of quicksilver suspended in air. Vines and flowers climbed the old stone archway that framed it, their leaves trembling with the breeze cast by the opening between realms.

Layla stood with Rue and Evelyn just a few feet from the portal. She clutched her bag tighter, already feeling the weight of this world beginning to loosen its grip on her. The ground didn't rumble. The air didn't shift. But something inside her had begun to ache with the knowledge that she was leaving. This wasn't even her home. She didn't know why she was feeling this way.

Rue reached out and hugged her first, tight and fierce. "I'm leaving tomorrow. I'll visit soon."

"Okay," Layla nodded. "Evelyn, will you visit?"

"Of course. We should make a coffee date of it and drag the boys along." She laughed loudly hearing Remington and Dacre grumble from nearby.

Rue pulled back and smiled softly. "The bookstore's

still yours. The life you had, it's waiting. Just... maybe a little different now."

Layla laughed, but her eyes burned with unshed tears.

Evelyn handed her a small cloth bundle. "There's a pouch of salt in here for protection. And dark chocolate. And a little bit of the fire whiskey. For emergencies. Love ya, little librarian."

"Thank you," Layla said, voice cracking.

"We won't be far," Rue said, tears sliding down her cheeks.

Layla glanced between them. "Try not to summon any more cursed books while I'm gone."

"No promises," Evelyn grinned.

Behind them, Thrush waited with arms crossed and wings folded tightly against his back, his expression unreadable, but his eyes never left Layla.

She turned, her fingers brushing his. "Ready?"

He nodded once.

They stepped toward the portal together, then through, and it swallowed them in a shimmer of violet light.

Stale air greeted them, carrying the scent of parchment and dust.

The sky outside the windows was cloudy, casting a golden hue across the sleepy town. Layla blinked and steadied herself, gripping Thrush's arm.

"I think I'm gonna throw up." Her hand flew to her mouth.

A large, warm hand rubbed her back. "Take some deep

breaths. It will get better." Thrush helped her to a nearby chair.

"Oh my god, is it always like that?" she asked.

Thrush frowned. "I don't know. Did you feel like this when my shadow dragged you through the dirt to Hell?"

Layla was shaking her head. "I think I was too shocked to feel sick."

He crouched next to her and Layla looked up.

"What happened to your wings?" she asked.

"They can't be seen here. There is balance."

"Oh." Layla felt her cheeks flush despite the lingering nausea. "I guess there's just so much I don't know about your world."

"We'll learn together. A lot of information had been destroyed or hidden before Meg took the throne."

"Rue's research..."

Thrush was nodding.

The bell above the door jingled once, though no one had touched it.

They both looked up.

Waiting on the stoop was Jed, arms folded, cowboy hat low over his brow, a faint smile tugging at his mouth.

"Took you long enough," he said.

Layla exhaled and smiled wide.

"We're back."

CHAPTER 51

THE WIND WHISPERED THROUGH DRY GRASS AND twisted trees. It was quiet here. Not even the birds dared to sing. They sensed a meeting was about to take place.

Layla stood with her arms crossed, watching Nero paw at the earth a few feet away. She glanced at Thrush. "Why didn't he tell me he could talk?"

Thrush smirked. "He didn't want to scare you."

"Too late." Layla said as they walked closer.

Nero lifted his head and whinnied.

The temperature dropped a few degrees, and from the tree line emerged a figure; tall, radiant, and impossibly white.

The horse wasn't just white. She glowed. Pearlescent light rippled through her mane, and her eyes gleamed with ancient awareness.

Layla's hand flew to her mouth. "That's... she looks so different in the light."

"Yes," Thrush said. "This is the White Horse."

"Is she glowing?" Layla asked.

"She kinda sparkles."

Then the horse spoke.

"You're late," she said flatly, voice feminine and echoing like thunder wrapped in silk.

Layla stumbled back, blinking. "She does talk."

"Yes, I talk," the White Horse replied, swishing her tail. "What did you think I did? Neigh cryptically and disappear into moonlight?" She made a nickering noise that sounded like a laugh.

Layla looked to Nero, then back to the mare. "I want to hear your voice."

"It's nothing special," Nero said, watching Layla as though she might run for the hills.

Thrush stepped forward, bowing slightly; awkward, hesitant, but with a reverence that Layla hadn't seen in him before.

"You asked to see us," he said.

The White Horse's eyes narrowed. "You were supposed to keep her safe."

"I tried," Thrush snapped, the tension in his shoulders returning instantly. "There was just so much I didn't know. I wasn't whole. I couldn't control..."

"No excuses," the White Horse said. "She nearly paid the price."

Layla stepped closer to Thrush. "He didn't mean it," she said gently. "He saved me. Twice."

The White Horse turned her full attention on Layla now and it was like staring into a divine abyss, light and shadow folding into one.

"You've changed," she said.

Layla stiffened. "I... I don't feel that different."

"But you are," Nero added. "You walked through Hell. You were bitten by the Astral part of his shadow. You fed your blood to a princeling of mixed realms. That leaves a mark."

Layla looked at her hand, remembering how it had gone black, how it had slowly cleared.

"Are you saying I'm not human anymore?" she whispered.

"I'm saying you're more than just a human," the White Horse corrected.

Thrush's hand found hers again.

The White Horse dipped her head slightly. "I knew it would come to this. I saw the spark in you. I was only waiting to see if Thrush would survive the fire."

Thrush raised an eyebrow. "And?"

The White Horse's eyes gleamed. "You did. But just barely."

She turned to walk away, then paused. "You still owe me answers. But for now... all is well. This realm hasn't had a bond like yours in a long time. Don't waste it."

"Wait," Thrush was unsure of what she was saying, "does this mean we can stay here? I still have to learn more about the magic."

The White Horse looked at Thrush then Layla. "You can both stay. The portal in Lame Deer needs a warden." The White horse stared hard at Thrush. "Don't fuck this up, princeling."

Thrush nodded. "Never," he whispered, disbelieving his luck that the White Horse would allow this.

Then, without another word, the White Horse and Nero turned and trotted toward the mountains. They picked up speed and began to run so fast that they could barely be seen.

Layla stood in silence for a long moment, hand still clutched in Thrush's.

"That was... interesting," she said finally.

Thrush grinned faintly. "I can't believe that she said yes."

CHAPTER 52

THE FAINT SCENT OF FRESH PAINT FILLED THE AIR as sunlight streamed through the bookstore windows. The bell above the door jingled every so often as a soft breeze pushed through the cracked front door, mixing late summer air with the scent of books.

Layla was surprised by the amount of books she sold in the middle of nowhere Montana. Seems the reading culture was strong here.

Layla crouched in front of a wooden shelf, carefully stacking a fresh shipment of titles. Her glasses slid down her nose, and she pushed them back up with a knuckle smudged in dust. She was humming off-key and softly to an old eighties tune Shay had played earlier.

Behind her, Shay balanced a precarious tower of fantasy hardcovers in her arms. "Tell me again why I agreed to help you alphabetize by subgenre?"

"Because you love me," Layla grinned over her shoulder.

Shay snorted. "Debatable. I might've just pitied you."

They both laughed.

Layla stood, brushing her hands on her jeans. "We're almost done with this side. Just the old mythology section next."

"Oh, speaking of old," Shay said, setting the stack down on the counter with a loud thump. "I talked to Jed this morning. He said it's safe to let you know that the Peabody Library is still functional."

Layla's head snapped up. "Wait, really?"

Shay nodded. "Yep. Still has most of its collection. Even some of the private archives Rue was trying to get access to. You could help her with that. Maybe even take a trip to go see it. I think you'd like that. The place is cool. I stayed there for a while, years ago."

A spark lit in Layla's chest. "That's huge. I could still help Rue. I mean, from here. With the right connections."

Shay leaned against the counter, arms crossed, eyebrow raised. "So, you're gonna start smuggling forbidden books from a haunted library again?"

"Maybe," Layla said with a grin. "But, like, this time I won't risk my job to do it."

They both giggled again, the kind of soft laughter that belonged to people who'd survived something big and come out the other side still standing.

"You really like it here, don't you?" Shay asked after a pause.

Layla glanced around the bookstore, hands brushing the edge of the counter. "Yeah. I do. It feels like... mine. Even if my view of the world's completely changed."

Shay snorted. "You and me both, sweetheart. I can barely remember my days of a *normal* world."

Layla turned back to the shelf, a soft smile on her lips.

"But it's okay because I have Jed and a whole gang of people and creatures who are family now." Shay moved closer, touching Layla's arm. "We were all brought together for a reason. And I'm glad you're here."

Layla hugged Shay. "Thank you."

The bell over the bookstore door jingled.

"We're not open yet!" Layla called from behind a stack of unshelved books.

A pause.

Then a low voice, familiar and dangerous in all the right ways, replied, "Good. I didn't come for books."

Layla's head popped up, a smile tugging at her mouth. "Thrush?"

Shay peeked out from the back room, eyebrows raised. "I've heard that tone before." She winked at Layla and grabbed her keys. "I'll leave you two alone."

"Shay," Layla started, flustered.

But Shay was already halfway out the door. "Don't do anything I wouldn't do!" she called, and the door jingled again as it closed behind her.

Thrush stepped inside and turned the lock with a click. A flick of his fingers and the windows darkened, the soft light inside suddenly tinted and private.

Layla crossed her arms, trying to look unimpressed. "Seriously? You're using dark magic to flirt?"

"Is it working?" he asked, grinning like sin itself.

She rolled her eyes, but her cheeks were pink. "You're ridiculous."

He walked toward her, boots echoing softly on the wood floor. "I missed you."

Layla arched a brow. "You saw me this morning."

"Jed had me throwing hay bales all day like I'm some kind of glorified farmhand."

"You kind of are."

"Betrayal," he muttered, mock wounded. "I came all this way to sweep you off your feet."

"At least you showered." She tapped her chin. "Mmm, and what exactly did you have in mind?"

He reached her, wrapping an arm around her waist, fingers warm on her lower back. "Something like this."

Layla squeaked as he pulled her gently to him, the stack of books behind her forgotten. He kissed her forehead, then the corner of her mouth. "I wanted some time alone with you."

"I noticed," she murmured, breath hitching. "What's wrong? Are you hungry or something?"

She searched his eyes, wondering how the whole blood drinking process was going to work while they both had things to do during the day. They couldn't very well lay in bed all day long, although... it sounded nice.

Thrush kissed her, slow and unhurried, like he had all the time in the world. Like the shop could burn down around them and he wouldn't stop touching her.

Layla sighed against his lips. "You smell like coffee and soap and... Hell."

"You love it."

Tugging him closer, she whispered, "I really do."

Thrush brushed a strand of hair from her cheek, his expression half-mischievous, half-hungry. "You know," he murmured, "I've been thinking about something."

Layla leaned back slightly against the shelf, suspicious. "That's always dangerous."

"I owe you so much for putting up with me. It's time for repayment." He smirked. "What's your darkest fantasy?"

Layla blinked. "What?"

Thrush licked his lips. "I want to know what you've dreamed about. All those nights since we first met," he said, voice lower now, a gravelly whisper meant only for her. "What you keep tucked away behind that quiet librarian look. I've seen the way your mind works, Layla. I've seen the stares. The smiles. The way your cheeks and neck flush when I notice you're watching. What do you want?"

She bit her lip, her cheeks coloring deeper this time. "You're serious?"

He nodded, stepping closer, one hand bracing against the bookshelf beside her head.

She looked away, flustered, and then back at him, defiant. "Fine. Someone strong. A little dangerous. Tall. Blonde." She was looking him over.

"That sounds like me." The corner of his lips tipped up.

"Could be. I read a lot of romance books though so..." She grinned back. "Make love to me against the book-shelves."

Thrush raised an eyebrow. "Here?"

She nodded.

He stepped closer, crowding her. "Like this?" he asked, voice dipping low.

He moved in closer, their bodies touching, her back pressed to the wooden case, the books hard against her spine. His hand found her hip, the other trailing along her arm until it reached her wrist, fingers threading gently through hers.

Layla swallowed hard, her breath catching.

"Thrush," she whispered, more warning than protest.

But his mouth was already on hers, soft at first, then demanding. His hand curled behind her neck, tilting her head, deepening the kiss. He kissed her like he hadn't touched her in months instead of hours.

When they broke apart, Layla blinked up at him, dazed. "Are we really doing this in the bookstore?"

He leaned in, kissed the corner of her mouth, then her jaw. "It's your fantasy," he whispered. "And the door is locked."

"And you're just fulfilling a customer request?"

He grinned. "Exactly."

His mouth found hers again, and the books behind her rustled as he pressed her closer.

Sharp teeth scraped her jaw and heat flamed in her veins. She reached out to touch him with her free hand. The other was pinned above her head by his hand. Fingertips traced the skin just above his belt. He was hot, his skin always so warm. She reached into his jeans but he pressed against her body so hard she couldn't move her arm.

"Careful, little librarian."

Thrush kissed her like the world had narrowed to this very moment; just her breath, her body, her heartbeat rising to meet his.

Layla pulled her hand free and slid her fingers into his hair, tugging slightly as she tipped her head back. She had never wanted anything like this, never craved someone the way she craved him now. He was fire and smoke and danger, and she wanted to be burned.

"Like this?" he asked against her mouth, voice rough with restraint.

She nodded, breathless. "Yes."

Thrush pressed his forehead to hers, gathering himself, as though the weight of what they were about to do mattered. And it did. Somehow, it always did with him.

Then he kissed her again, deeper this time, until her knees nearly gave out. She clung to him, to the shelf at her back, and felt herself melt into him. He didn't just touch her, he consumed her. He mapped her, remembering every sound she made.

His hand slipped beneath the hem of her shirt, fingertips skimming her spine, eliciting a shiver. She arched into his touch. Her glasses tilted slightly, and he gently removed them and set them on a nearby stack of books.

"You," he said, voice thick with something dark, "are my greatest temptation."

"Good," she whispered, tugging him down again. "Then we're even."

He fumbled with her waistband. "Why are you wearing jeans?"

"I can't exactly walk around without pants all day."

"Yes you could."

Layla giggled and helped him unsnap the waistband. Thrush pushed the jeans down her legs, ripped her shoes off, and then shucked her jeans off as she leaned against the bookshelves for support. He was on his knees, looking up. Then his lips were on her knee, his fingers curling around her panties and tugging them down her legs. He shifted, kissing up and up and up until he was at the vee between her thighs. His tongue was on her, licking until she moaned and had to hold onto the shelves for support as her knees threatened to give out. She cried out his name just as a loud knock echoed from the door.

Thrush's hand slapped over her mouth. "Shhhh," he whispered, rising to his feet. "The customers will hear you."

Layla nodded.

Whoever was at the door knocked again and yanked on the door. Layla tried to turn her head but Thrush clicked his tongue.

"No, no, you're all mine right now. Ignore them. There's only us. Me and you and the bookshelves."

He kept his hand over her mouth while the other trailed up her shirt, moving the cloth down until she could pull her arm out. He tugged the strap of her bra down revealing her breast. His mouth touched her shoulder and trailed down her skin, licking and nipping until his lips closed over her nipple and sucked.

Layla moaned behind his fingers which were still clamped over her mouth.

He pulled away. "Shh shhh shhh, little librarian," he teased. "You don't want them to hear."

Layla's body was on fire. No romance book she'd ever read was like this. It was like he was in her head, reading her thoughts and revealing her dreams. How many times had she wished he would follow Rue into the campus library so she could see him again? And here they were.

Fingers pressed at the softness between her legs and his mouth went back to her breast. Layla closed her eyes, hips rolling against his hand until the tension coiled tight within her body. Suddenly he pulled away. Layla made a sound in her throat. She opened her eyes to see him standing in front of her, disheveled, cheeks flushed, fingers sparking.

"Don't stop," Layla begged. "Please." She reached for him, unbuckling his belt and shoving his jeans down.

He kicked off his boots and pulled his shirt over his head. Then he stepped out of his jeans.

Layla's eyes went wide. God he was magnificent. Tall and muscular. She shivered.

He reached for her, tugging her close. Gathering her into his arms, he lifted her with surprising gentleness. She wrapped her legs around his waist, pressing her forehead to his as they shared the same air, the same space, the same need.

He pressed her against the bookshelves.

"Like this?" he asked, adjusting his hips, and pressing into her.

Layla hissed at the stretch. "Yes. Just like this." Her hands were at his shoulders, fingers unable to stop moving against his skin.

"If you keep tickling me like that, I won't last." He growled. "Grab the shelves above your head."

She did, reaching until the muscles of her arms felt stretched. And, oh, it did things to her body; feeling suspended and equally supported by him. And then he moved his hips and Layla cried out, unable to move like she wanted. She could only take what he gave.

"Please," Layla begged. "Teeth. Now."

Thrush smiled and lowered his mouth to her shoulder. "Here?"

"Lower," she instructed.

He moved down her chest to her breast.

Layla cried out again as he thrust into her.

"There," she cried.

And then teeth scraped her skin, the pinch barely felt with him thrusting into her, the tension of holding herself up, and the scrape of the bookshelves against her back. Her body shivered and shook as Thrush sighed and his body went taut.

That odd sensation came back in her throat, and she realized she hadn't felt it in a long time. Her mouth felt strange, like her teeth had moved. She rubbed her tongue over them and stilled.

He pulled her away from the bookshelf, still inside, arms wrapped tightly around her and he brought them to the floor. Layla straddled his lap. He slouched against the bookshelves, still inside her.

"What is this?" Layla asked, finger moving to her teeth.

Thrush was watching her closely, hands on her thighs as she pulled her lip up revealing sharp teeth like his.

A hand moved to her neck. "Thirst? Hunger?" he asked.

"I... I don't know." She swallowed hard, focusing on the red stain of his lips. Her mouth watered. "Is this supposed to happen?"

"It happened to Evelyn," he murmured. "I wasn't sure if it would happen to you."

Her eyes went wide in disbelief.

He moved his hips to get her attention again. The Bloodlust was stirring inside him and he wanted more of her—longer, harder, bloodier.

She swallowed again, her teeth feeling sharp against her mouth. "What do I do?"

Thrush's hand left her leg and pointed to the skin of his chest, just below the collarbone. "Press them here. Break the skin. Drink."

She licked her lips. "What if I don't like it?"

He chuckled. "I think you'll like it."

She shifted her hips and he groaned.

"Careful," he warned.

"I just... umm." Layla felt strange; her body felt hot and a strong gnawing feeling was growing inside her. "Something is wrong with me," she warned.

"It's the Bloodlust." His hands moved to her hips, up her sides, thumbs grazing her ribcage.

Layla moaned and threw her head back, shifting her hips.

Thrush's hand moved behind her neck and he sat up, pulling her against him. "Show your teeth, little librarian." He urged. "This little fantasy of yours will only get better. It might exceed all expectations."

Layla's cheeks flushed with embarrassment, but she felt him growing harder inside her and her body fought to move. Her mouth watered as she stared at the pulsing veins in his neck. She lowered her mouth to his shoulder, kissing, exploring.

"Christ," Thrush groaned.

She pressed her teeth against his hot skin and *bit*.

Warmth flooded her mouth. It was sweet, savory, like nothing she'd ever tasted before.

Thrush was muttering something in her ear. Prayers

perhaps. Or a promise between creatures caught between worlds; flesh and shadow, heart and hunger.

Their bodies moved in unison. Layla pulled away, blood staining her mouth. Her body felt strong, wild, uninhibited. She gripped the shelves over Thrush's head and used them for leverage as she rode him. He lifted his back off the floor, mouth connecting with her ribcage, then the sensitive skin below her breast. Layla had never felt anything like this before. He was looking up at her like she was a goddess. Hands tangled in her curls, drifted down her neck, and a thumb brushed her blood-coated lips.

"It's good, right?" he asked.

She could only nod before pushing off the shelf and leaning back, resting her hands behind her on his thighs, watching him as he watched her ride his body and take as much as she wanted.

When the moment finally broke, when they were still and breathless and leaning against one another, Layla rested her head against his chest, listening to the erratic beat of his heart.

"Tell me," he said as he kissed her hair, "did it fulfill your fantasy?"

"Beyond," Layla giggled. "So far beyond."

His fingers played along her spine and she shivered closer to him.

"I feel different," Layla said quietly.

"Is that bad?"

"No. Different in a good way." She looked up at him and his eyes had shifted to blue. Relaxed blue, not chaotic and shifting colors. And she realized, he'd changed too.

CHAPTER 53

Day??? I stopped keeping track. I think I'm a vampire now and that probably deserves a new notebook, but I really like this one, so here we are.

Pros:
Still not dead.
No longer being hunted.
Portal to Hell just a short walk from the bookstore.
Boyfriend has wings.
I might have fangs.
Coffee tastes better. Didn't think that was possible.

Cons:
Sunlight is... the same. Like, no issue here.
My blood might be slightly magical now. TBD.

My glasses keep fogging up when Thrush looks at me a certain way. (Not really a complaint, more like a hazard.)

But seriously, what just happened?

One minute I'm a librarian with a cursed book and a weird bite on my arm, and now I'm... this.

I'm standing in my own damn bookstore.

I have people who get it. Rue, Evelyn, Shay, Jed. Even Chel (grumpy retired Hellion™) drops by sometimes to complain about the weather and ask if I've seen the White Horse.

And Thrush?

I think I love him.

Not the easy kind of love. The kind that's forged in fire and stitched together with sharp teeth and blood bonds. The kind that burns when you try to walk away.

He still sleeps like the world's about to end. Still gets twitchy when the curse flares. But he talks to me now. He lets me touch him when I want. He lets me in.

And when he smiles at me it's like the whole universe stops moving.

I don't know what happens next. Maybe I'm a vampire, maybe I'm something else.

But for the first time in a long time, I don't care what label fits.

I'm alive. I'm loved. I'm dangerous in my own right. And I am exactly where I'm supposed to be. IDK what I'm gonna tell my parents.

Now if you'll excuse me, I think Thrush just locked the bookstore doors again.

—Layla
(possibly immortal, definitely in love, owner of one demon-proof bookstore)

———

THE DOOR CREAKED OPEN, AND THRUSH LEANED against the frame, eyes glinting with mischief.

"What are you doing?" he asked, his voice a low hum of amusement.

Layla snapped her journal shut, cheeks warming. "Nothing."

His eyebrow arched. "Nothing, huh?" He stepped into the room, his boots heavy on the old floorboards. "Is that what you call writing 'Thrush has stupidly pretty eyelashes and smells like pine and sin' in a notebook?"

Her eyes widened and she gasped, horrified. "You read my journal?"

He grinned. "All of it. I'm offended you didn't include my perfect hair."

Layla stood. "That's an invasion of privacy!"

"I've invaded more than your privacy," he said smugly.

She grabbed the nearest pen and chucked it at his head. He caught it easily, smirking.

"Thrush!"

"What?" He held the pen like a trophy. "I was curious. You leave it lying around like it's not filled with juicy confessions."

"I'm going to read your diary," she threatened, storming across the room.

"I don't have one," he replied smoothly.

"Then I'll read that little book you carry around all the time," she snapped.

His expression shifted into something unreadable. "If you can find it."

She narrowed her eyes and came at him like a hornet. Thrush laughed and raised his arms as she started patting his pockets.

"Careful," he murmured. "That's how rumors start. That's how things get *hard*. You'll make me thirsty."

"Shut up," she hissed, shoving her hand into the back pocket of his jeans. Her fingers closed around the familiar leather-bound book. "Aha!"

His smile faded just slightly. "Layla..."

She flipped it open and frowned. "Runes? Seriously? I can't read any of this."

"Exactly," he said, but there was a softness to his tone now. "It's not meant for anyone but me."

She turned a few more pages, slow and deliberate. "I swear if this is just a recipe for how to boil basilisk eggs I'm going to..." She glanced up. "Cut all that hair off as you sleep."

Then she reached the last page.

Her breath hitched.

The last page wasn't runes. It wasn't gibberish. It was his handwriting, messy and bold, like it had cost him something to put the words down.

The curse is quiet tonight.

She's sleeping in my shirt, curled up like she belongs in my ribs.

The shadow in me doesn't rage anymore.

I feel whole. And it's her. It's always been her.

I love her.

LAYLA LOOKED UP. THRUSH STOOD STILL, EVERY trace of smugness gone from his face.

"I wrote that after the cave," he said softly. "Didn't think you'd ever see it."

She hugged the notebook to her chest, heart pounding. "You should've shown me."

He shrugged. "It felt... too big. Too psychotic. Or something. I sound like a creeper."

She crossed the space between them, barefoot and blinking hard. "It's sweet."

His arms wrapped around her and she melted into his chest, the little spell book still between them.

"I'm still mad you read my journal," she mumbled into his shirt.

"I'm counting on it," he said, his lips brushing her temple. "Your revenge is kind of hot."

She pulled back, giving him a look. "You're the worst."

"You love it."

"I do," she whispered, rising on her toes to kiss him. "Princeling better make up for reading my diary."

He smiled darkly and lifted her off her feet.

"I'm still mad," she murmured, voice muffled against his neck.

He exhaled a half-laugh. "I'm counting on it. You're cute when you plot vengeance."

"I'm going to write terrible things about you in that journal."

"I look forward to reading about it."

She tilted her face up, lips brushing his jaw. "One day I'll crack your little codebook."

"Promise?"

She didn't reply, only kissed him again.

And just like that Thrush knew without spell, mark, or binding, he was hers. Fully. Forever.

Epilogue

The apartment still smelled faintly of fresh paint and wood. Layla had lit a vanilla candle near the window, and the gentle breeze carried the scent through the small, cozy space. The town of Lame Deer murmured outside, distant and familiar to her now. This was so different from her apartment near Loyola University, but she'd never felt more at home and in control of her life.

Layla sat cross-legged on the couch, her phone in hand, a wide smile on her face. "Yes, Mom. I know. I miss you too. I'm planning something. A trip. Maybe next month?" A pause, her voice gentled. "I'm bringing someone with me. He's... special."

Across the room, Thrush stood leaning against the wall with his arms crossed, watching her like she was the only light left in the world.

When she hung up, Layla looked at him, her eyes bright. "She's excited," she said. "I think she'll like you."

"And your father?" he asked, brows rising.

Layla looked away. "He'll catch on once he sees how happy you make me.

Thrush arched an eyebrow. "I think most people don't like me."

"That's because you're so tall and moody." Layla shrugged. "I like you. That's all that matters."

A smirk tugged at his lips, but something quieter and heavier lingered in his eyes. She noticed it, as she always did. And she crossed the room to him, slipping her arms around his waist. Her cheek rested lightly against his chest.

"I miss your wings," she murmured. "I liked waking up next to them."

"They are still there," he said. "We can make a quick trip back to Hell if you want to see them. The portal's not far."

He pointed down. Downstairs was the bookstore and the portal which they were now guardians over.

She tilted her head to look up at him. "Do you ever think about splitting the difference? You go to Hell during the day, do the whole... princely shadow thing. Then you come back to me at night. Like a nine-to-five job."

Thrush laughed, and it was rough and low and honest. "That's the most human thing you've ever said."

She smiled. "And you didn't say no."

He cupped her face, brushed his thumb along her cheek. "I'll go as long as the balance lets me," he said softly. "But I come back to you. Always."

They stood like that for a moment, tangled up in each other. Not perfect. But together.

Something thudded from downstairs. Thrush went still.

"Did you lock up the shop?" he asked.

"I always do," Layla promised.

He moved toward the door and jogged down the stairs.

Layla followed.

A gust of warm air followed the tall figure stepping out of the hallway that led to the portal; broad-shouldered, scowling, and radiating pure chaos.

"Chel?" Thrush said, straightening.

The Hellion looked around the shop like it might bite him. He was still in Hellion gear looking like some mix between special forces and a heavy metal cover singer. His boots were caked with Helldust.

"What are you doing here?" Thrush asked.

"I need to speak with the damn horse," Chel grumbled.

Layla's brows lifted. "The White Horse?"

"Yeah. Her." Chel huffed and crossed his arms. "I'm on vacation. Officially retired. Don't ask." He waved a hand. When his arm went to his side, he hit a book display and knocked it over.

"Shit."

"You don't seem thrilled about it," Layla said watching him restack the books.

Chel scowled harder. "Thrilled? No. I've been a Hellion for a century. Now Meg and Sparrow say I need to 'rest' and 'heal' and 'find inner peace.'" He rolled his eyes. "So unless your bookstore sells peace in bulk, I'm tracking that horse down. She owes me a good deal. One near the beach."

Thrush exchanged a look with Layla.

Layla smiled. "Well, you're just in time. We've got coffee, cursed history books, and a portal to the ethereal realms. No beaches in Montana though. Sorry about that."

Chel sighed. "Great. Just what I needed. A mystical coffee break."

The phone in Layla's pocket rang, interrupting Chel's grumbling.

She pulled it out. "Hello?"

"Hi! It's Rue," came the familiar voice on the other end; bright, determined, and slightly winded. Like always, the girl was always doing something suspicious with her research.

Layla smiled. "Hey, how are you?"

"Fine. Great. Maybe a little sleep-deprived. Evelyn says I've become a research goblin again."

Layla laughed. "So, the usual then."

"Pretty much. I'm calling because I need you to find me a book."

"Of course." Layla leaned against the counter and searched for a pen and paper. "What's the subject this time? Demonic tax law? Reaper etiquette?"

Rue snorted. "No. This one's serious. It has to do with Appalachian giants, child sacrifices, and maybe... angelic bloodlines. Specifically, ones tied to archangels who had children on the Earthen plane. We've always believed most didn't survive birth but I think there's more. Something buried."

Layla straightened. "Like... your kind of serious, or Meg-will-throw-you-through-a-wall serious?"

"Closer to the second one." Rue lowered her voice. "We think one of the sacrifice stones Evelyn found might be linked to a forgotten sect, one that believed binding a child of an archangel would keep the veil thin enough for possession."

"That's horrifying."

"Right? But Evelyn and I think it connects to the old blood rites they used in the eastern mountains. Maybe even the ones tied to the pools we've found in the mountains here."

Layla turned, scanning the nearest shelf automatically. "You're looking for folklore or ritual logs?"

"Both, if you can. And anything that mentions giants. That's usually a good place to start."

Layla's skin prickled. "Creepy."

"Yeah," Rue agreed. "Which is why you're the only one I trust to look. You can use the portal to get to the Peabody Library if you need to. You think you could get in today?"

Layla glanced toward the back hallway of the shop. "I think I can manage. Not much is going on here."

There was a pause, then Rue's voice softened. "Thanks, Layla."

Layla smiled. "You know I'd go to Hell for you."

"Right back at ya," Rue said, laughing.

Layla chuckled. "Fair enough. I'll let you know what I find."

She hung up and turned to find Thrush standing there with arms crossed, watching her with that half-smirk he wore when he was trying not to look worried.

"You're going somewhere," he said.

"Peabody Library. I finally got a personal invite." Layla nodded. "You want to come?"

He stepped closer, brushing his fingers down her arm. "Always."

Layla turned toward the giant Hellion who was lingering in the shop.

"Hey Chel, can you watch the shop for a few hours? Just make sure nothing comes through the portal?" Thrush asked.

"I didn't come here to babysit a bookstore," Chel grumbled. "I don't even know how to read."

Layla's eyes went wide.

Thrush laughed. "He's lying. He can read."

Preview of: These Thorns are Sharpest

*This is unedited rough draft.

These Thorns are Sharpest is another book in the next generation Veil of Shadows world.

This is a companion to The Sky is Starless, The Night is Endless, The Shadows are Darkest, and the original 13-Volume Veil of Shadows Series.

These Thorns are Sharpest
by M. R. Pritchard

Chapter 1

Blood was thicker than water. But Angel blood? That was closer to the inky water of the Black River in Hell than anything else.

There was a reason why Teari left her father's kingdom to serve the Archangel Gabriel. A real reason. One she didn't speak of. She didn't dare because in her world silence was survival. There was a time when power was bought with secrets. Times had changed, but the change didn't reach far. Some secrets were soul deep. There was a time when the Archangels and the Deacon's conspired to rule all. They gave off a holy impression, but Teari knew what had gone on behind closed doors. There was no holiness in what the Archangels were doing. Meg had put a stop to most of it. When Alastor and Lucifer killed the last Deacon just before the war, the glass castle had shattered. Babylon no longer held all the power. It had been restored to its rightful deity. A White Horse who resided on the Earthen plane.

Yes, Teari was a black sheep deep down. She'd always been too soft, too curious, too unwilling to look away. Too willing to stand up for what was right. Although, sometimes she had been eager to stand for the wrong thing. There was a time when she'd nearly made Meg, the Queen of Hell, her enemy. But that was before she had all the details. Before she realized Sparrow would be out of her reach and nothing more than a friend. A girl could dream but an Angel could not mingle with that prophecy.

Now, she was a healer, and simply that. She had been a soldier, briefly, it was part of her training to stay in Gabriel's kingdom. He didn't want a healer who could not protect themselves. Her hands were far more useful putting bodies back together rather than breaking them apart. Her stint in the Legion was brief, but enough to bury her deeper into Gabriel's kingdom, enough to give her cover. Enough to give her distance. She had made a commitment to Gabriel's kingdom, it gave her enough distance from her father's rule to pretend she'd carved out a life of her own.

She hadn't.

Not really.

She was still caught in his shadow. He still called upon her to clean up what he'd stained.

Think what they'll say about you, her father had said. *They'll banish you. They'll strip you of your gifts. And you'll come crawling back home.*

Home.

Teari shuddered. That wasn't home. That was the gilded cage where she was raised. Where she'd come into her healing powers. Where she'd first seen what true corruption looked like when stretched under divine skin.

She would never be like the creature that made her. Couldn't.

Her father, for all his radiance and scripture-wrapped powers, was not pure. He was far from it. Archangels could not lie but they could deceive, they sinned. They murdered their mistakes and scrubbed the blood away with her hands.

Teari had been the one scrubbing as soon as they realized her worth. She was always scrubbing.

And it was breaking her. She'd take a thousand years serving the crown of Hell as a healer over the scrubbing she couldn't escape.

Even here, behind Gabriel's gates, she felt the old rot creeping beneath her skin. Her father's claws were long and patient. Every time she tried to pull away, he yanked her back with veiled threats. The weight of the unspoken, of children who never received names, of women left hollow and grieving, of sins buried under marble and incense. It all hung on her like the heaviest of chains.

And while Teari kept her chin up and her mouth shut, it was taking a toll. There was only so much she could take. Only so much she could see. There was too much blood on her hands. Too many last breaths. Too many gravestones.

Archangels were not pure. Their souls were not divine. They still did bad shit. Awful shit. Teari's father was still using her to hide his sins. Still using her to sop up his mess.

Her bloodline hid a secret she could never escape. And as long as her father lived, she would never escape what the Archangel Raphael had done and continued to do. The judges of Babylon looked away for a few souls of payment.

Archangels were not holy.

They were propaganda with white wings.

She would never escape her father. He would continue to send messages sealed in gold. He'd never say what the mess was. He didn't need to.

Teari always knew.

It was always the same. She'd never forget the first. The place where she'd first learned how to hold a dying child. The place where she finally understood some Archangels will keep their hands clean and their bloodline pure. The place where she stopped calling herself a daughter.

Even now, she could feel the pull like a hook beneath her ribs.

The air shifted behind her.

"I wondered where you'd disappeared to," came the familiar voice of the Raven King. Sparrow had come for a visit. He was once Gabriel's Legion commander. A cursed man. And now, a King of the deceased Archangel Remiel's land.

Teari didn't turn. "You could call or message me."

"You never answer these days."

Teari glanced out of the corner of her eye. Sparrow was beside her, hands tucked into the pockets of a long black coat. Typical vampire brooding male. His black wings were tucked so close against his back she barely noticed them. Those had gotten him the title the Raven King. The only King in the Seven Kingdoms of Heaven with black wings.

He was trouble bottle in scars and beauty. He was one of the few beings in this realm she trusted. Him and Meg. Chaos and fire, both of them. But at least they were honest about it.

"You've got that faraway murder-glow in your eyes," Sparrow said, giving her a once over. "Having a bad day?"

Teari sighed. "Just... thinking."

He nudged her shoulder and a light trill of birdsong escaped his lips like a soft whistle. "You don't have to stay here."

She was standing at the edge of a shallow garden behind Gabriel's southern cathedral. Bare feet pressed into the soft earth. Golden sunlight spilled across the marble paths. Shew as here looking for peace.

"I must stay here," she replied to Sparrow with a sigh. "I won't go back to my father. Or, maybe I should run off and join Hell's kitchen crew. You all need a new chef down there?"

"Your cooking sucks." Sparrow laughed. "Meg would take you in a heartbeat. You know that."

Teari crossed her arms. "I'm not sure where I belong anymore."

Silence stretched between them, broken by the distant sound of cathedral bells from Babylon.

"Our fathers were monsters."

"Mine is still alive."

"You are not your father, Teari," Sparrow said.

She looked up.

Teari pressed her lips together, emotion burning under her ribs. She wished she believed him. But the truth was ugly. The things she'd done, the cover ups. No matter how far she ran, she was still the pure blooded child of the Archangel Raphael. And Archangel blood never let go.

CHAPTER 2

The castle in Hell had always felt like home to Chel. The Hellion barracks were better than the hovel he'd grown up in. The Hellion lair reserved for Hellions of high standing, including himself. High ceilings, leather furniture, old wooden tables and plenty of blood in the bar fridge. And memories from before the war. He couldn't escape the flood of images of battling Alastor and his chaos that had taken the castle. In the end, Chel was the only one who survived.

Now, he stood near Meg's office, Arms crossed, boots still streaked with Helldust and sweat from training. Smoke clung to his clothes, sharp and bitter.

Meg opened the door and ushered him inside.

"You're limping," she said, sharp eyes assessing him.

Chel shrugged. "It's nothing."

"You're leaking."

He looked down. His leathers were torn through the thigh. Blood soaked the edge of the fabric. The wound had sealed, but barely. It might scar. Another one to add to the tally.

"Flesh wound," he said.

Met stared. "That's Hellion talk for impaled."

He half-smiled. "Gotta be tough."

"I wish you'd take care of yourself better. You're the last one, Chel." Meg's expression softened.

Chel's smile disappeared and his jaw snapped shut.

The others were gone. Tukka, Klaus. Skeele. They had died fighting. All for Meg. And he had lived.

Meg stepped closer. "You've given me more than I had any right to ask for."

A large hand covered his heart. "It is my duty as a Hellion. My birthright. Protecting this throne, you, the young ones, it is all I know and all I will ever know."

One dark brow rose on Meg's face as she turned away from him and walked to a nearby chair. She sat and kicked out the club chair across from her, motioning for him to sit.

"You're tired." Meg threaded her fingers together.

"No. I never tire."

"Sit." She nodded to the chair.

"I'm not sure I should." Chel had a queasy feeling in his stomach.

"Don't be afraid." She slouched, very un-Queen like. "Rue says you've become attached to her kitten."

Chel shrugged. "Lucipurr is cute." He finally moved closer and sat across from Meg.

"My son says you're moody."

Chel scowled.

"You've been drinking. Drawing even. I didn't know you could draw, Chel."

He pressed his lips together remembering the night a few weeks ago when he'd had a bit too much to drink and it sent him into a downward spiral. Despair didn't look good on a Hellion.

"That was an accident." Chel's back straightened. "It won't happen again."

"You were bred to be a Hellion." Meg looked away. "But you've become something more. You're loyal. We've been through some shit."

"Part of the job."

"Maybe." Meg leveled her stare on him. "Maybe that was the old way things were done."

Meg had brought plenty of change to Hell after she took the throne. She'd battled Lucifer for peace. Her rule had brought hope to the creatures of Hell. She challenged the old ways of thinking.

Chel's back straightened again when he started to understand where this conversation was going. "It is my duty to protect you, your family, this throne. Nothing more. I have nothing more in my life."

"I don't need you to do it anymore."

That landed deeper than he expected. His mind went completely blank with shock.

Meg must've seen it in his face, her tone gentled. "I know you've been trying to connect with someone."

"There is no one." He didn't want to admit that all his calls had gone unanswered. All his invitations to the balls and celebrations ignored or a halfhearted excuse was given. Rejection did not suite him.

"There is a house on the Earthen plane. You've been there before," Meg reminded him. She reached into her pocket and pulled out a set of tarnished keys. They jangled on a keyring with a plastic pink flamingo. "Go there. Rest."

"I am not tired."

"Take a vacation then."

"Are you firing me? There is no greater disgrace to a Hellion."

"I am not firing you." She jangled the keys out to him again. "You'll still be a Hellion. I'm simply asking you to take some time for yourself."

Chel growled before swiping the keys out of Meg's hand. "I can't believe you're sending me away."

"You might enjoy retirement." She smiled.

"Doubt it."

"If there is a problem here I will call you back," Meg promised as she stood.

He looked up, a sinking feeling in his chest. Disgrace.

"Oh Christ almighty," Meg finally said. "I am not firing you. I am not even forcing you to retire. I'm simply asking you to take a rest, find peace, get a tan." She spun around. "Find a girlfriend, get laid and stop moping around this castle."

Chel's eyes went wide.

"I need you to stop and see the White Horse in Montana before you go to Florida."

"And ask permission?" He stood and followed her to the door.

"She's expecting you. She asked for you, actually."

379

Chel's brows rose this time. "What is really happening here?"

"You're going on vacation." Meg smirked. "But you might be going on an undercover mission." She clicked her tongue. "Sounds like fun."

"I'm not sure about this. I have not spent much time on the Earthen plane."

"You'll be fine. Rue said you fit in just fine on campus when you filled in for her bodyguard last year."

Chel swallowed hard, remembering how he'd damaged her tiny apartment just by walking through it.

Meg turned to him, settled her hand on his big arm. He went still. The Queen of Hell didn't like to be touched and rarely touched others.

"Thank you, Chel." Meg looked up at him. "I can never thank you enough for everything."

Chel nodded even though the awful feeling spread throughout his chest. He didn't like the idea of being sent away. He sighed and absently rubbed his aching wrist. An old injury that never seemed to heal right.

"You'll be just fine." Meg opened the door. "You deserve this."

Chel nodded as he left.

*

As he packed, Chel wondered if he should stop and tell his mother he was leaving Hell. He wasn't sure if she needed to know.

A flood of memories hit.

Then...

During the reign of Lucifer, Demon children were

not to be seen and not to be heard. Breaking either rule would result in severe punishment. It felt awful at the time but Chel would learn it was to prepare him for life under Lucifer's thumb. Chel learned early how to hide in the shadows. He learned how to avoid the light. Bred to be a Hellion and serve the throne, he spent his childhood years in training. It was the only thing that made his father proud. The only time he'd heard his father utter a whisper of delight was the day he'd completed his training. There had been no joy in the family household for years prior.

Chel would never forget that day because there should have been four people at the dinner table, but his sister's seat remained empty, as it had for nearly two years since she'd gone missing. It was the first moment in a long time that anyone uttered an emotion besides despair.

Demon women weren't known for their longevity. Many died in childbirth or defending their young from rage-filled fathers. It was a family dynamic like nothing else. Lucifer's reign kept his subjects in a constant state of dread. It trickled through day-to-day life like a dark tap left to drip and drip and drip.

Yelena was three years younger than Chel. She spent almost all of her time with their mother. Raised to be nothing more than a breed horse, she spent her time learning how to survive childbirth and motherhood. One day she was sent to the nearby stream to collect water for washing laundry and never returned. She was never found and it was assumed that she was murdered. A dark lull hung over Chel's family ever since. And Chel found he harbored an extreme dislike for any man who could harm a female.

His family was bred to be Hellions but something changed when Lucifer died and the new Queen took over. There was a shift in the edge that drove Hellions to violence. They held back, anticipated, contained their rage for only necessary times. They slept lighter and trained harder. New concepts had been taught like compassion and delayed reaction. Chel was not the same Demon his father was.

Chel would never forget when he stepped through the threshold, the familiar sights and sounds of his childhood greeted him with a bittersweet embrace. The air was still heavy with grief, the weight of loss palpable in every corner, especially the kitchen where his mother spent most of her time.

Chel's mother hadn't spoken much during dinner, her eyes hollow with sorrow. She sat in silence, hands clasped tightly in her lap as if trying to hold on to the fragments of her shattered world. She'd been like this since Yelena went missing.

His father was a brooding figure in his favorite lounge chair, radiating an aura of simmering anger, his jaw clenched with unspoken fury. Chel remembered the same Demon from childhood. He hadn't changed a bit.

"Utter bullshit," his father slammed a fork down. "I didn't send my only son off to be a pussy in the ranks." He reached across the table and grabbed Chel by the collar of his uniform. "You listen to me, you smile and nod but deep down understand that mentality will not save a soul. You need to be quick, exact. You need to kill. That is a Hellion's duty."

"Yes, sir," Chel had nodded and stared into his father's red eyes until the moment of rage passed.

There it was. The rage that drove previous ages. They were going to be different, better. Sparrow's teaching and guidance was always inspiring, but Chel didn't tell his father that. He finished his dinner and came to the realization that this might be the last time he visited his parents.

Chel's mother stood and began clearing dishes. She left the dusty plate at the setting next to Chel. Yelena's seat. She'd never cleared the place setting after all these years. It was like she was expecting Yelena to come running back home and burst through the door for dinner. She never came, she would never come. Yelena had been gone for years; kidnapped and murdered by wrath-filled Demons.

Chel's gaze shifted to the empty space where Yelena once sat, a void that echoed with the haunting absence of her presence. The ache of her loss weighed heavily on his heart, a reminder of the fragility of life and the cruel whims of fate.

As the evening wore on, Chel found himself grappling with a revelation that gnawed at the core of his being. His father's violent outbursts and callous disregard for Yelena's death stirred a wellspring of conflicting emotions within him: a potent brew of anger, sadness, and a dawning realization that threatened to shatter his sense of identity.

In a moment of clarity, Chel realized that he could no longer ignore the toxic legacy of his father's behavior. He could not condone the cycle of violence and indifference that had plagued his family for far too long.

He was not his father, and he refused to allow himself to become a reflection of the man who had brought so much pain and suffering into their lives.

"Do you have any news of Yelena's body being found?" Chel asked his father.

"Who cares?" his father shouted. "She's gone. Just another damned Demon woman, they make more every day."

"Yelena was more. Your wife is more. Do you not give a fuck about either of them?" Chel challenged the Demon. He spoke of the love and warmth that Yelena had brought into their lives; cozy evenings reading, dancing, picking flowers. The memories were a stark contrast to the darkness that his father's rage had wrought upon their family.

His father's anger boiled over and Chel stood his ground, refusing to back down. "I'm going to be better than you and if I ever have a wife or daughter I will love them more than you have ever loved anything."

"Get out of my fucking hovel with that mouth. You're nothing but a piece of shit. Hellions in my day didn't give a fuck about women or children. You were bred to serve the throne. Wait and see where this new ideology takes you all. You'll be dead in no time, and well deserved. Fuck off." Chel's father stormed off, disappearing to a room in the back of the hovel and slamming the door.

His mother hugged him. "You're a good Demon." There were tears in her eyes. "Yelena would be proud. I'm proud." She was taking off her apron and threw it aside. "I'll be leaving here now."

"I'll take you elsewhere. You can't stay here," Chel said.

She pulled a bag from under the sink. "I have only stayed this long for you, but I don't think you'll be back."

Chel shook his head. "I'll never see him again."

His mother nodded, wiping tears from her face. "There's a place I can go." She was shaking her head. "It's safe. Private."

"Good." Chel reached for the door. "Let's get you out of here."

His mother walked outside and Chel grabbed his gear and belongings. He closed the door to the hovel, taking one last glance at his family home. "Goodbye," he whispered.

Chel turned to face his mother. Walking closer, he wrapped his arm around her narrow shoulders. In that moment, Chel realized that he was not defined by the sins of his father, not bound by the chains of past Hellions. He was a warrior, a protector, and above all a son who refused to let the darkness of his father's legacy extinguish the light of hope that burned within him.

They walked down a dirt path. The sounds of furniture breaking and angry shouting came from the hovel. As they moved on, Chel vowed to honor Yelena's memory by forging a new path; one guided by empathy, tenderness, and the unwavering belief that he could be the change that his family so desperately needed.

The reign of Lucifer was over, the darkness that had infiltrated every corner of Hell was slowly dispersing.

*

Chel shivered as he stuffed a pair of pants into his duffle bag. He didn't have many belongings to bring with him.

He paused and decided that maybe he'd send his mother a letter instead of going to visit her. If he saw her, he'd be plagued by memories of Yelena for weeks. It seemed grief didn't pass when the innocent met malevolence.

He would send a letter. He rubbed his wrist. It had been aching a lot these days. Maybe he'd have someone write the letter for him.

*

Chel sat in a chair too small for someone his size, knees angled awkwardly, arms crossed like he might break something if he moved too quickly.

The bookstore was quiet. The kind of quiet that made you realize how loud you were just by breathing. Damn, he breathed loud.

Chel had exited the portal in the back of the store only to immediately be asked to babysit a bookstore for a few hours.

He glanced at the clock. It had been a few hours too long.

Dust filtered through shafts of sunlight, catching on motes in the air like ashfall. The scent of paper and floor polish wrapped around him. A bell above the door had jingled once when Layla left, and hadn't made a sound since. Probably because he'd locked the door and flipped the sign to "Closed."

He wasn't used to this. There was no way in hell he was going to try and use the computer and deal with money. Nope. Instead he tried to enjoy the peace.

There were no screams in the air. No roars of Hellions. No weight of orders cracking through the back of his skull. Just... books. Hundreds of them. All spines and ink and strange titles.

He reached for one, out of curiosity. Something about

ravens and riddles. The pages crackled like firewood as he flipped through, skimming a passage about lost sisters and prophetic dreams.

He didn't expect to like it. But he found himself leaning forward.

By the third book, he was stretched out on the little loveseat beneath the window, boots on the floor, flipping through a history of curses carved into bones.

No patrol. No reports. No sword at his side.

Just silence. And stories.

What the fuck am I supposed to do with this? he thought looking up at the wall.

He hadn't had time like this since—well, ever. His days had always been war and training, weapons and fire, endless lines of enemies and duty. He didn't know what it meant to fill a day without the rhythm of battle and hum of protecting others.

And yet... he wasn't bored.

He was unsettled.

By the time the shadows reached across the hardwood floor and the sky outside turned amber, Chel had gone through five books—three closed halfway through, one upside down, and another he kept re-reading the same paragraph of for twenty minutes. If Layla could see him now. He could read and he could read quickly. Something Skeele had taught him. Speed reading he'd called it.

He heard whisper and a crackle from the back room. Someone was coming through the portal.

Chel stood. He heard Layla's voice, then Thrush.

Layla stepped out first, cheeks flushed, curls springing

loose from behind her ear. She was already talking rapidly about the Peabody library and the Angel they'd met.

Thrush moved closer. Listening. He'd met the guy ages ago.

Then.

An Angel descended, his presence commanding yet puzzled. His wings spread wide, casting a golden glow over the chaotic scene. With a wave of his hand, the Demons were obliterated, their bodies disintegrating to ash. The Angel's eyes swept over the room, taking in the devastation and those who remained standing.

"What do we have here?" the Angel asked. "A Hellion. A Nephilim." He leaned to the side and focused on Rue and Remington. "Those two are something different." Then he stared at Shay. "And you're *barely* human."

Magic prickled in Jed's hands. He drew on it, ready to blast the Angel to another planet. He had zero trust for Angels of any kind. They'd only hunted and tried to kill him his entire life. He wouldn't let this one do the same.

"These children," the Angel said, his voice resonant and powerful, "who are they, and why do they bear such auras?"

Jed took a deep breath, his voice steady despite the turmoil and urge to kill. "They are under our protection. Their mother left them with us to keep them safe. We will protect them from everyone and everything, including you."

The Angel's eyes narrowed, his gaze shifting to Shay. Recognition flickered in his gaze and he took a step back.

"You," he said, his tone wary, "are part Crossroads Demon. Somehow. But you weren't born that way."

Shay lifted her chin, her eyes defiant as she swiped blue hair away from her face. "Yes, I am."

The Angel took a step backward. "No deals." He shook his head.

"This is not a crossroads," Shay clarified. "But that doesn't mean I won't kill you." She tapped the fire poker on her palm menacingly.

The Angel crossed his arms and he gazed quickly around the room. "You're all leaving?"

"That seems the smartest choice," Jed said.

"Can I stay here if you're leaving?" the Angel asked. "I need a place to hide." The Angel was surveying the library. "And I get the feeling you all can't stay here, not after this." He opened his arms to the piles of ash all over the floor.

"We don't own this place," Jed warned.

"I'll take care of it," the Angel promised.

"I have never met an Angel that I've trusted," Jed said. "Why should I trust you?"

"I've already fixed the wards." The Angel moved his hands to his hips, real proud of himself.

"I think we should take the deal," Chel suggested. "This piece of flying garbage could fend off more Demons who come here looking for us."

"Hey!" the Angel shouted. "I offer help and you insult me?"

Chel shrugged, unafraid and unbothered.

"I apologize for my friend," Shay said. "But we have yet to meet an Angel who hasn't tried to kill first."

The Angel toed a pile of ash before focusing on Jed.

"Not all Angels are of the old ways. Some of us just want peace, just like God intended."

"You can stay here," Jed finally said. "We'll collect our things."

The Angel smiled with relief. He turned his back to the grouping and began picking up pieces of the broken chairs and tossing them in the fireplace.

Now.

Layla spotted Chel and blinked. "Oh—hey. You didn't burn it down."

"Tempted," he said, then nodded toward the stack of books on the table. "But I got distracted."

Her brows lifted in amusement. "By reading? I am glad you're not illiterate."

Chel shrugged, but his mouth twitched. "Don't tell Meg." He exhaled a big breath. "So you finally met Jasper at the Peabody Library. What's he up to these days?"

"He was very strange. Said he was restoring the building and cataloguing books." Layla shrugged.

"He seemed lonely," Thrush said. "Guy needed some sunlight. Or a date."

"He's been alone there for over ten years." Chel stood and walked closer to his duffle bag that he'd tossed on the floor. "Poor guy is just sitting around and waiting for someone."

"Who?" Layla asked.

Chel shrugged. "That's beyond my pay grade."

Thrush gave him a sidelong look. "We were going to

390

drive you up to the ranch. Shay should have dinner on soon."

Chel glanced out the shop's front window.

"I'll walk," he said.

Layla blinked. "It's at least an hour."

"I've walked worse," Chel replied.

Thrush didn't argue. Just held his gaze a moment, then nodded.

Chel grabbed his jacket, hesitating briefly before tucking the smallest of the books under his arm. He didn't know if it was allowed, but no one stopped him.

As he stepped into the cooling evening, he felt something unfamiliar settle low in his chest.

The door to the bookstore clicked shut behind him, and for the first time in centuries, Chel wasn't headed to battle.

Lame Deer's main road stretched out in front of him, quiet and empty.

He walked until he reached the turn to head toward Colstrip. Jed and Shay's ranch wasn't far off Route 39. Warmth spread in his chest when he thought about seeing Shay again. It had been weeks. He'd missed her at the castle, seemed she visited less and less since they'd moved to the ranch. A cool breeze chilled Chel's skin and he remembered that she was probably canning and preparing for the winter months. She talked about it often enough that he should have remembered. She'll tuck in for the winter with Jed. The northern land of the Earthen plane would slow to a trickle of activity once the snow started piling up.

The seasons weren't as severe in Hell. That realm was nothing but a dark reflection of the Earthen plane but the snow never accumulated around the castle like it did in other parts. Probably due to the burning caves that the castle was built over.

Chel noticed a sign for Crossroads Ranch and turned.

The gravel path turned to dirt a few yards down, curving past a run of trees and dipping low where the earth sloped into fields. The sun had nearly slipped below the horizon, and the world had gone gold.

The stillness pressed in. Cicadas sang in the tall grass. A bird wheeled overhead. Somewhere far off, a screen door creaked and slammed. No monsters. No horns. No sharp teeth. His tongue brushed his own. Well, he had sharp teeth. He glanced over his shoulder, always strange not seeing his wings. They weren't present on the Earthen plane, not when there was balance between the realms. No wings could be seen here, not an Angel's, not demons, and not Hellions.

Chel didn't know what to do with the quiet.

Every step took him further from the life he knew. From the fire. From the edge of a blade. He'd never been given time to feel the weight of his own thoughts. Not really. Not like this.

Now, they crowded in. Every memory he'd repressed was fighting for his attention. Alastor's brutal attack in the Hellion lair, Yelena, his mother, seeing his Hellion brothers come back from the dead to fight in the war against Lucifer.

Every time he blinked, he saw them—his brothers. All teeth and loyalty and... dead. They were dead. Replaced with new recruits over the years. It had never been the same.

And what did that make him now?

A relic?

A weapon without a war?

He dragged a hand through his hair and exhaled hard. Dust puffed beneath his boots as he crossed a rickety wooden bridge over a small creek. Water rushed quietly underneath. Somewhere nearby, a frog chirped like it didn't know anything about the end of the world.

Chel slowed.

He'd never been to Montana. But this... this wasn't what he expected. It was soft. Raw in a way that didn't ask anything from him.

He passed a tree where someone had carved a name into the trunk.

He didn't know why that hit him so hard. Maybe it was the memory of chasing Yalena through the forest when they were children.

He paused to lean against the trunk for a moment, fingers brushing over the jagged letters. Someone had wanted to be remembered. Maybe that was all any of them really wanted. He'd left marks on the tree near the river where she'd been stolen from. He pushed the thoughts away and kept going.

By the time the ranch came into view—its porch light glowing like a lantern in the dark. Something smelled divine and the thundering of hoof falls echoed in his ears.

"Hellion," he heard Nero's voice. "You look lost." The giant black horse trotted closer to him in greeting and nodded his head. "You're just in time for dinner."

"Hello, Demon horse. You look quite at home in these fields," Chel brushed a hand over Nero's neck. "Quite at home for a beast of the underworld."

Nero made a noise that sounded like a laugh. "This is

some of the last true land you'll find on this plane, it doesn't care where I'm from." Nero nickered and pawed his hooves at the ground. "Want to race?"

Chel dropped his duffle bag and cracked his knuckles. "I had a standing chance with wings but now I only have these old knees." He tapped his thighs once before taking off in a sprint.

Hellion and Crossroads Demon horse racing on the Earthen plane was a sight for anyone. There was no winner, because Chel's knee gave out five-hundred yards in and he grabbed Nero's tail, causing the horse to twist and fall to his flank. He'd spent too many hours sitting around that bookstore today. Or at least that's the excuse he gave Nero as they wandered toward the ranch house.

Read: These Thorns are Sharpest next!

A NOTE

Thank You

To every reader who picked up *The Shadows Are Darkest*—whether you've been with me since the first Veil of Shadows book or you just stumbled across my work on TikTok at 2 a.m. THANK YOU! You are the reason this world keeps growing. Every like, share, review, late-night DM, and "I can't believe you..." message fuels my dark little writer heart. And I love responding with: "I wonder what's going to happen next?!"

To my incredible BookTok family: Mellystarr, massiel reads, ShadowDaddy/D, Linda, Kim.d.f.reads, Tameka, Tracy, Cass Marie, Shania, littlekick, sweetpea26_26, Del (I'm still thinking about that alpha rescue!), thatgalbritt, punkachoo, Short.n.sweet, Shannon, curious_kitten, momma Deb, SarLitten, Raye, Platinum_VERA, Okay-Lucy, DivaSoldierFoster, jennifer7746, Whit, Brianne, Mikayla, Brandi B, Ken, Like.A.Diamond, Mystery Book Bundles, and sooooo many more!! You all make promoting vampires, morally gray chaos, and slow-burn romance a joy.

To my ARC readers on Booksirens: Thank you, thank you. I love getting your first reviews and thoughts.

To my editor, Kristy: you catch the things I miss and all those extra commas, sharpen every shadow, and somehow know when I've been holding back on a scene. Thank you for pushing me to make each book better than the last.

To my family: you've listened to my rambling lore dumps, tolerated my writing marathons, my Livestreams, and never once questioned why I'm Googling things like "how long does it take to bleed out from a vampire bite?" You're my safe place and my chaos crew, and I love you for it.

Here's to more books, more worlds, and more late nights chasing the stories that refuse to let us sleep.

Let the Vampires Bite,
    Meredith

About the Author

M. R. Pritchard delves into the profound clash between good and evil, the mystical realms of gods and monsters, and the intricate transformations of ordinary people into beings of immense power. Her gripping narratives often unfold within the haunting backdrop of apocalyptic or post-apocalyptic landscapes, offering a unique blend of suspense and wonder.

M. R. Pritchard is a two-time Kindle Scout winning author, her short story "Glitch" has been featured in the 2017 winter edition of THE FIRST LINE literary journal. Her short story "Moon Lord" has been featured in Chronicle Worlds: Half Way Home (Part of the Future Chronicles) and will be time capsuled on the moon on the Lunar Codex in 2024.

Visit her website MRPritchard.com and Subscribe. You'll get subscriber only content, deleted scenes, updates, special previews of new projects, and book deals.

Also by M. R. Pritchard

The Night is Endless (2025)

The Shadows are Darkest (2025)

These Thorns are Sharpest (2025)

Standalone Fantasy

Thread the Bone

Thread the Bone Illustrated Edition (2025)

Science Fiction/post-apocalyptic:

Songs for the End of Days (2025)

The Phoenix Project

The Reformation

Revelation

Inception

Origins

Resurrection

Heartbeat

Asteroid Riders Series

Moon Lord

Collector of Space Junk and Rebellious Dreams

Steampunk:

Tick of a Clockwork Heart

Fantasy/Fairy Tale Love Story/Romance:

Muse

Forgotten Princess Duology

Midsummer Night's Dream: A Game of Thrones

Poetry/Short Stories

Consequence of Gravity

www.ingramcontent.com/pod-product-compliance
Lightning Source LLC
Chambersburg PA
CBHW021228190726
48289CB00005B/1226